# THE MOUTHLESS MURDERER

# THE MOUTHLESS MURDERER

## BARRY DICKINS

Connor Court Publishing

Connor Court Publishing Pty Ltd

PO Box 224W
Ballarat VIC 3350
sales@connorcourt.com
www.connorcourt.com

ISBN: 9781925138863  (pbk)

Cover design by Ian James, sketch by Barry Dickins

Printed in Australia

# INTRODUCTION

In the course of one life lived beyond belief although couched in the ordinary there once existed a gentleman named Ernid Ernst. Possessing an extraordinary name he looked for extraordinary work but after emigrating with his humorless parents from Prague forty years or so ago all he could find as a job was a common shift-working engagement in Sydney at Burp Lemonade Works who were determined to conquer Coke as the universe's preferred fizzy drink.

He commenced operations as a lowly vat watcher where his duties consisted mainly of observing it fizz.

He rose rapidly through the ranks and made it to the esteemed position of Logo. Without his really knowing he became the very drink he manufactured and his new life was hedonistic and ravishing and his fame bought him a wild ride he was incapable of paying for without a soul he could call his own.

He also became delusional after falling from lofty heights into the very vats he inspected with a great eye for chemical variations. His tumbling down into a particularly large lemonade vat sent him insane in next to no time and thenceforward he thought he was really someone else entirely such as Lee Harvey Oswald the lone assassin of President John Kennedy, and he thus endeavored to simultaneously promote his company's famous drink and put up with the added psychological pressure of believing he slew JFK in 1963.

The entire area surrounding his silent and humble parent's home was razed to the ground by sniggering local councils and by virtue of a government decree the new way to live in Sydney was in a hole.

The living in a hole wasn't as horrid as it might seem but there was simply not a single thing anyone could possibly do about it.

*The Mouthless Murderer* is fantasy and real simultaneously exactly as it is in Australia as we go to press.

We are dying of leadership and the poor suffer in ways tragic and unfunny unless you have the heart to laugh out loud at them, as the rich find easy.

**Barry Dickins writer**
**Melbourne 2015**

# Chapter One

## Mr Ernid Ernst from Prague

Not so long back, in fact a burp, a fellow of no import fell head foremost into a large steel vat used to pulverize Burp bottles, when they were glass and into this chamber of horrifying cleansing and rapid-fire crumbling he sailed and yet he lived to tell this tale. You'd be incorrect upon several levels not to call it mordant.

It is genuinely true and pathetic as well as sorrowful because the man had a fair bit going for him, not the least being his passion and flair for spontaneous speech. His name is Mr Ernid Ernst and he was conceived in Prague in the midst of an uprising.

His honest parents toiled in the horse-boning industry and to all intents and purposes they excelled at it. Peasants from skull to toe they boned away contentedly in an unremarkable quiet and serene slaughterhouse.

Ernid was a respectable infant who enjoyed the lessons at his school very much indeed and always wished to end up cleaning soft drink bottles in one way or the other since Burp was the big thing in Prague in the late 1950s and he could see as if he were a visionary that Burp would always be there, like the air except more addictive.

His parents only had one single pet, a pig. It existed in a snowy forest nearly all the time and just stood there barking at whatever they did to get attention. Ernid loved the pig passionately and adored chaining it up and mocking it.

He would poke half-incinerated sticks into its eyes and laugh at the effect until his parents read him The Riot Act, which they had learnt at school.

Prague was good at riots.

The parents were possessed of devils and some nights it proved arduous for a developing mind when the lad was required to observe and take ritual part in having the screaming demons removed from mother and father in tandem. The village priest shoved both mum and dad straight on the meat chopping block in the somber shed and using a mix of ancient exorcism with plenty of Burp he drove the wicked things out.

The usual screaming became nothing but a bore for the next door shepherds who were used to devils anyway, and saw them as just a necessary distraction from daily peasant existence where all you had to look forward to was hay shaping.

But the bitter experience of having to watch both parents having their brains opened with a chisel left an indelible impression on the child; and all his life he never forgot things like witchcraft, warlocks, seeing parents opened up with cold chisels and various sniggering phantoms flying out as though demonology were naught but a joke.

But his parents were made of sterner stuff than the odd exorcism and pretty soon they both got back to their meaningful chores such as pig washing. The hog was a girl, a big one named Lady who was so vast it couldn't quite make it through the door. The Ernst family adored it and wept to see it trying to batter the same door down with its almighty brow to no avail.

The lady pig was the quintessential comrade of the family and it was treated not really as a hog but a spirit of kindness and enterprise bargaining, for many in the wilderness thought of it a lot and fantasized on eating it.

It was a girl pig to be reckoned with all right, rather pink as it turned out and very snout-orientated for it loved to snuffle through corpses of dead villagers before their delayed burial and snout right through them hoping for a truffle; for the endless dead reminded Lady of truffles.

That hog was paraded through the ghastly gas lit unmade roads of the town as if it were royalty and by and by it curtsied and had apples cast at it by oafs.

Ernid used to talk in a completely confidential manner to it in his bedroom when he wearied of study for school and needed a hog to lighten up.

Years even decades that are blooms of years Ernid would mourn the hog and remember it with a vividness that passes all understanding for citizens who actually can't understand what all hog fuss is about. But the fact was that the particular pig came at a dire time in the evolution of a boy of Prague who was in desperate need to believe in something, and any pig shall do in a storm.

He recalled it bathing and relaxing in mud and even attempting to speak for it had that look of a hog about to talk and Ernid liked to listen to it making honking effects which only he was capable of interpreting and archiving in his mind for future reference, possibly when he got in some sort of a jam and needed honking.

His parents were forced off the peat farm by their unscrupulous landlady who daily had their front lawn filmed and then emailed to the owner of the peat works who was a practising vampire who lived in Translyvania by a bus stop.

It was seen that the rented front lawn was overgrown by a very considerable degree and that an eviction order was served on Ernid's father Burptek.

Burptek had seen it all before of course and laughed hard at the notice of eviction as it sailed straight through the jagged crooked tin letter box at the front of the peat works that had never had a single lick of paint put on it or a new roof – which happened to be urgent. A hail storm upon Christmas Day of the year 2013 collapsed all ceilings and the incredible size of the hail stones, particularly their width, was an agony for the Ernst family, and Pa decided to migrate at once to Sydney in Australia, which was what they did.

The pig was denied a visa even though it had a successful application for being weighed but not sliced. It was absolutely shattered that it may never go to Australia and sadly fell into a vast decline which required expensive anti-depressants, most of which were only available on a pig prescription.

The pig was expensively counseled by pig psychiatrists and pig psychologists and notes were taken as to a special dispensation and eventually even a special pen.

It had to bear living in the pen for years in the end as the Ernst family didn't have enough funds to shout it an airline ticket from Prague to Australia, as much as they thought it a decent idea.

In the end the Ernsts turned up at Prague Airport pretty early on April Fool's day of 1963 and immediately rented in Coburg where there are even worse peat bogs available than the eyesore they endured in the Old Country no less. They didn't last in Coburg and scraped up enough to shift to Sydney where they rented a house so old that Captain Cook was in it, although not in his original form.

It was Glebe Point Road that attracted them and the slums there really appealed to them. It was near employment in the realization of the great Burp Plant which offered thousands of variations of serfdom in order to boil up lakes of sugary soft drink the entire continent not only worshipped but needed more than oxygen, of which none was left anywhere.

Ma and Pa made the slum worse by just moving in and decorating, painting, sand-papering the balustrades although they patently didn't need it; thence they ate on the floor like the depressing peasants they really were; and many was the night they gutsed into potato cakes like you wouldn't believe right on the main floor and threw back chicken claws fried in fat similar to the lethal dishes immortalized by Elvis Presley.

Ma worked for Burp the first day she lobbed in Sydney, in the belching section where professional indigestion was practised and mastered by skilled staff that burped on the early shift according to dosages of strange chemicals and outer space additives not available on Earth, not really, and they are dreadfully expensive and highly mysterious and if used incorrectly, deadly or worse than that, if anything can be.

The newly arrived ones from ever so distant Prague didn't fit into life as it is certifiably accepted in suburban Sydney; they were nice and conventional but their next door neighbors were very rude Turks and living right next to them was horrid and they just got abused from dawn until acceptable dark.

The hovel rented by Ernid's Papa was to be demolished in order to be upgraded as a hovel. It was a three bedroom with one faulty toilet that scarcely flushed but hiccupped. The landlady never apologized for the degrading way the tenants had to live and increased the camera surveillance ever more in her crazed efforts to get the lawns mowed. The Ernsts couldn't afford a mower so the grass grew and grew until you couldn't make out the sky if you were out in the yard.

The terrible cheap wallpaper varied from tomb to tomb within the spectral dump, so much so it was a wonder to Ma Ernst that the wallpaper man could get it so very wrong indeed. The sitting room bore no furniture for them to sit on and boasted no television system to become distracted with. It was hard core reality rather than Real Estate.

The poor group were so poor of a night they sat on the floor and watched each other, sometimes endeavoring to go to Channel 10 by looking depressed out the window at a dead cactus which succumbed to a single solitary drop of rain.

In the morning of their first day they all awoke in a fetus position as though they were new born babies, although that is the feeling all European migrants have after an insufferable trip from The Old Country, whether by paddle steamer or walking.

In the situations vacant pages of *The Sydney Morning Herald* the tired family perused the tiny typeset boxed ads to discover the sorts of employment available in Australia; they were fairly lit up at first with cerebral imagery of Rodeo work breaking Brahman Bulls or else toiling as a telescopic hostess upon a jet with your hair up.

The sad truth was that there was nothing as interesting as back home in the shit-hole.

Ernid gasped when he saw an ad for a bottle pulverize person of either sex at Burp and after feverishly cross-examining his sick father about whether or not he looked like a bloke, it was agreed within the Ernst clan that he was much more like a man than a woman, so he wrote to Burp his personal letter, whacked a stamp on the brand new white envelope and posted it with a heart bursting with pride.

'I think you are pushing it a bit my love!' cried his fatigued mother as she pounded cheap flour on her flour board into a kind of archaic crumpet unknown in Sydney. She called them Gag and that was certainly the gastronomic effect they had on reluctant tasters. Mrs Ernst had successfully poisoned their landlady back in The Old Country with only half a Gag.

She was found deceased at the bottom of a well in the city square by a broom sweeper and yet Mrs Ernst had no charge to answer as they all cook like her back there.

'You and your Gag!' laughed Pa Ernst and he pounded the table with approbation until like everything else in sight it collapsed with a loud sigh and was no more.

Ernid had to get himself unconscious at night on a fold-up sofa which one night wound itself round him rather like a python and tried really hard to disembowel him. He screamed as it crushed the shit out of his anus until someone came.

He struggled with the fold-down bed he sure did but it was quite all the battling Prague family could possibly afford, he knew that if he knew naught else and just had to learn how to defend himself spontaneously whenever it attacked and lunged at him with a colossal force of will previously unknown in furniture. That particular sofa haunted Ernid the rest of his life with its savage will and by dint of its unpredictability.

A few days on from this Ernid gouged an impressive missive out of the filthy dun-colored letter box, apologized to the slugs and read it to his mother who was smoking dehydrated peas.

The letter went on to say that Ernid Ernst could commence at Burp the next day at six in the morning in Pulverize Section EBD.

It further said the work took the form of an apprenticeship and that Burp would require his pulverizing services in section EBD for five years. After that he may be shifted to The Bottle Top Section; which was vied for like no other section.

All he needed to do was sign a contract for life and do a health check first thing in the morning. He asked his father if he might borrow his bike to get there but his Papa made Ernid pay one cent each way for the privilege; and Ernid reluctantly did that very thing. Mind you it is hard to pay one's own Papa a cent for a ride on his crummy pushbike.

The evening before his birth by work Ernid tucked into more Gag than was good for him, but the whole family were homesick and wearied of stress and all that sort of thing, so they hopped into Gag and enjoyed spaghetti out of a hot can as a dessert that you have to be careful with as it is most rich.

They spoke of The Old Country and how far away it felt because it was. They spoke of Gag and how they were beginning to love it and they sipped tap water soup had from a sacred old family recipe handed down from time immemorial.

They even smoked crack that was also handed down from an old family recipe and after a decent inhaling of it threw themselves into bed for a good old fashioned early night. Ernid rather unwisely swallowed a bottle of Aspirin to get himself off and in the morning his ankles were all swollen up like the size of a house.

He dressed painfully and sipped his cereal and genuinely fresh cow milk that his inbred mother had personally milked from a passing cow. It was scrumptious!

He alighted the early morning shuttle to Burp with hundreds of similar Prague immigrants and because the whole prospect of work in a new country was so exciting he found he raved away like a right loon.

Thousands of Prague Burp workers clocked on at the main gate in correct Burp uniform winking at the overseer because that is exactly what workers are expected to do at a gigantic lemonade plant like Burp. Billions of young men and women winking and rushing to vats larger than the whole god damned universe!

'This is great!' Ernid enthused in the latest English his Papa had belted into his nut.

He assumed perhaps wrongly that everything about Burp was great. with the workers and the vats higher than their cholesterol levels.

He liked or possibly loved his fellow pulverizing team and really enjoyed first of all watching the experienced people leading by example and laughing hysterically as they poured millions of slaked Burp bottles on winches and cranes and funnels the same as *The Titanic* had as it sank.

The noise was erotic, every worker worth his or her salt had bad tinnitus within a minute of working there; the shrieking of steaming hot whistles for correct boiling operations and instantaneous starting times instantly deafened the lot, but they did not care as they were employed by the friendliest employer in the world; Burp was synonymous with feeling triumphant and developing a sense of giddiness and taking a punt on life. It was a scientific fact that cocaine gives people a high, not that there was any in Burp today but by Christ there used to be in 1867 when it kick-started!

In the Morning Tea Room Ernid listened as never before to the old dyed in the wool Burp staff who somehow could remember the early 19th century Burp Cola Fountains bedecked with laid-back ladies in fancy dresses whose beaux spooned Burp down their pampered pudding chutes in the most effervescent and graceful way, then belched.

One old gentleman recalled giving a big bottle of it to God; however he was fired after that. The Tea Rooms of course sold only one drink and it was the drink of choice, Burp, although it was not that much cheaper for the fevered proletariat than what you'd expect to pay in a sproggy milk bar.

Ernid clasped his young honest hands enraptured by the safety rail and the sight of thousands upon thousands of shiny and dull empty glass bottles. Light green they were in those days and still are these days because sales teams have proven that shiny light green bottles remind consumers of more and more refreshment.

Do people really need more refreshment? It is necessary to feel refreshed in a world that grinds you personally into glass crumbles of what you once were, what you once felt in your gleaming spirit and radiant soul. You felt once immortal before consumerism was invented to drive you right out of your wits.

The great metal cranes dumped shards of bright vicious Burp glass into ashes of light and many a worker applauded as the mountains of empties hit the deck with sounds indecipherable and fragrances unbelievable as the mouth of Hell.

Security teams kept workers and sightseers well away from the vast volcano of Burp bottles skidding and knocking and crashing straight through each other so to speak, molten glass now and very soon new Burp bottles in the handy 125 mil size.

Ernid watched rapt as spent and cleansed Burp metamorphosis was over and mint new pallets of the stuff was reborn like Jesus Of The Stomach Ache.

Great overhead groaning chains and block and tackle, tons of it, got slammed into giant trucks of it out on the private Burp Freeway to The People!

Speaking of them the raging thirst for Burp drove them further than their cars could and their insatiable requirement for their appeasement never ceased.

Crate after crate of the belch and hiccup brew was mechanically dispatched by larger and larger cranes that thumped uncountable pallets of it directly into semi-trailers more powerful than the need for what was bubbling away inside them.

# Chapter Two

## In Pulverizing Section It Felt Like Prague

There could be no possible doubt whatever that the sensation Ernid discovered in the Burp Pulverizing Section was just as though he'd never left Prague. It was home certainly and he experienced a certain kind of camaraderie he thought was all but gone. The workers didn't like their dreary work but they loved it despite its great gruesomeness and noise because the income was realer than starvation and ruin.

It felt good to receive a complimentary pair of cotton overalls and a t-shirt with The Pause That Refreshes emblazoned across its chest; each worker got a couple of those on their first day and they were coveted after dismissal.

Yet no one was fired during Ernid's time in Pulverizing Section, in fact more were put on since the greater popularity with the drink gained momentum and in Ernid's first week at least fifty new workers, all from Prague, got their start, and rejoiced to be in regular work that would probably last until they died, but most didn't and just kept doing it in the vision of owning a home not far from Burp.

In fact many workers lived in streets linked by architecture to Burp and thousands upon thousands of them drank Burp after work from special faucets connected to what used to be their water supply; many a birthday party was celebrated right next door to where work was and if there is one thing people worship it is work.

Loyal staff were not too fastidious to shower in Burp or bathe in it at home; it was just such an intimate feeling to surrender to the overwhelming force for human good you don't receive any other way. Lawns and shrubs were watered with it and cars were washed and polished with it; the family dog drank it out of the tap with gusto and animal gratefulness because there is nothing like it.

Mind you the starts on Ernid's shifts were real killers, with a six in the morning clock-on-time it was hard to stamp your card absolutely

pinpoint accurately after being in line for twenty minutes with your fellow automatons; some of them sipping Burp as they started as dull as gurnard at the time-clock on the wall.

However Ernid enjoyed the brisk mechanical stamping of his yellowish card, he grooved upon the precise hit of the black carbon ribbon printing the exact time of commencement. It mattered very much to him that he felt secure and anonymous as a cloud of atomic fallout.

By 6:15 he was pulverizing bottles and overseeing the great crush of boiled crates of Regular and King Size or Family Size bottles which were being dumped louder than is imaginable into the greedy steel vats below him; below his enormous and irksome rubber boots that seemed heavier than a joke in his old village whose name he was beginning to forget.

The great sloshing vats actually began to rise alarmingly only to descend the very next second, shaking the glass more than violently and vigorously until all of the trillions of empty bottles turned to a hot mush.

The strange substance was then piped to Forming Section which was where brand new Regular and Family Size were manufactured in what at first seemed like a chaotic way but after a while seemed perfectly natural, even refreshing.

Many workers envied those who toiled in Forming Section; it had more panache, more clout possibly due to the instantaneous newness of the glass. The applications to labour in Forming Section never ended and middle management were hard put just trying to read them all, but they understood the rationale.

'I love doing this!' was the first recorded utterance of Ernid Ernst on day one in Pulverizing Section, as he humbly pushed a bright red button to operate an overhead scoop-thing which dropped a hundred tons of glass into powerful crushing rotors at the bottom of the vat. He would have hated to fall in.

The worry here as in all sections was the noise. He tried to make the necessary adjustment to great sounds of splashing soluble sugar vastly being mixed directly into billions of thirsty bottles lined up on ten mile long conveyor belts but it wasn't easy and he often got minor headaches but wrote them off as experience, and he loved experience.

The whole effect of making the beverage was euphoric in the high extreme of not so much physical pleasure as a cerebral need in him always denied to him back home, where all available family outings were visitations to bomb sites.

The way of American Capitalism was practically magical and of course it was astonishing and pleasing to contribute to Australian culture since the people here seemed not to have one before Burp.

It gave more than it took and it was impossible to imagine weekends with it being sipped by relaxed teenagers who leant up against turbo-charged cars made in Detroit and the famous bottles silk-screened on banners and hoardings everywhere you looked. People sipped it in the movies or had it on the toilet if needs be.

It wasn't just the drink of choice for the young because the old folks guzzled it inside demented guest homes or they drank it as they clipped a hedge; they drank it whilst love-making because it put youth into them and encouraged more highly-charged intercourse at the relatively timeless age of a hundred.

At Morning Tea in Pulverizing Section it was the way of that section to engage in the act of oiled human wrestling: the new chum had to really wrestle naked the workmates and give to the act of wrestling all that was in him or her or transgender.

Ernid had a thin if feeble build and didn't really feel like a violent wrestle but it was expected so he had to just go and do it despite not wanting to.

'Here', said a chap from Labeling he'd never been introduced to, who had wandered across from Labeling to test his arm and considerable Armenian leg on those from other rival sections. 'Put on oil!'

So Ernid put on wrestling lotion like cheap olive oil, all over his meagre frame. It glossed until he was deemed perfect by the much bigger competitive others eager to win the best of five throws with oiled-up workmates on a freezing-cold day in the Morning Tea Rest Rooms.

The foreman in Pulverizing himself took him on in the best of five holds. The man was a veritable giant to be sure and his over-glossed biceps momentarily presented Ernid with a splitting headache as he lumbered at him to the whoops and cheers of his underlings who greased like anything to get ahead.

The foreman must have come in at 125 kilos of solid fat, wearing his olive oil with magnificent pride as he came at Ernid in a dramatic sort of way, each massive calf shining more with each incremental step.

The foreman had jet black curly hair like a Rocker in some ways and the way that he grunted and beat his enormous hairy chest was frightening even for those sycophants who'd seen him do it at a thousand factory wrestles. Some even booed him but that just made him happier and much worse in look and vocal range, like a big monster devoid of all human form.

Ernid wasn't quite ready for him as he was still engaged in the deed of applying the wrestling oil to his skinny legs and modest chest cavity that didn't have any tattoos on it, nor indeed a solitary hair.

The foreman grasped Ernid in what was understood to be a legal or legitimate hold or lock and lifted him right up and then viciously speared him to the concrete. The workers cheered wildly and collected bets because of course they had laid money on their vindicated foreman.

The bout went on for around thirty minutes because Ernid had wrestled lots of times in the Old Country, in fact it was the sport of choice in his village apart from pneumonia or whooping cough that wiped out half the population in winter.

Ernid got his fit foreman in a neck lock that proved a winner because the foreman's eyes nearly came out like organ stoppers due to the pressure that Ernid applied.

It was interesting that the workers cheered him on when they saw that, saw the fitness in so dismal a physique but also marvelled at them.

The foreman vindicated himself by throwing Ernid into a wall by the hair and the crowd wildly cheered that hold, although there may have been one or two of the older men and ladies who saw that act as a breach of the rules. The two shook hands after so many falls and Ernid, nursing a sore body, was told to get back to work, even though he felt honour bound to cheer on the next lot of mat men as they were called at Burp.

Still the vigour and courage of the wrestling did him good and ever afterwards he was treated with dignity rather than disgust and contempt usually afforded new workers the whole planet over.

He started to feel wanted by Burp because of his newfound workmates, some of whom were girls by the way, and with their Prague pasts and hairnets some of them turned him on; they liked him automatically as often occurs in factories and one in particular blew him a special kiss as he did his pulverizing.

Her little name was Anna and she was very good on the eye; she labored in Labeling and loved doing it so far as all her workmates could see because she had a special way of winking at each 125 ml bottle as she adhered its special lettering with industrial paste that was set at 5000 degrees Celsius and was not thought especially dangerous.

Ernid continued with the wrestling at Morning Tea each day until he beat the leading hand as well as The Foreman no holds barred, both of them to cries of rapture from the mob who always urged them onward to seized victory and locked hurtful back and buttock. Ernid felt vindicated.

He met with Anna one day after work and they strolled together at dusk towards a remarkably flat and uninteresting field where he attempted to kiss her but she desisted claiming they hardly knew one another. He heartily agreed with that news and kept his hands extremely to himself. But she dared to kiss his modest bicep and after that he wasn't so certain how to proceed.

She was so pretty and shy but very determined-looking and aware of where she was going in life – straight into Marketing.

They discussed Marketing for hours as she munched his left ear-lobe in a most arousing way, firing him up like a small bottle of Burp that was a teeny bit too fizzy you may say. He fell in love with Anna at once and needed her baby, hopefully a Burp worker.

She was devastatingly attractive and she took him home to meet her parents, both of whom thought they were forklift trucks.

They of course worked at the plant and their modest home bore Burp ads all over.

They dined on Burp Pie that Anna's mother wrongly thought she'd invented, but it is common in that part of Sydney, not that different in concept from Beef and Guinness Pie except for its fiery black and brown sugar content and zillion little popping bubbles.

It was nice to have love even without its meaning and from the moment he tried to kiss her but naturally failed, he adored Anna and liked her hard-working family whom he saw as an extension of the Burp family and all Australians so far as that goes.

Anna got a trifle frustrated by the Ernst family on the rare occasion she was invited to dinner because none of them spoke directly to her and seemed inanimate. They were always down.

Pa was perennially obdurate and just stared at Anna with his tongue hanging out as though he were in a permanent trance, which he probably was as he only thought about soft drink or soccer, which he played each Saturday, dreaming he got the Red Card as that would lend him some cachet or even admiration for being a somebody.

Ma served up her famed Gag without a single variation and although Anna politely nibbled a bit of it, she spat most of it out at once into her handkerchief out of sight, hopefully, under the tablecloth. But Ma noticed. As did Pa.

Ernid's brothers and sisters ate their Gag with ravenousness and then played out in the busy street dodging Burp trucks or sliding door vans of it which rattled past on the second. There was a no-splash clause in each worker's signed contract which was rigorously enforced so that any worker spilling a bit was fired straight away.

Anna got a bit hot out in the miniature garden and showed Ernid her thigh which excited him although he had no concept that there were two of them. He rubbed it expecting it to gleam but it was simply common flesh and it didn't; nevertheless he never forgot Anna showing it to him under the stunted apple tree.

Anna appeared to want sex with him and invited him to tea at her parents' home one night. They were too old to do a single thing except sigh so they both sighed a great deal as their variation of Gag was dished up without fanfare. Ernid drummed his fingertips on the table.

Her father worked for Burp in the newfangled pop top can section where the precious fluid was poured into molten tin and then sealed mechanically for the nation's fix.

Canned Burp became even more popular than bottled and even

Greeks understood it.

Canned it was and every single Australian milk bar stacked up great crates of it in fridges or just kept it in the scorching sun out the back with a rug over it.

The milk bar proprietors loved canned drink as it was easier to shove into the fridge, easier to grasp and to sell to the desperate public who started purchasing the stuff in a six-pack that was considered sexual or groovy when the cans came out.

Capitalist scientists engaged by Burp realised their captive audience was endless and endlessly fascinating for Market Research Department was the global willingness to guzzle their brand in any new way such as parboiled, heated up for scoffing in Nova Scotia or swilled in bulk in handy one ton boxes with attachable plastic easy-to-get-at tap at base.

Indeed frozen Burp was demanded by all chilly continents continually with respect to consumers' rights to hoe into it around the clock. Ever since its creation almost 160 years ago in America it has helped clinical depression and very nearly eradicated human anxiety. It is more than merely palliative.

The dying are given it to cheer them up on their death beds, coming in the physical form of a drip or taken as an ice block.

One Tuesday evening Burp presented screenings in hundreds of cinemas dotted throughout their plant and these entertainments were keenly looked forward to by loyal managers as well as the bottom end. So to speak.

Anna fell hopelessly and completely in love with Ernid and to win his heart she tempted him to come over to her parent's place for a scrumptious supper of Cola Cutlets with a side dish of wilted spinach done in Fanta, which was brand-new and the research was showing that orange-flavored Burp was a hit everywhere it was tested and found to completely satisfy.

Her honest parents politely tipped a modicum of chilled milk on the family meal which happened to be All Bran; but the incensed mother screamed something shocking when the father ill-poured it. She was outraged and all purple in her face because he had tipped a little too much on one side of her proffered bowl.

# CHAPTER THREE

## ENGAGEMENT FOR BURP'S SAKE

It was wondrous to become engaged to the rapturous Anna whom Ernid was simply crazed with, dreaming of her particularly when he was right next to her, which seemed odd to her but she had gone out with so many conservative youths and this dear boy at least had a bit of go in him. He was her first love who was eccentric.

He wasn't so especially good-looking in any way but the big mouth put her in mind of Mick Jagger and was considered sensuous by his wrestling team at work. Many of the men saw him as a turn on and they dreamt of him too.

He was perhaps six feet in the old measurements in his silk stockings and he was terribly emaciated complete with a concave chest which lent him a depressed piano accordion look at his front. He was also bronchial so Anna feared he might keep her awake if they became betrothed, which they did anyway so she just had to wear it.

He dressed casually, too casually for her liking, and she put pressure upon her fiancé to dress in a more considered manner, such trousers as black or purple imported corduroy matched with a striking sort of vest topped with a celluloid collar if she could find one in one of the better city stores such as David Jones.

She wasn't happy with the eyes that God lent him in the instant he was thought of, they being a mismatch where one was hazel yet the other bore a cerulean blue hue that was opal-like and many who looked into it were aghast at its rabid intensity; it was like the eye of a coral snake.

She herself dressed impeccably but conventionally, naturally, and frowned at the short skirts that were becoming popular with other Burp staff. One lass in Sales chose to wear a blinding green mini skirt which resembled a blade of grass.

It was decided that sexual congress might be a positive thing after they had courted for a year without touch as 'going the grope' was called at

Burp. They had very hotly kissed at the movies and panted like asthmatic mandrills for each other just about everywhere they went. She was just 19 and happily so was Ernid so they scraped up enough for a motel and got into bed together buck naked.

She read to him to relax him a little but she chose *How To Make Money And Influence People* written by Dale Carnegie the famous American author who seemed an authority on almost everything except light heartedness; and that was probably just what the young nubile couple wanted as they were both determined virgins.

She showed him her clitoris and he thanked her with a written note. It was utterly hopeless trying to get to know one another with nothing on so after about an hour of rugged unhappiness they dressed and played rope quoits in the quiet of the evening. Ernid let her win and she knew that he did, although she gave him oral sex in their bed and once again he hand-wrote a highly formal note of appreciation.

Meantime at Burp a recession had savaged the great firm and many thousands of workers were unfortunately let go. People got the envelope everywhere and it was particularly cruel in Pulverizing Section where a hundred dedicated serfs were booted out with merely a buck for each year they'd toiled there. Ernid was a favorite of the gods and his manager Miss Purves, who vigorously and obviously flirted with him, actually promoted him just to stick it to his more experienced workmates.

Ernid was surprised one day to peep into his tiny crisp pay envelope, shake the notes and coins out onto his workbench and discover it was much more than last week's pay by a long chalk. Miss Purves made him the Leading Hand and dismissed old Bob Treacle after years of loyal service. Old Bob got drunk immediately at a pub over the road from Burp and wiped himself right off with fifty straight rums and Burp, but he drank with nobody but himself, being stupid.

The new leading hand was expected to show leadership by experience and Ernid was good at showing safe work practices such as how to put heat proof leather gloves on whenever undoing volcanic hot faucets and bending down pretty low on the overhead cat walks to scoop up thick particles of preservative which clogged up the sieves that led to purification corridors and vast arrays of copper tubing that fed the dye into the whole river of the stuff. It could be tricky work at times, that's for sure.

Ernid led by example just as his own troubled family had to do during the hard times in The Old Country, where with only the pampered pet pig to give them rest in their battered minds, they just had to deal with massacres and freezing to instant death should they accidentally fall into a crevasse, and so on.

The jolly pig came back to gently haunt him during the first days of his upgrade in wage and responsibility at the new job. It once squealed as he clocked on although there was no visual or intellectual evidence of its being at Burp. It was more an apparition of the poignant pig.

Although Ernid openly talked to it on his shift the rest of his fellow workers didn't enjoy open conversations with imaginary beasts that much; they rather wished that he didn't do it. Ernid certainly had his faults but I mean to say here – don't we all?

Because of his unblemished record over the year he'd been at the plant his bosses decided to shift him into Bottle Tops.

He loved the intriguing work required of him on very long and arduous shifts of scanning by human eyes the lake of fizz as it got shunted and pumped via powerful jets and piping into waiting hot and cleansed bottles on a shrieking ten mile long conveyor belt. The result was that a machine imported from Atlanta, which was very efficient, personally hit the metal lids on.

He was delighted with the sights and various assertive metallic stamping sounds that somehow seemed familiar; such as the boots stomping away on concrete footpaths that the Nazis hit the eardrum with to horrifying effect by way of sheer force of will and propaganda that crumpled anything in its way.

Ernid sang ancient village songs to the hiss and beat of the armies of soft drink bottles as they rattled at him like waterlogged and droning live creatures. He began to see soft drink as politics, which it is in marketing of course, and he scurried fast as possible in his enormous rubber gum boots along his perimeter to stare without ever blinking at his devouring glass audience.

Anna was herself shifted into Bottle Tops which excited her because it included a free vinyl hair net that she coveted, in fact she had always coveted hair nets and wore one on her own wedding night.

Mind you it got terribly humid in Bottle Tops which is entirely understandable given the manner in which tin is heated to over 4000 degrees and then stamped really hard in a pleasing clamping action over the nude light green bottle's throat. But after several million of them right in front of you it gets a bit of a drag.

Sometimes Anna desired Ernid during trial runs of various experimental Bottle Top metals the company were interested in; and she panted for his touch in the most brazen way and tried to feel him up as he checked out the bottle tops as they raced along under the fifty thousand finely tuned bottle stamping guns.

'I want you Anna but unfortunately not now!' he would lament and she would just have to wear it. But they worked side by side without congress practically all of the long day and Ernid when copulating with her at home called her 'My Little Lid!' which aroused her without any foreplay. She thenceforward demanded to be called 'My Little Lid!'

His father was a problem as he deliberately became Type 2 Diabetic. He used to grizzle about it about the home and go crook whenever Rolly Polly Cake was being presented as the dessert after the piping hot Gag got down past the gullet of the perennially starving gob.

Pa Ernst was seriously sick though and in the days before insulin at home came in the annoyed family kept him in the rabbit hutch and cast him a carrot if he were good.

Mrs Ernst caught the illness too and in the end she also lived in the hutch, which she liked and preferred to her bedroom because of the easy access to carrots.

At Bottle Tops management installed a Croatian as the new leading hand and sent the much valued Ernid to training camp in inner Sydney in their effort to boost the boy into a higher soft drink stratosphere, which he liked. He collected them.

Anna missed her chap something shocking but she was never late at work and keenly operated the boiling hot metal lid stamping machines in a steady blur of hydraulic steam and sugary hisses.

To toil in Bottle Tops was seen as special by the uneducated masses who worked there, for many of them just watching something get stamped was like being born in parts of Europe or remote China where there is no escapism except more toil which merely leads them to oblivion and even more anonymity.

The Croatian chap fancied Anna and one day placed his only bicep on her shoulder and commenced to whistle a Croatian propaganda melody in her earhole; she slapped his cruel face and he wept like a baby in front of all the others, which was a shame.

Training school or college afforded the young fellow the golden opportunity of improving his mind and although it was intensive and long, each day of strict adherence to classes saw him lift his imagination as never before. On the first morning he had to get blindfolded with all the others in his team and what appeared like communion drinks in tiny glasses filled with Fanta were presented to the pupils.

The idea was to identify the new taste of orange that the soft drink scientists were perfecting in the lab.

'It isn't peach!' whispered hoarsely one of them in an over-excited sort of a way.

Others of the students thought it tasted more like mandarin but that verdict was poo-pooed.

Revolutionaries within the company were trialing raspberry and not merely orange but blackcurrant. It was grim times for commerce and Australia itself almost went up its own oriface during the Credit Squeeze of 1961; the only way through was a confident experimentation with sparkling fun flavours, it was thought.

Training School taught Ernid enough for Management Status and he was earmarked for Director Of Flavours, which would net him more income than his family had ever counted before. He tried hard to dress sharper and speak wittier although his whole background lay in clinical depression that was recognized as sport in his village.

Some of the theories he studied were the pursuit of greater knowledge of the ancient and the modern relationship that has always existed between money and lemonade. He studied original Hebrew transcripts discovered in Cairo in tombs which showed the earliest understanding of the gullet, the bowel and the large intestine. He was good at tracts.

He read of the ancient Egyptian intrigue for soft drink or carbonated papyrus which when diluted with crocodile moisture produces a surprising taste not unlike Fanta.

'Marvellous!' he enthused as he pored over primitive likenesses of milk bars executed by slave-artists in the employ of the great Pharaohs.

He also got enthused by Marketing and quite rightly saw it as the only pathway to international success; he could see the only writing on the wall worth looking at – that Burp would sell like fury in every milk bar on the Earth; that the very name of it was imprinted on the parched lips of all on the dying planet.

Not only was it important but necessary because people about to be executed in soccer stadiums demanded a can before getting machine-gunned, and martyrs in every civilized and uncivilized country of the world spoke the word Burp just before a public garotting.

People needed it much more than the burden of their own loved ones and had their parents forcibly removed and a big fridge full of it shifted in to replace them.

Burp was the planet and Fanta the heavenly stratosphere.

# Chapter Four

## Burp Cutback

The sheer ferocity of the 1961 Credit Squeeze delivered a knockout punch to Burp in Sydney that sent fearful vibrations through every lemonade plant in Australia; including Boon Spa and Tarax.

The tiny Italian lemonade works situated in Thomastown kept pumping out the sour soft drink called Bisleri and since thousands of Italians dwelt right in Thomastown it was considered certain they could trade their way through recession even if the Italians decided to cut back on their incredible consumption of Burp.

All through the plant was gnashing and wailing with the gnashing worse than the wailing. The usually cocksure managers weren't as sure as normally they were, nervous and agitated and paranoid; the sack was just round the corner, some bosses actually deferred to the lower orders to check out what they felt exactly, and the irony of seeing such a thing wasn't lost on Ernid.

He well remembered the tanks rumbling into Prague in 1956 and the firebombing and he even recalled the shock of newsreel footage, usually grainy with crummy sound in bad cinemas where people pigged out on garlic to cease considering Adolf Hitler and the monstrosity of his ideas that came true all through Europe.

The pressure of anticipating the sack always brings about the actuality of it and so it was that all staff at the plant got into a right old state. Their futures were more up in the air than the carbon dioxide that made their fizzy.

Ernid was suitably sad and chastened when the last oiled-body wrestling match came about at their lunch break; the look of fear was in the men's every expression as they disrobed and oiled their brutish frames and got stuck into each other. Some put fatal pressure into their neck-locks until their opponent died and was speedily interred in the plant cemetery.

Usually in the tradition of oiled labourer wrestling there are one or two light-hearted moments between thrusts and eye-gouges and various blows to the spleen or the head-butt; but today it was just be brutal and wring the guy's head off sort of philosophy; the fun went out if for Ernid and he didn't rejoice in his horrifying head-butts.

The problem was the pain wasn't the same.

You ought to have seen the desultory looks on the tense faces that belonged to Burp; the wrestling-room didn't possess the old familiar pong of Deep Heat Muscle Cream any more; the toilets didn't flush and the wrestlers declined to put their underpants on and were so halfhearted about it that they wrestled nude to the exhausting taped music of yodelling

Ernid found sexual fulfillment in reading and commenced to memorize every back issue of *Readers' Digest* which he could find no fault in; he sat indeed of an evening in his favourite antique reading chair and experienced orgasm after orgasm just flicking through sections of it like 'My Most Unforgettable Character'; although he couldn't recall just who that was.

His wife was understandably cheesed and began dalliances at the plant, mostly with Pacific Islander Fork Lift Truck Drivers that turned her on in the plant garden by showing off their gargantuan buttocks.

She had money, her own savings out of Bottle Top Section, she joined The Credit Union and paid for the first ever costly tanning capsules to turn on the Fork Lift staff who fancied her.

She began dating a one-armed Pacific Islander Fork Lift guy and they would make passionate love in his parked Fork Lift Truck that really gave her sexual energy, partly because he got it going as they did it.

Mother and Father Ernst startled Ernid and the rest of them around about this stage of the game by becoming Anglican as opposed to Catholic; they thought it was cheaper.

The New Way Church was where they now felt free to worship partly because it was right in the shopping centre and you could always get a park, though they both walked.

The church itself bore an enormous razor sharp point to its apex manufactured of rolled copper-sheeting and many a passer-by marvelled

at both its sheer height as well as unbelievable sharpness of metaphysical gloom as well as physical sorrow architecturally-speaking since hundreds of filthy scavenging sea gulls perished completely as they flew into it and were decapitated, leaving bloodied feathers stuck all over it.

It was a tiny but fiercely loyal congregation who prayed and sang the melancholic hymns each Sabbath no matter what; and Ernest's young and highly impressionable eyes would flood on hearing the sacred songs he knew cheered no one up.

There was an old woman organist who played winningly up the back somewhere and it was worth it just turning up for her, otherwise the misery of the songs might be forfeited forever thought Ernid as he made his humble way there for the first time.

The famed hymn 'We Can All feel Bad If We Want To' was being sung as he bowed and went into the putrid dark.

Sad fellow travellers through life did not greet him or show a single solitary thing as the stranger among them sidled by to his choice of wooden pew. They were all mostly Burp workers and Ernid was slightly dismayed to discover Coles Black Currant Juice being served up as part of their Communion accompanied with a Jatz Cracker on a plate being passed around. He received rude stares when he failed to eat them.

The Minister was Mister Almond Cracker who was perhaps seventy or so and whose over the top deodorant preceded him before he came on from behind a dark russet curtain and just stared at his flock dead.

He certainly seemed crucified and the very second he stood so still the gathering copied his exact expression and looked dead as well. Ernid stared at the congregation and couldn't see a single smile amongst any of them, apart from the Minister who was now mindlessly beaming at them in a mummified way before he delivered his hand-written sermon that was always incomprehensible. Ernid's parents sat a bit too close to their son and cheered at the wrong times because that was what you did back home in the church of their village. Ernid's father began to bleat.

Try as they might the rambling sermon of the Minister actually made little or no sense to anybody assembled there; this particular Sabbath it had to do with dangerous intersections that the Minister had hand-drawn with a large black Texta pen on the back of an enormous length of brown cardboard that once contained a washing machine.

The Minister likened the rigid pursuit of Jesus to a busy intersection and handed out the big expanse of cardboard for closer scrutiny but there wasn't a single worshipper there who could see the connection. It was just a washing machine box.

After an hour and a half of dispiriting hymns it stopped and they all filed into a big cold hall to feel bad. There was awful coffee or awful tea.

What the congregation was after were the buttered Teddy Bear biscuits that each Sunday a kindly volunteer came up with and put hundreds on plates. Mother and Father Ernst felt slightly awkward when South Pacific Islander teenagers boxed viciously right in front of them and succeeded in belting one another about in a truly upsetting way, with droplets of flying gore going on the coffee cups and sugar spoons.

They hadn't expected boxing in an Anglican church very much, not at the same moment of meeting the elders and trying hard to hobnob.

'God Bless Burp' was emblazoned on a very big white banner and practically impossible not to take in as Ernid munched his buttered Teddy Bears in a rapt way and tried to mix; but that seemed practically impossible for some reason that was real.

When he and his parents strode back home they had no sense of having gone anywhere; and that was a key impression that he was beginning to sense just about everywhere he went in Australia.

It was pretty different at the plant because he was being promoted and sent from new section to new section, constantly learning new facets and understanding new faucets.

He tried to review the Minister's sermon with his suddenly ageing parents but they just wanted to avoid being squashed by a Coles truck as much as possible, it being no fun being run over on a cold day.

Maybe due to the killer workload and incessant long shifts, the demands on his hours that came in the form of rosters that never ended, the work or home work he was obliged to take home by way of written 10,000 word essays on camaraderie or how he felt about Fanta as opposed to Burp – something was tiring in him and he was just twenty years of age but felt all washed up.

He no longer had a sex drive and of course Anna was enjoying extra marital affairs in the Fork Lift Section and their marriage as a consequence was shaky. She sometimes raved at the table about the prowess of her lovers at the plant but Ernid just shut it out and got on with his hot Gag that they dined on without a single variation eternally and remorselessly in the manner of all newly arrived migrants.

In his bedroom he wearied of Anna's lurid descriptions of hot sex with Fork Lift Truck Drivers and although pleased with her orgasms asked her from time to time to play table tennis with him in the cream brick double door garage; she pretty much always agreed and when they played singles into the wee hours he called her a good sport, which I suppose she was.

One day at work they installed him once again in Pulverizing Section but as Care Taker Of It which was its exact title; and he was required to not just oversee the mind-blowing power of the crushing of the bottles by giant iron and copper arm-things and put up with the great grinding noises the vats created when all the empties went in, but he also from time to time had to climb right down into these vats and so on.

Occupational Health And Safety personnel had sworn that these mile high vats were safe and sound but to arrive right down into them on a rickety steel ladder in big gum boots was not for the squeamish. But he always did what he was told and so he grimly but determinedly descended the horrid ladder to the very bottom of the fizzy empties that ferociously gargled at him like insane dogs.

Many staff observed Ernid descend the great big vat and were pleased it was him more than them who had to do it; the sound alone was like Niagara Falls if you could picture lemonade cascading in it rather than pure water.

He arrived at the bottom, hundreds of yards down in there and gave the thumbs up sign, something he'd never seen before in all life but knew instinctively to do it as it was the right thing under the circumstances. But what was he signalling?

It was like a fabulous end to human understanding when instead of bending over in relative tranquility to examine the metal base of the gigantic empty vat in his instruction to check for rodents, mechanical rods arrived out of the walls rather unexpectedly to say the least, and these one ton rods made of tungsten mixed with pure copper struck him about the teeth area and repeatedly assaulted his rather large jaw, rendering it not on.

The gore of course poured out of his missing face and torrents of the bright red fluid began to fill his great gum boots till overflowing; he was at a loss as to what his function might be now that he felt deceased or at least not that great. He lay inert at the base of Vat 4 and sort of heard or overheard the shrieks of horror emanating from the mouths of his loyal workmates.

They saw to their shock their friendly leader lying in a vast puddle of his own gore where he should have been bending down examining the base of the vat for health's sake. He didn't look all that healthy.

The effort to shut up the fast-propelling arms or rods used to smash the glass bottles had literally knocked his block right off until there was virtually nothing left of him. It took ages to get the rods to settle and cease their erratic vibrations and basically shut the whole steel vat down whilst he lay there as dead as a door nail.

As the hurtful copper and other metallic rods shot right out of the vat ever downward and went right in him and then more grinding apparatus followed suit coupled with hyperactive mops that ground into the blood-spattered base where he lay in agony, the new awfulness was the shocking fact that he was being observed by staff in Pulverizing Section who saw exactly what was occurring to their troubled workmate.

Their woeful and demented faces moaned inaudibly towards Ernid who helplessly and hopelessly tried hard to make some sort of connection with them; for there they were; hundreds from Pulverizing Section who knew as they beheld him writhing it could so very easily have been them in the same boat. All they could do was wave goodbye and leave it at that. They openly wept as his spent and mangled body was eventually lifted on a winch that in itself didn't look that steady.

The plant medical team pronounced him deceased several times in the company's private operating theatre, their own priest who doubled in Pulverizing Section gave him The Last Rites even though there was nothing left of him. Unexpectedly he rose through his tubes and medical support with an iron will very closely related to peasant life and the verdict was altered and they said he was alive. He was.

Ernid had lost his entire jaw in the accident as well as most of his throat and the missing bits went as far as a lung and his oesophagus and all up it was a near thing. But he was still kicking.

He was slid into an ambulance on several drips clutching feebly his jaw in a bag.

But nothing of course shuts a lemonade conglomerate down and the upset staff in Pulverizing Section were soon mopping up where their workmate had lain and all the pumps and sieves and great pipes of thundering hot dye and syrup and sugar commenced to tip loudly into the vats as horns sounded and overhead bright lights blinked on and the night shift began in deadly earnest.

Ernid remained rather unconscious in the plant clinic but he felt okay about new parts pretty much; he was professionally put in the picture and accepted that his new experimental mechanical jaw could do him good. With no head on just about he read about it in medical-science literature that lay on resting stations which looked like coffee tables to him.

He was a prototype, a new lemonade toiler, a man of tomorrow and as the arduous rehab classes took over from scampering up and down lemonade ladders all the time he started to enjoy crude elocution classes and could by now pronounce the word Fanta in such a way it was understandable but not very coherent to the untrained ear-hole.

Ma and Pa gathered as only they knew how, on either side of him. The factory clinic was actually one big rest room containing the injured. He didn't quite recall what had happened to him or all around his stricken body, just the awful sounds of the pulverizing and the mess it all made of a human being.

Ma said he looked practically identical and he tried hard to nod to that, and Pa agreed that he could look far worse but Ernid just tried to shrug that remark off but it was a limited shrug to be certain and it could have been seen as assent if it were neither of his parents looking at him for the exhibit he was. He looked like crap.

He felt dreadfully stiff all over and sore just about everywhere he tried to stretch. He was all blurry and indecisive and limited to a great degree in jaw and throat movement; he soon would be in the gym and doing weights to gain muscle tone. But still in all he didn't feel too crash-hot it has to be said.

The Specialists moved in on him and studied the missing bits after he had convalesced a month at the expense of the firm, although he assumed he was covered by Medicare Private his wife had forgotten all about keeping up the necessary payments and he had lapsed utterly.

He could vaguely remember his ATM number but he couldn't think if he banked with the Commonwealth or ANZ.

What exercise regime he did like was weights and treadmills for they put him in mind of The Capitalist System and he always respected money in this formidable new continent. It was odd to him that although the average Australian was mythic overseas and seen to be generous with their cash he had seen no sign of it since his arrival eighteen months back.

One particularly grueling morning after a hard workout at Rehab he was just resting on his beloved treadmill, chatting to Robert who'd lost a jaw too, when Anna swept in with her new boyfriend the giant guy she'd been seeing in the Fork Lift Section.

His heart squirmed if heart can do that; and they most likely are capable of squirming when the emotional shock is great enough.

It was very hard to accept that she had left him for a Fork Lift Guy.

The new man was brilliantly put together like someone who worked out all the time and was just so laid-back and cocksure within himself; he positively glistened as his powerful visible chest hairs stood erect, deliberately it felt.

He not so much gracefully but effortlessly strolled about the various operating theatres having a good sticky at sick and perished lemonade staff who had fallen foul of the latest thinking in machinery. One had no head on and a soft drink straw was inserted right in his neck and yet his bereaved family mourned him as if he were intact.

In the medical centre although he was in vast agony and feeling pretty mortified that he was so very close to death, that an oxygen drip and morphine stand stood right by like comrades in arms to help him get through the extra powerful saw they had used to get the remnants of jaw and bone and gristle and what-have-you well clear so they could commence fitting an artificial mouth on him had sort of hurt him.

He was sat up nice and ramrod straight and a gaggle of specialists fussed or swarmed around his half-face (as it were) and there they forked into him and fiddled with this funny tube of him, lifted away coagulated this and rotted that; it was rather like putting the rubbish out on rubbish night.

He was of course unaware of anything medical-cum-scientific proceeding in any possible way, he being heavily sedated with powerful dope, and it took two complete days to give him a service that included a lube and fresh radiator fluid and a check of his headlights, or eyes that had been badly biffed about by the rods.

Others were in nearby Rehab and were getting looked at to put a new foot on or a complete new head that might have come in from any land on Earth; possibly Outer Space where arms and feet were being grown by specialists in this sort of thing.

Ernid's parents set up camp in the operating theatre in a small rather cute tent and there they slept, or alternatively munched their heated Gag.

At one stage of the game Ernid's father got up off his haunches and asked his unconscious son if he too would like some hot home-cooked food from Home.

The clinicians forbade him to speak and drove him back into his tent and cautioned both parents about getting in the way of medical science.

The fact was that Ernid Ernst was nothing more than a busted model of a man that needed a new mouth, chest cavity and possibly brain and definitely a new lung because a copper pulverizing shaft had completely skewered it like you would not believe. It was practically astonishing that Ernid was alive after his ordeal.

He sighed in his deep, deep sleep since his olfactory senses could detect that Gag was around and he vomited up blood a few times, which made an awful mess and the cleaners were summoned into the operating theatre to speedily mop it all up. They also put a fairly nice Turkish carpet under his single bed to jazz it up a bit.

Eventually the much-taped and much-anticipated big parcel from overseas arrived and the postman had the delivery docket witnessed and signed by the three specialists in New Parts.

If you have ever seen a new radiator go into a car then that is virtually what occurred next as the new parts team undid the bulky parcel from Detroit and pulled away all the styrene-foam and rubbish and lifted it on an overhead winch straight into him with no more mucking around.

They linked filters to both lungs, the badly collapsed one and the alright one, they tightened up reasonably simple to understand screws with dirty big plastic handled screwdrivers, they wiped back every molecule of excess gore until they got access to the gaping hole in his head. The specialists had to be sponged down it was so hot in there; and one ducked out for a smoke quarter the way through it as he just needed to get outside to think straight.

The new mouth of Ernid could be claimed on Medicare Private which his mother scrupulously kept paying despite an invisible income; she it was who used to scrounge old Burp bottles and get the tiny deposit on them at certain drop-in-centres. This was how she kept the family going whilst Ernid fought for his mouth and a fair bit of the rest of him. It was how she maintained the Gag the family shovelled into themselves at every chance.

'A One, a one, a one two three!' cried the Chief Spare Parts surgeon and the entire team lifted the winch that contained a fibre glass mouth and neck and chest cavity directly into the patient's gaping holes.

In a jiffy it was correctly attached and screwed together and bolted up nice and just right; you couldn't really fault any aspect of the procedure. Radiator Coolant was tipped in next in a speedy way, his oil level dip-stick was scrutinized and several brand-new spark plugs were put in him, which was the hardest part of it all.

He was thoroughly sponged down and dried with a leaf-blower and allowed to go into Rehab at once. They even gave him a latte.

As his impressed but tired parents accompanied him to Rehab a new recipient of a mechanical steel and latex jaw was brought in, rather unwillingly it must be said here, and vigorously hurled onto the waiting operating table that had a small reading lamp by it and a copy of the *Herald-Sun* to peruse if patients felt like that sort of thing.

The new jaw was stiff at first and Ernid had to try to get used to it as best he could, although he mourned the old mouth and missed eating, not just home-baked Gag but things like steamed dimmies.

The experts showed him himself in a portable mirror and he stared without any recognition at the new human model of his former self; the way it looked so hard and shiny he realized it needed to be broken in a bit and looked forward to having a wrestle with another jaw recipient to rough it up a bit. It really needed to be broken in.

Two experts showed him a likeness of a pie and said 'Bite!' and so he tried to bite but the drive shaft of the jaw still had some stiff particles of styrene foam jammed in them and it was all too stiff to think of coming at a pie, hot or cold it would have been impossible, just about, I would have thought.

His new digestive tract was of tractor tubing and allowed some give and take in the deed of swallowing food or the sipping of fluids like Burp, which he slavered for with his every atom. Things do go better with it.

In the end he was given a decent oil and put in a wheelchair and taken into the plant gardens to briefly convalesce but even that was a bit perfunctory. The others with new jaws on in their wheelchairs performed road rage upon him and battered him to bits right in front of family and admirers of the stricken accident victims.

And victims there sure were in the industry and not just Burp who boasted an unblemished hit record in safety programs that only enhanced its immortal name.

From the delirious days of their original alabaster drinking fountains of the 1870s when the grateful thirsty public slaked their need of it by scooping out a cup or two in the most luxuriant way to the present day when you may purchase it upon the surface of the moon.

Marketing Scientists have grappled with the problem of outer space sales ever since operations began 150 years ago, but now there isn't an outlet in outer space that doesn't boast a perfect record for freshness, availability and gassiness.

A worry for the revival of Ernid arrived when upon the operating table it proved impossible to cool him down to the correct heat in order for him to work at the plant once more; in their determination to restore his health they tipped half a bag of party ice into his new neck and former jaw area and that seemed to work.

He actually murmured at one time and tried to get up and put his pants back on but they administered more party ice diluted with powerful Aspirin capsules and succeeded in getting him down to an operable temperature. The mechanical jaw was fitted in and the metal gearbox and clutch that drove it placed in his chest.

To eat or drink he only had to push a simple button in his shoulder and to give himself a charge he only had to patch himself into an ordinary power point, either in the comfort of his own home or out strolling using a remote, at least this was the plan and naturally the concept was new and the scientists said there could be teething problems but would have to wait and see just how he went.

Part of his regime at Rehab was to drink as much fizz as was practicable without becoming over burpy and it was agreed not to indulge in more than a slab per day.

When he came home his concerned parents put on a big banquet for him that for once skated around the problem of having to eat and digest Gag.

They presented their son with a complete Sunday Roast which included pork and crackling that Ernid loved passionately. He commenced with a miniature pea but as he attempted to come at it in the new ceramic and wire teeth a bright red light came on and a sound like a brake siren arrived; similar in intensity as a van with a sliding door trying to reverse out of a lane.

His parents noticed of course but cheerfully put it down to modern medicine and the prevails therein; as they tucked into the juicy pork and baby roasted potatoes they passed around the literature the clinic had given them when they left and tried really hard to study the dense descriptions to do with recovery and digestion.

Ernid wept at one stage when a hot sprout became lodged in his mesh denture and its stubborn folded leaves grasped the new-made lower gums with unbelievable hurt to its owner. His mother hit the vegetable down his experimental throat with the back of a fork.

He found the pork really hard to get at though the mouth sort of ate it for him and it was good at swallowing, the machine, and after half an hour its recipient had consumed three good thick-cut slices as well as a big bit of pumpkin that was a fair bit easier than he'd ever thought possible. The gravy sailed down in one mechanical and grateful gulp.

'Thank you very much my beloved parents for the outstanding pork shoulder roast as well as the steamed baby sprouts, they were fantastic!' gasped Ernid as he wiped the mouth that he couldn't feel with his tissue from the family tissue box on the family tea table. He was so glad they were there as he didn't want to get gravy all down his new throat, that would be depressing and he's had enough depression to last him a lifetime, even several of them.

'You surely got room for ice cream and jelly my love?' said his mother as she dished him up a bowl of fresh ice cream adorned with a generous pile of quivering raspberry jelly; the others tore into their serve at once but poor Ernid just nibbled a fraction of the jumpy desert and wept when the insane coldness of it reacted with his gullet and offered him more pain than is acceptable these days just about anywhere on the planet.

He wiped his artificial mouth a great deal in the small family bathroom then stared hard at the contraption within his head and noticed he'd lost his soul. There was nothing left of his old familiar look, his natural buoyant look had fled and he felt gutted.

Nothing hurt within him or anything like real discomfort but he wasn't him anymore, he was a robot of medical science, an automaton who lived inside a machine that tried to nibble food for him but he'd lost his booklet of instructions.

He combed his still shiny hair, at least that felt pretty real and comforting and assuaged some of the new fears which sprang out of his consciousness such as whether he could get a lady.

Anna had set his divorce in train and had shouted him a six buck legal separation kit from the post office; he'd written to express his gratitude.

# CHAPTER FIVE

## THE BURIAL OF A BURP TOILER

Not so long after Ernid's release from the clinic he was invited by post to turn up at a funeral for someone he worked with at the plant who had fallen similarly into a glass bottle pulverizing vat. The guy was on a double-shift and though that was long the wages of course were a reward in economic tough times; he was glad of it in fact and his family lived pretty good on the strength of it.

It was a dismal industrial affair in the end as the priest got his name wrong as well as his calling, that of bottle crusher and said at his service he drove trucks.

At his request he was interred anonymously and nearly all of him laid to rest in an unmarked grave in the company of the many accident victims who had gone before him. Staff had been struck ferociously over the brain by large heavy pallets and others had succumbed to falling into dye that tinted the liquid concoctions the public vied for.

The dead man was slid into his crypt on a rope and covered over with crumpled bottle tops which acted everywhere around as landfill. The man's family were so distraught that they threw themselves in after him, not that it did any good but at least they made their point.

Ernid was requested by Pulverizing Section to say a few words of comfort to the grieving family but his mechanical teeth had jammed in first gear and would neither open nor close so he just grunted as best he could in his limited command of English. He needed a new clutch.

He tried hard to state that the dead worker was a good person who was popular with the rank and file and not too bad at inter-factory ping pong; he had apparently been Ernid's table tennis partner and together they'd defeated Fanta in the finals. He had a stunning forehand.

It commenced to pour with rain and it was observed by mourners that the very air smelled of fizzy.

There were some splendid moments in Ernid's elegy that he's penned on the reverse side of a packet of blackcurrant juice for the occasion, but mostly it had faded and was nigh on impossible to read aloud through his speaker phone.

Indeed the voice of Ernid resembled tin foil being squashed loudly and incoherently because no matter how hard he tried nobody got him. He tried to pull the mechanical mouth out at one time because he couldn't be understood on any real level, but the false mouth and artificial jaw were indestructible.

In the end his father read the remarks to the stricken grievers but his peasant accent and goat-herd-mentality made understanding him not that possible; and people threw manure at him that they had collected before the service started in the anticipation all the eulogies would be duds. Pa was pelted with it and never really recovered from such a public embarrassment.

* * * * *

Ernid convalesced poorly at The Plant Rehab partly because there were too many recipients of crushed faces and most limbs of the worker's bodies to be taken seriously by the company. They tried hard to put their injured first but with the remarkable ballooning of the global market and sheer pressure to expand in all departments to keep up with staggering demand by consumers the inevitable result was that some of the injured didn't fully recover and were sympathetically sacked.

Whole surrounding suburbs near the plant were filled with the many seriously hurt staff who'd either fallen into machinery like Ernid Ernst or been clocked by a darting Fork Lift Truck or got seriously stricken by drinking too much of the Burp.

There were indeed lots of families who'd been badly harmed at work in some way or another. Some completely gassed by lethal fumes had found Rehab difficult as it was hard just to breathe on the way from home to work, let alone go up the pub and try to socialize.

Sad to say The Pulverizing Section Company Choir folded and was badly missed because each Christmas they presented *Traviata* or *The Pirates Of Penzance* to a much cheered crowd who slaved away in any one of a thousand sections of Burp.

Because times were simultaneously awful for workers and fantastic for shareholders there were mass sackings and greater profits, the injured as ever came equal last and so it was that honest Ernid was required to shift back in with his often moody parents who would have gone as far as a wheelchair for him but not the 24 hour care he so desperately needed. They'd had him.

He liked at first the novelty of trying hard to get off to repose in his old bedroom, that one with wall posters of Croatian soccer heroes and a rather hot one of Marilyn Monroe clutching a kitten over her crotch that was a favorite of Pa.

'Oh', he used to say as he squinted at it, 'That's hot all right!' But it wasn't really, it was in dreadful taste and one felt sympathy for the kitten held in camera where it was probably hot and smelly.

He took ages to get off to sleep in the cage-like mesh jaw with its limited actions that were so predictable and actually hurt him whenever he attempted to speak or smile or just shut up without a locking sound that it made. He was given a padlock made of brass to clamp it shut but often he felt like talking as most new automatons do.

He would attempt to patiently read something late at night, usually something light-hearted like the hospital brochures he kept on his bedroom bookshelf. They were not hilarious naturally enough but it felt progressive just digesting all the technical data and studying the artwork that accompanied the rather dry text.

He read that he could easily rust for instance or perish if he ran out of four stroke oil. He had to learn to swallow in an entirely new and original way, a peanut might take a weekend to get down and he loved peanuts and dreamt of them all the time as if he were an elephant or a bison.

His legs and arms were just the same but it was the head that was hard to cope with, he could feel the unreasonable coarseness of crusts which he once adored to disintegrate and masticate with a peasant's will and strength of purpose because all peasants love crusts; however with the new technology he could scarcely get at them.

He wept really hard to view the recalcitrant crumbs bedeck his sore neck as they fell out of his new mouth and made a bee-line towards his balls that got terribly scratchy when he ate a salad roll and basically buggered it.

The hardest aspect of his regime in the morning was to shower as the hot water might rust his grille or seep into his chest cavity and destroy and degrade his lungs. The soap in the shower seemed more difficult to obtain a lather with but that might have been due to Pa cutting back on Life Buoy Soap that being deemed too expensive so the family had to have their scrub-up with dog soap.

It was nearly impossible to proceed with a shave because his chin whiskers and long throat hairs tried in their way to get into the mesh of his artificial mouth and in one of the brochures he read that was bad. He loved shaving and just had to be more careful, that was all. Generally speaking he had to live completely differently from now on.

He stopped singing in the shower in deference to listening to taped recordings of opera and he began to try to speak much more clearly and studied voice clarification techniques and also daily imitations of famous actors out of Hollywood such as Robert De Niro whom he could sort of do, or Mickey Rourke, but was nothing like him.

One morning his life was changed when a lady social worker dropped over and sat demurely on the family sofa and softly explained to him that from now on he would have to exercise his Hollywood impersonations at a more serious level as well as do weights connected to his jaw so that he could masticate with authority and, hopefully, enjoyment.

She withdrew a small set of leaden weights from her bag and attached them to the new jaw and instructed him to recite 'The Lord's Prayer', which he did straight away and did it in one.

He rather enjoyed playing with the jaw-weights and liked to try to swing them over his shoulder because that felt groovy, but the lady told him off for mucking around and straight away a tiny tear arrived in his real eye. Thank God I've real eyes he thought to himself.

She taught him how to sip chicken noodle soup with nothing on and he grimly thanked her, and she showed him how to relax with the new device and speak crisply, whether he was impersonating Robert De Niro or not.

He realized the social worker was attractive as she leant over the coffee table in her neatly buttoned but skimpy cotton blouse; she struck her incredible white teeth sharply with a lead pencil and hummed a

Himalayan Marching Tune to herself.

'You really need to look after yourself', she smiled although it was hard to see whether that smile was actual or just professional in many respects. He loved her.

She assured him he would in time grow accustomed to the gear changes in the teeth and told him to put the mouth into first when he ate a hot pie. He said he would never forget her sound advice and as she leant over he realized she was hot.

She chatted about control mostly and the need to check emotions and feelings of inadequacy now he was a cripple. She tutored him in the need for par-boiled vegetables, particularly baby sprouts, and he nodded assent that he realized they were good for his bowel; he also laughed at his own expense that he had one.

'You are lucky you do not have a mechanical anus', she grinned at him and actually stroked his right knee; that made him feel wanted.

Maybe she lusted for him and was sick and tired of being a put-upon social worker; he hadn't a clue about that aspect of her and all he knew about her were her charms such her softened eyes and nice bust.

She spent over an hour lecturing him on hygiene and the need to never overlook cleaning the wire mesh that was his mouth, to utilize wash-up-detergent in all its hard to get at bits such as the metal trapdoor thing that shut him right up with a definite clang sound. He never failed to un-padlock the security chain around his throat and was pleased when the social worker gave him the new combination to it.

He commenced to groan the more she leant over him and showed her charms. He realized just how long it had been since Anna had been on top of his sex organ, speaking of which he hadn't seen it since Rehab where at least he could urinate through it without experiencing agony. He was tired of it, no doubt on that score.

She bent over him and kissed his mesh passionately and he experienced an orgasm; he reciprocated by reading her a melancholic essay out of The Old Testament until she too achieved an orgasm. After that she hurriedly left his old parent's home and did leave her mobile number, which he could fleetingly make out in a way and tried to commit it to memory.

He sat at his spick and span kitchen table and read the instructions upon his medicine packets, put his magnifiers on and read each letter as if he were a Greek scholar; far from it of course, as he was just a laborer at a soft drink company; that was it, full stop.

The act of swallowing your medicine isn't always so easy what with all the sachets being hard to undo when you are in the nude; as Ernid mostly was when he did his tablets first thing of a morning. He had manufactured himself a hearty brew of tea and added a solitary white sugar, which his social worker had warned him against, but he felt he could lash out for once and enjoy life.

He gulped the forty different big and tiny capsules down, the swallowing being hard to do on his own. He scrunched his eyes hard and thought of his new lover, the social worker who'd leant over him.

After all the tablets had gone down the hatch he could feel the sense of leather deep down in his throat, and the smell of it, and he wondered whether the doctors had turned him into a belt or not because he felt like a belt.

He cooked a few Truss Tomatoes in his frying pan and made whole meal toast on which to support the fruit that looks more like a vegie.

He found it rather fun to sizzle them and plop them on the toast but when he sat to eat them the pips got snagged in his unfeeling ceramic dentures and he found himself coughing like a fool.

He was starving so proceeded with the repast but it was certainly painstaking.

He sipped his morning coffee but the stuff was tasteless as the scientists had put in new taste buds that were made in America for similar victims of industrial mishaps that he certainly knew about.

He cried again because the old familiar taste of coffee eluded him entirely; it might as well have been tea or lacquer thinners. He wept hard into his own wrists and was pleased that they hadn't been lost in an accident like his mouth and throat; his own hands looked so friendly at his real eyes that cried really powerfully as he realized that 'modern medicine has a lot to answer for' as his mind phrased it silently.

He called the erotic social worker, a thing he never expected to do in the course of his long day trying hard to get better, and she said she'd meet him anywhere. That excited Ernid Ernst very much, the prospect of love with the social worker, and so he concentrated hard on his new exercises, some of which weren't that so easy.

He felt much better at the plant rehab centre where many hundreds of implant recipients met to do the treadmill, the exercise bike, weights which were made of iron in the shape of big family bottles of fizzy. He loved the others immediately because their immediate pressures and fears made him lose himself; and after the accident that was exactly what he wanted to do.

He boarded the sturdy treadmill machine which was set on high; he requested a lower setting so the gymnasium instructress set it on 2, which was just the shot.

He got off to a nice steady start by hallucinating he was strolling somewhere friendly like one of the streets around his father's residence; where owls hooted obliquely in their way and sometimes springtime was available and his sore lungs opened up to take in the fragrances of bush wattle or land fill or open sewers that all seemed like old friends from Prague days.

The friendly mindless nice treadmill skipped along on its wide black conveyor belt and he traipsed after it to peacefully reach his destination of normalcy, something he needed more than oxygen or new drugs that sometimes just backfired; no matter what the specialists claimed they could do once they were in your system. Some very dominating drugs remained in your body forever, even longer.

He loved to joke with blokes worse off than himself and one or two had no head on, their heads had come off in some trifling accident such as a truck hitting them in the loading-bay whilst it either loaded up or violently unloaded. The new head ones accepted their sorrows, took the bad luck in their stride and screwed a basketball on.

There being no air conditioning in the plant gym it got fairly warm in there and the super fit and cheerful gymnasium ladies sometimes stopped organizing the exercises and handed the perspiring basketball head ones a small drink of tap water; these diversions were brief though and soon it was back to the grindstone again, flat chat!

One night he met the social worker at the Miami Motor Inn and they had wild intercourse together whilst knocking back a quart of scotch and delighting in a bag of grass she had bought somewhere, like a milk bar or a bus stop.

She looked hot when she came in the motel door and pashed on with him, not minding the metal jaw that much, although a lot of clattering she commenced to kiss him softer as she didn't want to dent her brilliant white teeth that looked just like tombstones to Ernid.

He enjoyed the lurid sex sessions at The Miami Motel with the sincere social worker whose name he failed ever to remember; he connected her with he *Titanic* for some reason though she didn't resemble a ship. He instigated the passion by lightly opening and shutting his mesh and latest tungsten mouth and it drove him to distraction when she fiddled with his little mouth-padlock and eventually undid it.

He did experience a difficulty relating to her emotionally, especially verbally as he could barely make a word of sense, so they usually made love eating pizza.

He didn't want to marry the lady that much but needed her body to remind himself of his own former one, and in that sense they hung out together but she had another real lover whom she adored wildly and one day Ernid was invited over to see her at her home and the lover was there.

Ernid was miffed that this was the case and stood at her bright doorway riddled with hot and burning tears of rejection, not that the social worker was really rejecting him; it was just that she had a new guy and he had a real mouth and was attractive and always had spare tickets to the opera.

Amongst the beneficial things the social worker had done for Ernid was to get him a health card so that his daily medicine costs were almost halved at the chemist shop. He almost laughed with relief when the lass at the register struck the controls with a positive 'ding' noise and handed him twenty in change out of a fifty.

'That's a lot happier!' she crooned and he heartily assented that it was and he shook her tiny claw and struck off up the footpath clutching the big bag of pills and then he sat in the park that he liked and took his tablets one by one.

But this time however the pills proved difficult to swallow, nigh on impossible and he hurt himself just getting one of the tiniest ones down his corrugated throat; he could feel the mechanical steel mouth absolutely rejecting them in some way; and he also felt a cramp coming on as if he were experiencing a wild seizure or spasm or death, which he didn't feel like.

He managed to get half of them down but the sweeping feeling was nausea no matter how hard he tried not to feel that. He despaired as he vomited the tablets up again in a yellow spray of rejection and was pretty concerned about what passers by might say; or whether he'd broken the law in some way.

'Jesus Christ, all over me shoes!' he cried as the billowing tide of crap swept downward onto his fairly new gymnasium shoes, wrecking them. He reluctantly held them both under a tap and tried to get the flowing water to sweep the crap off.

But the sick patch stuck irremovably to most of his laces and he despaired of the entire predicament.

'Modern medicine has a lot to answer for!' he said once again aloud, even though it isn't usually the right thing in contemporary society to speak aloud because ordinary citizens believe you're insane. 'We are meant to keep our mechanical mouths entirely to ourselves!' he actually shouted aloud, which is against the law in point of fact.

He knelt and wept as he tried to clean up the sick, the mess of mechanical medicine that kept him alive although destroyed him simultaneously. He reached into a bin and retrieved some old newspapers from it and gave himself a decent wipe down as best he could, but the tablets with their guarantees of a cure had violated the real him.

A passing drunkard offered him some grog but he said he wasn't up to it and the drunk told him to go and fuck himself which is what medicine was doing to him no matter what he did. He went into a friendly café and ordered a small bottle of chilled soda with an accompanying wedge of lemon and a straw and ice and tried to like that.

But the sensation of chilled ice presented him with a migraine headache and besides that the lemon was off so he paid politely and left without leaving a tip; and he usually left a tip because he was a nice guy.

He went back to the park in the gathering darkness and strove to swallow all the medicine right down because the social worker had foresworn him saying he must keep up the correct dosages lest he grow terminally ill; he didn't want that and after the last big one successfully disappeared down his purring throat he felt vindicated and considered his prospects, not that he had many of them.

'Where oh where do I fit into this society?' he again commenced to cry aloud as he walked sort of around in complete and near-perfect circles; he had no idea just where he was or where he was off to, but the walking felt good and it presented him with a sense of purpose. He ended up walking into a very cheap motel just up the track from Miami, which held too many memories.

He paid politely at Reception with a credit card his bank had pressured him like anything to procure and he decided to keep the receipt for taxation purposes because he had an appointment with his accountant coming up.

He read for a while but was distracted by his tablets that he laid out on the coffee table right by the tissues; all the packets seemed the same as what he was used to, the obscure titles and sometimes a whole lot of tiny cautions and tinier lettering no one could possibly follow. He stroked all of the packets of them and sighed deeply from way down inside his now android being.

'Why do I have to take so many?' he asked himself but of course no answer arrived and they seldom do in lonely motel rooms. He undressed and lay naked under the enjoyable bed sheets and reluctantly stroked his mouth with an extended fingertip.

'I'm now a machine!' was exactly what he uttered. 'Just a god damned device!'

He fell into a most profound sleep crowned with nostalgia and purest nightmares to do with his former contented self, well, relatively speaking contentment let us say, and in the visions he patted the old beloved pig of home and washed its snout lovingly in the wood chip bathtub, only to witness its unexpected death by firing squad and then he dreamt that he was responsible.

The stunning truth happened to be that he had become not merely a man-machine but an experimental being who may be able to dress without bother and put on his underpants and his socks and bend low to do up his laces, but his face was over. He looked like nothing on earth, a freak and he knew it. He saw his future and it was his forced involvement in a play he didn't want to write; or else a freak show.

He wandered along a sombre embankment all by himself and wished he had a mobile telephone on his person in order to speak to someone, basically anyone would do because of the isolation and alienation he felt that wildly churned and punished him.

He wondered what it was that he'd done incorrectly to deserve agony of mind and body.

By and by he came along to a park bench where a lady sat with the identical mechanical jaw he'd had put on. They seemed instinctively to know one another and there was a palpable intimacy between them. She smiled with the aid of the newly implanted foam rubber lips and with a jerky sort of a gesture she invited him to sit by her all alone.

She was stunning-looking apart from the hospital jaw but she was beautiful to him, of that there could be no doubt and he tried to talk to her but all he could do was to embarrassingly gulp. She gulped too but they communicated.

'Where did you have your accident if that is not a particularly rude question?' asked Ernid as he sat himself down alongside of her. 'In a pie factory!' she said and blushed and looked down at the innocent green grass as though more conversation lay there at her real feet. 'I understand', ventured Ernid, although he had no idea about pie factories or any mishaps in them. All he knew was that pies were a global hit.

The eating and consequent consumption of a pie can be unimaginably difficult even when the pie recipient has normal teeth, but for an artificially mouthed man it is quite impossible. Ernid dined alone as per usual and ordered the pie of the day which arrived topped with a big blob of tomato sauce and nothing more to speak of.

He requested steel cutlery and even a steel serviette as he liked propriety as he grew sicker and needed to practise perfect etiquette so as not to be depressed; he had long loathed depression and anxiety for the fools they are because the person who is so bedevilled with them offers ever more energy to them day by endless day. The only way to recovery is to completely starve them to death, then they quit your body and mind, what's left of it.

He had no idea what café he had the pie in except to say that it was remarkably rude in service and dreadfully expensive; he didn't score a pea or bean with the mains and in the end the pie came only tepid in temperature with horrid white plastic cutlery all around it. The salt and pepper to bump up the taste of the mince came in hard to get at paper sachets that his artificial teeth couldn't hope to penetrate. He ate them in their difficult to understand un-get-at-able paper coverings.

The girls that served him demanded to determine if he wanted a latte with his pie and they caused him to openly weep with a blend of humiliation and sorrow that you can't get good service anymore, not even in a café that sells mince pies and nothing but.

'I wished I had a real mouth with which to defend myself!' he blubbered and even as he blubbered the uncompleted pie was withdrawn from him and vigorously chucked in a bin in the kitchen that was dominated by cruel people.

'You will still have to pay for your pie!' screamed the waitress and shoved the bill onto the awful mince which had the white plastic fork and knife stuck in hard.

'That's okay with me!' sobbed the poor man but he happened to be utterly broken in his dwindling spirit and felt he didn't have a soul to call his own.

Like a beaten creature he asked for a doggy bag to take the remnants of the terrible pie back home, but his mind was off the pace and he was beginning to hear the sounds and voices of natural and unnatural horror that would destroy him.

In the complete end he composed himself in compost and slept with his medicine in it, his body in a perfect birth position, pre-natal almost as though his deformed body had been somehow eclipsed or forgiven by the fates. He never felt safer than living in a compost heap and made a mental note never to vary from it. He went to work next day completely invigorated due to breathing up so much nitrate and bulbs and what-have-you.

That morning was important for Ernid as he had an appointment with Management, in fact a meeting where he was offered a position in Public Relations as the perfect figurehead of recovery in industry. He became famous for reconstruction and determination to get to the apex of his calling.

Management impressed him with their ideas and for the first occasion in his existence he had the moment, he had self-respect and pride even if he had half a face. The truth was that he was indifferent to a whole look and saw each evening on the news bulletins the horrifying blown-up bodies of children in Syria and Afghanistan and just about every suburb in Australia. The world was at war with its entire self it seemed to him as he tried to suck a juice through a straw that was beyond comprehension.

He liked Management in their masculinity and vanity of dress, their hard corporate look and fastidious look, their absolute certainty was a real excitement and a thing to definitely try to imitate and possibly upstage. He was determined to be handsome and since he was once handsome he figured he could cut it.

As he listened enraptured to the advice of his superiors whom he saw as gods he realized he was not so different from the men right in front of him; they even liked him and he relaxed in their power and glory because they wanted to use him up.

They seemed so thoughtful and genuinely concerned about the fate of his ageing parents who both were good and faithful servants of the great plant of Burp.

One of the Managers touched him friendly on the knee and he purred because that touch was exactly like his father's sure and kind touch or caress.

'We want to take you places, Ernid', they cooed and he instantly felt to go with them to these lofty heights. He wanted security as much as a new head and just nodded his acquiescence and thought being kind was best for him. Being kind he realized is all anyone is ever remembered for. All the rest is vapour.

He was the go to man from now on, a photographer's delight. A man of more than many parts and even sexy; it was said that he looked sexy with the artificial mouth and that through marketing he would be seen as the new James Bond.

He thought that was going a bit far but he liked the idea of him being likened to a super hero in some way and becoming rich and powerful. He would be able to afford divorce and perhaps nicer clothing but he would never leave the compost heap, no way known. That was sacrosanct.

He was presented with his own posh office as well as twin secretaries known as the two Maria's who kept his diary and many media appointments. He was given a chauffeur and a mint-new Rolls-Royce whose roof was canvas and could collapse just like his new mouth. His pay was put up and now he was the new deal all together and he felt much better within his self.

He was a natural speaker and his voice-box was adjusted quickly to Speaker Phone in such a way he could get closer to his own microphone or boom it if he wanted to, he was briefed to work the room wherever he spoke; and this appealed to the natural performer in most of him.

The odd thing was that the public sympathized with him as his plight was theirs also because Ernid had a way of looking vulnerable; it was a mechanical hurt expression complete with sorrowing eyes that appeared to revolve to enlarge their melodramatic looks. He really knew how to use those old blue eyes of his to lethal effect.

At a huge public forum on body parts at The Sydney Convention Centre he drew an estimated crowd of forty thousand fans as if he were a football match in the finals.

There were all sorts of excited individuals present who lavished praise on him, who hung on every ground-out-word and cried when he needed an oil.

The two mechanics speedily squirted machine oil into special dip-stick-holes in his chest and screwed in two spark plugs really securely to give him a bit more oomph.

The crowd laughed till they were sick as he strode purposefully up to the microphone and groaned about what modern medicine had done to him. They had cause to fall around and to wipe their wet eyes with their crumpled hot tissues that were continually handed out.

The funny thing was the more earnest he became the more they fell about and pointed at him, not so much in ridicule as gratitude that his condition was so strange but also common in today's throw-away-society. Really close to the microphone he said he missed his face and they all grew silent and he didn't do any more but just look at them, not with respect but pity.

'I feel sorry for you!' was what he intoned and his perfect body language coupled with the natural tragedian in his ancestry made him woo them. He said he sympathized with their plight of trying to make it through each day and that he prayed for them in his beloved compost heap of a night with his whole mechanical soul and spirit that came in the form of long life batteries.

Life in Management did not corrupt him in the slightest it must be said. He remained a machine which was what interested Management in the very first instance; he was not very interesting, in fact he was so dull he could have led the country.

His high wage didn't alter his idea of economics because he continued to live in his small compost heap even though his chauffeur dropped him off at The Hilton Hotel just over the road from said compost.

Inside the compost heap he took off his expensive tweed suit and ironed trousers and carefully rested his costly business shoes on their appropriate rack. He put on his pyjamas and was often so absent minded that he successfully brushed his teeth with Colgate his favorite brand of toothpaste; he had practised and practised the formerly painful deed of brushing his industrial teeth and now it didn't hurt him.

He gargled into the compost hand basin and liked the gargling and held up to the light his bottle of mouth rinse to glory in its refreshing and intriguing taste; he placed his new toothbrush in its appropriate rack and went to bed by falling right over.

His bed was the ground at the very bottom of the rather warm compost heap but he was an improvisatory person.

He zipped up with great pleasure his sleeping bag and with his strong arms nestled neatly behind his great big head he fell asleep upon the instant. He immediately dreamt of Anna but she was now the lover of his Social Worker; which put him out a bit and because he didn't want that dream much he just lay there in a stupor.

The only worry about moving away from a naturalistic residence and choosing to dwell inside a hot compost heap is the fact of slugs, worms, snails and leeches arriving to get into you in their disgusting way, but he could relate to them and held them in the highest sort of respect and then they seemed to leave him alone, quite alone which was what state he was acquainted with.

Management had billboards erected the country over featuring him on them extolling the hygienic virtues of bottled Burp and although he never looked that happy in them there was something charismatic about his grin, even though it was as artificial as the rest of him. People liked him for his playful but slightly sinister quality and children went for the chomping look to his false front teeth with the sense of Frankenstein's monster no less.

Billions of hits on Burp's web site guaranteed his fame as their grinning but mean looking figurehead who gargled their brand all the day with a real zeal but also the appearance of remote indifference was just the image the company was after and he was introduced to a wide radio audience that allowed his amplified gulping sound to become the most recognized effect on the airwaves bar none.

His epiglottis became the mystery sound on Radio 3AW and most listeners guessed it after a while and then his robotic visage went on global television as the most famous image since Jesus Of Nazareth whom the company exploited sipping eagerly their brand and winking at consumers.

Ernid had life by both poles or social extremes now he could easily withdraw into relative obscurity living under a compost heap; or else he could match wits with the best of them in all media including live at vast Burp convention centres.

A new confidence was instilled in him when it was his shout to install his aged parents in a pleasant block of flats not far from town; he had their old place trashed and made a tidy profit out of its position which was poised over a poisoned creek which was renamed 'The Gap'.

He found with his new high profile and low profile life he didn't need very much on him when he went to work at the new advertising agency Burp Plus.

He merely put on his snazzy grey suit and fashionable pointy shoes and waited for a cab.

But on the way in one day he complained bitterly to the driver of shattering migraines and after pulling over for an attack of biliousness into the drain he wiped the sick from his visor and signaled the driver to hit the road. He turned up for the usual interviews and film shoots depicting the paper drinking straw pressed into his visor, obviously sucking up the Burp that he represented and giving the thumbs-up-sign.

He went to visit Doctor Tulp who seemed fairly concerned although it's always hard to tell with doctors; their concerned faces may simply be too much golf.

The doctor at least bulk-billed the sickened public or if they lost their Medicare cards as people do from time to time, then he savagely charged you fifty on the spot.

Ernid had his cards on him and undid his wallet on his hip and almost grinned out loud when he beheld such trivial comforts as his driver's licence, truck licence and fork lift truck one, although that didn't look too much like him on that one.

He sat and told the doctor that his sleep patterns had been mucked up by his dramatic jaw reconstruction and that he invariably woke at two in the morning due to the funny noises ringing in his head.

'What sort of sounds are these?' inquired the tired-looking doctor as he sipped a scotch and water most politely, but it did seem a bit early in the morning for something like that, thought Ernid Ernst, not that he'd say anything.

'Well doctor", replied he, 'the thing is I do get off to sleep real good about eleven of a night but about two in the new day my visor starts banging open and shut like a gate in someone's backyard you know?' The doctor didn't know as he had never seen a gate or a backyard. He had kept a limited life.

'Why would you keep the visor on, if you please?' asked the doctor as he monstrously yawned and Ernid saw big splotches of tears of boredom or tiredness form in his reddened eyeballs. He was starting to fear for the interview as though the doctor was the one who needed guidance and not he. The visor slipped down hard just then making a loud penetrating banging effect like a gunshot.

'Why have they put that visor-thing over you?' said the doctor helping himself to a second shot of scotch and lighting up a small cigar with a practised flourish and then puffing like an incinerator immediately; great orange sparks flying out of his own mouth that licked against Ernid's weatherproof protective visor.

'It's just to keep grit and dust out of my lungs and other components' smiled Ernid as he fiddled with the plastic shield bolted firmly over his head; he actually wished they hadn't put it on as he thought he looked grotesque enough as it was.

'Just lift it up would you please?' the doctor intoned as he placed the empty glass of whisky down on his neat desk and extinguished his half corona cigar with a hard grinding noise that made Ernid jump a bit.

'You look like a motor scooter courier', chuckled the doctor, and then he got up and consulted some books in his library, choosing a couple on the subject of mechanical parts such as mouths, teeth, tongues, air brakes, clutches and carburetors.

'Does your mouth hurt you in the night, dear chap?' he queried and tried hard to look his guest in the eye but the annoying plastic shield-thing was right in the road.

'Well, doctor, not really but early in the morning when the birds sing around my compost heap I am awoken by bell effects such as you'd hear should you be strolling by a cathedral'.

The doctor examined the visor with incredible care and eventually used a Philips Head Screw Driver to undo it; it fell on the floor with a light thud-sound and they both stared at it for a minute at least, as if it were part of them.

'I'd get rid of it if I were you', advised the red in the face doctor as he whisked around as he heard the ill moving rapidly towards his rooms like a remote wounded buffalo.

'Here they darned-well come again!' he almost shouted out loud.

He frantically scribbled a new prescription for Ernid to fill out at the local chemist shop and ordered a new set of X-rays from the hospital at work, although it seemed extravagant to Ernid who had just about had a gutful of fuss. He tipped the doctor fifty cents before the mob booted the door in and madly scrambled for his worn out attention. 'Just one at a time if you please' said he.

Most of the seriously sick public that came in had chronic injuries sustained at work such as a back that was entirely broken, an arm which declined to swing, one ear because the other had melted in a microwave oven at a cake shop. They all of them shrieked for his limited attention, some looked slightly put out that he looked so old as well as inattentive. Some hit him.

In the end the frightened doctor hid under his desk and watched helplessly as the crowd of desperate people ripped prescriptions out of his book with glee, hurtled out the door which had been much abused and kicked by their impatience until it came off. The crazy crowd wanted to lynch him and one of them showed a tow-rope but by this stage of proceedings the poor man had fainted away in a complete swoon.

Ernid could easily hear the mob yelling and clamoring for justice as he walked into the X-ray rooms of the plant clinic and had his head done.

He had been through it all a million times and just lay on the table waiting for the staff to do him with a dirty big camera.

He expected film X-rays and was a bit amazed when they told him it was digital.

It didn't hurt him the shots being taken of his head but he was pretty sick and tired of it all, as often happens when you are examined non-stop like some sort of an exhibit kind of thing, like an object for that is precisely what you happen to be after all.

He could sense new troubles coming up such as the way the television news bulletins kept on being transmitted from his brain to his tongue; and the way he was with his damaged voice box beginning to speak the weather directly off the television presenter, man or lady it never mattered much. He'd become a mimic.

Under the warm and slightly prickly compost heap he read the news and weather to the uncomplaining mineral life that existed there; in tandem you might say with the various snails, slugs, spiders and grass hoppers that were his friendly tenants.

His impersonations of ants and daddy long legs was spot-on and he knew it. He could easily talk like the moon, for instance, and even sound like the sun and that has never been achieved before so far as any of us really know.

One night under the compost heap he for some reason spoke the commentary on the John Kennedy assassination from every viewpoint as if he had been there, right in Dallas. Covering it for a wire service like the BBC or any of Rupert Murdoch's newspapers. He felt upset reciting all the statistics and analysis of it but kind of high.

He realized the assassination was an implant like a voice chip that somehow had been fitted into his jaw when they did him. When they altered him from mono to stereo.

He loved the warm sound vibrations emanating from his jaw's speaker phone and realized being able to broadcast assassinations would make him popular and famous and possibly end in his own one if he didn't watch it.

A compost heap when you meditate upon the topic is the perfect venue for a mental assassination or an unpredictable massacre due to the chaos of disintegration and the fevered re-ordering of politics. Somehow in all of his trials and procedures and scientific and medical history an implant to do with rare archival super 8 filming of the Kennedy Assassination in Dallas in 1963 had gone into him.

Under the stuffy and detestable clods of warm earth, cinders and rotting veggies he was in a private viewing room of his own mind. The footage was taken by a fellow named Zapruder who shot the movie by the motorcade as the American President came along to the whoops and cheering of many thousands of patriots that fateful day.

Over and over Ernid was required to stare into the grainy horror of that day, relive the fearful murder in his tired consciousness and see the President's loyal wife endeavour to throw herself over her stricken husband's shot body in her desperate bid to save him, to no avail.

The security men and secret agents screamed out loudly in Ernid's head and the stunned mob moaned as one. He saw repeatedly the shock of the slumped body of JFK and heard repeatedly the loud single gunshot emanating from the Dallas Book Store Depository Building, where the assassin had hidden to get a good hit on that awful afternoon that stopped the world.

The first time he saw it he wept hard under all the rot. As he went to bed more and more in the vegie patch the more he became accustomed to it; however it was traumatizing and he sometimes wished that he didn't have to look at it.

He went to a psychologist and that was a relief although he had said to Ernid that he too was having the same sort of flashback; he too was in Dallas with the motorcade and also saw the shot go through the President. It was thought that it was common and luckily this time Ernid was bulk-billed on his card and that felt much better than having to squander another fifty buck note on the spot.

Because of the endless pickle he'd been in ever since he started working at the big lemonade factory he was sort of used to chaos and saw it as inevitable, almost beautiful and glorious in a life he supposed was the servant of Capitalism.

He had born a Capitalist 25 years ago in a little village out of Prague and all of his aunties and uncles believed only in cash, with credit being evil and charity crooked. He loved to glean a buck and that was his raison d'etre.

Next morning after the first of personal interior screenings of the notorious Dallas motorcade assassination he washed his face under the park tap, dried his chestnut coloured hair with the back of his freshly-ironed gent's handkerchief and put on his suit he always kept in a plastic bag; got down on his hands and knees in order to iron his pants on a fallen log, tied up his shoelaces and skipped off to work at once to Marketing Section which was ten floors above Pulverizing Section. He felt feted. He was.

# CHAPTER SIX

## THE WELL INTENTIONED SOCIAL WORKER

There is something sinister about any meeting in the Capitalist System but today's briefing was particularly nasty with Managers demanding breakthrough marketing ideas before five in the morning. The flesh is weak at that ungodly hour.

Many managers writing up new programs to do with destroying Pepsi and Slades Lemonade by boosting popularity of their own ancient tried and true sort of fizziness.

The men all wore pitch-black three-piece suits with aggression and stared at Ernid with a kind of drool as though he was just the droplet of novelty they wanted.

He was made to walk along a platform so management got a sideways view of his head and as he obliged they saw their future. He could become the face of their Burp in actuality. Their brand heals the lame would be their new logo, even the cripples amongst us may pause to sip their refreshment guaranteed ever so much less burpy than rival lemonades. They would put him on every billboard on the planet.

One particular irate manager actually beat another up by employing big fists to the edge of his face to express a point in global strategies; instead of being suitably shocked the audience of underlings applauded most passionately. Many red-faced managers screamed into the public-address-system that lemonade was war.

Drinks were next and polite slaves handed out their own product employing tongs with which to add ice; even a sprig of mint was added to jazz it up.

Heads rolled next day when the great company dumped five hundred middle-order-managers without talking to them in any sort of way which included signage.

Buses of the sacked were dumped right in town; Ernid went with them as his bosses in Marketing wanted his report on how that went so in fact they could do it again whenever they felt like it. He was told it was expeditious.

He visited the one-bedroom hovels of the sacked.

He saw and reviewed what melancholy it looked like to go to bed without a cracker, to arise without sleep to no possible income. To cry all the day and well into the night and to hallucinate there was income where none was. He witnessed mass evictions where he beheld landlords personally toss renters out of unlit slums and bailiffs chase the old folks into the unkind night that reveals all her sufferers continually.

Whole roads and streets were being disgorged and old rental properties torn down and left vacant. Each road had vacant blocks as ugly as sin awaiting a reconstruction that was to be apartments for the upwardly mobile; the rich.

He felt it would a dereliction of duty not to write it all down sincerely as he possibly could with pen or pencil or else dictate precisely what it was he saw into a tape.

He wept to see so many roads pulled up like cheap plastic champagne corks and no history nor laughter left behind. He realized the perfection of commercial power over defenceless workers whose only education was tears of shock and grief in the making.

The thing about him was that he was a new being, a terrible creation of medical breakthrough and the personification of machine-men who could still not only toil in the global Burp industry but kick a goal and have more children who would automatically labour for the same plant.

But the footage screening behind his sore eyes frightened him and dismayed his waking thoughts. His imagination was over now no matter how he thought it was never in the abstract but rooted in reality. He was modern history with nowhere to run except the recent past; someone else's past; in this case JFK's past.

Under the immortal compost heap late each evening the screenings continued in his poor brain that was the fatal result of a bungled jaw reconstruction. He was forced to view terrible events like the shooting of a popular American President and like it or lump it the screening was always on.

He got himself as comfortable as he could under all that compost and although it was lovely and warm he sometimes resented sharing his bed with termites and snails and greasy beetles that he recognized as the same sort that can easily withstand a nuclear explosion. That he identified with these creatures is a matter of public record because from now on he commenced to keep a daily diary.

It was hard to write under the compost heap of course, and many a time bits of gristle or bone got in his eyes to test his willingness to write first up in the morning, but when else and where else can personal reflection be practised, even rehearsed for a relaxed reading for God?

He gnawed his writing fingers to their considerable stumps as he tried hard to express his sentiments like a buried gentleman.

The brightness ingrained of the Zapruder film gave him terrible headaches each time the film was shown; he knew each grainy over-bright frame off by heart. The pan shot of the cheering crowd dissolving to the head of the president coming right off. He often wondered how the camera could possibly remain in the filming hand of the Zapruder man?

He wept ceaselessly with the shock of recognition each time the awful film came on, yet in a way he eagerly looked forward to viewing it once again because it was by now his history, his idea, he was the accursed assassin.

Yet he always hopped up early like a veritable coil out of his compost heap, showered at his parent's place, dressed then shaved his new machine-jaw and really enjoyed the sensation of fresh ceramic skin. He put on overpowering after shave and ran for his bus.

There were just so many meetings at work and he was now an integral component of the company, his ideas were taken seriously and when he spoke with the aid of the new jaw he was eagerly listened to and well liked by most of his public relations team that was like an army. People called him love names such as 'Captain', which he enjoyed immensely.

He was sent to Indonesia as the machine face of Burp and the first night was in K.L.

He disliked the heat which he found exhausting, the high humidity clogged one of the gears in his jaw so it was really tricky ordering a meal in the oppressive air conditioning that merely made the motel muggier. No one could possibly help him.

In the middle of his first night he realized his jaw was playing up and was all loose inside so he employed a tiny plastic-coated screwdriver to adjust its strong grip and fiddle with its bolts which were choking him a little. He also lightly sprayed himself all over with a local deodorant until he smelled nice as a rose in a heat wave.

He always presented well and although he spoke very slowly and hesitatingly the marketing team in the motel, mostly locals who wanted to make good, applauded him in the foyer as he gave a power point presentation to do with sugar, thirst, money.

'Sugar equals thirst and thirst equals profit even if it leads to chronic diabetes', he chortled, and then coughed hard into his patiently-ironed gent's handkerchief and looked at it. There were big spots of blood and he realized he had pneumonia as well as all his other various setbacks. 'Bugger it!' he gasped to himself.

He spoke eloquently about the global push for relaxation with diabetes and got a huge hand for that and gaining confidence by the minute he mocked rival brands like Pepsi and said they had lost their fizz. The audience wept to hear it.

Unluckily for Ma and Pa back in Sydney both got the boot and were vigorously escorted by guards to the perimeter and dogs put on them. They were badly mauled and had to hitchhike home in bloodied rags like dead rodents. Pa said to Ma he'd gone off Australia and wanted to sell up and fly back home to Prague on the first available jet. Ma said she wasn't sure and pointed out that poverty is pretty much universal these days.

Pa sat at his cheap relaxing chair in his sitting room and tipped out his pay. He had been given a week's salary for every year he'd toiled for Burp.

He laughed at what he called 'buttons' which were the dull brass-looking two buck coins that tumbled out of his envelope. 'Enough for rack of lamb', he joked, but Ma took that seriously and made a mental note to purchase one at the butcher shop.

She had to take several Panadol and lie down, close her sacked face for the afternoon after the unexpected dismissal at work. She immediately

dreamt Ernid hadn't fallen in the big steel vat and that he was still the happy boy he always was before they migrated, and she talked and laughed with him with his normal jaw on in their old tongue.

Pa was not that old that he'd not try out for a new job; he was seventy but looked more, yet felt young so he was pretty insane when you think about it. He didn't have diabetes or high cholesterol or high blood pressure from all the free Burp at work but he was fairly burpy and he didn't like it. Just living made him uncomfortable.

All through Indonesia his lemonade company had placed huge banners up bearing his mechanical face and made a highlight of the fact that the right fizz makes a man of you; the correct lemonade not only refreshes its consumer but defies melancholy.

Ma and Pa dreamt simultaneously side by tired side in the park where they now abided, so like thousands of displaced Australians in time of spontaneous and calamitous eviction and demolition. The country had changed since they turned up here and no welcome mat could be detected anywhere. Australia was Nowhere.

His parents appeared to age in front of his eyes, now so worn down by the changes and tribulations they simply couldn't keep up with. They had no say in the token price of their home and just dumbly got out of it when their urgent eviction order landed in their letter-box. It didn't matter whether they read it or understood it. The local council had instruction to bulldoze it ASAP.

Pa tried hard to convince both his shop steward and manager at the plant that his entire family were engaged there and had only really come from the old country because of the promises of secure new work in Australia that they'd seen just about everywhere in their village – even local pigs and chickens had placards adhered to their bodies to advertise Burp.

But it was no use to be righteous or indignant and no one at work gave a toss about people heading for sixty years of age, as Ma and Pa were although they looked a hundred.

They reconciled tough lean times and bought a tent in a hardware store and set up in the sopping-wet park where Pa was frightened a beast that was untethered might come at them, but luckily none bothered although they could both hear howling and baying in the dimly lit and misunderstood woods that could have had a tiger or two in them.

Ma still made fresh Gag in the tent and its pong nauseated others who had similarly set up camp in the unlit park, the biliousness on sniffing the infamous meal had driven half a million citizens in the old country to commit mass suicide but still Ma made it.

Its chief constituent was frog and that at least had some sort of nutrition in it, the eyes probably, the rest was incinerated onion.

Ernid was in Indonesia overseeing propaganda for his company and giving speeches the firm had written for him which were delivered in shanty towns that usually boasted a well and ice for Burp.

Sometimes he attracted audiences of fifty thousand who liked the way he looked and enjoyed his monologue extolling the virtues of his soft drink over rival brands. He seemed and was so different in the way he spoke and winked at them like the robot he actually was. However they sensed an interior friendship that was at odds with the visor and other adornments hanging out of him. He was nice.

The company as in days of old installed Burp fountains everywhere so luxuriant and otherworldly and hundreds of people lolled along savouring the sparkly product and revelling in the leisureliness of its endless availability that they just didn't see the point of working for a living anymore; and the country went into a decline in industry.

Logging stopped in rain forests for instance because natives just sat under coconut palms sucking lemonade all day and didn't want to do a single other thing.

The product overtook everything in its bubbly path and the economy slipped almost immediately after the latest figures of sales were recorded for the plant in Sydney.

After Ernid featured in a mass hysteria television ad for his product that had him singing a foolish song and winking the country was finished.

Pa and Ma began to drift into crime in their cooperative efforts to keep on living and they put on masks in lanes and robbed passers-by at gun point.

They ate well on this ruse and even put on some weight it has to be said.

Pa in particular took to devouring junk food to cheer himself up and looked like a blimp to Ma who just stuck to the Gag.

Ernid would just obey his managers and tirelessly promote product in villages to witch doctors and so on or else to cyclists or brain surgeons he met by sheerest chance.

He knew he was good and even if it were mechanical he had the gift for public address and he knew it; he also knew how to make cretins drink more product which was exactly what his superiors were after in their passion for income that had no bounds.

The trouble was the night, the unforgiving evening when he tried to discover repose in the motel or temporary vegetable gardens he rested in. No matter where he was the movie started up and he sat up horrified and stared aghast at his own interior motorcade containing muffled cries and super 8 distorted screams of anguish.

Sometimes the footage only lasted a second or so, other screenings went on and on, rewound, re-edited, the same thing only worse, with the poor President's head coming right off and blood sailing everywhere. Ernid just had to hack it but the effect on him became not merely psychotic but pathologically violent. He wanted to murder, too.

He tried hard to beat his sensation down but it arose no matter what solace he tried.

Each radio bulletin he listened to was about a murder or an attempted kidnapping or the speedy robbery of kindergarten fund-raising-cash from a collector's tin of small change. The world was insane and violence was a bore of course and everything was debauched.

As for dress he was becoming a bit perturbed actually that Management failed to notice just how grubby he had become and all tattered he was. He was beginning to skip the morning shower now that his father's residence had been pulled down and he even forgot to do his hair or brush his revolving steel and ceramic teeth. His own visor was dull and nothing about him was up to scratch pretty much.

But to all of this Management didn't bat and eyelid and so long as he clocked on and off at the right time he was seen as a role model and not heading for unwanted retirement like the armies of those heading for the gate. The plant began to put on thousands of automatons like him that didn't give any trouble and cost less to exploit.

And they posted phenomenal profit margins this year and their eager-beaver shareholders were well satisfied with yummy dividends and brand new Audis.

Their flavour team invented new tastes and blindingly brilliant colours to cream the market and the thirsty public threw the new hues down the second the supermarkets hurled them in their refrigerator-cities; for that is how best to describe their vastness.

New lines included Marijuana Burp that really tasted like dope; Panadol Burp that relieved stress and frontal lobe memory abatement. Others the public hung out for were Ocean and Neap Tide that tasted like that which their title summoned up. The most popular new drink was Aggression that had real bite to it and it was rumored it came from lion blood.

Ernid was diligent with his banking and liked to do a check once per week at NAB which was near the compost heap anyway and easy to get a park near, particularly when you walked there. He realized he had lots in two different accounts but rather wished Anna was still with him in some sort of a way. He felt vulnerable as well as mechanical.

He was always picking morsels of food out of his mesh grille gums that collected fragments of minced pie and bread crusts had from repellent Vietnamese rolls the proletariat were forced to devour at their break in the busy strips that ran around the gigantic soft drink factory. He hated pork buns because whatever was in them coagulated him so he swore right off them.

When he turned up at Strategy Meetings that were more and more his work it was apparent to him that a new ruthlessness was in the stuffy air of the frantic meeting rooms. The big Managers were being leant on by bigger and much more important Managers in The States to hammer Pepsi until it was no more than an old belch.

Infants at primary schools were presented with free bottles of Burp upon their first morning there with a straw in it; the blind infants were given an instruction note in Braille on how to drink it quickly and become more focused and energized quickly. The deaf were given it in sheltered workshops with a heightened audio sting built into its microchip to wildly increase its hissing effect and turn them on.

Ernid's face was everywhere and he was the inhuman visage of Burp because Management realized that no matter how strange he looked he possessed an innate heavenly innocence that the guzzling and perennially thirsty public required right around the clock. One image had his wired face downing a family sized bottle of it and the contents going all down his visor and him saying in a speech bubble the word 'Ah!'; and it really caught on, that one.

It did feel great to head back home to his faithful damp but not too bad compost heap and make a nice cup of normal tea, a bit of toast and take a squint at the paper. He always did his teeth of a night with Colgate like billions of people around The Universe and then off to bed hopefully not to have vile nightmares or burp.

He slept profoundly with or without sleeping capsules and didn't roll around much although at times termites attacked him slightly.

Bugs bit into his left thigh and their viciousness put him off a bit and cockroaches managed to arrive in his quite tender ear canals so that he found it hard to hear. Not that he was desperate to hear things other than human voices right above his crypt home and by and by he got himself off to repose by reading his telephone bills that were forwarded onto the compost.

The living in various heaps of filth caught right on and many citizens copied his example; pretty soon there were compost cities around the great Burp plant that so dominated every single son and daughter in the land. They were more than economical and warranted no upkeep other than getting into them like the living dead.

But the internal screenings battered him and confused his memory and mind and even if he sat and took it easy in a park, in the timeless manner of lots of uprooted Europeans, just sitting on a friendly wooden whitewashed bench he could easily hear, like tinnitus, the ringing of a bullet in Dallas ages ago.

When he heard he saw the deadly projectile and tried to dodge it to no avail; and the footage-bullet fired off in his considerable heart; for it was said he had a big heart and he sweated something shocking after being forced to see it again far in him.

As he tried hard to relax after an unexpected viewing he would try to enjoy leisurely walks around the wide perimeter of the plant but the screening kept coming on over and over again to drive him out of his damaged wits, and he screamed sometimes.

His aged parents were shown by The Department Of Human Services just how to hop in a hole, much like a throw-away-grave really and save the fuss of looking for anything more substantial. Their particular compost heap was two-story.

They could easily climb upstairs and fall asleep right near the surface of the concrete footpath, hear or at least sort of overhear what folks were saying or muttering or joking about, and also hear the birds whistling and conversing in their way via warbles and run-throughs of cheap music. Ma liked her two-story compost heap and was very vigilant in respect of its maintenance. She intended spouting put on as that would have blown her mind.

Every single street and road in their area now boasted single story or double story well-maintained compost heaps that were raked over neatly and even had smokestacks to them so that homecoming people on their exhausted way from the factory could just make out the friendly smoke curling out of pipes.

This was the homecoming all Burp toilers had to look forward to at day's end, the new Totalitarian Regime was in place and workers could be fired for speaking; they were there at work in order to listen to Management as never before. They were to dig the wax out of their ears and pay greater heed. That was all.

Streamlining was in and human voice was out, to be replaced by gossip such as whispers of death and agitations of mortality; the flavour scientists had invented a new batch of lemonade guaranteed to deliver mind-altering cheerfulness at work but the effect altered immediately they arrived at their compost heap residences and felt depressed and suicidal with hardly any appetite to eat their Gag.

It was practically amazing that Ernid kept the balance of his mind whilst suffering so many unscheduled and unendurable screenings. He just bopped along in his eccentric fashion, always sort of cheerful although he could get a bit down if his jaw gearbox got stuck in first gear or the clutch kept on slipping so he couldn't speak or yawn.

Management bumped up his pay, he got a new more aggressive accountant to save on tax and he squirreled away about half his weekly wages in his desire to see The Old Country again; he was in his compost heap hallucinating on crags and mountains and the old familiar massacres he knew by heart.

One night he dined with Anna in a restaurant and she saw the new confidence in him; he now used a decent if slightly overpowering deodorant both under his arms and on his testicles to prohibit bad karma and that worked.

He was dressing nicer and his shoes were so giddily polished she received a migraine looking into each of them. She slid his visor up so she could see his friendly face and she saw he was using toothpaste to greater effect because his mouth was not rancid like it used to be when they were together.

His teeth clashed up and down like a drawbridge as he made the points he needed to, he had control mostly of what he wanted to say but at times broke right down as he described living in dirt full time. She got a small brush out of her bag and used it to wipe him down.

'Must you live under the earth all the time?' she politely inquired of him as he vigorously brushed clods of clay from his shoulders and squished a bug whose extreme wriggly ways made her feel ill as she sipped or tried hard to, at least, her tea but it slipped and wet her palms, and he observed a new ring on her finger, not his.

'I see you are married but remember please that we are not divorced,' his machine mouth said to her. To his disgust she put a straw in her cup of tea and slurped it in that awful style. He needed to beat her for that outrage.

He was forgetting her name and status and his former relationship with her, her face was not known to him other than an image that had pulverized his own one; she was just like The Pulverizing Section at Burp in that she had torn him to fragments too.

She nibbled her raisin toast and said she thought he might try to live as a normal person does, in a house for instance, with a yard and some bushes in it, and how about a pet dog and a library? He found that his plastic visor kept on skidding down low over his face, annoyingly and persistently so he could hardly make her out in a filmic jump-cut sort of way. He saw her as needing editing, like old film stock that was rotting.

He became furious as she raved on about her new guy and their holiday ideas and how much she needed him, she giggled at his request for a divorce and told him off for being so old-fashioned as well as idiotic. He was hungry although his boiling hot soup of the day kept on hitting the visor when it slammed on his mouth and in the end went everywhere. He tried to mop it up but ended up bitterly weeping.

He went to the big city court quite alone and his divorce was legalized since he wanted a crisper portrait of his future, if any.

He was mechanically dismayed to find about seventy people in the courtroom all going through a legalizing of separation, some glad of it, others not, and at one stage when he saw a black guy and his excellent-looking wife get divorced he felt like interrupting proceedings and pleading with them – and she had a baby – to stick it out.

There were all kinds of broken and down in the dumps ones there, some almost weeping with pure sadness they should end like this, many with a sort of 'who cares?' expression and some with a mixture of pathos and arrogance as if determined to get it over.

His go came and the judge read out the solemn fact that she found his marriage failed and that from that finding he should pay their children's school fees, but of course kids had they none. It cost him six hundred bucks on the spot, like a parking infringement you might say, and he forked it out in new lovely fifties and shoved his receipt in his alligator skin wallet as a keepsake.

After leaving divorce court he saw the losers leaving alongside of him, all looking absolutely appalling and he wondered if any of them sort of regretted it.

Foolishly perhaps he drifted into a white trash underground bar with a whole lot of soiled white collar alcoholics and he pulled up a broken stool with only two legs on it and commenced to wipe himself right totally out.

He asked the morose publican for a triple scotch over ice with a ten ounce pot of heavy and he also bought a lovely fresh pack of smokes with a green lighter and he then settled in to let things drift as only drunkards can let them drift.

He sipped the acrid but also sweet scotch which instantly reinvigorated his brain whilst at the same time totally relaxed it and his tired and strung-out body.

He drank the expensive drug straight down the pudding-chute and then sipped the pot of heavy beer and dragged seriously onto his first fag in donkey's years.

The friendly nicotine personally thanked his mouth and nostrils for taking time out to inhale the gorgeous tobacco. He remembered how it made him relax and made a mental note never to give it up as a healing-force for the brain, lungs, kidneys, etc.

All night saw Ernid in that bar sipping and sighing and puffing away and brushing out the long cylinders of vile grey ash onto the provided public ashtrays. He didn't want to get into a conversation with strangers, he just wanted to forget Anna and maybe chew up half a kilo of cashews.

He probably drank a little too much because after several hours he hadn't the fuzziest clue who was there, who wasn't or how come he wasn't in his nice compost heap looking at 'The Green Guide' to see what was on the television later that night.

Three big gross senior managers wandered assertively towards the barkeep and pointed at the most costly bottle of bourbon and it was theirs straight away, if not sooner. They were such errant pigs they ordered full big bottles of ale, long necks, and sucked into them as they chucked the whisky back quick as quick without the bother of speech.

They were so big and fat they stuck together as a matter of fact; they laughed at rude and vicious things to say in the manner of most managers, then they told lies and gossip to do with work which was at 'Burp' Pty Ltd.

Ernid was so intoxicated that he understood them, he knew them, he realized and remembered their type and he also figured just why they came into the same pub. They were just a very blurry and menacing new form of machine-like-machismo who hated ordinary rank and file toilers at their own plant. They had greased and fawned on their up through the piggy of power to become masters of menace.

He couldn't but help overhearing their ideas on mass sackings in order to implement such a drastic alteration to the company that men and ladies in human guise would no longer do things like go to work anymore; 'Burp' Pty Ltd would be fully automated within a year and the only thing human would be bosses like them.

His left ear and his right one blushed red to hear their ideas on retrenchment globally that would guarantee billions in profits at the expense of helpless and sincere toilers who drove fork lift trucks, dyed the vats with sickly red and golden sugar, bottled it and freighted it and put in trucks vaster than cities.

Who for years refrigerated it and emptied it in lakes of other lakes, who hit the big cork into trillions of fancy memorial bottles to celebrate its invention 150 years ago.

Innocent toilers of the company took orders from hard men and harder ladies who had them by the throat in regard to personal security and rental-payments so they had a resting place known as home; so they could feed and clothe diabetic children.

One of the pigs-at-trough said through one of his tusks: 'The best thing for us is to install machines to boost profit and have the security staff march the toilers to the big gate and then fire the idiotic security staff!' That remark received a huge oink and guffaw and earned its originator a fresh jug of heavy that he guzzled in a gulp and a hog laugh filled with the squeal of glee and hysteria.

Ernid smoked one after the other through his visor with the ash and sparks of red-hot-tobacco flickering across his stern mesh front grille. He turned his back on the managers and purchased a big bag of grog in the greasy bottle shop and got in a taxi to go to several of his latest homes.

'Let me see', said he, still seeing those buffoon pigs of managers in the dingy bar, 'Shall I go to the apartment tonight or the compost heap?' The Asian driver kept on asking him where it was he wanted to go but he was so pickled he just laughed and pointed vaguely to mist in vacant lots where not long ago people's homes stood.

'You must have some defining destination, surely?' said the cab driver and Ernid got him to pull up near a bridge which happened to be there on its concrete own.

He grasped for his old wallet that somehow was on his head and it fell in a mud bog, he scooped it right out again and found it difficult to undo the zip in it due to all the mud and ooze on it. He gave the guy fifty in small notes and the driver screamed away into the chloride night.

It was hard to relax that night under all the hot and rotting filth of the compost and his racing-around mind offered him mayhem and sometimes he honestly felt all used up, which was quite the correct emotion really. He was only an exhibit, an experiment in marketing and profitability for his maker.

And the bugs and slugs and termites bit into him with appreciation for disaster which had become his only acquaintance.

His side was all sore from their terrible gnawing and he groaned aloud through his visor and tossed and turned in his pit in a remorseless kind of a way. When he woke he couldn't find the bathroom in order to take a refreshing hot shower and then he finally remembered you don't get a shower in a compost heap any more.

At his morning briefing that morning he felt irritable and not himself, partly because of the slugs in his arm which seemed to be bearing their young there; partly because he felt he needed a break. The humming of insects was upsetting him and bees swarmed out of his blood-shot eyes- not that Management cared.

He looked bitterly across at the well-manicured team of bosses and felt a stab of remorse and envy for their better position in life, their sex-drive, probably, their speed boats and get-togethers. He envied them not their considerable income but their superiority and cocksureness, especially the ladies.

He was escorted thence to a projection room or corporate cinema to watch a new promotion that upper management were excited about. It depicted armies of himself guzzling the lemonade that they made through the metallic face that was his own. He watched helplessly as the computerized cartoon overwhelmed him.

The imagery was every consumer on the planet guzzling their brand disguised as monsters and they appeared to be marching in columns like robotic Third Reich things and smashing up milk bars in their fever to get at the drink that had brainwashed them all throughout the ages.

There was looting and destruction beyond description mixed with violent and urgent music that seemed out of Hitler's hit list.

He commenced to sweat as he viewed it but was aware it was going over fantastically with the bosses who applauded it and did head-banging in rapt approval of it.

'This is it!' they cried in unison. 'Yes!' they moaned loudly. 'This is the real us!'

He excused himself and went to the toilet in order to relieve himself, but when he arrived there instead of the rare and brief physical comfort of the lavatory he discovered graffiti to do with smashing Burp entirely from the planet Earth; this destructive message was sprayed right across the wash-up-stand that he loved.

As he strove to wash or embalm his hands (as it felt in fact) he read the upsetting vandalism as yet another shock to his system. The words were so hateful he didn't know how to digest any of them and just mentally ignored them and did his hair as best he could.

There must be a sub-group here at our plant that hates lemonade, he thought as he headed back for yet another urgent meeting. 'Murder Control!' the message of hate had said, clearly said in powerful crimson-coloured spray-pack. He wondered who they were that wrote it as he rang the cleaners to eradicate it ASAP.

That night as he arrived at his comfy compost heap he saw that every single home in the area was demolished and that the suburb he dwelt in had turned into a million compost heaps that had replaced them. He was living in land-fill like the rubbish he was.

'Where did everyone go?' he thought aloud as he viewed everyone coming up, spiraling up through their rotting mounds of dirt to either wave to one another or take in the fresh washing from power lines that luckily were still standing, but he noticed that the crows which always rested on them were hanging there dead.

He watched dumbfound as people chatted to each other over their one or two bedroom mounds of dirt, exchanged pleasantries and gossip about who had cracked it for a three or even four bedroom mound in The New Deal.

Some mounds or compost heaps were trendier than others and a few had white washed wooden picket fences surrounding them and yet others were plain as manure.

He thought it extremely unjust that there was so much uneven distribution of assets in modern civilization and he entered that thought in his new diary that he kept in his breast pocket and constantly referred to in his efforts to stay sane.

It is surprising just how quickly people make the necessary adjustment to change and drastic rearrangement of the concept of home; he saw people living in perfect contentment in a washing machine or relaxing in a coffin nobody needed any more.

'People really know how to improvise', he mumbled to himself and again entered that philosophical observation in his pocket diary with a tiny pencil that stayed in it.

He was out walking past all the compost heap village when his brain backfired and he commenced to feel so programmed and violent with dreadful desires to hurt and maim ordinary things; he kicked a tulip and spat on a nice lady because some force for badness and of harm propelled him to do it. The surge of satisfaction overwhelmed him like the addiction to the drug ICE.

He insulted a lame old couple waiting for a bus inside a bus stop, he called them terrible words and made them cry and that cruel deed excited him and so all that morning he said rude things to every walk of life including restaurant proprietors and farm animals. He insulted a racehorse at one stage for no other reason than to see it break right down emotionally, possibly without ever getting over it.

The screening was now continuous and brighter and louder all the time; and it had been adjusted so it ran faster and the perspectives had been fiddled with; it seemed and was more real.

It occurred to him he needed a holiday and was simply overtired but the desire to hurt people, plants and beasts drove him to a new level of hate and rage.

He destroyed an innocent butcher shop.

He knew he needed to frighten and maim and murder and in the end there was nothing to be done about his programming so he throttled babies and laughed at the lame and urinated upon the blind.

It happened to be after work so nobody noticed and no one cared what he did any more. He set fire to a kindergarten and terrified a priest. He looted a milk bar and cast spears through its owner. He buried a dog that looked perfectly okay.

Whilst he was enjoying the rampage his parents had an early; they always called it that when they went to bed after the news on the ABC on the television set. 'Let's have an early!' said Pa to Ma and off to the bedroom under the compost heap they went. They enjoyed a passionate sex life together, and after achieving climax they read to one another and watched the television again as there wasn't much to do.

On the evening news bulletin to their shock they saw decapitated dogs and cats hung on trees with the investigating police officers weeping to see. They were aghast at the craziness of the imagery and to make matters much worse they saw their errant son in handcuffs being shoved in the back of a division car.

'Soft drink figurehead loses it!' was the text on the bottom of their own screen. The story was shown repeatedly overnight and the son was refused bail as he had just gone too far, it was thought. He was put into solitary confinement.

What he had done was move too far away from the control he obeyed at the plant and because of the continuous JFK screenings in his head he requested a psychiatrist, who when he entered the cell seemed as mixed up as Ernid .

'I think I'm slightly overworked at the minute', said Ernid through his blood and mud spattered visor that he was heartily sick and tired of. He wanted to destroy it and he wanted to destroy himself because he was now beyond The Pale.

# Chapter Seven

## Imprisonment

He was naturally imprisoned for his spree and was denied legal representation as well as hope. He signed under considerable duress an Anti Hope Contract with The Supreme Court who took a very dim view of his crimes which included the trashing of an altar inside an Anglican Church because it depressed him to see infants being browbeaten by self-appointed Messiahs in the name of a vindictive God.

His others charges were attempted manslaughter of a hen in public and the pulling down of lemonade billboards promoting his own product. He had been in a punch-up with a guinea pig, a fight he lost by the way, and he had brawled with old ladies whom he deemed rude to him because they laughed at his new mouth in public and were entirely unrepentant.

He got ten years for causing public disgrace and of course his bosses wrote him right off, never to guzzle another can with him or hang round together or play a few rounds of golf on the day off, like a Sunday let us say.

His prison cell was so miniature it closed as soon as it opened.

He sat on a tiny hard uncomfortable dark dusty green bench supported by metal chains which bore his name and compost heap number on each link just to stick his punishment right up him. He had no friends so he wasn't that surprised when none came in to see how he was going. A bird talked to him through the razor wires that ran around his small sky-coloured window; that favorite hue of Liberty.

He didn't know how to relate to his officers apart from lifting up his visor and saying 'Hi!' to them, but they vowed they didn't get that word and of course they didn't understand that it is the most beautiful sound in English.

He was regularly both beaten then forgiven as it was a Catholic

Prison and that kind of thing worked well with ordinary supporters of vindictiveness. He liked being beaten and hurled into brick walls and rather thought it could help far younger offenders to come clean and confess to their sins.

He loved being refused the right to speech and this gave his mechanical mouth a break and he was glad of it in other prosaic ways too, such as realizing his jaw parts could break if he raved too much and that his intricate gears and mouth-clutch could become worn right down if he continued to converse.

The great aspect of imprisonment meant he could still work for his managers so long as he related to them by séance or email and that his wage was put into a trust for homeless lemonade toilers in the area. His personal pain finished up inside the cubicle when officers gave him an extra yard to exercise in; and it was portable too so that he could walk in the certain knowledge he had that extra liberating room in front of him.

He proved a model prisoner almost from the jump and since the delusions gave it a rest he found peace once more in his overworked noggin; he recognized that feeling that only peace contributes to the stressed body and obeyed the sensation of passivity and began to like life again except he had none.

Of a night suddenly the screenings were gone and some nights he was completely dreamless and whimsically wondered what all the fuss was about. He became luxuriant in jail and related easily with his fellow prisoners, some looking just like he did with fidget wheel minds and cuckoo clock tongues and what-have-you. He liked the inmates there and played checkers with them or enjoyed talking together like a whole line of electric typewriters banging away.

He grew rapidly accustomed to his cell and the somber truth of its claustrophobia made him relax in a new sort of a way; he found he could stroll into its darkness and by smoking Ice he could surrender entirely to glades and forests, nooks and streams as if were really there; they weren't paintings done by mouth or anything like that but actuality in the cell that could be construed as a beacon of learning.

One night he would never forget was a month into his stay and the well-oiled metal gears of his bottom false teeth locked right up and he developed extreme lockjaw. He telephoned for assistance and a dreary dentist paid his cell a visit and tried hitting them with a chisel as you would a jammed starter-motor but they stayed locked.

The dentist said he'd be okay so long as he remembered to put oil into his sump of a morning and check the long bendy dipstick to make certain he was full and ready to run. The upper gears of his teeth were just beginning to jam, the dentist said, but he also concluded that they'd be okay as long as he looked after them properly.

The constant addiction of ICE was keeping his savings at a low ebb you'd have to say, and his brain was crazier the more he got stuck into it. He liked it and it made him feel immortal and do stuff like fly over a tree or a country so he continued to experiment with it despite its fantastic dangers that included death.

He taught the inner and outer selves of himself to withdraw utterly and completely from drugs like ICE and concentrated upon reducing the JFK imagery which occasionally came on as a late show behind his eyes to horrify him once more; it was a thing he failed to get used to and even one frame of the movie made him shriek like an ape.

One afternoon he escaped and made it into the city again disguised as a postman upon a red push bike and was so deluded he really believed it was his calling. He robbed a bank later on in the same day and was shot but it wasn't too bad. He limped away to a gulch and bandaged his gory wounds up tight using a spare pair of underpants like a tourniquet.

He lay in this grotesque gulch for a week and listened carefully to the whining police sirens and saw the searchlights piercing the inky heavens until he was sick of looking at them; in his head the dreaded JFK assassination started up again, much brighter and louder than ever and he struggled really hard to get to sleep in that damp gulch but even though it took him all night he managed to dream in a nice old gulch.

He decided a life upon the run wasn't ethical to any degree, as well it would crush in his parents the slightest hope he might turn a corner, any would do quite nicely, so he handed himself over to the authorities in order to complete his original jail term and thenceforward be a good guy.

There were literally thousands of gents and ladies performing the same task when he arrived at the local lock-up, and many men of his build. He was spectrally skinny, had been in factory accidents, lots in lemonade plants who had artificial jaws put in and new legs and feet installed. One guy's collapsed chest had a fireplace put around it with live kindling wood slightly ablaze and he just had to resign himself to that particular mode of expression.

A girl had an old-fashioned telephone put in her forehead as she had got wiped out at a pub and been struck with understandable brutality by a bus; she like most of the others had made the adjustment physically but hardly psychologically because she kept on dialing the same number; which was 000.

Men he worked next to at the plant had been in weird incidents and accidents, one had a vice for a head as his original one had been struck by a pallet of empty Burp bottles and had come off so the medical team thought it provident to make him safer. They manufactured a lathe for one of his arms so he could go back into the workforce, which he agreed to do most rapt.

Ladies who got their hair caught in a machine which hosed away old logos with boiling-hot-steaming-water and had forfeited their entire back had been given a false one made of styrene foam and just had to lump it; these were the ones who had robbed convenience stores or shot someone or any one of a hundred misdemeanors – they were keen to do time so they could come good and be of use in industry again.

Some workers lost both legs so came in stolen wheelchairs or else they'd scraped up just enough money to rent one of them to arrive at police headquarters,

Many had no head on and just mumbled into their replacement basketball ones.

Ernid finally got to the end of the line and was thoroughly frisked and his wallet slammed on a desk alongside of his bus tickets, wristwatch, socks and pointy shoes and he was duly handcuffed and given a ball point pen with which to fill out some very detailed forms. People jostled for enough space to complete them and that was a hard job in itself as the unpredictable ball point pens were chained hard to the desks they were on.

At least he hadn't murdered anyone, not yet at least, and he would give it his very best shot not to as he realized it was pretty bad to do a thing like that, take someone else's life just because they were right in your road. In the future random murder would become a leisure in America and Australia, its sycophant sister country that copies the gun culture, the everything culture.

He and ten other new head men were formerly charged with serious offences such as the garroting of a grub or the dismemberment of a table tennis team or the mindless torture of a Frankfurt salesman on a remote and blood-soaked beach at night.

He did his time in a tiny cave-like dwelling that The Department Of Corrective Services were giving as try-out somewhere near the border, very near Albury.

The prison was modern and experimental in that the air conditioning was based on dangerous conditions experienced in 18th century collieries and fatal silver and gold mines that pumped deadly toxic fumes into the mouths of their own miners.

It boasted a rigged table tennis centre where you couldn't serve properly or expect to win.

There was a play-writing-section where original literature was openly encouraged but there were no prizes or any scholarships and nothing was ever praised or published.

There were in each choking and cramped cell overhead television sets which only showed harness racing, the same race over and over with Greek commentary.

There was an Anglican Chapel where you could feel even worse if you liked. There was a psychiatrist available to you around the clock however he was suicidal and hardly ever of use. Ernid exercised on the daily coin-operated treadmill and realized on those walks that was the extent of escape.

In this new holding centre the officers weren't friendly nor unfriendly but relatively Fascist in between and some of them fell in love with the criminals they were supposed to keep in check. There were even pregnancies to women prisoners who might have been there for baby theft.

# Chapter Eight

## Forced Emigration

Not that there was shock left in Ernid Ernst but whilst toiling away in The Sandwich Section of Prison he received the bad news that his parents, whom he loved very hard, were to be forcefully migrated back to Europe because of the racist policies developed by The Government. These made it extremely unlawful to live in Australia.

This included anyone of Indigenous background whether pitch-black or medium grey, the lot were shoved on big boats and basically told to go to Buggery; and ironically that happened to be where they originally came from.

It was a round-up conducted by paid thugs who became high priests of forced emigration, scuttled back to the land of their often difficult birth. It was highly emotive for anyone passing by who happened to catch the obscene action initiated by our heads of state who only loved British-looking people and hurriedly got rid of the rest.

It was sobs and lamentation time and many who were not selected for ships passed out in a dead swoon to see so many innocent Europeans kicked and badly roughed-up in the new stewardship of nice people who just didn't look correct.

It was hard to look right in the head because those who mattered in the State decreed that there was a right look from now on and that look or physical likeness had to be British Establishment and no coloreds or eye-ties otherwise known as Wogs.

Boat after infernal boat lumbered off toward shark-infested-waters overflowing with people who had the luck to be born or conceived in Prague and Oslo.

Ernid in jail listened to The ABC Radio news bulletins which featured descriptions of ordinary nice citizens being toughed-up and then kicked onto gangplanks that took them into cavernous prisons which were filled with vermin.

It took two weeks to get back to Prague what with bubonic rodents and giant sea slugs that could wrap their sloppy tentacles right round the ships and squeeze the living Jesus out of them.

It was the initiative of Australia at this time to not only force-emigrate persons originally conceived and then of course born in Prague and let them basically fend for themselves there, even though their economy wasn't too crash-hot, the Australian Government had become so conservative that it decided to ban sex.

Intercourse between consenting nurses in hospitals was the one box which wasn't ticked appropriately and from now on it was decreed that men would mate with other chaps and ladies would have no intercourse whatsoever, apart from thinking about it on a bus.

Ernid found himself back at the plant after performing years of community service programs such as the speedy and popular digging of ditches, making roads look nicer, installing personal alarms on inpatients and outpatients in hospitals; but for the most part his voices sadly grew worse and not even psychiatrists or psychologists could help him out of the inextricable foul mess he found himself in.

His old familiar compost heap was taken off him rendering him homeless; the Government auctioned uncountable amounts of compost heaps, some two story and others even condominium and they enjoyed a surplus in the first time in living memory. Citizen's recollections were auctioned and delivered in albums to the successful bidder. Life had turned into a bidding-war.

The Conservatives that led by example, which was their only saving-grace, auctioned to the public anything not nailed down; they sold their own chalets and multi-story skyscrapers to the highest or the lowest bidder. Trains went for a song and school buses a pittance. Sets of play-equipment sold well, particularly see-saws which went for a buck so long as the successful bidder took it away themselves.

All industry was sold at auction and that included airports that made cheese and mustard sandwiches. Train stations sold and bus stops went in next to no time so that the buses didn't stop much any more or people cast manure at them in an effort to get them to pull over so you could get on them.

Human blood donations were sold by public tender so that each hospital in the land was instructed to bottle it and barrel it at once so that pick-ups might be organized for quick delivery to overseas shops where it sold faster than inflation. The Koreans purchased every single droplet of Australian blood and South Korea and North Korea engaged in a bitter war over whose blood it was.

The very streets which simple-minded-citizens trod on were sold to overseas interests so nobody could go anywhere, not that the Government minded, as there is nowhere to go in Australia anyway; at least that was the thinking.

Roads sold for half a million each and were delivered to either South or North Korea where they assimilated into existing native roads in such a deft way no one could possibly tell the difference; the tar was seamless and even smelled the same no matter what you did with it. The Government sold roundabouts so Australian drivers couldn't make a right-hand-turn.

Criminals with a track record of bestiality were turned into Government Consultants and murderers retrained as Police in a desperate bid to lower inflation as well as the new crime rate which was going through the proverbial roof.

There were emotional scenes in great convention centres where depressed people were sold in job lots and transported to Tasmania where they no doubt belonged and then found their way in the timber industry as pine tree consultants or owl experts.

The most innovative idea was to arm school children from Prep up to year 12 with sophisticated machine guns, some automatic, some not, and infants who failed to show at target practice behind their schools were hanged.

Draconian alterations were going on in every sector of the community and there was not a single solitary thing you could possibly do about any of it.

You couldn't even leave Australia because the ships and jets had gone overseas to new homes that wanted them; for some reason they wouldn't let on.

Police were trained to be interesting, perhaps fascinating and so many ordinary criminals got into the right training programs in order to quote from Oscar Wilde.

The study of Oscar Wilde was made law.

Instead of seeing, as you used to do in the old days for example, happy children swinging off to State School and heading for their first lessons, you now saw forced target practice organized by volunteers at The Tuck Shop.

The saddest sight for Ernid Ernst himself was the collection of compost heaps that folk lived in and had made the necessary adjustment to cook in and sleep in and bear their young in. People are incredibly good at adaptability and don't really stress too much when they are required to exist in mud and grubs so long as it's got two bedroom and running hot water. A driveway would be great if that's possible in tough times.

Great Government-made trucks scooped up every single one and two bedroom compost heap in such a way there was no shadow or story of where it had been or how many people lived in it or read the paper among the cockroaches.

It became the latest treat to live nowhere and have no hope. Folks just bathed in heavenly lavatories and rinsed their hands in puddles that formed where roads once existed. The Government led by example as they lived nowhere too, selling offices as quickly as lilac shoots form, that sort of thing.

And the people saw that it was good and took their cue from the devastating infrastructure, the enforced guidelines for temporary living.

Free intermment was tremendously popular with kids. The new way of governance was to work like mad and hope for death; and the schools pushed this line also; with clinically depressed teachers also teaching in a clinically depressed state. Anxiety was available in coin-in-the-slot automated ticketing machines on railway platforms, or at least where they once stood.

Popular culture stopped for good and escapist television programs ceased to be replaced with live crosses to interment or cremations for old pets that couldn't walk any more. The restaurant trade positively boomed when free dead duck was presented cheerfully to the rank and file dead duck devourers. Sports cars were driven off cliffs or set alight.

Reading was censored so that only The Three Bears could be studied, and that in audio form only. Meantime Ernid had done his community service order and because of his shame and disgrace his employer put him back in Pulverizing again; not that he really minded. He felt at home in Pulverizing Section. It was an old trustworthy friend of many years, it sure enough was.

Every billboard had the great word 'Coalition' on it in big print with a leader's face that resembled the spirit of Totalitarianism. People loved to be meek, put down, shoved around, think nothing of their dreams or themselves and the policy makers for the party knew this to be an unshakable truth. People are weak.

Parents attended their own press conferences and children at school studied Fascist Theatre and learned by rote the rhymes of Mussolini.

Pets became masters of repetition and Government Thinking so that they woofed the appropriate words at will when the lemonade van went by.

Ma and Pa now rented a pot hole in the centre of a road and were delighted with its position, its aspect you might say, as it was right next to a park that had been recently detonated so that all that was left of it was a smoking ruin, which put them immediately in mind of Prague during the winter of 1944; brother was that tough.

The streets were unrecognizable as there were none; the roads ditto and most buildings smoked and cinders rained down to make matters unimaginably worse.

In the atmosphere of a closed set in Hollywood there was nothing going on except melancholic neatness and the pong of disinfectant which saturated even the bank notes the public used.

It was an intensely wary atmosphere of knowing your place and of showing no initiative whatsoever; it was so awful Australians reveled in it because they have always been lovers of bosses who hold them beneath their oily contempt.

Australian Government by now had dropped every other industry and focused entirely upon human misery; that was where the money and the power were and those in charge knew it. Gone was infrastructure for in was Burp. The economy depended suddenly on indigestion.

The global appetite for their brand of lemonade over the past year had triggered off an expansion in vats so that the giant plant in Sydney was now one big vat that was capable of processing and producing so much Burp that the brand beat Pepsi as well as Slade Lemonade easily, with outlets on the moon and there was heated talk of putting one on the sun, but keeping it cold would be expensive.

Ernid's brief foray into crime was forgiven, as was his time in jail, and the new management installed his eerie likeness on every label and crate and pop-top-can and carton all over the world; he was already famed in Indonesia so now the company had his wired face on buildings in London and New York to guarantee heady sales and magnificent profits. The slogan 'Wired For Burp' went viral.

He had a new doctor who cured him of flashbacks so that he never thought again of his industrial accident. He was on pretty heavy drugs that made him want his own product more than ever. He was the perfect logo for putting on weight and keeping it on possibly for the duration of his existence.

He had lost touch with his former wife but connected her with a Croatian Wrestler whose face and body remained but made him nauseous, understandably. He had no clue as to where his old parents now lived; he presumed in a hole somewhere and he was right about that. They lived in a secluded one bedroom gap in the road right next to 'Burp' Pty Ltd; and they had the fortune to get their old jobs back.

It was in New York he gradually realized he was being stalked by an agent for Slades Soft Drink who had their plant in Keon Park in Melbourne, they being a very ambitious soft drink group who wanted to conquer Burp to monopolize the global demand for burpy-ness.

He was staying in Manhattan in a rather pleasant hotel with two secretaries named Noel whom he rather liked, and they made a nice change from Bimbos he usually traveled overseas with. The Noels worked him hard though, and because he was good on his feet they arranged to have him speak on fashionable radio stations as well as

powerful television shows. People loved 'Wired For Burp' as well as him and he was everywhere all at once.

He chose to put on his lean powerful body that was over six foot high in the old measurements continuous drip-dry-suits of fashionable rayon which he gave a light iron after gallivanting about on the Upper Eighties all day on his talk shows and appearances. His hideous bizarre face appeared in *Time* magazine explaining the virtues of his brand.

'Not bad these one!' became his catch-cry and he invariably said that on talk shows as he playfully scratched a flea in his head or bit into the arm of his presenter; although sometimes he required a leash.

It was the dumbness and innocence of him that the public liked and admired; he seemed a robot but more like one of them because he was stupid. He threw back lakes of Burp on television to much clapping and women threw their under garments at him.

One night after an arduous shower he could have sworn he heard a big body of a man make himself or itself a coffee in his kitchen; as he muttered ruefully about rust beginning to arrive in his throat-vents and irritating mould get in his ceramic dentures and to cling to his plaster tongue he dried himself right down and went into the kitchen in the mechanical nude to see what was happening.

He was annoyed at the build-up of pollution on his firm transparent head-visor and he sprayed it with new anti-scum which worked at once; of course it did. He believed wholeheartedly in products. He himself was one of them, the new breakthroughs that come onto the market every day. He screwed a new spark plug in his brain and coughed a little then he put his underpants on.

There was a strange presence in the kitchen and it seemed to come his way like a funny inexplicable sensation of possibly danger and instability; he dressed properly in his favorite rayon suit and laced up his pointy shoes that he liked more than any other form of temporary transportation.

What was after him in fact and in deed? It made him feel bilious to think about who could do him harm after all the promotional work, and hands-on-work such as his long stint in the hazardous Pulverizing Section – he felt used up in a way whenever he examined his NAB Passbook only to see a few desultory bucks saved in it. He was always impoverished and at thirty years of age still didn't own a credit card or boast any debt.

He was tired of being the poorly-paid figurehead of The Burp Company Pty Ltd; and although he had a kind and friendly heart and a most sweet outlook at life in general he often wept to see how unjustly others fared under the colossal hammer of commerce. He was just trying to keep going and to take care of his rapidly ageing parents. They seemed to age in front of his eyes. They did.

He heard footfall and then the odd sound as if someone wet from a shower was dripping right alongside of him, a spectral thing rather like himself, possibly it was a side of himself he'd never seen before; his own ghost attacking him. He threw down some Panadol and tried to take it easy but it wasn't really that possible in his present state.

There was definitely a being next to him, that strange wet-sounding-person or fellow automaton who was toweling himself down a foot away. He decided to scream but nothing emitted and he dialed 000 but the phone didn't connect. He was terrified by nothing but a sound; but then again perhaps lots of people had been terrified of his single sound which was his plastic windscreen-visor slamming down violently.

Could it be an agent from Pepsi or Slades Lemonade located in distant Keon Park in Victoria? That felt more likely and he began at once to tremble something exquisitely, almost like a quivering dessert such as a jelly, let us say.

He could easily detect a pump-action-shotgun getting loaded although he couldn't see it. He could hear feeble or remote giggling or obscene guffawing but no one was there and nothing could be detected in any sort of a way. He was obviously hallucinatory but wanted not to be. Then he saw a man get up.

He was dark like all lemonade salesmen with a dark hat over his dark eyes; everything about him was awful and so threatening offset by him holding his head under his arm.

He spoke through his normal mouth as he clutched his head in his big right hand, and his voice was friendly, which blew Ernid's mind.

The man was clear as a bell and inserted beautiful scarlet-coloured-squat-thick cartridges into the shotgun and asked Ernid for a Burp. Ernid hurriedly searched the tidy kitchen for a Burp but he was in such a state that he couldn't even find the fridge. He could not understand what he was doing physically, mentally, any other way and he could detect muffled boot-steps coming his way, and a weird voice that in itself did not make a jot of sense.

He could sense great danger, particularly in respect to the sound, unmistakable effect in his ears of the big bullets or explosives or whatever they were, going into the firing-apparatus of the shotgun and he could definitely hear the weight of his assassin standing up because the murderer obviously chose to have crook knees and he could hear in particular his creaking.

His mind completely panicked and he could feel not just perspiration beginning to arrive in the vinyl black toupee he had on today that felt like a long-playing-record on his boiling-hot-skull, but he was now sweating and swaying as the guy got a darned sight nearer.

He had never been murdered much before and it wasn't much fun and the panic made him want to rush and to run. He could feel the fetid breath of his hit-man on the edge of his neck and those tiny neck hairs commenced to vibrate and sort of sigh on their own. He ran away, yes that was the only option available to him, and it was original so he ran like mad into the street where it was most windy and inclement.

It felt beneficial to just run and to escape a shotgun attack upon his person. His heart pounded faithfully and his kidneys functioned not too badly, and his face strained as his calves protested but he knew it was no good asking his assassin to explain his intentions; what use was something like that?

His mechanical jaw throbbed and pounded with the extreme effort of being much physically faster than his follower. Meanwhile the tiny intricate copper keys in his throat agitated and the false ceramic tongue hurt and hindered him as well. He ran by a disused railway works and leapt over hissing locomotive steam and still his pursuer came at him apace.

They both ran right through a bus yard after that, dodging reversing buses whose drivers tooted and hooted their horns and sirens at them; he was happy he was fit and well and he figured he'd just outrun him in the end – although where was that end?

His mind raced with the want of rapid answers but none came of any kind. Why was this happening and why was he targeted at this late stage of proceedings?

Although it was two o'clock in the morning a tea room was trading, in fact there were contented families inside it nibbling fresh scones and yummy looking lamingtons rinsed down with piping-hot tea. He felt like joining them straight away and did so.

He and his assassin sat down a tiny table apart and perused the menu both asking for piping-hot tea with a serve of hot fluffy scones with raspberry conserve on the side and fresh whipped cream. The assassin went outside to smoke and that gave Ernid some respite. He sure looked angry in the open doorway the dramatic way he inhaled his foreign-looking-cigarette and doing large sighs the way smokers do.

Ernid was so frightened he wet his underpants and had to request the toilet key and find the god-damned toilet which was right out the back in the slippery pitch-black. He wound off fifteen feet of lovely life-saving lavatory paper and then he softly patted his groin down until the effect looked right and normal.

He stood up and pushed the cistern button and experienced severe flashbacks from The Pulverizing Section instantly; he thought in the toilet he was back at work except that it felt like years ago when he first started. He brushed his machine teeth brightly as possible with his portable folding toothbrush, combed his nylon black vinyl hair and stepped back into the tea room again to have the scones.

As the friendly waitress placed them down before him he could hear wolfish laughter emanating from the chair next to him where the hit man was enjoying his own scones, although the murderer's hat was yanked down over his non-intellectual-looking-forehead so he couldn't see that much of him even at close proximity like that.

What was off-putting was the shotgun, the manner in which it leant against its owner's chair, the grimness of it. Ernid was more frightened of the noise it would make than of being food-poisoned by the not-that-great-looking-scones and the decrepit whipped or soggy wilting cream that had an insect wriggling away in it.

The heavy staccato breathing of his assassin put him off the scones as hungry as he was, so he pushed them right out the road and sipped the hot tea which relaxed his jagged nerves to a point where at least he knew where he was.

He hurt a lot; in fact every muscle pained him especially the muscle of the memory and he was of course experiencing flashbacks faster than the heat went out of the tea.

He was seeing the dreadful pulverizing accident again and witnessing himself as it were being pulled out of the great vat of powdery soft drink bottles that were a billion degrees in heat and awful in intensity. He reluctantly bit into his fluffy scones to distract his paranoia.

The instant he politely munched a very tiny fluffy scone a droplet of his forehead blood dropped on the top of the scone with a vivid redness. He added some cream and mechanically gulped it down in one swallow which was difficult.

His assassin applauded him and he could see very plainly the man had white gloves on now, so that the applauding was muffled such as hands manufacture at the opera.

He threw down a second small scone which was entirely coated with his gore and he wondered why he was so starving-hungry at a time like this?

As he consumed scone two he could hear a shotgun shell being loaded into a nearby weapon of vastness that was just a friendly tea table away. He just kept on staring down into the blood-covered scones that he liked, in fact he was enjoying them and started wondering how many he'd consumed by now, blood or no blood on them.

He looked finally across at the tea room hit man but he was gone like hope. He had clearly liked his scones, the hit man had, since he had devoured them and Ernid could see that the chap had paid for his snack and left a quivering twenty buck bill that kept flat under the imitation silver sugar bowl.

Ernid decided to order a mince pie to settle his bad nerves. It came on the spot without sauce to it so Ernid leant over the delicacy to munch its vitamins and was startled to see more forehead blood drop all over it. It made a right old mess, it really did, and poor Ernid was embarrassed.

In a voice of his he scarcely credited was from his mind he said 'Excuse me please miss would you but there appears to be much blood on my pie!' But the exhausted baggy-eyed-waitress sighed as she took away his tea-things and Ernid mopped his dripping-with-blood-forehead, paid at the register and left no tip as he wasn't that satisfied with the level of service.

It felt pretty nice to step out into the un-minding street where no assassins were. There was only a miniature broom truck that busily swept detritus up such as human beings who were a week late with their property-rental.

These electric bristly broom car-things were rather cute-looking to Ernid and their drivers looked so perfectly contented as they busily swept up bodies that he rather felt a jab of jealousy that it wasn't his calling; what with the scratchy sounds they made and the hum of their whining motor and the guys in them eating a Kit Kat.

The street was cold and lonesome but no murderers were to be seen anywhere except on his mind.

Relatively normal-looking people who in their way resembled him without the apparatus he had to wear. He had begun to hate his own see-through visor and as he melted into the general scheme of things, apart from the pursuer, he started to brighten up somewhat. He went and sat in a little green park and there he met a woman lemonade worker.

She was neither mechanical nor that human-looking but somewhere friendly in between. She sat so very close to him that it positively excited him and while she didn't exactly smile at him but rather examined his heart by inserting her right palm inside his business shirt, he had to think therefore that she liked him without knowledge.

Her hair was long and very blonde and was by now looking handsome and fascinating in her way. She could have worked in Sales or Costing or Receipts maybe, and thought they might have had shepherd's pie in the café once together because he remembered distinctly that she liked peas and tomato sauce. That was his remembrance of her and he also loved her because she was simply with him.

She moved up a little closer to his side on that whitewashed park bench and kept on holding to his heart her warm hand without it going anywhere; it sort of felt like a dove of love had perched there and he was dumb to do anything at all about it. She was mysteriously intimate with him; he hadn't been close to anything lately but a common old hit-man who was still eating his hot pie.

She smiled far into his face and she stroked his plastic sun-shield in a way he liked, humming some obscure folk song that he seemed to remember and which connected with the poppy dance of home at harvest-time. He missed home but had no concept of it. She was home.

She lightly caressed both his visor and the cruel and monstrous grille that kept him in; he always felt trapped within it, for it felt like the perfect embodiment of The Capitalist System in that he had to feel snared and caged and intimidated by a force of will nobody can ever begin to like or comprehend. You just give into its awfulness and aspire to an inner freedom that they can't get at. Which was his beating heart with this woman factory worker now kneeling on the park bench right next to him.

Her bare shoulders were on him and she kept lingeringly kissing the wire protective grille in such a way that he wept at her exertions; she was a pantomime lover and had no need of speech lest it destroy the mimed moment.

He at long last put his protective right arm around her warm waist, kissed her soft face and asked her what section of Burp she worked in. She didn't answer in any spoken sort of way but reached her lips into his conveyor-belt-throat and kissed all of his inner parts until he fainted.

When he awoke the hit-man had replaced her and was looking at him with a terrible intensity and greater certainty of purpose than he had just before in the tea-room. Where had the factory girl gone, he wondered. He missed her company terribly and disastrously; she had vanished only to be replaced by a reptilian gentleman with a shotgun. It didn't seem that fair.

To his horror the hit-man knelt in precisely the same way the girl had done just a second before. He lifted his weapon to the side of the face of Ernid and pulled the trigger just as Ernid had seen in his recent nightmares and a few American films that are supposed to be amusing but generally aren't.

The great wad of pellets went right by his left ear and took out a weeping willow tree just behind him, in fact Ernid could see hundreds of birds intensely flap upward and in fact scream. Everything screamed, distant witnesses and the lake, they screamed.

Ernid's ears were bleeding badly as his eardrums had been destroyed by the close proximity to the blast. He hopped up like a frightened bunny rabbit and ran for his life across the park.

The hit-man ran too, ran with him and fired another charge with part of his scattering pellets striking his big broad back. That really hurt him a great deal, but then somehow he lost his pursuer and after twenty or so minutes of grave danger he found his hole in the road, flew down into its labyrinthine comforts and put the kettle on at once.

Just to be on the safe side, as he was beginning to love and think about security as opposed to insecurity, he pulled the plug of earth hard down like really hard in order to feel even safer. It made a pleasant 'pop' noise actually as it shut him in where he stood on the end of his ladder to the road.

In his shut-hole he sipped gratefully his tea bag and boiling hot water, finding it amazing how tea bags work on the human heart to give their possessor the peace they need to keep on going through The Capitalist System.

He kept sighing as he tried hard to take a look at the paper he'd bought earlier that day in his wandering ways, but he had hardly any real concentration left as he kept on hearing that dreadful weapon go off right near his bleeding ear. He put some wads of soft paper tissues over the damaged ear and collected his dripping gore in that improvisatory way like most Australians do in daily life these days.

As he deftly patted the friendly unjudging tissues in his bloodied ear he hallucinated upon the factory girl who'd caressed him in the innocent park; she re-caressed him now in his cold bolt-hole and he could smell her hair once again and also the incredible fragrance of her loving but very temporary arms that were white as snow and had draped themselves just for a minute around his lonely body.

As he turned to the sports section of his newspaper a hand pulled the big paper page down to his level. It was the girl again who was smiling wistfully at him; she was definitely present and she lightly brushed the sports pages away so she could kiss his machine face in a much more passionate manner than in the park. She desired him.

Her lovely natural blonde hair cascaded into his mesh teeth again with a reverberating sound, with each remarkable blonde hair making him happier than he was on his own.

'I work in Costing', she murmured into his sore ear-hole. He said mechanically 'I thought you did. Didn't I see you once in the café at work?'

She said they'd enjoyed a plate of hot chips together and that he'd been gallant enough to give her a big bite of his mince pie, not to mention half his Burp that workers got free with their meal-break in the café.

She got out of her purse a nifty little bright yellow handled pocket screwdriver and undid his chest and inserted two brand-new batteries in his heart and he surely thanked her, she did the cavity up again and he heard it clang shut in a truly satisfying way. 'Now I am complete!' he giggled with new pleasure she'd given him just now.

She kissed his every mechanical part and pressed her hand on his knee for some reason that has to be intimate, he looked up and she was completely gone again.

But this time she wasn't replaced with his assassin which came as a very great relief as he was sick to death with stress.

He drew a bath and got in it piping hot and scrubbed his machine and partly real body with a very costly artificial bath-sponge and that felt fantastic, it really did.

He luxuriously soaped his still-on windscreen and made a mental note to add wipers because lately it did nothing but rain in his area. He would pay a visitation to his motor mechanic, not that he had a car or anything.

With his long legs resting on the end of the big bathtub and the steam relaxing all of him, the steaming hot wind shield feeling much newer and easier to see through, he realized that he truly loved his hole in the road like never before, that it not only felt safe from the violent outside world but that it loved him like the lemonade lady.

# CHAPTER NINE

## A HOLE OF ONE'S OWN

He liked and probably adored his hole in the road and didn't care one way or the other if his neighbors in their holes were pleasant enough towards him or treated him like vermin; it was in fact a time of relative solace and of finding his feet, so to say, and all he wanted to do was take it really easy after all that had occurred to him.

He rang work and begged for a full day off so he could do up the hole. He didn't get through to anyone real, just as he wasn't real, he knew that much, but he left a nice message on his manager's answer service assuring him he'd be in first thing tomorrow at 8am on the proverbial dot.

He carefully swept up the dirt floor of his dirt home, and that simple job in itself occupied the best part of two hours. He placed a nice mat beneath his tea-table and slid a clean-looking dining-chair opposite his own one just in case Lemonade Woman dropped by; as he felt sure she would; and of course she did after he'd settled in and done the hole up and even make it trendy.

He rinsed his only Blue Danube dinner plate with care in the sink and then he wiped it shiny-clean with the aid of half a new toilet roll that he found somewhere. He whistled through his wired jaw, some rustic melody it was, a snippet from Prague and he got right down on his arthritic knees and painted every single wooden underground door dark green.

He tidied the bed-hole as opposed to the bedroom he once possessed and he neatly folded the sheets he'd purchased at the op shop in the main strip; he imagined the sight of his new lady companion sighing for him in the simple hard bed.

He brushed his nylon hair in a new way and wore it up today in the perfect tribute to Elvis.

He picked up all the fluff from the earth floor and blew the excess coal dust off the coal dust. He loathed coal dust.

He got out a bucket of boiling-hot-water and swiftly wall-papered the living-room and though the flock-pattern looked okay in its way.

He decided to change the furniture rather drastically in a revolutionary kind of way, and through a gift for interior design he shoved the couch nearer the wall.

He put on excellent fresh underwear and slippers and then the phone rang shrilly and persistently, it must be said, for the bell tones of it hurt his damaged ear drums.

It was his manager insisting he come to work at once as there had been a serious complaint about his work-attitude. He rang for a taxi and went in there.

In the office of his several managers he remembered not liking many of them, and that feeling was reciprocated by most of them since he was a detestable robot who they thought was getting a bit uppity and were in general thoroughly tired out by him and his stupid visor that made him look like a tennis person in a way, it was thought.

'You were in Promotions for ages weren't you Mister Ernst? Why did you vote to go back into Pulverizing Section? Also you are a jail-bird, are you not? We're not sure you've the correct qualities we require for our figurehead any more. What on earth happened to your ear?'

He sat and wept right in front of them with the agony of pints of his head-blood tumbling out of him, no matter how many infernal paper tissues he shoved in his sore ear the blood just kept on arriving from the damaged canal within it.

'You can be quite exasperating, Mr Ernst!' they called in unison as they gathered round him. You could see they needed to kick and to beat him.

They all crouched round his blood-shot eyeballs offering him a new job in the same company he knew he worshipped; as well as needed to pay rental on the hole in the road.

'We want you to go into schools as our Educational Officer and complete a four year Internship with twice the pay you are on at the minute; what in fact do you say to that offer, Mr Ernst?'

Next day he stepped automatically and briskly into a gloomy Catholic High School and was made to go to The Mass the second he signed in there c/o 'Burp' Pty Ltd.

He was shoved down onto the shivering cold marble floor and made to look up at Christ being publicly admonished by the Romans who weren't keen on Him.

The lead light windows depicted vast floggings on His poor old back.

He was literally frog-marched into The Year Sevens and whilst the eager-eyed children gawked at him he had to give his presentation on a whiteboard-thing with a squeaky marker that of course had nothing in it but a squeal-noise, the hopeless dry old thing it was.

'Good morning children, my product isn't on your tuck shop morning tea list at the moment but that shall be rectified and at once; now let us have a show of hands who has Diabetes 2?' They none of them dared to put their limbs up.

He raved on to them about the need for enormous reserves of pure sugar going straight into the growing healthy bloodstream and he assured them that even with deadly Diabetes 2 they could throw down a slab, no risk!

He told them it was refreshing to have illnesses because the human person needed something yummy to look forward to, such as caffeine with which his product was laced. He told them dying folk sipped it through a drip.

'Burp cheers the human school person right up!' he enthused and then he daringly demonstrated just how fast he cheered up with two gallons of it in his gut, without a single solitary belch as well.

Pallets of his brand were slid into the classroom and Burp workmen aggressively handed out family sized bottles of it to each gaping child who looked thirsty.

Staff gargled it straight down without even looking at the brand name on their free bottle, they were so stressed they just kept drinking it, even on the toilet they got stuck into it.

Little kids crying to no avail were tossing it back and hurling away the empty bottles, and meanwhile the staff fought the kids for more of it, and there were unedifying punch-ups.

Girls punched on and threw one another about the room by the sticky lemonade infused hair.

Ernid had to wear both a hat that looked like the family sized bottle as well as the suit that made his tall body resemble a great big bottle as well; he didn't need the sack from work and so he heartily gave his assent to the pressure of doing it. The happy kids poured Burp from his own body and gusted into it so they were fit to burst.

He worked hard all day and prayed for a good report but management didn't say a word to him; and he had to hope he'd be okay.

He really liked using the black marker on the white board and he exploited his own training so he could speedily draw diagrams and charts and logarithms to show the human need for carbonated sugar and also point out the perils of sudden almost catatonic withdrawal. The kids liked him and he was popular with the teachers because he handed them free six packs of it on the house.

Back in the hole that night he retrieved the battered diary he usually stashed in his desk, put his reading spectacles on his nose, that felt a bit battered as well, but through the almost opaque lenses he saw those hectic ruled pages, his diary no doubt, and by virtue of running his eyes along the pages he saw just how hard he'd been at it.

He had only been at 'Buzz' Pty Ltd for three years but felt like a veteran already with so many changes, shifts of position, from Pulverizing Section to Marketing and then out on the road to be the figurehead for them; yet he only had a few bucks in the bank, no girlfriend and the ghost of a friendly lady who caressed his lonesome hair in the little park not long ago, in fact it felt present so it was present.

He dined upon Lonely Beans, his favorite dinner which was apparently delicious, you only needed to heat it up and plop it on your hot buttered toast and he sipped hot lemon mixed with honey and he knew that would ward off hypothermia.

The Lonely Beans had a little paprika in them to give them some heat and they in fact were so hot a few of them went down his shirt and deep-fried his hairy nipples, and that deed made him jump.

As he washed up the dishes a knock came from the door on his hole that led to the road; so he walked up the stairs to answer it and opened the road-door to his hit-man again.

The hit-man was smoking an overpoweringly strong cigarette and had his sombre hat over his cratered visage, as per usual, and he wore a very dark overcoat that bulged with weaponry such as a machine gun, grenades, machetes and Zulu head-hunting-spears. It was as if they were old friends the way they acknowledged each other with a grunt and a wink, or a half-wink is more accurate.

It was a strange meeting and an odd etiquette indeed for the suddenly well-mannered murderer to take off his hat and coat and sunglasses too, take in a way his sinister self off and put a freshly-ironed nice clean cotton apron around his firm waist and assist with the evening meal. He put the double-barrel shotgun on the table next to the cruet set and the silver wear that Ernid had salvaged from his separation.

The two placed the spoons just so and the pretty forks and knives correct and right, butted up against the rim of the dinner plates where they would have their Last Supper.

Ernid politely poured his unexpected dining companion a glass of Golden Circle Pineapple Juice. He delicately poured himself the same fluid and they ceremoniously chinked then laughed to burst the tension I suppose.

They went into the small laundry exactly together and shared an old had-it black plastic comb to part their hair, they washed their faces together and Ernid passed his friend a most fresh bath towel and a block of fairly impressive soap. The hit-man thanked him most passionately; Ernid thought at the time a little too passionately. They went into the sitting-room and they both sat down.

'I love Lonely Beans!' exclaimed the assassin as he beheld the ever so friendly hand of Ernid spoon a considerable pile of them onto the perfectly cooked toast that was wholemeal because Ernid was trying to lose some weight and was guilty about putting on some weight. He wanted to be bean-pole-like.

'Can I tempt?' asked his murderer as he gingerly poured some claret into a glass; then he poured himself one and they smiled and double-chinked.

They sat down in perfect peace and tucked into their really hot Lonely Beans and winked at one another. It was not awkward.

'What did you get up to today?' asked Ernid of his guest who just tapped his hideous bulky machine gun by way of answering the question. He smiled in a benign way and said 'Not much. Work is down this year and I'm never that sure when the next hit will come from. I haven't got much in the bank at the moment'.

Ernid offered vanilla ice cream topped with canned and sliced peaches and when he bent over the man to present it the assassin instantly wept.

'Have I done something wrong?' asked Ernid in a very concerned way. He loathed wasting canned fruit and was brought up to yearn for it mechanically sliced with a knob of ice cream poised on its precipice.

'You are making me feel special, even wanted!' blubbered his grisly guest and then of course Ernid didn't know quite what to do – so in the end he didn't do a single thing.

They had a game of draughts in the end and then the murderer cleared away. It felt so civilizing to see the guy do the dishes nice and hot in his old sink.

'I'm dreadfully attracted to you, do you know that?' cried the man and he then blew his nostrils hard into his immaculate checked blue handkerchief and looked at it.

'Are you a figment of my imagination?' inquired Ernid and it seemed he was because the chap just looked at him stupid. 'Maybe', was exactly his answer that night.

They realized they were beginning to have not much in common and for the next bit of time they merely sat and stared at the wall; and that's an indication of the awkwardness as well as alienation both were perhaps feeling. The clock on the fridge that Ernid wound for his morning alarm seemed to tock terribly loudly, almost like a death knell.

'So do you pursue many lemonade toilers?' asked Ernid of his unwanted guest who had become wearied of his level of high emotionalism, and to demonstrate this he sponged up the dining table in a marked manner, glaring at him as though he wanted him to leave right away, never mind the cup of tea at the end of the meal.

'I just toil for an agency', admitted the killer, fidgeting with the bowler hat that Ernid hadn't noticed before. He couldn't make the adjustment to its look and the murderer now had a public service look about him.

'We just go to work like everybody else in the system but we murder instead of toiling putting parcels away'

'I used to work at the post office when I was a kid', said Ernid brightly, and the hit man also brightened up, in fact he appeared luminous for a change on the subject of parcels. 'I always wanted to put parcels away', he muttered. 'Or something more interesting that what I'm doing at the minute'.

Ernid didn't know what to do with him so he showed him around his hole in the ground, but the guest looked flat as a pancake no matter what he looked at.

'These are my boyhood cricketing trophies I won at our local church in my little village', smiled Ernid but the murderer had gone in a deep decline.

'I'm very sorry to have chased you and aimed my shotgun at your head and stuff like that', confessed the guest as he continued to blow his nose.

'That's all right my friend', whispered Ernid at last and he smiled at him; but that genuine show of affection took the man by surprise and he sat down very heavily and wept like a tap. 'I just do what they want me to at my agency. I never want to kill anyone. They have a very great power over us at work and none of us want to get the sack. They make us watch violent films and tell us the eliminations are for the good of the firm. They in fact dope us so we can kill people and if we are in the end successful they put us on full-time and we attend screenings of holiday homes'.

At this he wept loudly like a crushed beast and his leg kicked the leaning shotgun over making it go off deafeningly, very deafeningly that is for sure.

'Maybe you ought to look for a different sort of a position?' suggested Ernid and he again smiled at him to demonstrate friendliness. 'What else can I do?' beseeched the weeping murderer and started to actually nibble his sodden handkerchief until it was unrecognizable as an object of clothing.

'You could be a public servant if you wanted something different', said Ernid and he undid the old fruitcake can and pulled its irritating warped lid off and hacked them both off a juicy wedge. The hit man ate a sodden bit of it made more sodden by his fit of grief; thus it was difficult for him to get at no matter what sort of fork he employed.

'What in the world are public servants exactly?' asked the man as he continued to attack the cake. Ernid would not have been surprised to see the guy stand up right by him and shoot it, raisins and all, but he just shoved it down.

'Well' said Ernid 'They don't do much really except feel oppressed by a higher order whom they don't understand or recognize. Their work seems meaningless to them, just unreadable data on their voracious computer screens; and they have a very high amount of suicides per year'.

'Maybe I'll do it then', sobbed the man and was so distraught he dropped his waterlogged gent's hankie in his half completed cup of tea out of sheerest nervousness. 'I don't want to keep on with my current job because I used to be a practising Christian you see, and going around murdering lemonade toilers is just too much stress. I think I shall do as you suggest and try the public service. I shall go in there on Monday morning'

With that the gentleman took his big heavy impressive shotgun and left; and Ernid was actually relieved that he had gone up the hole in the ground and left him in relative peace and security. He certainly was a strange fellow but then again Ernid understood just how strange he was himself. He didn't want to criticize anyone else on the grounds that he could be found wanting as a bona fide human being.

He examined the room for proof the murderer had been there but when he looked in the sink, and the wash-up-water was still hot, very in fact as he wiggled his finger in it, there was only one fork and one knife and one spoon in it; and just the one dinner plate where he fully expected two. It was likely no one had come.

There was no evidence of any one else having dined on Lonely Beans with him at all, that it was missing out on his medication that drove the hallucination and nothing else but. He was just so certain the chap had been there and that he'd relaxed with him, seen him looking tragic about his dreadful position and had honestly suggested moving into the public service and trying to discover a new outlook in life as well as philosophy.

He sat up reading *David Copperfield* by Charles Dickens but couldn't stay on the page. He had no idea of time passing and couldn't recall what time it was that the murderer paid a call; he felt vaguely pleased he was gone though and so he went up his stepladder and felt like something sweet in his mouth so he visited the local 7 Eleven convenience store just up the way. They never ceased trading and seemed to him the perfect spirit of Capitalism or Totalitarianism. Were they the same ?

Inside the gaudy shop he found some delectable chocolates that to his surprise were made in Prague and had come all that distance to be gobbled up in Sydney.

He chose a few packets and added the daily newspaper to his bright red shopping basket and waited patiently at the busy register to be served.

It was the occasion of his thirtieth birthday and where better to celebrate the fact than in a blinding convenience store filled to the very brim with murderers of all persuasions from American Red Indians to Lebanese Gangs who seem obsessed with image such as ferocious-looking neck muscles and powerful leg muscles. The 7 Eleven store seemed a breeding ground for casual violence and he was feeling apprehensive and even frightened in a way.

Like all the others he stood at the register waiting to be served, and he became well aware that boredom was breeding like a sewer right around his shopping basket that contained tea bags and painkillers – the only two objects needed to sustain life in the suburbs. Two Pacific Islander chaps punched one another really overwhelmingly right in front of other shoppers.

They really laid into one another, hammering one another into froth for getting nearer the register before the other one of them. This is seen as an outrage in their culture so they continued their brawl in the crowded parking strip out the front, with a big crowd cheering them on. They eventually bit each other all over their quivering bodies and lay in pools of their own gore to wild and desperate applause from the mob.

The way they fought so savagely put Ernid in mind of the time he witnessed aggression at a bank where a customer punched the lights out of a fellow customer for being served first. It resulted in death of course and a futile ambulance visitation.

He just didn't deign to pay at the busy register for fear of being executed by a customer.

He was also well aware of the gluttony and sugary addiction of children in the store who were grossly overweight; they screamed for a treat as they raced round the shelves in their hunt for a sweetie or several of them. They didn't request any permission from their parents but just hit lids off Milo cans and swallowed every particle of it in the one gulp of pure addiction.

Crazed church elders sat on the grubby floor and thirstily drank bins of Fanta and of Burp without bothering to pay for it.

It was hard to get by in the store because of internal brawling and a lynching but eventually he made it across the rubbish and bodies in the overcrowded car park.

All the way home he saw violence come out of nothing and he wondered just why it was like that.

Home was best, hole was best, so he wandered past frightful brawls and dodged ambulances which seemed to pause only to slurp the gore. There were bodies everywhere due to excessive drinking and blowing dope and buildings in Australia were beginning to look like ones all over America. It was a copy of The USA.

He said hi to a woman who stabbed him hard in his pelvis. He staggered back to his safe hole and hoped he'd shut its front door and that the hit man wasn't back to remind him that he was in love with him again.

He got into his bathroom hurriedly and in a panic enshrouded a fairly new bath towel round his skinny stomach, briefly wondering why he never put on any weight with all his sugar intake at work.

He managed to cauterize the wound with antiseptic rinse and the towel round the gut really helped. The feet he was standing in were lurid red of violence all around him.

After he managed to feel better and the wound was dried right up he knelt by the foot of his single hard bed and clasped his palms together in deepest prayer. He asked God to cease the violence that was synonymous with sugar.

He prayed his fool head off and wept like mad to hear God but as usual there was only tinnitus and nothing else. God is soft drink.

He tried hard to scrunch his eyes in bed and hallucinate nice things, but no matter how hard he tried the sights and sounds of brawls and angry citizens made him feel restless and even fidgety. He missed Prague.

He missed lots of things like his parents, he didn't have their new phone number on him, partly because he was naked under the covers. He made a mental note to find to try to find them but other things kept cropping up.

He had no idea any longer as to what happened to actuality to make it fictitious; and as well as that the people's faces that he met were novels . He had read long ago in a public library that all fiction is true but how could he possibly believe in anything as far-fetched?

He was no doubt whatsoever seeing that which isn't there and not just doubting whatever was left of his mind but his own human eyesight felt dubious to him; he loved to be alive in all its various aspects and had no need of bothersome hit men who just came and went out of whimsy.

He went to the toilet mirror where it all started and carefully examined his head; he saw a friendly sort of machine composed of a winning sort of smile but the grin he understood was machine-made, machine-washable.

He gulped hard and paused to listen to his epiglottis functioning with a suction effect rather like someone in a kitchen using a rubber suction-thing to suck all the rot out; so he chose to gulp dramatically once more but that time it hurt him and so he stopped it.

He craned ever forward to the mirror to behold the wire mesh of his mouth and saw that somehow a sliver of bathroom soap was in there; so he looked like an old-fashioned soap-saver that his Grandmother used to rinse Gag off their plates in The Old Country.

He looked more closely and in the end he saw all kinds of tiny hairline fractures in his forehead as if he were reading too much.

He stroked his exhausted face and felt love and respect for whatever he was from the operation onwards.

His tongue of plaster he was acquainted with by now and had no problem coming at soup but he did experience a difficulty trying to hoe into cheap raisin toast with economy jam stroked on in time of gloom.

He had made the adjustment to the bird cage like door of his mouth and got used to hearing it slam shut whenever he ate something; but late at night the screenings would start up again and he screamed violently to himself as he saw the head of JFK come off over and over in the Hell of his own peaceful-once-bedroom.

He assumed the Zapruder footage was somehow inserted by error during the procedure at the hospital but it seemed cruel that it was on for all time.

Sometimes it jump-cut from sequence to sequence and at other screenings it remained identical to its premiere in his frontal lobe.

The sound track was louder especially the gunshot and it made him wince once or twice as it rang out in his brain, smartly followed by muffled screaming and indistinct cries of disbelief. He failed to understand just why it fell to him to keep on witnessing the terrible deed of cowardice over and over again. But witness it continually he did, whether he was in his earthen hole or on his way to work at the plant.

He could even be in the middle of urinating when the loud gunshot rang out singly or it arrived in a vicious volley of bangs and smoke, then the loud cheering becoming public sobbing and the screech of security limousines and police cars making a colossal racket in his sore ear drums. He believed it would drive him out of his mind and that maybe that was already happening.

# Chapter Ten

## The Outcome of Ma and Pa

Ma and Pa just learnt to roll with their punches and when they both arrived at The Commonwealth Employment Service they were not so surprised to see a line of a thousand people all looking the worse for wear. They were all trying to apply for the old age pension although most of them were children. These kids were completely starving and so thin they could easily see through each other in line.

There was pick-pocketing within the long line of Dole Applicants and many desperate thieving hands were whipping through crumpled personal items secreted in broken old pockets; I suppose it was a pocket of fading hope in a crumbling universe although there was scarce verse in it and only bitter rhyming.

Ma and Pa had tried really hard that important new-hope-morning to look the goods but their poverty was only too apparent even to the mostly perfectly jaded eyes.

Ma had a grubby old misshaped dress on over her grotesque lingerie hand-stitched in her village by senile Nuns and it didn't really cut it on the big day.

Her shoes too were ugly and improvised out of football boots with the ancient leather stops still in them, so that she made rather a racket on the wooden scuffed floor.

Pa just stunk.

When they reached the counter they were a year older and they kissed one another to celebrate the fact of it. Ma got a hand-drawn birthday card out of her filthy grubby pocket with pear juice all through its lining and she handed it to Pa but he said that he simply couldn't understand it. 'I'm senile my love!' he blubbered and she said she could see that in one look.

They were escorted into a mean cubicle together and their door was heavily bolted. They were then doused with powerful disinfectant and set fire to after which they were presented with a styrene beaker of beef tea and forced to smoke, even though they didn't.

A low order public servant beat them as another one of them showed them the correct way to smoke, starting with the drawback and ending with blowing fumes out of their dilated nostrils so that they coughed and spluttered something terrible, and were a sight to see, with their cascading toxic tears tumbling down their white and frightened faces.

All throughout their inhuman Government assault they were to complete very complex forms in order to seek the pension as they were of course entirely eligible at the tender age of sixty-five per each. They had both lost their work at Burp and were hysterically impoverished and had sore eyes from looking at each other.

More Commonwealth Employment Officers came into their cubicle and realized what they needed to do and got into it immediately and kicked them almost to death, all the while asking whether either of them needed assistance to complete the paperwork.

Pa had very poor handwriting indeed and made a complete mess of his application form and ended up drawing public hangings from memory in his village.

Ma was publicly garroted and left in a lift-well although afterwards informed she had been successful in her application for her pension, and although she was blood from stem to stern she gave Pa the victory sign with swollen and disjointed fingers.

Complex forms they certainly were, with literally hundreds of millions of personal queries in respect of their sex life and how bad they always felt.

Pa did his best to fill in the upsetting questions that demanded neatly hand-lettered answers as to his intelligence in old age, why he liked his wife and why he thought that 'Burp' Pty Ltd had sacked them both. He was also cross-examined by wording he couldn't follow as to why he was escorted to the big gate on the afternoon of his dismissal. He wrote sincerely that he had no idea why he was walked to the big gate;

and less idea as to why his honest wife had her jaw broken just before she was hurled onto a bus which took her to a mint-new-housing-development.

He found it hard to complete the tricky questions writing all the information down on his hands and knees on the floor and it was annoying that someone's cake crumbs had been underneath the many forms, making the hand-writing nigh on impossible to complete. One question asked him how he felt about trying to fill in the forms in this awkward kind of way.

In the end he was declared dead of paperwork, of forms in fact, and he lay deceased still gripping the faulty fine liner of The Australian Government in his going-green-fingers as rigor mortis, the beastly virus, had arrived all through him.

His body was stiff as a plank and he was interred at The Australian Government's expense in a Potter's Field where our country's anonymous poor are shoved.

Ma wept unstintingly by his plain tombstone trying to get the fact of his strange disappearance, she placed likenesses of tulips around his awful grave that didn't even have his name on it. Just Lemonade Worker 230,000,000.

Ma didn't know how to get in touch with the spirit-world in order to contact Pa and she just lived obscurely in her two bedroom hole until she could focus on the obituaries published in 'Burp' Pty Ltd Magazine; that was one of her meagre delights.

There was no wake, not that she knew of because her employer didn't believe in the sanctity of life or even its meaning; they just speedily swapped a deceased toiler for a living one and could find no fault in this arrangement because it was a winner.

Ma was sent a pallet of Burp which she sipped in an incoherent manner all the evening through as she watched the news on the broken television set.

Ma was in bad pain in her hole and her phone had been restricted so she could only call herself, that wasn't much use so she just began to compose self-explanatory letters to herself on onion paper, in fact she was down to her last slice of onion paper.

She gulped the last three painkillers in her palm and tried to get down and kneel on her muddy floor in order to get through to Mother Mary, but she was a different call.

As a peasant she knew life was unfair but it had never been quite this unequal, not to her elephantine recollection.

Ma mourned Pa bitterly and quite correctly saw his departure as a waste of her time, although there was his time to consider as well, all the times they'd fornicated in the village or out in the open or in the woods where they first learned to speak as they undressed. She was old and just lived on in the hole without his meaningless company.

She recalled that he sometimes uttered the archaic word 'Hi!' to her but she didn't really know what it meant. She had been sacked and he was dead so she wrote those two deeds in her daily diary with a pen embedded on a chain; that chain always put her in mind of her son's new mouth; but she had no idea the repair of the mouth had turned him into a perfect monster. But to her he didn't look too bad. She'd seen worse but couldn't recall where. Possibly in her vivid nightmares.

Next morning she dressed in widow's black and visited Pa in Potter's Field, the new home of people who weren't known by name anymore and just were the friends of the stones and stories and minerals under the earth.

She knelt before an unmarked grave and sent up loving signals to Heaven where the angels had full-time-work; the rarest thing in The Whole Universe!

She crossed herself and tried to envisage poor dead people without the worms or slugs and tried also to remember some of them, even the ones, especially the ones who'd been pressured into committing suicide.

The more Ma sent up messages directly from her soul and her heart the more tranquil the dead became and their souls also became peace-filled instead of having awful thoughts all the time. Jesus Christ, did she pray!

She was a bit concerned as she perused the morning newspaper that morning and read about a witness observing a man with a visor and what looked to be a wire-mesh-jaw that flapped up and down at a rapid rate terrorizing schoolchildren. He was seen to mime that he had a weapon on him and was pantomiming shooting them all. There was another positive sighting of him sitting down in a drain eating a foreign substance.

His face was obscured and his bearing looked like her son but she couldn't be certain partly because he was a good boy who worked hard and tried to do his various jobs; they included of course being mythic as the logo for 'Burp'.

She concentrated on decorating her hole in the ground so that she mopped and wiped and used the straw broom to good effect all round the place, especially the hard to get at places such as under the table where her broom got stuck on its legs; that really annoyed her although there's not much you can about legs.

She even polished the squat black dull-looking telephone that hardly ever fetched good news, hung up all her dead husband's tee shirts and thought of him lying out there all alone in Potter's Field, with no one to talk to. That would be lonely she thought and put her slippers up to enjoy an instant coffee.

Ernid was taking new medicine to offset his admitted rage attacks and that included anti-delusional medication with chronic side-effects including over-the-top-remorse so the swallowing patient could do practically nothing for a week except to weep, and that can be fairly exhausting in the long run. He also took new 'Anti-Thought' capsules that were big and tricky to get down but they did block out imaginings and improved his logic as well as geographical sense of direction.

He was giving a power point presentation at work in their central office with about two hundred managers and dignitaries assembled, and he made a promising start it must be said, even getting a few laughs when he cracked a joke about sugar addiction and the world contagion of diabetes two and all of its other variations. He graphically mimed a schoolboy guzzling 'Burp' and staggered about like a fool but it received rapturous applause and instant recognition.

'Gee he is funny, that guy is a hoot!' they chorused and pounded their palms together in resounding admiration. A publisher's representative offered him a contract to write his memoir and a hospital's representative offered him an appointment telling him he looked insane. He laughed but politely declined that one.

He did not speak of the mind pictures and Zapruder footage screening virtually non-stop in his head these days, not wanting to blot his copy at work, and even though he was separated and childless he wanted to get along with his life and try to learn such things as yoga and mediation and even mediation before too long. He had joined the table tennis side at work and had a good strong backhand, it was thought.

But even when his side at work competed against a rival lemonade company like Slades in Keon Park the voices troubled him, especially if they lost. That was when they really kicked in; he saw the whole home movie then and it was now much closer as if he was in the very front row at a cinema where it was showing.

'It is strange how it kicks in when we lose the men's doubles!' he said to himself in the car park outside Slades Lemonade Company where the others got into their cars to go home. He had to pay for his own jet flight back to central Sydney and rather regretted the cost of that.

He was in a spot of bother with his property manager, also called Anna who although she was a lady insisted upon being called a Landlord; and that was okay with Ernid as he was progressive in his attitudes towards his superiors. He saw Landlords as perfect beings.

But Anna was making things tough for him by having his particular hole filmed by a chopper if it looked un-looked-after in any way; then her p.a. at the real estate office sent the incriminating evidence on to the actually owner who was 'Burp' Pty Ltd; and if the film depicted a slovenly look to the hole in any way he could be evicted from it without further notice. He dreaded that.

Although his hole in the ground was precisely the same as thousands of others they seemed to target him for an eviction and pressured him by phone and personal letters sent from his own work. Holes were becoming more desirable and harder to obtain due to the ever-shrinking property market. His vision was to buy his hole outright and live in it into old age and traditional burial with an empty Burp bottle.

It was a quiet Monday morning and all around he could see happy schoolchildren heading off to something they loved which was education and books and swings and slides. He saw columns of them running down the so-sunny footpaths like contented ants all heading for teachers they loved and looked forward to being with. He decided to be a bit late for work and strolled across to the emerald-colored park and consider the birdies.

The agreeable mixture of singing birds and warbling bees and children's laughter made him feel immortal and part of something; like the force for good which he hadn't really felt at his strangely empty employment. No matter what new things they taught him he was incredibly unhappy and often wished they'd get on with it and do him in. He smiled at those birdies and marvelled at their spiritedness, the way they seized the seconds and then piped them away like little whistles and flutes.

Maybe stop work, maybe stop the terrible interior movies, maybe start being happy just like these creatures or forgetting the stresses of 'Burp' Pty Ltd?

He wanted a revolution and being perfectly joy-filled was the only way into it.

The birdies were teaching him a new job no doubt whatever.

What had he to lose but his mind and that was already gone and vanished on behalf of medical science? What he was he actually didn't know or care about any more and he was, as far as he understood a living example of rigor mortis. He was dead but a machine with a mindless quality of reaction and stimulus and all the smashed feelings of loneliness; but it was a mechanical despair like a machine fault that needed a service desperately no matter what the price.

He was invited to deliver speeches at medical centres pointing out the new power of parts for damaged persons, legs and memories, minds and toes, ear canals and ear lobes, frontal lobes and tuned-up senses of direction, without that there was a legitimate fear the recipient might stroll before a locomotive and be no more, say no more, remember the procedure no more; but then again be billed no more.

He liked to talk even with the irritating squeaks and squeals his teeth produced when delivering his sensations too close to the microphone; he had a high voice naturally but that was well before his accident at work, now the implants had produced in him a grating effect, a sub-human sound like a cyclone wire gate shutting hard in the wind, a repeat cyclonic hum was what he was.

He really liked to talk, as I have said, and made good robotic eye contact with his guests at these meetings and forums on the subject of parts present and parts future and the crowds that came to see and listen to him clapped his whirring witticisms and bone-dry ad-libs which came perfectly natural to him. He loved to joke!

One fellow had lost his entire body in a road mending machine which he fell into without meaning to, poor thing, and all that was left of him was one shoulder. The medical men and ladies constructed a portable platform for that section of him to perambulate upon; and he applauded Ernid heartily by striking the shoulder on a kettle-drum that happened to be there at the forum.

A lady had her legs replaced with bronze walking canes and let nothing stop her trapeze work and another lady spoke like a goldfish because of some aquatic misadventure.

There were prematurely ageing traffic control persons desperate to appear youthful again and there were babies with old people's heads on somehow who could now recall The Cold War.

He had an offer to write his memoir and the friendly publisher assured him it would sell; he popped the contract into his breast pocket and because he needed fresh air all of a sudden he disappeared out into the street for a much needed breather. He marvelled how his old lungs still exhaled only to inhale.

He hardly recognized that street he was standing in since all the known edifices had been demolished practically overnight with only the detritus of gates and entrances and wire fences where citizens had existed; all was rubble.

He strove to take it in even though he knew 'Burp' Pty Ltd intended the end of our planet, and that the sugar economy would result in fantastic suffering and fantastic surfing in waves of joylessness.

The only thing left of people's homes, their residences in fact was a mint-new free family sized bottle of Burp deposited on what was once their letter box. The brains at 'Burp' Pty Ltd saw the value of leaving large examples of complimentary sugar on people's letter boxes in the sure knowledge it would get them hooked; and fast.

He stared at the almighty power of their idea and he felt awed and

grateful towards those in charge at work, that all countries could be united in Diabetes 2. He picked up his large bottle on a section of blown-up front gate just hanging on as a reminder of normalcy that his own hole in the dirt symbolized. He drank the lot in a big gulp and brushed excess fluid from his mesh mouth with satisfaction and lust for more of it.

He in fact gutsed the entire bottle of its horrifying contents and then gazed at all the others on his street doing likewise. He watched them all register pleasant surprise at first seeing the free big bottle of it; then the quick drinking down of it and the sighs of pleasure mixed with poisoning and addiction to sugar boiled in toxic water that the whole world wanted to slake to the very last droplet indeed.

Vast rubbish compactors were now trundling along and their great hydraulic arms hoisted persons still caught in the act of slurping and these arms hurled many empties as well as their fevered imbibers straight into the compactor-part of the trucks so that thirsty addicts got mixed up with empties and the lot was violently compacted in a right old mess.

He lifted up his home dirt door and went down the ladder to take it easy but his teeth were killing him, really killing their possessor. He hurried to the medicine box he kept on the small tea table, scurried about for pain killers that he decanted, swallowed fifty of them and rinsed them back with a swig of Burp. But the pain remained and a new panic set in. How many panics were there?

In his head the lethal JFK screenings and then the wall of his sitting room screened it on a giant picture of the hit, then the images were to be found in his hair and on his own tongue and he could easily see more images of JFK on his hairy fingertips as well as on his pants. He had become the assassination and the assassin also, but who were his targets?

He had read lately of mass murders in cities similar to the Sydney he lived in where anonymous murderers took away lives of perfect strangers such as old folks and families but until now it was just them and not him. Now he was seized by mayhem so he threw down another twenty Panadol.

The awful physical agony grew merely worse and it positively shocked him to see just how many capsules he took, how many he obviously needed to buck up a bit; however there was no bucking up of any sort so he had to just lie there on the bed and feel stacks worse.

He moaned but the groaning became a dissolving of everything around him; that his books groaned also and his bed mattress went into despair and his socks wept and he found it tough to handle so he got in the shower and took it as hot as he could bear. The boiling hot water burned his red-raw-backside so he cooled it down and did his hair with an economy shampoo he was pleased he owned, as he owned hardly anything else.

He toweled his hair down and his body too, then he dressed and went to work in order not to be very late. To his surprise many workers punching their time cards were wearing mesh mouths just like he was and he found a sort of camaraderie.

But as he shouldered along with them to get to his meeting that morning with his planners he became somewhat frightened again.

# CHAPTER ELEVEN

## PROJECTIONS

At this time he commenced to view and be in a life which was a series of light-hearted as well as serious or dramatic slides or projections and nothing more than that; he couldn't make the distinction between reality and aberrations or mental pictures and the world as it actually is. It's spherical.

He continued to exist in his hole and enjoyed it as much as possible, of course; he tried to see the engaging side of life, the brighter side of the moon so to speak.

He kept on going to work where management had crushed his spirits a trifle by taking away his image from their powerful product, dropping him all entirely from all promotional engagements because he was seen as ugly.

Yet the swilling public liked him and loved his global image as his machine-body was the very object of their passionate identification with refreshment and bubbly personalities; it cost management a lot to remove his face from billions of bottles but he never went on can or bottle again and only the word 'Burp' stayed on their drop that kept drinkers infatuated and giddy with pleasure.

He was installed in Packing Section which wasn't much fun and involved twenty-four hour repetition and moronic sameness; he had to shove cans and bottles into cardboard boxes on a jiggling black vinyl conveyor-belt all the day and well into the night. After all that drama and fame he was nothing.

All the halls of nothings filled up all the endless cardboard boxes repeatedly and not so much eagerly as rapidly in order to keep their work;

that work paid the exorbitant rental on their one or two or three bedroom hole-properties as well as fed them and paid for car registration and all sorts of necessary insurance.

He didn't mind much that his year-long celebrity had been removed like a cheap tattoo but he remembered with great affection giving what he assumed were inspired and motivational talks to boost the popularity of his brand; he misremembered every single event over that past year, from the point in time where had been headhunted for fame, but without any security that perhaps should have gone with it.

He found as he sat at his morning coffee break in the finger of sun in the loading-bay that he had been immortal, on everybody's lips. He was a drink himself because everyone on the earth that drank 'Burp' swallowed him with it.

He remembered but not with bitterness or remorse how children dressed up as him, how they too wore visors and put on mesh wire teeth they bought at the milk bar or at the many registers of supermarkets.

How could he have been so instantly recognizable only to vanish next day; all the cans without his strange and sort of funny face on them; all the crates that bore his likeness and all the pallets swung onto vast ships to export 'Burp' around the globe that had him on them. He had been everywhere and now was nowhere.

He gazed at other hurt and damaged workers and saw many like him, just the same as him in The Packing Section or The Pulverizing Section or Accounts Payable or Marketing Section and they had defects like him but they seemed okay about them; they just got on with the job as they had families to feed and protect and love like anything, even more than anything.

Some lemonade toilers picked up the cardboard boxes of 'Burp' with strong rain-proofed machine arms that they seemed satisfied with; others of them scratched artificial calves or wind-up-legs that resembled clothes-hoists. He felt love for the battlers who had so many problems and whose lives were burdensome.

Some bosses sacked workers mechanically, at least it felt like that for loyal teams of lemonade toilers who had given their hearts and souls to 'Burp'. They were bussed in great droves to the big gate and dropped from the company register of names; they were acquainted with being given the sack and many of them came from families, whole generations of sacked workers.

The funny thing about his fame was that it was just the same as being not famous. He began to see the great similarities between product and the sack and profit becoming nothing; he was now on the team of nothing, not that he minded it much.

He experienced fame flashbacks in the busy mindless loading bay; and he saw again Her Majesty The Queen herself the day they had a can of 'Burp' together at Buckingham Palace; and he recalled she called it 'Not too bad!'

He missed the projection of Her Majesty badly so he wallpapered the bedroom with her. Her image wasn't difficult to come by at all and he managed to buy an enormous one with her tile teeth looking just great. He ended up dining with her, so to speak.

In the loading bay he sort of found himself in the drudgery and unimaginative conversation of his zombie workmates who just humped boxes and big crates onto the backs of trucks and operated powerful cranes to get the big stuff on them. The way that dumbness works fascinated him and he was keen to not just love dumbness but to contribute to its cause. He swore to himself he would never think again.

The days sailed and whistled by and he discovered contentment in the misery of work and the passivity of sameness. He played ping pong with workmates of a Tuesday evening against other factories in the area such as paint manufacturers and aggressive envelope makers; they were cheats actually and hard to beat but he loved his silent workmates and thought of them as brothers and sisters, even aunts and uncles.

'Burp' Pty Ltd began to flood the lemonade market with new variations of soft sugary fluid and with the sure knowledge that many city workers cannot possibly spare the time to open a soft drink can or flip a lid from a bottle. So they invented an aerosol lemonade which could be inhaled at any time when the need to get high kicked in, with serious 'Burp' addicts that can be just about all day.

So 'Aero Burp' came in and conquered the world market immediately and forever.

It was user friendly and cheap and you got higher on it than other physical versions. It was kept in the addict's pocket or worn behind the nose.

Addicts swore by it and if they were asthmatics they deployed a puffer like Ventolin simultaneously with 'Aero Burp' to stunning effect. Soon the whole world was pausing outside a milk bar, anywhere, even Antarctica and having a puff or two and enjoying the after-belch more than they had done with the fluid version.

During films being screened patrons had a quiet puff that no one could possibly object to; it was a surreptitious puff and no louder than the dreamiest sigh in a cinema.

The next novelty was lemonade in eye-drop-form that tired motorists enjoyed because they could feel drugged immediately in heavy traffic; some of them squirted a few droplets into their sore red eyes at red lights when their automobile pulled up.

All the new lines of 'Burp' were parceled and addressed and flown to every city on the planet to ensure the profit poured in; and it did indeed pour in with shareholders delighted at their investment returns.

His outlook upon life changed right before his very eyes: he was more contented than he'd ever known before; he looked and smelled great and his appetite came back like a miracle; he no longer used his Ma's recipe to bake, boil, fry Gag that he was so sick and fatigued by. He decided to forgive his employers for taking him on a roller-coaster ride of ups and certainly downs that in a sense led him to despair, beyond it even. Was he at death's door?

The recollection of immortality or greatness faded like an aspirin snagged in his throat; he often took them to make certain his blood-pressure didn't get 'a bit up' as his General Practitioner warned him it would if he gave into stress in all its snickering forms.

He wrote to his Ma even though she only lived next door, using a large very thin almost transparent sheet of onion paper and employing a blunt black lead pencil to seek information as to how she was getting on.

It was a quiet Wednesday after his shift in the loading bay was over, about ten at night it was when he absent-mindedly dropped the note in the bright red post bin right next to her place. She had done up her hole in the ground to a certain degree and had bent down low to plant a bush and install a nice cement bird bath with a painted whistle-note on it like something from a cartoon of birdies.

Inside her hole she was in the rather foreshortened bath that looked more like another mental projection than a real bath, however she was too impoverished to employ soap so she scrubbed herself as radiantly as possible with spit; just like in the village in the snowy woods where people were so hungry they ate words.

She immediately began to feel much better now that the ingrained filth was coming off her vile hard old wrinkled and disgusting body; she hated being enfeebled and lame and with all the annoying gangrene but as she often said 'You just have to hack life!'

She took an age and a day to slow-motion-dry herself down and she realized how arthritic she was becoming; her arthritis was in her rheumatism it was that bad.

She took her own good time dressing and re-put the identical dirty rags back on and even she was offended by their dizzying smell that could easily kill you.

She wrote to the Old Country but forgot what village it was in as well as the exact name of the country, but she accepted that she was as silly as a wheel; and there was not a single thing she could darned-well do about her insanity. 'You just have to hack life!' she vehemently sighed, annoying herself in a marked manner.

She put on her pom-pom fluffy slippers and went into the grotesque kitchen and set it on fire. She hated the kitchen anyway and danced like a bear in the flames, and so on.

She then, after the naughty fire went away, went out, disappeared as they do from time to time, got out the steam-iron and made pancakes all round; even though she happened to be the only one there.

She made the pancakes so flat and thin you could easily see the ironing board straight through them all; they were more like crepes than your traditional pancakes, actually, when you got right down to it. She ate one and threw the rest into the street, which was how her insane old mother used to do them before she shot herself.

Ma relaxed and put her feet up and remembered happier days, even nights, even afternoons or public holidays when she was part of a happy family, her tribe, as she put it, when they all chopped down large pine trees and denuded the landscape. When she conversed with her pet pig that a neighbour stole and tried to sell at the market, but there were no takers as it looked not right to anyone who knew pigs.

She didn't have the foggiest clue where she was, like all Australians.

She wished her son would knock upon the door of her hole. He had a key to it that she had cut by a key man she didn't trust or like that much.

She was really liking having a good sit, that was free in The Old Country, as sitting in the village was a sign of affection for the body, trust, you name it; and she was a person who had always sat. She could relax that way as opposed to standing, for example, and she thought there was too much standing in the world which was why the Earth was wearing right out and becoming thin on its crusts.

She thought for a minute there she must have gone to bed sucking a tough toffee, which what she usually did whenever she went to bed, because she could easily sense a thing that was hard protruding through her gums.

It was only eight at night so she wasn't really that ready for bed, and she could feel this awful thing in her mouth like a tooth rising up or a fang possibly, as though she were a bear.

But bear she was not and a mother she was and one who loved her mechanical son who had been the figurehead at 'Burp' for one thing, known around the world, famous as 'Burp' was famous, even notorious.

She tried to feel exactly what the hindrance was but it just felt odd, that was all so she giggled at the concept of a new tooth arriving at her old age, but she was frightened and understandably of anything new.

She went and peered into the bathroom mirror, if any object might reveal the truth it was that friendly thing that usually depicted the visual truth of any object; she gasped aloud as she beheld a wire set of teeth when she flexed her shocked mouth. There were bolts screwed into her new jaw and a sun shield was coming out of her worried forehead which was like a mixture of a lady's tennis shade and a windscreen-thing.

She felt obviously to emit a piercing scream but none arrived; she just had to hack it for she was turning into a monster like her son, and what he wanted to know at once had he done to warrant an atrocious head on him like a bird cage.

She lightly patted her brand-new-mechanical mouth and snapped its jaws together to create an unpleasant snapping effect that was not pleasant for her to hear. She wished hard it wasn't there but it certainly was, for all the world to view and gawk at in the ancient manner of gossiping peoples.

She went to the cluttered kitchen sink and finished washing and drying her dishes. She lived all alone so there weren't that many of them, but she couldn't locate the sponge with which to wipe greasy food off one plate that had still remnants of irremovable Gag in it, even the pastry surrounding the main dish was glued hard to the surface.

She employed her new mesh mouth to do the dishes and cutlery with, tipping plenty of bright green detergent into her grille and locking its two halves in the manner of a wash-up-device and lo and behold her sink was ablaze with delicious and dancing bubbles. She got to and washed the lot.

The new jaw and machine molars didn't hurt in any way and as she was old in her body she didn't feel like pondering just why the change had happened; she just accepted it and wanted, as they say in the world or in the street, 'to move on'.

She managed to get herself off to sleep without a fuss and made a mental note to have a word with her neighbours about what befell her, but she didn't have rapport much with any of them really, and they just lived in a labyrinthine way in their particular hole in the ground and watched the television set with their slippers up.

As she drifted off to pleasant and fulfilling repose, a thing she loved since it cost nothing, and as well as that you didn't need to keep receipts for it was on the house pretty much. Her last images that screened in her cinematic mind were of the free family sized bottles that 'Burp' had deposited upon everyone's letter box in a huge operation to ensure they remained needful of opiates like soft drink.

She felt hardly any pain in her face apart from the sense of metal bulldog clips coming through her forehead, which hurt a bit but she was a hardened veteran of sufferings and wrote it off as an aberration and some new initiative of industry; she believed in industry if nothing else.

The black metal bulldog clips, or clamps is more accurate, came straight through her forehead lending her the look of a notice board but she got herself completely comfortable and ended up sleeping on her left, her favorite side even though she only had two to her entire being. She unashamedly snored loudly.

In the midst of her dreamless evening she had to get up in order to urinate, and so she silently cursed her own bladder, as they all did in The Old Country, and had to go to the small toilet and relieve herself of too many cups of tea.

To her shock the new forehead bulldog clamps came right off as she reached for the toilet roll and they struck the toilet water with considerable force and noise; she could feel that they had come loose so she had to get down on the cold floor and find them right down the bottom of the cistern. She swore in the old language.

She managed to dry the clamps thoroughly and get them back in but they didn't feel or look as good to her as she studied her latest reflection in the bathroom mirror.

Her teeth were too prominent, she thought, being mesh and steel with a large air vent in her throat that doubled as a speaker-phone with a dial tone for local calls so she could ring with hands free.

She had the most passionate desire to consume 'Burp' immediately if not sooner., so she sat next to the gas heater and got herself right and drank a family bottle in one swig and felt the good of that. She laughed uproariously to herself when she looked at the empty bottle and remembered how much of it she had made for them, the bosses.

She had applied for a new position as a Dyer.

She went back to her simple but comfy warm bed and dreamt she was involved in an exam at work to see if she was acceptable in the dyeing section. She dreamt in bright yellow and saw it as a sign or an omen that she would soon be involved in new flavours such as pawpaw and tropical pineapple.

She got her jaw right in the fold of her pillow and there was no more fuss with the forehead bulldog clasps that stayed in properly for a change as she continued to dream or hallucinate that she was back at work; she even pulled the edge of the squat hard pillow as if it were a time card clock and she was happily clocking on for her exciting shift in Dyeing Section.

Her phone rang shrilly in the early morning and even though the bulldog clips seemed in properly and so on, she gave them an extra push to make sure they wouldn't come off and answered the call, using her new machine mouth to try to form words that could be perceived as right ones on the other end. It was her boss, someone she didn't know at all.

It was a demand to come in immediately on her new shift in Dyeing Section and she was reminded that she would be docked a quarter of an hour's pay for each three seconds of lateness. She was never late, even her own birth was a second early.

As she dressed she gave her visor and metal grille a good polish and awaited the plant bus with the other toilers who looked the same as she did, all of them having mechanical mouths and sunshields and bulldog clips adhered to their foreheads; only the bus driver was normal but no one liked him.

It caused her some concern that a hundred toilers looked the same and had become perfect and acceptable robots without characters or imaginations, although she thought it best she didn't imagine anything except her evening meal which she devoured like a cannibal; she felt like a cannibal in several respects not the least of which she looked like one, she thought as she gazed at her crazy face in the window reflection.

The passengers on that bus chatted eagerly to one another as they compared forehead bulldog clips, new ceramic teeth and chest speaker phones that were hands-free. They clutched their sweaty time cards in anticipation of clocking on and listened carefully to what the un-robot driver was saying about departure times even though they hadn't arrived yet to toil there.

To her absolute indignation one of the female toilers pashed on unashamedly with one of the male toilers and they kissed hard on their wire cages and embraced the new order of things, robotically complimenting one another for good looks and mechanical wit. People were so excited that the plant was ready to receive them that one or two fainted in a dead swoon.

For once Management were pleased to see them, and the old and new toilers were surprised to be greeted and made a fuss of, they sure were, and so all the workers sprinted away to their different work-stations and in fact no one was a single second late. Management were overjoyed.

Ma ran herself stupid getting to her morning briefing which took place in The Convention Centre which was an enormous vinyl carpeted hall that could comfortably seat a multitude. She noticed just how many fellow toilers had their bulldog clips on nice and tight and that their pay slips dangled from them ever so tightly. Management had a female stand-up on and she was trying a bit too hard to be satiric.

'Don't you just hate it when you are sacked these days of mindless repetition and no job vacancies just about anywhere? Isn't that too much!' the comedienne laughed and perspired and did not go over.

There was a brief question time to do with redundancy packages but no one learnt a thing; so they put the comic on again.

Ma trotted off to Dyeing Section as forewarned and politely took her position alongside many veterans of exotic soft drink hues. She marvelled that they looked like pineapples as they scooped up the tons of dye by shovel and in a no-mucking-around-way they hurled the stuff into bubbling carbon monoxide vats that had the poison removed.

These veterans were extremely muscular and so fit that sometimes they hurled the blinding dye over the rims of the 500 foot vats and missed altogether in their desire to do it right. They sung dwarfish chants the whole time to get motivated and the big pineapple fizzy one came up a treat with all the yeasty action and bubbles and what-have-you.

Ma at the age of sixty-six was to stand bravely on the end of a plank way up high and personally do the shovel into the big pineapple one. She wasn't scared and used to doing dangerous stuff so she didn't spill a drop of the gaudy dye on her trembling shovel.

The fact that she was on tip-toes didn't dissuade her one jot and she chose not to think of tumbling into the volcanic lemonade as so many others had done, mostly gents.

She not only was gifted at tipping in the powerful dye that created pineapple flavoured lemonade but began to swat up on food dye technology at home after her toil ended with a colossal hoot of the factory siren sounded so alarmingly.

She went along to her local library and renewed her lapsed membership which was the only thing free with The Liberal Party Leadership initiatives. She was almost over-stimulated just staring at the oceans of food dye stories, facts and myths on coconut flavour.

She was permitted four books to borrow so she took home with the librarian's blessing editions of the complete remembered history of bun dye for one book, it in itself running to 1,000 pages and of course most lavishly illustrated by ancient monks who used quills to decorate illuminated manuscripts on buns brought back from The Holy Lands.

In her practically sober kitchen, in an unlit way to make reading harder and so on, she craned her weathered old neck over immortal bun descriptions and recollections given by bun addicts since Time started; way before Jesus Christ.

She studied orange food dye being made in time of Cleopatra and how she herself, the Queen Of Egypt liked to sip it on a great barge being drawn by midgets who had a crush on her but were far too meek to do much about it. She it was who invented Fanta.

She had a great mixing bowl on the kitchen table with a ladle of finest plastic so she set to work with respect to the bibliography of dyeing and read feverishly about the provenance of purple because at work she had heard Management were keen to beat Slades and Pepsi with the push for cobalt purple and call it 'Zorro' Burp after the iconic masked Spanish rapier-wielder.

She tipped a little of this into a lot of that and observed the hypnotic hue come to spinning life. It took an hour altogether in her improvised laboratory but she figured it was well worth it; what doubt could there be when she saw how bright it was.

She ended up making a batch of half a dozen bottles of ultra sparkling deep but surprisingly light purple soft drink to which she pasted a label with 'Completed Zorro Mixture' and put it to one side in order to concoct coconut lemonade.

She beat several fairly fresh coconuts into a fibrous paste and added sea water and vanilla essence and a pinch of sugar and a modicum of crushed marijuana that she'd bought at the local milk bar, poured the lot into a big bottle and then tasted it with a rush that the heady stuff gave her as soon as it sailed down her new throat.

She labelled it 'Coconut' and put extra sticky tape around the pasted bit of paper.

She came up with 'Scarlet Lake' for her final fresh flavour and used various tints of red roses that came in a fine powdery form; she added solidified memory loss that came from the local chemist shop, and also some radiator stop-leak. It was a lethal but winning combination to be sure.

She placed all the new invented flavours in her zip-up work bag and left it by the door for first thing next morning. Super-confident her managers would be pleased with her magical efforts she went to bed and experienced dreamless repose, her favorite brand of unconsciousness. On the other side of the city her son Ernid had succeeded in getting himself lost.

He was a long distance from the plant in fact and in an overexcited and practically exhausted state he had wandered into a gigantic warehouse and asked for The Pulverizing Section only to be told they sold washing machines direct to the unwashed public. He then fainted.

The police were summoned and pretty soon all the warehouse mashing machine staff heard loud sirens that put them off their work of carrying them about, in many cases on their backs from pillar to post in the way of most warehouses. Ernid was cross-examined as to why he turned up there.

'Where do you think you are?' the cops asked him.

'Isn't this Pulverizing Section?' he gurgled with saliva rolling from his grille and all down his front.

'This is a washing machine complex and you have no right to be in it!' yelled the policeman and he withdrew his collapsible baton and commenced to brain him.

They kindly shoved him in the back of the van and delivered him back to 'Burp' where he was docked a quarter of an hour's pay the moment he fell in through the doorway. He apologized for being a tad late and requested an hour off in the sick bay due to feeling just rotten but this act of grace was denied him.

He showed the shop steward his new police bruises all over his back and arms but there was no interest in any of it as he was escorted briskly to The Loading Bay and cautioned against shirking. 'I don't shirk in fact!' he bellowed and was fined ten dollars for the loudness of it. He was beginning to wish he didn't work there.

As he humped crates and vast cartons from the mouth of the production line along a yellow line to the other mouth of a semi-trailer he hallucinated he was a hobo somewhere gallant such as Mexico. He saw a sombrero on his head and everything novel that could possibly occur to him post trauma-accident, post new mouth.

In his bumbling way he was happy with The Loading Bay life of meaninglessly shoving big crates up onto endless black conveyor belts and watching stock disappear into trucks larger than ocean liners, but there was certainly something missing.

At Afternoon Tea he might ask the work-mates what futures they envisaged as they sucked on their sugar hit and smoked a Cuban cigar.

But there was fearful news delivered on the overhead television set in the depot shed where his team had their break: the new Australian Government had decided in their cups to sack every single worker as from first thing tomorrow morning and begin to hire Mexicans. Eight million lemonade workers were sacked on the spot.

The very depot shed was auctioned with the shocked workers still in it finishing their cups of tea or free soft drink. There was pandemonium all through the plant and a lot of that came from bosses who were sort of in the firing-line themselves as it had now become the very thing to fire managers with staggering salaries and basically downsize every single staffer.

Ernid however was spared and glad of it and when he took a breather outside the plant on a rare and extravagant piece of lawn he made himself sit still and watched all of his workmates go out the big gate as the perfect testament to preserving industry.

He knew a lot of them and a tear arrived upon his nostrils as he heartily waved farewell to the ones he personally knew, but he cried hard for them all and loved the ones he did not know.

When would the Mexicans arrive, he wondered, and scratched his sock that was annoying him slightly, half expecting to see a wheel under his cuff but there was just his work-shoe which came as a distinctive relief to see something so normal for a change.

The media were there at the gates that disgorged all the workers and television cameras were trained on the relentless exiting and studying the faces of the fired. Tape recorders captured the shuffling of fired feet, the clouds of despair and dust and sorrowing and frightened factory worker's faces all showing the great strain, the burden of rollicking homelessness and overpowering sense of human waste.

He didn't get the envelope of goodbye but he felt very acutely the sting of the boot, as he waved fruitlessly to the enormous vans and buses that whisked so many honest hard-working toilers away towards unemployment.

There was not a solitary thing he could possibly do but to love them and hope for them and to pray for new jobs for them, but he knew in his heart of hearts no jobs were available for all or most of them and that they would be probably evicted soon for being in arrears with rental.

The buses of sacked just went on forever and ever, never-ending. but all he could see was dust and departure and sadness and hopelessness en masse.

He saw himself in all of them, men and women who loved the firm and expected loyalty which 'Burp' Pty Ltd didn't have to display to them.

They each got four weeks of pay for every year they had toiled there for boss's profits.

'Burp' Pty Ltd was leading the universe in unexpected sackings and rapid fire bused departures, while other major companies, not just lemonade ones, simply followed their example of gigantic unfair dismissals.

In the distance there were vicious pit bull dogs put onto recalcitrant toilers, with much moaning and excited yelping. Ernid hid his eyes and ears from it, he really did.

# Chapter Twelve

## The Meeting of Restraint

It was offered to him at work now that it was all Mexican that he could earn himself a few bucks a week by consulting services just as retired Mexican Ministers did when they were either fired or just wanted to get rich quick. He still did his daily and nightly vat work and thoroughly mopped up the dirty broken glass as per normal, and that was a task he loved due to peasant parentage; but he moved into consultancy as well to glean a coin and stow away savings for his and his mother's futures.

He firstly was expected to show up at The General Annual Meeting Of Restraint and show also suitable respect for his Mexican Superiors, not that every man Jack of them were from that part of the world but these days most were, and he thought of himself as Mexican to show more respect to his superiors.

He had never really enjoyed formal meetings and felt all kept in, so to say, when he was to speak or mildly put up his hand to register that he had life in him. The experience he'd had of get-togethers was pretty miserable actually now he thought of them and hurried off to another of them, albeit larger and even more formal and important. Why were meetings considered important? He was keen though.

He was in his best three piece suit and the pretty rose-colored tie he chose from an array of dress ties he kept hanging over the foot-rail of his single bed; he tried not to move in bed to save energy as he'd watched programs about conserving energy at all costs to save our planet. He was pleased that he had ironed both his socks and hard-to-get-at shoe laces because doing something like that always impresses management, as he knew that it would; and it did, too, just as he thought it might.

Five thousand crucial managers in first rate imported sombreros sat rigidly on a stage so stand alone and dedicated to the feeling of a colossus and being not just put in your place but being made to feel as you came in that you were without meaning, and you weren't.

The stiffness of the grim sombreros and their purpose made all there silent and apprehensive about outcomes; the atmospherics were of unforced paranoia and paranormal betterness of Mexicans no matter what.

All the lower orders including dyers and palette lifters and fork lift truck drivers and elevator drivers; assemblers and bottle-top-hitters-on and label-paste-nobodies and sales reps and canteen ladies and cleaners and fifth year apprentices and sub-managers who longed and prayed to be real managers, they sat motionless and stared hard with gritty sore eyes due to dust at the Most Important Ones on stage.

World War Three had started, that was the silent feeling of fear that the importance imposed upon the thousands of rows of lesser beings who were there to hear of the latest crisis and the Mexican plan to save the beloved plant; although to many workers their loyalty to it felt constrained and artificial at times.

Shareholders were at the rear of the great hall of importance and were allowed to vote on motions but it didn't become a General Annual Meeting in the traditional sense as it was just something you went to of your own free will or got sacked on the spot.

The CEO of 'Burp' Pty Ltd herself got up in drop dead personal panache and tapped the microphone at the tip of the illuminated stage and hawked up. The people there daren't move nor attempt to understand or dream of fidgeting.

'We are here today ladies and gents to learn of some exciting breakthroughs in global marketing that may be just as thrilling for you as they happen to be for us at the top.

'We have all made the adjustment to Mexicans and have welcomed 100,000 of them into our workplace!'

Unreal approval.

'We know the market well enough to see that Mexicans ever so work much harder than people born in Sydney and even though lots of us are Australian by birth we feel privileged to be the inferiors of Mexicans and can only hope and pray that that is okay by them. Have you noticed how on-time they are of a morning, everyone?'

Enthusiastic sombrero throwing.

'A lot of us born in Australia or possibly Prague have had it more than easy for far too long and as the global market swings towards ever increasing demand for consumers we need to take their lead and obey their style and copy their morning punctuality and that way 'Burp' Pty Ltd will not only cream 'Pepsi' but still be pumping out mega-profits a hundred yards hence!'

More clapping and screaming and looks of hysteria.

'I need you now to show leadership and good humour by shaking hands personally with the Mexican next to you!'

They all did.

'I need you now to rise even in your wheelchairs and give them a hearty hug! No meaningless hugs now! Remember 'Burp' Pty Ltd has its great and noble eye right on you! Welcome Mexicans To 'Burp' Pty Ltd!'

It was duly chorused and duly noted and recorded in the big book of Restraint.

Various second order bosses also thanked the Mexicans for crossing all borders to make it to Sydney and throw their hats in the pool, in many cases literally speaking.

The overheated CEO then made a strange speech demanding restraint being expected and performed from now on until the end of time. They sat rigid and cowed completely.

'We must show a degree of tolerance towards not merely Mexicans who toil for us but may indeed make their move to take over our company in the long run. It is the truth socially and scientifically and morally and religiously that sugar infused bubbly soft drink can cause mental disturbances linked to depression, anxiety, obesity, flatulence, suicide, despair and unreal cravings for a four bedroom residence. We are onto it and upon our promise you may all rest assured!'

The on stage cheering didn't really take place as every single Mexican did nothing but fold their arms and stare without interest out at the jubilant crowd. Drinks on the house came next with Ma's Timber Lemonade voted Number One.

Her ham off the bone Fizzy came equal second and people milled around casually with a cold decent drink in their hand or front claw.

Ernid hadn't had much to drink but on his way home he experienced unusual hallucinations to do with burial and witchcraft so that he gulped about and tried to work through; these sensations culminated with a fiery passion to murder people, any people, and thus he walked into the city to do people in as swiftly as he could.

He stalked having never done bad things like that, then found an old car salesman sitting on his bottom in a park munching his own bun. He would do, obviously, so he went across and had it in his mind to strangle him with no motive.

But the little friendly fellow just kept on munching into his nice bun and was really enjoying the coconut icing on the crest of it. He just looked like a little schoolboy to his potential assassin so Ernid gave up at once and apologized for coming at him like that; and the little chap gulped a bit but said he didn't mind.

His leather-like forehead seemed to possess its own ideas while his damaged frontal lobes were sending his ruined brain deranged messages to kill.

He really gulped overpoweringly and exceedingly felt the remorse any robot should feel just after attempted murder; possibly he had been programmed to murder people or possibly pine trees or mulberry trees or puppies or pussy cats. He had no idea how these feelings arrived in his banging-away-heart to a point of loudness actually that he was surprised people didn't hear those banging beats of his.

He strode purposefully away and crouched at an all night crouching coffee shop where management decreed that the only way a coffee customer should be served was if they wholeheartedly agreed to go into the full crouching position based on frogs about to leap by a pond in some way. People loved crouching coffee!

He joined at once the long line of potential crouching coffee wanting people and he pre-crouched in line in eager anticipation of soon sipping in a crouched manner.

In the end he ordered his latte and it was served by a crouched coffee person who appeared to have a strong seizure as he threw the coffee at him directly.

Ernid paid crouched and went away crouched and sat on a crouched rock and sipped in the most acutely bent over way you'd expect to witness in a month of crouched Sundays. He loved it and each sip relieved the strong stress in him.

'I obviously have to conquer these fractious feelings in my heart to kill my fellow man!' he uttered to the listening moon who never looks away from poor old us.

'Why do these feelings come to me to murder anyone I look at?' he pondered and wondered, almost out loud which is what I guess pondering is really made for in the end.

He actually wished he'd ordered two lattes as the caffeine hit was removing each signal of hurt in his soul. He eagerly licked the last vestiges of cream and coffee liquor out of the base of the glass and fought off a naughty burp. He beat the feeling down to kill someone and went and sat in a church that had been recently renovated and demolished at the same time. It was a nice new ruin and he felt safe in it for once.

He clasped his sweaty palms in fervent prayer and knelt on the rock-solid foundations of that church building, shaking from terror at what his damaged brain had been requiring his body to do, and trembling something exquisitely like a brand-new rose on its grateful stem on the second of October, his favorite date.

'Dear Loving God, lately my brain has ordered me to carry out assassinations on bakers and others who exist in our fragmented but noble land; I have myself no intention to do these hits but a force within my mind is really pushing for it. You have no idea how terrible it is to be so instructed and so innocent at the same time. Could you please just for a second grant me some tranquility?"

He actually felt like signing his name to it but then remembered it was said and not penned.

He knelt in his honest and shaking new way in the dilapidated pews, experimenting with one pew over another until a bit of peace came. He wanted the murderer to be banished right away. He couldn't cease his big gulping and even the gulping in his wired throat made him feel bad.

No one was in the church but he and all he could vaguely see with his tired eyes mostly shut were ends of beams and smoke and incense pots all upside down, pews upside down and Christ the right way up. He stared at the plaster figurine of Jesus and wept as though to bust as he looked at the bust.

The sacred words 'You mustn't hurt a living organism!' emitted from the plaster mouth of Christ and Ernid wept harder to hear it in full and not the abbreviated text message.

'I don't want to hurt anything my Lord", he caterwauled and bit his own right shoulder in self-disgust. 'But I feel doomed to follow my commands!'

'Don't be a fool!' advised Christ and then its mouth clamped shut hard.

After utterly and completely drenching his shirt and vest with his overflowing and acidic tears of such hurt and anguish he began to run his long slim fingertips along all the names of people engraved into the icy cold dark brown solidified pews; these cut-in-wood names were clues to souls who had fallen there like front line soldiers and nurses who'd given their bodies to their country.

He could sense just who they'd been and find their hair and eyes and cheeks – their personalities carved into sepia tinted ossified but incredibly alive wood. He stroked all the signatures with clammy extended fingers and his briny tears made the pews even saltier by a thousand degrees. 'Who are we all?' he inquired of the old names in the putrescent pews. 'Where are we off to?'

At least he had rejected the impulse to murder and was glad of that tiny victory as he strode without life back to his hole and hopefully put his jaw up for a while, he was absolutely conquered by life's unprecedented ironies and badly needed a bath that was so hot he could read in it for maybe a whole night, adjusting the cold and hot faucet as he felt like. He was tired of discomfort and the misery of stress, he really was, in fact he'd had it lately.

For the very first time since he was christened he enjoyed the church and everything about it; architecturally it was the same as the time of the monks and metaphysically it felt identical in his receptors no matter how badly damaged they happened to be. He was pleased no one was there. Not even Christ.

He had the place to himself so to speak so he kept on clutching his red moist palms like the terrible grip of a vice and really got himself into a right old state. He wept so hard the burning tears felt drop-forged and each of them scorched a memory of how he was before sense disappeared out of his funny old world that wasn't fun anymore because the stakes were too high, they sure were.

He got himself way down in a baby-getting-born position and prayed to his scrunched-up-sore-eyed version of a kind virgin who would fix his body. Who would save his old friendly head and screw it back on properly so he could be himself once more; he was so sick of the shock of the new interior and exterior flywheels and black tin bulldog clips embedded in his forehead.

'Oh please Mother Mary forgive me a sinner who is ugly and a machine now and possibly forever, I hope not because I need my so-friendly face back and have suffered too much with the medical one, the scientific one, you know what I mean? And my mother wants her face back so we can go up the milk bar together. You can do it dearest Mother Mary and then no one will point and chuckle at me. Already the public think I'm unkind and I'm not; not in a month of Sundays!'

# CHAPTER THIRTEEN

## PUREST FORGIVENESS

Where he lay after he had slid off the Antarctic pew which developed stalactites in it from the extremely low temperature, even for a church that is, the colder than it seemed possible gritty tiles stuck in his concave chest thus making contact with his personal God ever more possible. Though he was feeling not that crash-hot he had the closeness and peace which had been denied him ever since his jaw procedure, and so on.

He figured the church must have forgotten to switch on any heating since he just couldn't get himself hotter in any way. He stared up at what he thought was a non-functioning wall-heater but it was really a plywood warped collection box 'For The Holy Ghost'. He realized it was a donation box but wondered how the coins could be physically presented to God.

He lurched ever downward like a consumptive seal far out at sea and forlornly bellowed at the unfairness of his fate. Then as the ever-flowing-tears ended in a honk effect deep within his new throat he beheld a very kind face coming his way holding a lamp that smelled of kerosene and bearing a staff; the other thing he felt was the exhaustion of seeing things.

The wandering spirit was a man of the church, no doubt about that fact, for he wore humility like a badge of high office, in fact he sniveled and hesitated because he probably had The Flu and his long swishy brown robes looked very impressive. His pleasant face betokened an earthly angel on the old age pension, somewhat, and he reached down and with a massive forearm pulled Ernid to his feet.

'You will be alright my son', the friendly hallucination said as they both perched on an engraved pew down near the front, fairly close to the altar, and the feeling he gave was one of trust mixed with brotherhood you'd have to say.

'You need a holiday!' he laughed and as confused and exhausted as he was Ernid laughed with him; he was the most delightful chap!

'You have been saying and thinking fearful thoughts about the medical team that saved your life, you have forgotten to write and thank them properly for what they have done so professionally for you; all you have achieved is chronic self-pity and a bad attitude towards surgeons who think only about saving lives. If I weren't an apparition then I would kick your bottom'.

Ernid couldn't read him that was the trouble for the monk-looking-gentleman looked terribly nice to him but there was to him a weird violence as well; he didn't want to look ungrateful or anything like that but he just didn't trust his motives. The monk-looking-gentleman smiled at him at the foot of their shared hard old wooden brown pew.

'I know I must jettison my hate, that is what of course frightens me!' wept poor Ernid as the church person hugged him to his vestments and tried to stroke his sufferer's hair but his rheumatism was just horrid at the moment, and it pained him so much he could scarcely bear it. But then saints have to bear pain constantly because they love it and are good at it.

The caressed hair put Ernid in mind of his father's loving touch upon his head when he was little and they lived in the village so peacefully, if poorly, in fact they were so poor they used a harvester to sow thought.

'Your mad hallucinations are no worse than many others', smiled the chap as he straightened himself up a bit to save on curvature of the spine, which is terribly expensive in this day and age. He put his strong and protective arm around his young confused friend who seemed like a companion in many ways.

'Your problem is that you believe you have had a rotten time every single second of your day and probably way into the night. The more you

employ some decent toothpaste on your false jaw and give your plastic see-through-visor a darned good go over with a mixture of wash-up-detergent and then a staunch hard wipe with tissues the better you're going to feel, okay my lad?'

Ernid wasn't so sure where any of this was going but he automatically liked and trusted him so he agreed to rinse his teeth more thoroughly from now on; and to buy a better make of tissues and generally look after himself better. The monk looked pleased with him and offered him a nice-looking toffee.

'I like that kind of toffee but they are just impossible to eat!' confessed Ernid and the monk understood that but he said to him 'Try to understand toffee!' And then Ernid really didn't understand where this situation was heading.

'You've just got to stop seeing yourself as a perpetual victim that's all!' The monk or stand-in for one bellowed at him with a fist raised in hate, and that looked incongruous for a man of the cloth. 'You are just so annoying in your pathetic self-interest and delusional faith in despair!' The man was going all red in the face with his puffed cheeks resembling a glass blower as he beat up the pew.

'A blade of humble grass has more love than you, dear boy!' he groaned and then collapsed. Ernid had never before seen so melodramatic a monk. It was now his turn to comfort someone so he scooped the man up, surprised at his own strength actually, and helped to prop him back properly on the seat where he had his tongue sticking out.

'I must examine the grass again', whispered Ernid and made a mental note to give grass more time in the future, and all of nature in fact more of his time, particularly willow trees which he had always doted on.

'There is no doubt that global warming is destroying the Catholic Church', whimpered the man and he pressed the wrists of Ernid hard to add to his point.

'I can't exactly see that, I'm sorry', said Ernid and pulled his sore wrist away from his new comforter with an extracted effort. He was starting to hurt him but he knew it was only in his best interests. He just didn't want him to touch him but that was a groundless fear.

'I think I know you and that you have been on a rampage because of what the surgeons did to you after your shocking mishap', cried the man in a loud voice so that it echoed lots in the musty fusty church where at least they could hear one another properly, not like outside where there was nothing except exploding soft drink trucks, or at least they sounded as though they were detonating in a serious way.

'You're not the only one, that is to be cherished, to be daily remembered, and you must see your operation as a miracle, for that is what they did for you and you could so easily have perished on their operating table. But they lifted you back to life, didn't they my son, so you could clock on again! Isn't that right?'

He nodded that it was right and he hugged the monk-like-man with all his power.

Possibly this monk would give him a turnaround and his future would as it should be offered to him; a life lived to the full but without angst.

He was so sick and tired of feeling stressed and waking up irritably, he confessed this fact to the monk but something like sorrow snagged deep in his throat, and even though it was completely artificial the grief was tantamount to death; and the more truthfully he spoke with all of his natural heart to this hooded oddity in the church the more he felt vindicated.

His virtual lung-passages were opening up and his nostril flared like a lover as the man chatted so sweetly about the forgiving nature of nature strip grass; the spiritual need for bees to be worshipped at every chance and for all the aspects of the natural world to be not just embraced but recollected after meeting up with them all.

In short for the first time since his accident he felt great.

'The agony shall of course depart from your worn down body as you go forth and worship clouds and skies of every sort and feel the sea again and the various breezes once more; in short the beauty of the natural world shall cheer you up a fair bit!'

He had the perfect mental image of grass and saw it and sniffed it and even grabbed it from the cracks in the heartless timber floorboards.

'You must not ever think of meanness again since the new culture is meanness; always remember dear boy that all you shall be ever remembered for is your kindness. People forget the rest such as money and position and who is up whom. Be always unvaryingly kind and assist poor folks all you possibly can and the peace you so desperately seek shall be afforded you. The angels are on your side!'

He embraced another fellow human being and although he hadn't ever done a thing like that before it sure felt right as well as good; his own father was gone to heaven and he didn't know the password to gain access to it; yet here was a stand-in who cared about him even though he was a monk.

He more or less fell into the street and tripped over a couple of starving hungry families out in the dust who were scrounging as best they could for sustenance of many kinds and not exactly stooping to public begging but not that far off it.

He felt a new human being and the more he looked into the saddened and sore eyes of the dispossessed the more he felt grateful for the simple hole he lived in, even though the rent was being quadrupled next month, no reason given by the landlords.

He at one strange stage tried to drift and dwindle and emerge through these sad groups of homeless people and then a dreadful thing happened. The more he reached into his pocket and his heart to help them financially and emotionally the more they physically overwhelmed him and crawled right over him in their sobbing way; he felt like an insect being devoured by put-out-wasps until there was stuff-all left of him!

The demented demeaning moaning of the poor creatures devoured his mind via his overwhelmed ear holes and the way they came at him so remorselessly in a pagan sort of way as if to physically munch him up, crunch him up made him feel just dreadful, indeed he was so scared of them he tried to reason with them and couldn't get through to any real degree because they were real and unreal but they were certainly on him!

'Please it's not my fault and it isn't fair but you can't have my mind and body!' he yelled and yelled that same drastic sentence at the ghouls yet still they tried to eat him up body and soul. The fearful apparition never quit its nauseating intention and just kept on breaking off pieces of his body and wolfing them right on down!

He panicked rather and missed the monk at once and in the seizures of moaning and the determination to groan he didn't realize where he'd disappeared to, but he looked around and there he still was in a kind of miniature jade-green oasis or church park for the tranquility of worshippers. The monk sat there with a tiny smile and an even tinier book in his hands, as he waved at Ernid.

'What kind of book do you have there?' asked Ernid of the monk-looking-man and as it was a friendly sort of question the fellow replied 'It's a diary actually in which I enter most of my thoughts on a daily basis with a fold-up-pen; and whenever I'm feeling ecstatic or grateful to God or maybe down in the dumps I go ahead and write my sensations in it just to feel better. They're not so expensive so why don't you keep one to record how it is that you feel from day to day. It's so healthy!'

'I have these fearful feeling to kill people!' sobbed Ernid and threw himself down in front of the monk like a deranged supplicant. 'Ever since the accident in the vat!'

The monk assured him it wasn't his own fault and that mood swings were perfectly normal when you considered The Australian Government lately and how there is no one to love in The House Of Representatives or in The Labor or Liberal Party.

'It is just something wrong they put in you', he enthused and clapped him on the back as he writhed on the dewy grass in a most woeful manner like a fellow having a fit or something. 'You only have a bit of brain damage that is all; you are still reacting to possibly some uranium your surgeons planted in you to cheer you up!'

He wandered home by way of a drop-in-centre that had lost all of its funding, it was dark and ghastly in there with broken blinds flapping like ironies and disappearing perspectives no matter where you looked. He felt led there as if some strange force were leading him to a particular appointment, maybe with destiny.

He saw there was only a child at reception whose eyes were like sunlight only more extreme as well as pretty, the child asked him politely who it was he wanted to see but then he didn't know that; he just said that he felt to be there and wanted to say hi to folks if that was okay with him, and the boy said it was okay.

He wandered around all sorts of eerie rooms and eerier wards where floorboards were missing and doors hanging off door frames by only one screw, that sort of thing, and in the end he entered a room where two children, orphans both, were so impoverished that they were playing tennis with a dead dog.

They had improvised a tennis net hung between two chairs made out of an old tablecloth and using racquets made of fly wire screwed into paddles they continually hit the dog's head over the net in a state of boredom.

'Haven't you lads anything better to play with around here?' he asked them both and helped put the body and the severed head of the dog in a bin. He took them to a friendly sports store and bought them brand-new tennis racquets and new fluorescent balls and they hired a court and played for hours on it in gleeful rapture.

They sat after the game on a bench by a fence and agreed it wasn't nice to play with a poor dead animal, giving the head a fit and noble burial. They wept to realize it had been run over recently and hoped he was in heaven, running around with all his doggy mates. 'People can be so cruel!' bawled one of the boys. 'So cruel and stupid!' added his companion. They admitted they were bored and felt shocked by the callous game they had played. One of them blamed it on the media these days.

'No one is nice, that is all', he observed of contemporary society. 'The newspapers teach us meanness and offer no solutions whilst police admit they are Hells Angels who sell ICE and there is so much terrible road rage that we have no real safe place in which to play. It all makes kids go inward and computers and boredom kick in bad!'

Ernid agreed this was the case and was enjoying the fact that the boys didn't remark on his face or make any observations in respect of the look of him, the sun shield on him or the mesh mouth and dull-colored ceramic teeth. They were unjudging of him completely and he felt in a way protected by them both, his new mates!

One boy began to weep dramatically and very openly about his chronic shame over what they had been up to. He couldn't believe they could be so cruel and idiotic and even though they had buried the head he still felt racked with guilt over it.

'But you have apologized to God who is love', whispered Ernid Ernst and smiled warmly at him and added 'You are a kind boy just caught up in the vicious media!'

The three of them then stepped into the drop-in-centre together and were startled to see they suddenly had bunches of just-picked-flowers in their arms, such as daffodils, roses as tiny sweet-smelling buds that had just been born or conceived, little bright green ferns and steadfast scarlet geraniums that go on forever, and so they kept on distributing flowers to the needy and the more of them they gave then the more flowers bloomed in their arms.

One of the boys suddenly laughed and a pretty archaic vase appeared in his arms which he automatically filled with the geraniums and ferns and handed out to a pensioner who said she hadn't eaten for a month; no one believed that but she got the present anyway.

He had no idea of the physical that is time passing by simple degrees of not abstraction but feelings for nostalgia of the sun, and he wasn't certain any more of the days of the physical week or beginning the physical diary containing physical or real pages and a physical or real fold-up-pen with which to enter his thoughts. Suddenly he was with two boys who seemed friendly enough for the moment, but might they turn upon him and possibly murder him?

He broke out in a freezing cold sweat as he eyed off the boys who were now in the deed of playing badminton and patting a friendly feather over a net, but where they were doing it was in his old backyard in the rear of Prague; in the old village in snow and snowy cathedrals with pigs watching on that game of village badminton.

He went over closer to the boys who were now engaged in the ancient act of reading the daily newspaper and Ernid got his head in really close to what it was they were reading and it was to do with the latest public hangings in New Guinea; and there were gruesome photographs of such an appalling event; and people wildly cheering.

'Do you think this is right?' asked the boys in unison as the three of them fell away from the page, reeling in horror and they then turned to the daily horoscope and checked out their star signs, then had a go at the cryptic crossword with the cute collapsible black lead pencil; and they were overjoyed at how many correct ones they got. The New Guinean execution was instantly forgotten.

He walked through the miasma of sad wards and then the two boys became two girls, not that it was a bad thing as Ernid had always wanted to have a baby girl but it hadn't really worked out when Anna left him long ago; not that he missed her any more because as she had often said he was impossible to live with; but he didn't believe so, he was just a robot like any other one of them in today's world.

The girls were indeed twins and had stately walks and stately conversation when they felt like speaking, which was rare, so the trio walked through bedroom to dimly lit bedroom and there they comforted the homeless and presented them all with arrays of flowers that they plucked anew out of thin air in the most magical manner; in fact it was highly theatrical and peace-giving.

'Blessed be the peacemakers', whispered one of the twin girls as she handed a blind old poor lady a fresh-baked pudding or possibly it was in the end a fruit cake in some way. It was positively stuffed with yummy fat raisins and juicy sultanas, and the sick old homeless lady mumbled 'Miraculous stuff!' as she sniffed it – the first time she's smelled fresh hot fruit cake in many a long year.

They headed for another darkened room where two old ladies who were totally blind sat next to one another in silence trying to comprehend just why that was; they were as old as time and most wrinkly and unloved but they had each other to be comforted by and to donate comfort to if they felt like that, and mostly they did, it must be said.

The two girls talked to the old couple as if they were the most intimate of friends and pretty soon there was giggling and joking going on in the most pleasant way; it was as though they, the four, had always known each other.

The girls handed them early Christmas gifts of lovely shawls and hand-knitted socks and beautiful linen tea towels and lashings of bottled whisky, so many things, and soon the gloom had sped away and gone for all time.

Not just the gifts but the kindness of words the human voice may make in toughened times, the nightingale in the human voice when it's switched to kind.

The girls brushed ever so patiently the elderly citizen's scruffy unloved white hair and they implemented expensive shampoo into its twice-bitten fleas that munched their scalps.

In the end the girls strongly lifted the ladies up and escorted them to be bathed properly and did the old ladies like that for a treat!

They then gently toweled them down and refreshed their old bodies with talcum powder, put new clothes on them that weren't hand-me-downs and were lovely to slip into and so on.

Ernid watched all of this in dumbfounded awe and saw that he wasn't really a machine or a freak but a human with feelings of love for his fellow person.

He observed the fear get taken away from the vagabond women and felt their amazed joy as new clothing got put on them as if they were royalty; and they were royalty, what else could you call it?

He smiled benevolently at the friendships being formed in a living throng around him, the sweetness people are more than capable of, their instantaneous need of love like demanding and chirping baby birds, but the overwhelming thought in his brain was that he needed to be kinder because he knew that quality in a robot was all that would ever be remembered.

He wandered back to his peaceful depository, his hole, and as he quietly descended the curly metal council-designed staircase he saw his hole in an entirely new way. Sure it was only a rental property controlled by the council and a bit cheaper for local lemonade workers, well not that much cheaper, and it was true that he could be evicted any second for any logistical reason, but he had made it nice and there was nothing much else he could do whilst alive.

He didn't know what really to do so he put on the vacuum cleaner and sucked up the excess of particles of lint and gravel which was seeping in to put a bit of a dampener on it. He cleared away all the newspapers and remembered he hadn't looked at them much, just studied the zodiac which informed him he was heading for a disaster any time, and that worried his circling mind somewhat.

He picked up some horse riding instruction manuals which happened to be on the earthen floor which he also hadn't studied much, and he was a bit annoyed that by now the gravel drifting into his home from high overhead was commingling with pounding rain and now his floor was thick black mud; so he put on his rain hat and rain coat and big floppy black rubber boots to continue his overdue housework that was now vital to his wellbeing.

He felt puckish so he went to the bread cupboard, that in itself was hard to do because the warped door of it had in some way had jammed in some awkward sort of way; but when he succeeded in opening it more of this beastly gravel stuff flew hard into his inquiring face.

Puckish and puckish he certainly was so he managed to switch the toaster on but the power and gas had been disconnected by irritated energy suppliers. He said 'Drat!' aloud to himself and in the end was required to eat biscuits spread with crunchy peanut butter to sustain life. He loved them and as his robot teeth crunched into them he said to himself, again aloud for better impact 'They can't take my peanut butter away from me, at least!'

He was no doubt whatsoever in a siege situation, what with essential energy sources being cut off whilst he was sleeping probably, 'That would be like them, wouldn't it' he muttered for the third time and then cancelled all muttering as it didn't do any good and as a matter of fact he didn't like whining; the whole of Australia was going down with a big whine-sound called 'Going crook!'

The beastly gravel storm was blowing by now with such force that every single hole in the roads and streets where somehow people managed to eke out a living in the most foul and primitive of conditions just scraped through to the next shift at the plant if they hadn't been sacked in deference to the Mexicans who were everywhere just about. The old fashioned Australians were not in the hunt and were practically starving to death in their own holes, two or three bedroom.

He climbed into his filthy antiquated shower but the only thing which finally came on was a blast of stone cold painful red gravel which hacked into his back something fierce and caused great welts to form and probably bubonic plague to come. He leapt out of the gravelly shower and dressed in his gravelly roughened clothes as swiftly as was practicable and ran down the street that rained red gravel from the fiery heavens.

He felt his by now rusted jaw with the grille on his mechanical mouth now fouled by mould and a kind of green fungus he could feel with his false tongue. He was literally falling apart at the seams and it really came as hardly any surprise when the whole jaw and attachments tumbled off right onto his gravelly-patterned-carpet and he could feel a chilly draught blowing through the hole in his neck; he feared a cold or monstrous sort of Flu might arise.

In a way he felt liberated now it had slid right off and just lay there like rubbish with no history of their brief life together. He was relieved and not saddened by its departure, sat in his awful kitchen, put his cold fingers to where his jaw once was and envisaged all the other people who'd lost mouths in industrial accidents. How did they cope with the daily efforts such as going grocery shopping or picking up the kids from crèche or simply running the car with a new head on; everything became harder as they got older and had to work longer hours to pay exorbitant rental to merciless landladies and landmen.

It was as if he were being politicized and made aware of the fabulous inequalities which have just about destroyed the poor old planet, he was for the very first time at the age of twenty-three years of bitter and sweet experience able to feel sympathy for the caged fowls we've all become; the battery hens of both hemispheres.

It occurred to him to look for his mother, after all with the thermonuclear storm pounding away outside, the strange gravel apocalypse as well, and the weird sticks of lightning Thor himself hurled down on the metropolis he had slightly forgotten all about her; and as he continually loved her he blinked only the once and there she simply was in his holey home, just smiling at him there.

She had gone through major surgery or maybe been struck by lightning because she was well again and looked great, her eyes were all clear and the bulldog clips had been successfully removed from her fairly unlined noble forehead.

'Have you had your body all fixed up?' he asked her ever so humbly. She nodded and he had to leave it at that, for all his faults he was not just a robot but a gentleman to boot. To have perfect manners is not so easy and he had to reboot himself, man and robot, first thing of a morning.

'Where did you find the cash to get all fixed up?' he inquired like a timid titmouse and she explained that she had gone into casualty at the local clinic, into casualty in fact and they had quite cheerfully removed all temporary machinery from her at once and sent her off by emergency stretcher to a beautician and that was all there was to it, really, and her son wept to hear it.

'You always have top insurance cover, mother!' he exclaimed and they hugged one another and she kissed his awkwardly made mobile mesh mouth. Then the cage over his mouth fell out and he had it still hanging on, only just, by one small metal hinge.

'Do you think that they would do it for me?' he cried all down his heaving chest in such a dramatic way that she wept on seeing him do that.

He confessed to his old mother that indeed he was wearied of suffering and that alienation was his breakfast of not champions but his demons, of which there were many. 'Would they tidy me up?' he bellowed and his giant very powerful hands scrunched into the back of her blouse in a way that very nearly hurt her. He was by now fully kneeling on the vile floor and staring up at her full of agony.

She fiddled about with her blackened by Capitalism purse and the grips were hard to get at, but she opened it up in the end and retrieved an appointment card with his appointment on it; written in blue fountain pen ink to see her own beautician at nine in the morning, a Saturday so he didn't have to go to work or anything like that.

He made her some scrumptious cheesy macaroni with slices of actual fresh salmon whizzing round in it. She loved it and had seconds, making sure she saw him eat his serving, two servings indeed and like the loving creature she was she fed her son daintily through his visor and mesh teeth and could obviously hear it descending into his hungry stomach. 'There!' she called to him and playfully patted him on his gut.

'There!' he echoed partly because he couldn't possibly think of another word to say, and partly because 'There' was his favorite word.

He was glad of his new crisp snowy-white appointment card to see a new specialist in body parts at the hospital and wondered whether there were any new theories and ideas in new jaws and human biting apparatus.

'There have to be', he enthused.

His mother was sitting on a reasonably comfy chair looking terribly relaxed and watching The Channel 9 news bulletin and nibbling very humbly a date scone with the latest Government regulation scrape of margarine patted across its slithery surface; he put a nice rug over her knobby knees and they watched the latest horrors together, this being at six in the evening around about.

They led with a global hysteria vignette about mass sackings which made rather uncomfortable entertainment; the imagery depicted a great exodus from all industry but whaling. The Japanese had never whaled harder and the grisly footage showed workers gleefully hacking up giant whales on a big boat expressly constructed for the creation of sushi.

Billions of whale blubber sushi were being sliced into tiny bits and rolled up in freshly boiled white rice before being frozen in the hold; hundreds of cooks in white dust coats and transparent gloves and ventilation masks were doing it on blood-soaked preparation benches whilst lakes of beautiful tragic bright red blood was hosed overboard in the name of culinary delight.

The Japanese sushi seamen sang songs of cash and prospering industry as they performed their staggeringly ghastly work on the unfortunate creatures who honestly had no idea what was going on. One minute they were splashing about in the sea and the next minute they were sushi heading for busy up-market cafes globally.

As the camera went in on the bloody slaughter of the innocent lovely beasts Ma asked whether her son knew why things like this were occurring when a person could easily purchase fresh sushi down at the shop that was entirely vegetarian; and no whale sacrifice was necessary. Ernid replied that he didn't know and they left it at that, the two.

The next story was the ever popular crashing of modern automobiles straight into shops, homes, hospitals and flower shops and nursing facilities. This segment possessed sound as well as vision and the viewer and hearer witnessed the current practice of ramming your car at high or low speed into someone's home just to see if they're in.

Mostly it was old Italians doing it out of boredom and yearning for

The Old Country possibly, maybe they had formerly toiled as Formula One racing drivers and were now senile and figured they may as well go for it.

You saw them persistently hammering through plate glass windows of supermarkets manufacturing enormous amounts of shattering sounds, the terrified staff leaping about in their bid to avoid them, the customers clearly wishing they had shopped elsewhere, the dazed drivers not remembering where they were or why they had depressed the accelerator instead of the clutch; but mostly it was discovered by police that the cars that had offended were automatic anyway.

The last segment was the most upsetting and showed half a million Mexicans being sacked at the plant and having vicious wolves put on them as they skulked around the big exit gate in very sulky moods the lot of them; their sombreros had fallen in the dust and many had been bitten by mounted police horses the size of houses. Police were using extendable hard batons on their backs even though they were passive.

'I think I recognize that particular Mexican!' emitted Ma and she got down on her hands and knees and focused her field glasses on the television screen. 'Yeah, I know him too, Ma! He used to work in Pulverizing Section alongside of me. It's amazing he didn't fall in too!'

The lines of disappearing Mexicans went on forever and ever, all with a disappointed look and looking older than they were, which is how life is in their country. They were being clubbed and beaten and not offering any resistance of any sort; they were the most completely passive Mexicans Ernid and his mother had ever seen on television or live.

The story cut to management pointing out that The Mexican Solution hadn't really worked out and that the whole lot could return to Mexico immediately with a week's pay in lieu of toiling without a contract. The poor things wept blubberingly as they crawled up dark and awful gangplanks and boarded ships without heating.

Ma asked her son what he made of such extreme inhumanity and he said he didn't know. He was good at not knowing and made a mental note to stay that way.

The next item was to do with ICE and showed the damage done to hordes of Australian kids who were so addicted to it they robbed their own siblings at knife point to buy more of it.

The story showed tons of it hidden in illicit bags of rice that had come from Indonesia and sniffing dogs yelping and stiffening as they identified the horrible substance; the drug squad spokesman pointing out that it was Australia's biggest drug bust in modern history, as if that were something to be proud of.

That item cut to darkened up footage of kids using it all over the country, even kids from the bush used ICE to stay in touch with their community.

'Isn't there something pleasant on?' inquired his fatigued mother so he switched the television over to The ABC where there was a high-rating program on about mansions and castles being lovingly renovated so the rich could prosper.

'Let's go with this show!' cried Ma in solid jubilation and they settled in to observe the pitfalls of the privileged landowners striving to nut out a way of staying that way.

There was a chubby blonde lady who had expertise in mediation with the rich who inherited 12th century moats and barns and lakes and stables and castles with seven hundred draughty rooms in them, all falling apart from centuries worth of neglect, and she was at loggerheads with the white moustache brigade who owned these things.

'This is much happier a show!' cried Ma and nearly knocked her tea over and trod on her last remaining fragment of scone.

The inheritors of castles and moats were gloomier than any other form of life in Great Britain and did nothing but go crook about their lot, and they really had a lot, and the friendly but persistent chubby lady in the blonde hair tried hard to convince them of opening up their bizarre castles to the public, turning their ruinous residences into income by virtue of holiday homes, but she was getting nowhere.

'But we hate the lower orders!' smiled the rich in their fetid breath as they guzzled into another salmon cracker rinsed back with a sip of sherry.

'What have the dispossessed ever given to us stinking rich?' they pointed out with unleashed ferocity, and then the nice lady couldn't think of anything to say.

There was a connection with the cruel old squinty eyes that made Ma feel frightened and she crossed the room and put her trembling fingernails right through his young wrists for security, as she knelt at his slippers and pompoms and said 'This is the most frightening segment of all!'

# CHAPTER FOURTEEN

## THE NEW APPOINTMENT

It was dull and early as Ernid stepped into the brand new clinically hopeful Reception Area of Justice Hospital which was surprisingly built by funds from the local council mixed with other monies from the stinking rich who lived on the right side of town as opposed to the wrong side where people like Ernid rented to no avail. He by now had amassed nearly a quarter of a million dollars worth of rental receipts.

He had prepared excellently and had come to the hospital in Fervent Parade with four days' worth of change for the car he sometimes drove when he got sick and tired of buses; he kept his Skoda in the humble lock-up-garage and even though it was falling apart with rust he kept it in registration and insurance, pricey as that was, and it felt just great to give it a kick in the guts and motor into what was left of the city.

It was incredibly quiet in the waiting room and you couldn't even hear the bubbles going up and down in the water cooler or people sigh. There was a placard which read in big print 'No Sighing!'

He sat there as meek as could be clutching his very precious appointment card and waited for his name to be called, although he was forgetting what it was for some reason he couldn't crack onto.

He politely gawked at the other people sitting there like patient shadows of their former selves. They looked okay but he did notice that they all had mechanical jaws on them topped off with soap-saver-like fine wire mesh sharp grilles and teeth for obviously chewing with. They sat timidly there with false heads on in a way.

There were no racy magazines to take a squint at, nor were there any medical breakthrough journals that publicized the latest in foam rubber minds.

He gazed in a bored way at the goldfish that fluttered around in their bowl and he saw that they had new jaws on too just like he did; and that they also didn't know what was going on. He wanted to pat them.

He was ushered in to meet the specialist who warmly greeted him with one hand.

'Lost it in an industrial mishap!' he barked cheerfully enough for both of them.

With his stump he indicated a plush chair for Ernid to take it easy in or on, whichever suited him.

'We have exciting news dear man', the surgeon uttered as he puffed away on an electric cigar. 'Since your old reconstruction there have been fantastic breakthroughs in medical science and we are now preparing ourselves to get you right back to your former identity again by implementing a new flesh like fiber glass called 'Actuality'.

You shall dress and go to work looking just great, in fact like your old self only there shall be no freak show!'

In the coolest and calmest way he entered theatre where the nurses greeted him by name and the team of specialists said 'Hi!' in an unforced way and he hopped onto the operating table like he was in a reunion. The mood was festive as if it would segue to a banquet or a really splendid party; he was so warmly welcomed he didn't want ever to leave them all.

He was given a slight sedative in the arm that they assured him 'would take the sting from things', and it did of course as he was positively floating on air as they comforted him and adjusted the cables and gauges and gazed blinkingly at this or that gismo.

'Blood pressure is a bit up but not dangerous!' said a nurse who was fussing with a needle and patting a pillow for his head and the overhead lights came on much brighter, the intent faces craned ever nearer and the head surgeon smiled at him with an unthreatening grin like a virtual Cheshire Cat he was. And he said to Ernid, who was becoming stressed, 'Listen my friend you've got to go with me on this' and there was something so gentle as well as authoritative about him that it worked and Ernid surrendered utterly to everything in that theatre.

He had never been calmer and didn't need pajama pants or the top to instil a feeling of security, as they made him feel extremely safe and trusting of those professionals he sort of knew but certainly couldn't see. All he could make out was an opaque kind of friendliness towards his face, a remembrance of his face.

They fussed about with tubes and things and put him gradually to repose in such a way he felt they were still with him in the invisible certainty of prayers; he fell back to that old feeling of faith he'd experienced at his village church when people seemed part of a family; even the donkeys did and the sticky beak chickens that sat in the old altar.

The sounds of instruments seemed padded in some way, the voices sounded like muted harmless conversation or gossip which wasn't malicious, while the buoyant nurses and indefatigable surgeons set to work upon him like a talented jeweler tinkering at a rare and invaluable pocket watch which needed urgent attention. He loved every single thing they said and if he could have applauded then he would have.

They loved him but anonymously and some knew he was Ernst of the family of Ernst and they even knew he came from some part of Prague, out the back of it possibly, and to his unconscious delight they murmured and one of them darned well sang a well-loved and much-remembered village song that he tried hard to join in but sadly couldn't given his physical condition on the operating table.

They reached across him and over him and passed this thing and the other thing and used objects of great newness in thinking to cut the jagged jaw right off his body. They scoured completely and swabbed him sparkling clean and sprayed him ever so lightly with the kind of aerosol people employ to iron business shirts.

They spoke friendlier to him than anyone could to a new-born-baby and one of the girl nurses combed his downy hair up in the front like a little wave. They loved his old jaw coming off and they cast bitterly the foiled and strangled useless old mesh of his mouth; they tidied him right up like he was new and not a robot anymore.

They fitted him with a donor mouth so he was the world's first recipient of that and they put in a brand-new voice box fitted with double Dolby sound system.

He was given on his hip a new remote control that he could put on a charger overnight and with two good Double A batteries he could eat for six weeks no worries!

He was almost conscious when the new donor tongue was slid in with various intricate saliva glands and other attachments to keep it going in and also out, there was a painless light installed in his mind to keep him upbeat.

He sighed a lot and they sighed in perfect sympathy with his modulated FM Voice Box and also they installed a brand new record library that played Long Playing Records and Singles and he could, when he was recovered, either join a record library and play rock or free fall jazz; it was entirely up to him.

When he came to he was winched up nice and straight and apart from a sore back he was a new soft drink worker.

The nurses crowded in around him like family or a family of fresh flowers and it was so patently obvious they were personally thrilled with the success of the operation; his senior surgeons would have hugged him if they could but they just couldn't because of protocols but one of them wept with humility that he'd come through one hundred percent.

The new him didn't take a second to break in; there was no trauma in his body, the old was out and in with the new high tech body parts, all of them waiting for a recipient and he was it, Dear God Almighty!

He had to lie still a long time; that was all they knew for it to take, but his throat and mouth didn't hurt him any more and he could hum a song or really belt one out. He was as good as new as a cleaner swept all the wrapping paper and cellophane and spare screws off the sheets and primped his big pillow higher and more comfy.

They asked him to say something and he said 'Cool, Man!' as if he were in New York.

There was no adjustment to make and no psychological conundrum as he had come through as a fait accomplis.

Specialists from different floors and wards came in to see their star patient and what they saw was a new man, someone who'd been through all mills.

His face was un-freaked and his hideous bulldog forehead clips had been removed so that he no longer looked like part of a post office, although there were signs of old bent and crooked staples in his now fair and you'd need to say very handsome visage.

'I feel brand-new!' was the only sentence he could utter and seem useful to describe the revolution he'd been through just now in theatre.

He was capable of having a shave and so sat up in his skinny ward bed and ran the lovely sharp razor over his beard which he was sick of at any rate, and he gave himself a proper do-over.

He left nary a whisker on his handsome-again face and even managed to extricate those old awfully stubborn nostril hairs that always made his eyes wince.

He toweled his face down with something so soft it lay in the realm of a dream and then splashed a tiny drop or two of rather posh-looking after shave on.

'I smell like a baby's bottom!' he laughed and then a nurse thoughtfully combed his jet-black-hair until it shone like victory.

He lay in the now-comfortable bed with his powerful arms resting behind his head and watched the busy nurses rushing to and fro dispensing favours to sick people everywhere, while they listened attentively and made up small jokes to disappear the problems of frightened patients; they were as good as gold on very long shifts.

He gazed at a busy cleaner, and he had his troubles too, having contracted polio as a boy he dragged a useless leg along wherever he plucked up trash. He grimaced as he knelt to empty garbage bins and now he was chucking old false jaw components and bits of mouth-sprocket and facial hinges in with all the other rubbish. He did it with a groan but he himself was an example of grace under pressure.

The Sleep he went into after just one day of intensive care was drugless and profound in its sheer simplicity because he felt not just refreshed but completely born again, no longer delusional nor depressed nor racked with guilt over imaginary murder, while in sleep he was quite back in the village again in the Old Country, with his friendly pet pig, in the bath with him even.

They let him sleep for twenty-four hours in his ward with nice blankets over his never-restless legs and lovely cotton sheets both under and above him. His pillow was more than comfortable in that it positively rowed him to safe shores and all the voices he perceived in his unconsciousness were love words as far as his psyche went, and it went overboard with rest.

In Rehab a day or two later he did the treadmill with ever-increasing confidence, his strides enormous as he strode directly away from trouble to an imaginary snowscape based on remembrances of the village of long past.

He did the exercise bike with rapture and whenever the grinning gym instructor made the simple adjustment from not fast to fairly quick he found his still-youthful legs bounding around with the clip-on-pedals that he adored and could more than keep up with. He loved the exercise bike with all his heart and soul and could understand why some recovering ones felt crummy when it someone else's go.

The hospital was a new world to him with a special meaning and he made friends as effortlessly as rain glides down an outpatient's window-pane and they know they are cleared to return back home again. Everything about the place was wondrous except for the lectures.

After ninety minutes on the treadmill and exercise bike and doing the weights and learning basically how to roll his new head again – and like the first time they'd put one on it wasn't simple; it didn't hurt him that much but it just felt sort of awkward and slightly inconvenient.

Six new mouth recipients were ushered into a small tutorial space and then the white gowned lady lecturers arrived and instantly the fun of recovery disappeared in a puff of female importance. The ladies were on at least a hundred thousand a year and possibly the corruption of their income impacted on their outlook; it was hard to say but immediately he looked at them Ernid lost his confidence.

They each gave an incomprehensible power board display about the perils of recovery and the imminent dangers of not playing the game; not taking your medicine on the dot of consciousness in the new morning; not exercising the brand-new-mouth at every chance.

They used a lecturer's cane made of pointy cold white marble to adhere the patient's eyes to the dreadfully important words that hardly anyone could make out; it was a whiz of white board markers with no ink left in them.

Ernid was more interested in making friends with fellow recipients of new mouths because he was alienated in his way, practically like them he supposed; and he needed people more than ever; even or especially ones with new mouths like him so he could begin to take his confident place in the strange society he existed in like flotsam.

But the ladies raved on only about what perils lay ahead if proper maintenance wasn't shown towards the invaluable components of their mouths and necks and spoke ominously of death by not eating, self-starvation in housing commission one bedroom flats and even self-strangulation if a mouth-less man couldn't get a girlfriend.

They were very depressing but very bossy and the six recipients dropped their new heads until they were on the desks they had to sit in so uncomfortably and for so long.

They were informed that fun was out of the question and that they could never ever ride a pony again or go to Luna Park or expect passionate kissing; and everybody adores passionate kissing.

They were cautioned against sudden hay fever attacks at unseasonal times of the year when a darned good sputter could make a recipient's new head come right off; then where would they be the lady tutors asked with a frown.

The worst part about it for someone like Ernid was that the men weren't expected to ask the slightest thing about the predicament they found themselves in, the great physical and metaphysical adjustment they had to make before they could hop on a tram again or go to a movie like the rest of the population.

All he asked was 'May I expect love?' to which no answer was presented and he actually heard the ladies' real mouths shut like tin letter boxes in the wind.

'What may I expect after a year looking after my sick old mother in a two bedroom hole in suburbia?' he asked them but again there was no answer but silence and some gasps of disapproval from the other blokes who shook their new mouths savagely as if to say 'Belt up why don't you?'

He found one of the lady tutors cute and observed that she had a low top on so that her curvaceous bosoms were exposed to the new mouth men, and that she actually chewed gum in an American Movie sort of way. The way she leant over to talk so negatively to the men was supposed to turn the poor things on, but it didn't and she was just up herself.

The lecture was so completely different to the fun of the exercise when he loved to feel his blood circulate through his arteries even if one or two were down. He loved the camaraderie of the gymnasium and the chit-chat he liked and truly needed as he existed in a vacuum like the other men who had fallen into similar glass crushing vats with rods going straight into their heads just like him.

At the completion of the new mouth lecture the men were told off for being men and then handed some brochures and unreadable diagrams about the extreme hardness of digestion from now onward. Generally they felt useless together as they got on the tram like beaten dogs with droopy tails. 'I'm not turning up at one of them again1' cried a man as he groped for his ticket to go into town.

Ernid sat in a cold park with a fellow recipient and they sort of enjoyed their own version of a chit-chat being roughly the same age heading for thirty with a wealth of experience in the lemonade game. He looked a bit like Ernid the other guy but his voice was more modulated as though he had toiled in advertising, and he had as it turned out. He was in Public Relations.

'Do you find it hard having a mechanical gob? ' he politely asked as he stared ahead at basically bugger-all.

'Well', replied Ernid also politely 'This new one I had put in is ever so much more sophisticated than the earlier model which had dreadful gears in it so I had to chew in first gear and then swallow in second and excrete waste matter in third. The new model has no fault to it in any way and I look like I used to do before I fell in'.

'That is how it is for me too', smiled the guy and grinned hard at Ernid with a blinding smile to show off the new whiteness of his implanted teeth that opened and closed like a sentence in literature. 'How much exercise bike and treadmill do you do at our gymnasium?' asked Ernid innocent as a happy boy, which he was again.

'Well I do two lots of ten minutes as a rule', said the man as he relaxed on the park bench with his new companion. 'Straight away after that ten minutes on the bike I go to the treadmill as if summoned!' he chuckled and a tear of merriment travelled down his refreshed reddish cheek which then travelled for free to his right knee where it became a pool.

'I like that', laughed Ernid. 'As if summoned; that's fantastic!'

They enthused about the exercise bikes and the wonder of the treadmill and the mouth exercises they had to do such as group gulping, group swallowing, group gargling and especially group singing. The hospital boasted a new mouth choir and Ernid had heard of two women who belonged to it who'd fallen into vats like him.

But it was 'Brill' as his old demented pretentious Grandfather used to call something good such as death by firing squad when the Germans were crawling all around the non-sewage back blocks of cratered Prague in their robotic determination to murder anything that moved. He was very up himself the old Grand Pop.

It was 'Brill' to be clear of mechanical infection such as cancer of the plaster tongue or bloated back gum or prostrated arm in a permanent sling or just plain sick and tiredness that three-quarters of our country suffers from; the other third fear their jobs being removed from them and that gives them enormous reserves of paranoia-energy you can't get any other way, not really; it's a great initiative of the Government.

At rehab he felt generally normal again and socially fit to talk to another chap, even a lady although he hadn't been getting many dates lately, but that was due to his rehab appointments and all the caretaking of his creaky old mum who was so dirty she washed in dust.

The confidence fled back into his new model. He felt upgraded and incredibly of value so he took his decrepit mother into a fancy city store and shouted her some new duds.

'Here, take two Grand and whack on something fancy!' he couldn't resist a chortle and his impoverished mother of seventy literally ran towards canyons of skirts and beautiful billowing blouses that were not projections for once.

He stood before a dressing mirror in the Gent's Section (how different it was to Pulverizing Section!) and he tried on a fine three piece sheer cotton suit with matching shoes that looked a trifle like a suit as it turned out. He really enjoyed pushing his drop-dead gorgeous glossy black hair up at the front and got right in close to the mirror as his new face winked at itself.

'I am back!' he laughed and happily paid in cash at the register, wondering where in the world his sudden cash came from; maybe he'd always had it?

He got across to Ma and hardly recognized her as she was so exquisite and for once wasn't just standing there in a sheet of drool.

He had no concept of time or dress-code and didn't understand whether it were Sunday or Monday, time of rest or time of work, so he just got going that's all.

He decided to just walk things out, not review life any more, and wear nice clothing and maybe meet a woman. It had to be possible and maybe it was to his advantage not to know where he was off to.

He went walking at a most leisurely tempo along the main road and noticed the neighbourhood had all of its hole-doors shut fast adorned with just wheelie bins for the great compactor to collect with its Herculean Hydraulic Arm that he sometimes felt envy for because of its colossal size and the way it declined to break down, not once in his knowledge.

He strode by nothing and ended up nowhere with flying red gravel pounding down. Through the blazing pollution he thought he observed Martian Space Rockets belting about but wasn't that sure of it; the way life was nothing could have startled him less than alien rocket ships hovering over his city and an intention to land.

He ventured into a tea room he hadn't noticed before in a street he hadn't seen in his mind, or in his present state that was bordering on a complete blank, truth be told.

The tea room was run by aliens with antennas in them taking orders for a range of refreshing drinks, mostly hot ones such as blackberry coffee and tulip tea, so he tried to get their attention by tugging at an aerial on one of the gloomy alien waiters and she just muttered and got out her notebook to take his order.

Her face was like a hot crumpet so he spoke directly to the holes in it in the pleasantest manner possible, although it happened to be the

hey mate, where'd you score the pie?

busiest time of their day or possibly night; she seemed friendly and was preparing to enter his order on her pad. He stared up into her hot crumpet head and could see it had plenty of honey in it; and as well as that effect the crumpet was blowing smoke it was that hot.

'Excuse me Miss but you seem to be a bit too hot as there is smoke arriving from your crumpet holes', he discovered himself saying, but was also beginning to experience jumping-of-mind powerful flashbacks again which he'd assumed wrongly were over. He felt bad all of a sudden, in fact terrible!

She adjusted the ribbons on her pretty antennas and buzzed like a bee in an amused sort of way and whispered to him through her facial aperture that had so much lipstick on it with an American accent, 'Say, honey, haven't I seen you before? You sure look cute!'

He tried to pay attention to the huge hard-to-get-at-menu that was the size of a barn, but as he turned each page over he saw fragments of the old village where he'd played leap-frog as a lad and with his friends had constructed snowmen and even snow teenagers which were hard to build, actually, because they kept changing their shape all the time. The bee waitress touched his relaxed knee with her feeler in such a way he got terribly excited, then she whispered sweet nothings in his burning-hot-ear.

'Are you trying to hit onto me or something?' he purred to her as she bent over the table to clear away honey pots and the discarded arcs of leftover burned toast and incinerated crumbs; it was fascinating to see a girl or bee like her pick up so many objects in a fraction of the time generally allotted to complete such tasks.

With a sigh she swept into what he assumed was the busy and noisy kitchen.

He stared hard at his plate and unbelievably there were three piping-hot crumpets sitting on it covered with delicious fresh butter and just a scrape of fresh honey; she had willed it there!

He shrugged his brand-new-just-made head and snapped into the breakfast or late lunch or possibly supper. He stared at his wristwatch and saw that its delicate hands were running around in a clockwise as well as anti-clockwise fashion as if it were a line drawing of a timepiece and unreal. But it was real all right and he ignored it, cleaned up his yummy crumpets and wiped his new mouth with a serviette.

She reappeared and bent down low over him, hummed hellos into his red-hot-ears and reached over him to scoop up the used crumpet plate. As she picked it up with one of her feelers she looked him in the eyes and buzzed more friendly overtures of welcome, even adoration to him, then flapped her little transparent wings and flew very fast to the kitchen full of bee waitresses and wasp chefs.

He paid at the register to a fat and most grouchy wasp with a stiff bow tie on; he had never liked fat grouchy male wasps who grouchily took your hard-earned income and rammed it into their profit margins as if it was their own frightful baggy pants.

The rude wasp sneered as Ernid's money spilt into the chasms of coins that all winked repulsively up at him. 'You look a bit funny mate. Did you just get a donor head?' That awful remark really crushed him and he just about fainted, in fact he could literally feel his usually reliable legs shoot away under him and only through sheer force of will did he cling on.

He didn't bother replying to the intemperate insect who just kept on making similar remarks to honest citizens who came there expressly for their famous hot crumpets and honey; customers could just as easily have cooked them at their homes but loved the café because it was 'going out'.

For some reason he sat in the cobblestone alley just outside the busy café of crumpets and rather regretted ever venturing into it. He saw just how busy they were of course and earwig customers kept alighting screeching taxis and snails slithered in to be part of the scene while ants took their orders when the waitress bees fell over from heat exhaustion. That kitchen was so hot in there!

He was feeling overheated and loosened his tight silk gent's tie so he could get some air in and also began to loosen his fashionable collars. He could feel something rather like a fainting-fit come on him and figured it was just hay fever or the unseasonal warmth of early October, although he wasn't certain what was wrong with him. Huge droplets of perspiration fell from his furnace forehead and he felt really bad again.

He had dreamt of cracking onto a nice bee lady recently and she was it. He slumped in the awful alley on his grotesque rubbish tin and a hat fell off his sweaty hair that he hadn't put on before he left. He reached into his jacket pockets desperately and retrieved half a dozen packets of prescription tablets for his head condition and swallowed one of each.

The sweat was water falling down on him from his smoldering scalp to his shoes in gigantic drips. He made perfectly certain the drugs went safely back into his jacket pockets and that the packets were tightly bound so nothing could fall out. He fought for any available breath like a gasping alley-bound-pugilist might do.

He was just about out for the count and slumped at a strange angle against his friend the rubbish can when the pretty bee waitress came out and saw him in a bad way; she kissed his sweaty head with two gentle warm feelers and buzzed about him.

She orbited around him and produced loving and protective humming signals in her efforts to rejuvenate his hot and collapsed form, showing him every possible form of buzzed sympathy and patting repeatedly his too-hot-face as she went to a nearby tap and gave him a glass of water. She was incapable of human speech but showed insect love and bee kindness.

She put one feeler round him, escorted him and playfully ruffled his even blacker glossy hair. He had observed flecks of grey in it of late but now it was so brilliant as though it were part of his new self. 'How many selves are there in one lemonade toiler?' he asked aloud but by this time she was humming sweet nothings into his red-hot-ear, such as 'Hmm and more Hmm. How about we go sailing at once. I know how we can do that if you have a mind to go along with me on it!'

He loved the friendly manner with which the bee waitress held one particular insistent fore-feeler around his waist and just kept it there. 'Oh, bee!' he exclaimed. 'Always do keep that feeler there as I have been so lonesome of late!' She held her other feeler around his staunch shoulder and thus they strolled down to a real pier as opposed to the projection of one.

He saw their flighty shadows on the wall of a boat shed and was glad he had bumped into her at the fashionable hot crumpet house. She was darned nice to look at and she caressed his lonely head with that top feeler of hers until they got to a ferry.

It was neither night nor day but something nice in between when they got on the boat and he was knocked out that the lady bee had treated him to the fare.

It didn't matter much to him where they set off to as he just wanted to be with the bee. They rubbed and got excited together, feeler to new jaw as they went across the heads where the tides meet and are very rough indeed, but all she emitted was 'Swell!'

They had a huge kiss as the waves hammered together like clapper-boards to signal the take of a scene on a movie lot. She at one stage drove him mad by inserting one of her feelers into his ear hole and placing the other near his wallet. He was so over-excited he kissed her everywhere, feelers, the lot and her deeply recessed eyeballs spun round in a dazed and delightful manner and what passed for her mouth emitted the sentence 'I go for you!' in perfect bee.

It felt modern to adore a bee physically so they shyly traipsed away to a dingy motel where they could obviously express their feelings towards one another in privacy, as a bee needs intimacy as well as singularity to make love with every single feeler.

He tipped the wasp at Reception five dollars fifty cents for signing them in anonymously and being a decent sport about it. The garçon wasp who did room service eagerly carted their honeycomb up the floral carpeted stairs to their love nest.

The girl bee smiled as she fluttered to the big double bed and both her orb-eyes winked at him as he let down her straw-colored-hair. He just felt great as she undressed purely for his pleasure and perhaps well-being because he hadn't climaxed since his errant wife up and left him for dead; that deed felt like eons ago at least.

He undid his bag that had in it a spare set of false teeth that had no need of hinges. It also had in it two new pairs of relatively costly plastic toothbrushes, good quality toothpaste, two cups to spit into after doing your teeth of a night, some Mickey Mouse comics and a badminton kit if they felt like some light-hearted-escapism or maybe a bit of fun at the beach. He had a couple of thousand in cash and a maintenance booklet on new head upkeep that looked a bit dull, really, but anyway it was in with the rest of the stuff.

She the bee was surprised to see a pistol right down the bottom of his carry-bag but he deftly pushed a hand towel over it so it was not there again, just something maybe she assumed she saw in a waking dream.

She by now had taken her feelers right off and it was his turn to be startled because he had no idea that bee feelers were attachable; she kissed his new white as snow face with extendable lips that seemed unreal to him but he was sure glad of them on his much unloved and never smooched face. She placed her stinger on his groin and wriggled quickly into a nightgown that had a honey motif.

She the bee endeavoured to disrobe him although he was beginning oddly perhaps to struggle with the idea of sexual intercourse with an insect, consensual or whatever it was, and he could feel a certain unwillingness crop up so far as his feelings were concerned. He instinctively pulled away from her as she hovered right over the top of him and appeared to be nesting in his hair.

'Please, it's been a long time', he sighed with a visual remembrance of long-gone Anna his former wife who left. 'You are terribly exciting my bee but perhaps we could settle down a trifle and just watch a bit of television together, then when we are settled we can make love.'

The bee it must be said reacted poorly to this suggestion which sounded like an excuse and she drove her red-hot-stinger into his bottom with the maximum force; and she then repeatly stung him all over out of a fit of pique. 'Hell hath no fury like a bee scorned!' he moaned as he dived for cover under the sofa cushions of their hideaway motel room.

He dove his nose straight under those big thick hard compact cushions but the bee bit hard and very often right through their embroidery; it really hurt him badly which was its raging intention, naturally enough.

He made up for that disillusioned insect's crushed feelings in being sexually rejected like that, and she poor being had to button up her gauzy blouse and put her stuff back on. 'It hurts terribly to be rejected you see?' she buzzed.

'I know about it', he sympathized and playfully nibbled an eye-orb but of course that deed only drove her into a frenzy of lust as she dived full-length at him in a foam of desire and tried to get his trousers off although he strove to keep them on; he wanted to keep everything on until he was certain that he loved the bee with all of his heart and soul, let alone spirit.

They kissed tenderly and made up for lost ground but it wasn't the same at all.

'Maybe we don't really know one another that well this time around?' he soothed and she came around for she put her left antenna upon his strong right shoulder in the most elegant and classical way a bee could do such a thing to a man.

As he embraced the amorous bee he was beginning to drift somewhat as to what their intentions were and why he lusted after her in the crazed way he did; he kissed her gauzy wings once more just for the dreamy effect it produced within him and she tongue-kissed him on his second mechanical mouth with deep passion.

'I go for you my love!' she reiterated because he already knew she was hot for him, but he couldn't give himself completely to her partly because it didn't seem natural the more he thought about it. She said that she was disgusted with him and with that she flew out of the window never to see him again.

'What a flighty little bee!' he summarized and gulped a little as he was having bee flashbacks and seeing all of the hot deeds she was doing to him in the name of love.

He had her card and figured he'd give her, how else could he put it, but a buzz?

It was late and the hot bee had fled the coop so he returned home feeling somewhat fatigued by all the goings-on lately. Some appeared real and yet others certainly were not and it being a funny time for just about everything lately he decided to do nothing in his safe old hole; possibly consume a salad roll or take a look at the paper or something like that. He was sick of emotional upheaval, very sick of it.

It felt more assured being home in a hole of one's own once more and having still a feeling like concussion or extreme faintheadedness, as well as conflicting inner versions of what had happened lately, namely the paramour insect and the new face and neck and nose-muscles

Time passing and time not going anywhere had become more like an obsession and the strange way an hour if lived to the full seemed more like a millisecond was stranger than fiction.

On his tidy-for-once tea table he had laid a rather pleasant set of archaic tea cups used in the reign of one of the Egyptian Dynasties and he made a mental note to start collecting unusual beverage containers and possibly start to have people over; he honestly felt strongly to entertain but didn't really know anyone socially.

He sat and sipped beautiful hot tea. He couldn't remember having made it but he did recall how nice it felt on his always-sore-throat and then he snapped hard into a buttered slice of Ethiopian Raisin Toast and probably put a bit too much force into that very bite since his false teeth broke in two.

The sound of the uranium bottom denture striking the dish on the table made him jump swiftly realizing the lower plate was fractured. He had put it down too eagerly munching something and that had to be the toast.

He read an instruction brochure upon fastidious upkeep of movable mouths containing teeth that came in the shape of a fret saw or a rasp or a carrot grater. Then he became saddened in that he remembered having excellent teeth in the village as a lad and the fact that he could munch a twig or even a log in half.

He actually ran his original thumb and fingers of his hand along the well-made microgrooves of his just manufactured mouth and could feel in a tactile way what his mind already knew – that it was near perfect.

The fit was good and the snap in it was terrific. There could be nary a doubt that he could cut up a fillet steak and masticate its juicy portions in an appropriate manner as the ceramic molars were tight and very springy, even lethal, and he was pleased he wasn't a practising cannibal.

The new chest cavity speaker phone worked brilliantly and he always took calls as the medical scientists were sponsored by a fashionable telephony group based in California who were really at the cutting-edge of the latest technology; he could easily dial anyone back straight away or ring himself to see how he was going. There was a plastic cradle affair welded to his left hip where he could replace the headset.

'I want to be the new man!' he declared to himself and stamped his right hand down hard on his private tea table to amplify the point he needed to make at once.

As he sipped a hot drink of inexpensive coffee he gazed up at the overhead wall clock and saw that it was two distinct times. It was both midnight and six in the morning.

It was both Sunday as well as Monday. He completely panicked.

'Oh, oh!' said his new deep voiced speaker phone.

He hurried himself into the shower but the electricity company that controlled energy all through suburban Sydney had disconnected his power-source as he was a bit late with his payments; he had somehow or other lost his check book and mislaid his savings passbook. So far as he could remember it was still in his locker at work.

In the stone-cold shower, whatever the real time was, he soaped himself as well as he could and counted his spare change with his big toe; the car wasn't going with a seriously flat battery and he wanted to be able to catch the plant bus by the seven in the morning turn-up time.

As he dried himself down with his best household beach towel to his complete shock he began to experience flashbacks of the JFK assassination again.

'Oh, not again! Not with the new mouth!' he screamed half-afraid someone might hear him in his hole as he could have left the manhole cover unlocked and it might be possible that a passer-by could make out a muffled domestic shriek or two.

Neatly attired for work in his special dry cleaned three piece suit and his silken tie done up in a Windsor knot he managed to ascend the spiral staircase to the outside world, still seeing that which isn't there and panting and gasping, if there's a difference, on the bus seat with fellow lemonade toilers all examining their watches in the grimmest sort of way. 'I'll just die if the bus is late!' moaned a guy staring with incredulity at his timepiece.

He fainted as the bus came in a minute late but felt better immediately he got on, for it is the getting on the bus that rallies depressed and anxious commuters.

He got himself his favorite seat right behind the spectral driver and in the packed bus the horrifying hallucinations came on him with an even greater force than ever before, as he stared like a frightened rabbit at the motorcade murder projected on a guy in front of him, the gent's white business shirt doubling as a cinema screen and the lone gunman in the Dallas Book Depository Building firing off the single shot with a bang.

Then there was a succession of bangs and more and more murders. He could easily make out on men's shirts on that fatal bus, thousands it seemed, and always the William Zapruder home movie footage flickering away on commuter's clothing, even on their faces and neck muscles, there was no escaping it!

As the bus screeched and violently braked down some vast chasm the bang noise got greater and the public screaming got more intense. Ernid could not follow that the travellers themselves could not see the hit occur as it was projected right on their bodies, on their clothing and faces. The driver looked like Oswald the Murderer, he really did.

He rapidly commenced to scream out loud as opposed to inwardly which is quite the trend these days amongst white and blue collar workers, and as a consequence all the other travellers commenced to scream with him, tearing their demented clothes right off because of all the lurid projections within them; even when suits and skirts were cast upon the floor of that bus you could still make out Oswald The Murderer in them being shot by nightclub proprietor Jack Ruby.

The driver screamed the most as well as the loudest and in the end the crazed bus went over a bridge and crash landed in a lake complete with uptight geese who had never witnessed anything like it and in a way wished they'd never moved into that lake because you couldn't get tranquility anywhere, goose or any other species.

The police were soon on the scene and plucked hysterical commuters from what might have been a watery mass grave.

Wonderfully no one drowned but they were still writhing away and moaning on their way to hospital to be treated for public loss of focus.

He turned up at 'Burp' Pty Ltd at around one in the morning and the time clock worked perfectly, everything did and the hallucinations had by now dimmed a bit as he was only seeing part of the assassination, so he looked forward to just getting on with it and hoeing into his shift.

Mechanically he drifted to Number 1 Vat where he really felt at home because Ma now toiled there right next to him. Her head was on just like his new one, and together, mother and dutiful son they got down the terribly long ladder and with their black rubber boots on up to their knees they started kicking excess jagged pieces of unpulverized glass into big bags that they tied up and took to one side.

This was highly skilled work and required usually years of acute training but it had to be admitted that the Ernst family had a natural capacity for jagged glass bagging and putting away.

Through spy holes their overseers peered down on them doing it and made a mental note to keep them doing it forever and possibly ever at the lowest rate allowable.

Ernid and Ma used their powerful black rubber boots to stomp on the off-cut knobs of recycled lemonade bottles and were really in their element, it had to be said.

They daintily dodged the long hard copper rods that swept the bottom of the great vat and made a game of bagging all the rock-like-glass and stacking it thoughtfully.

'This is just like the old days!' roared Ma and she slapped her thigh with a bag of glass and Ernid heartily agreed with that.

'I don't need to be a figurehead!' he pronounced and Ma slapped him hard on his broad back with a big bag of fragmented glass.

They heard the morning tea siren that went so loud that many new staff soiled themselves at both the abruptness of it as well as the loudness and so on of it, but like everything else in the factory there was nothing you could do about it; all workers knew was that it was a rule to drink hot tea and have a munch on a biscuit at ten.

To his surprise there wasn't a Mexican in sight, not a single solitary sombrero to be seen in the cafeteria nor a jumping bean among the eaters of traditional fare.

'They've sacked all the Mexicans don't you know?' whispered a shocked cleaner and it is the cleaners who know everything in modern life, especially industry.

Ernid looked up at no Mexicans and saw that they had been replaced by Germans. There could be no possible doubt of any kind as to the sight of them all; sitting rather too close to one another in the crowded cafeteria and occasionally giving the Hitler salute. It was all somehow a bit too much, the removal after the hiring of perfectly acceptable Mexicans to create the lemonade and then replace them all with Germans.

He was summoned to an urgent meeting with two bosses in the boardroom, hearing his name over the public address system. In fact it just about completely cancelled his acute hearing and his poor eardrums throbbed and quivered as he loped up the metal spiral staircase to the boss's room.

Mr Burp himself was there with his precise twin Mr Second Twin and they peered at him over preposterously thick black seeing spectacles. They were both rock-jawed of countenance and their bright pink jowls were a fright to behold as they spoke to him in tandem with identical voices that boomed with confidence and unquestioned authority. They both clasped their hands at exactly the same time and both peeped at exactly the same kind of watch.

'It's interesting that we're here', remarked Mr Burp I and his twin brother nodded but not too much as didn't wish to pull focus. 'We here at the very top of 'Burp' Pty Ltd have been well aware of your ups and certainly downs at the factory; and we have liked equally your recoveries and determinations, whoops that's plural isn't it? And anyway since you came here you must not ever fear or believe that no one is on your side.'

The twin nodded in equal agreement even before the first twin had finished his opening remarks. There was something otherworldly about them and yet at the same moment when you conversed with each of them you felt as if you were back in the late eighteenth century because of their high celluloid collars and breast pockets topped off with spotted daffodil yellow silken handkerchiefs.

'What of course we both enjoy about you Mr Ernst is your durability; we have sort of road-tested your tireless body and limitless spirit and observed you get through many deliberate obstacles that were placed in your way just to see what you are made of; and we have to say that as our figurehead and as a vat toiler you are just terrific!'

They both patted him on his back several times beaming and winking a lot at him and reiterating that he was a great bloke lots of times, until they honestly didn't know what to do with him and told him to get out and go back to work at his vat.

'Shut the door on your way out!' they shrieked together as their dentures flew out and shattered on the wall.

Philosophically he repaired to the big vat and climbed down the slippery steel ladder to check on the size and quality of the jagged pies of glass flying around together, as he watched the enormous pipes full of used bottles slide and ooze and thump into the boiling-hot glass. At one stage with his eyes bright red from sadness he could just make out an old soft drink label with his robotic face emblazoned on it as the figurehead of 'Buzz' Pty Ltd. It was a real kick when he saw that.

The plant had ever louder and more nauseating punk music piped right through each section of its operations. Down in the five hundred foot vat most toilers just put up with the abuse and got on with their duty of unclogging the great chunks of flying soft drink bottles and trying to steer the smaller bits of oily sludgy glass down the plug hole; they cried sometimes of course from the noise of the awful punk music but they basically just had to put up with it. A terrible murder attack occurred in Ernid's brain causing him to go completely berserk and attack a fellow toiler with an ice pick.

He rapidly chopped at him several times declaring, 'You get out of my head!'

Luckily enough he missed the guy but an overseer saw it and made a note of it.

He murdered without end and wasn't at all satisfied until he'd butchered every member of staff in the entire Vat I Section where he ran his rampage; all the while he clutched his own assassinated head in the firm belief it was the damaged goods of JFK and that somewhere in the bloodied vat the killer Oswald was cowering.

With hundreds of throttled and decapitated bodies flowing with a mix of blood and pineapple lemonade the authorities finally collared him and had him abruptly handcuffed and charged with affray. He then woke up right down the base of the lemonade vat with a right old migraine because nothing of any sort had happened; he had just blacked out and seen stuff again.

He dragged himself up the bright clean ladder all the long way to the top and his fellow workers were glad to see him. Nothing had happened and they were happy to see their old mate again, although he wasn't looking too good. One worker piped up and said 'Are you okay Mister Ernst?'

He replied that he was okay but needed an hour in the sick bay and maybe a word with the plant doctor.

He made his groggy way to the place of recovery, the sick bay. The whole plant only had one, and it was occupied by a similarly delusional lemonade toiler who just like Mister Ernst possessed conspiracy theories and thought he'd murdered JFK. Apparently it was common.

Ernid could easily hear the deranged occupant crying out through the sick bay wall in the most lamentable fashion, with a psychologist in there trying to nut him out, and a nurse giving him a powerful sedative, apparently uncut Burp.

'I didn't mean to kill him, it was just a voice in me that made me do it!' sobbed the chap inside the chained-up sick bay and it immediately occurred to Ernid that it might not be so rare to be delusional and incur living nightmares which had no bearing on reality. Maybe there were whole cities of imaginary murderers who did it in their minds and apart from that absolutely bugger-all happened that was outside the law?

One after the other the confessors to the JFK assassination came out of the little sick bay with their hands up precisely like the movies and documentaries he had seen all his life; people merely worked a bit too hard and that was about all there was to it, really. He felt a pang of pity for them as they shuffled towards the police van in chains. They would be going straight to court to be charged with affray, even if it was just shouting and weeping and beating themselves up in front of others.

Finally, late in the afternoon, it was his turn to see the lemonade company chief psychiatrist, a diabetic.

'How long have your particular JFK delusions been going on in your mind?' the fellow inquired as he scratched his knee, but Ernid failed actually to answer as his new mouth had completely jammed and it didn't open or shut any more. He just stared at the men with his mouth agape in its stalled position and tried to shrug his shoulders in his usual way, but they didn't work either, just like the goddamned teeth.

The nurse came along and tried to lie him down flat but Ernid protested at that and cried like a recalcitrant baby at not being left alone. The nurse then showed personally a whole heap of positions he might go in but not one of those positions appealed to him, so he just sat in a triangular way.

They gave him a prescription for 'Not There' capsules which worked straightaway: you just swallow three big brown glossy pills and the delusions don't come.

He was also given half a day off so he went in relative peace to the bus stop and hung around waiting for it to chug in. The new peace and the new order of things made him feel elated and very sleepy so he was pleased to see the bus come in with hardly anyone on it.

It felt good to be aboard the bus, redemptive and ever so normal and the pills had kicked in and nothing was screening in his lobes, although he could hear people in his forehead munching caramelized popcorn loudly, ever so loudly in there and laughing at a movie somewhere maybe real like an boutique multiplex cinema.

He tried hard to ignore the amplified caramelized popcorn guzzling but he found the sound effect of it growing much worse, with interior movie fans choking on imaginary popcorn and irate babies screaming for attention just as they do in life.

He needed to scream but hung on till it got into town and sat in a deserted parked donut van where he experienced a really heavy psychotic episode like a seizure or a fit.

Two psychologists examined his mind then took him to one of the last cinemas left in town after the gigantic rapid fire developments had made Sydney disappear completely. The deadpan psychologists shouted him a tub of popcorn and took in the latest five star documentary on JFK delusion which went down exceedingly well with most of the audience dressed in the part of Lee Harvey Oswald or Jack Ruby.

The crowd appeared to know every frame by heart and often applauded heavily and cried or mass-laughed whenever a best moment cropped up; Ernid wasn't relating to it all that well and fell to the carpeted floor and went into several awful seizures until the psychologists took him home and threw him through his front door. 'That's about all the time we have for you today, dear boy!' they cried and drove off in a screechy way in a taxi.

'Back to Square One!' he faithfully announced to himself back in his unminding hole once again. His old mum was there so they tucked into Gag in the same old way.

He was delighted that the goddamned black metal bulldog clips had been removed from her forehead, although he missed the sight in a way because he could always hug her and put all his fluttery receipts safely in its sure grasp.

'Nothing's coming after you and nothing's happening!' piped up Ma in her stoical way and gulped half the spoon down in company with the big bit of Gag she had her greedy eye on.

It was pretty dispiriting actually if you too could have been there with them to see the way nothingness destroys normal domestic life and the great ogre of Boredom staggers in to frighten and appall all that stands in his path.

Normally over their revolting meal of Gag they sipped it and did chit-chat as they called limited conversation in the Old Times. You were fully expected to speak even if you were a peasant, especially if you were because there was stuff-all else to do.

Ernid had taken to using a diary not so long back and he now fastidiously entered every single infinitesimal detail and appointment in its faint ledgers: the amount of Gag he ate only to jettison and the way someone looked at him at work or ignored him in the cafeteria and how his locker was getting on, that sort of paranoia.

As his bored-stupid mother stared remorselessly into the wording on treacle cans and tried to read the fork from beginning to conclusion her son put on his cheap magnifiers and read her instead. He put down his faithful diary with its appropriate pen and plastic ruler and read her body.

She was completely obscene, which he could see in half a glance easily, for the bulldog clips she had put back on dully glared at him from the centre of her massive swelling of a forehead just waiting for gas bills and electricity accounts to get clamped in. She had had it removed, the awful thing, and out of sheerest perversity the old thing had put it back on again to spite him just about.

Her hair he read too and noticed that it didn't make a jot of sense: from the first paragraph to its conclusion of sorts, her idiotic hair was just stream-of-consciousness.

Her eyes bore an evil look, a wicked look of wariness and hay fever mixed together, while her whole bearing was unbearable and unbelievable and she oppressed him big time.

He had often read to his startled fright in the morning newspapers of terrible crimes perpetrated upon similar grotesque mums who had oppressed their honest sons, especially Christian sons, and the whole thing snapped as the son did them in.

Did them in with anything at hand such as a machine gun if it worked all right or dropping a great weight on them such as an anvil if they existed in a barn, or the demented and much-bullied offspring just beat and kicked them to instant death as they couldn't stand their look.

He hated her very fiber and expression of pig-ignorance; he hated her varicose veins a lot and even the way they went to work together on the bus; and even or especially there they couldn't think of a single word to say to the other one of them.

He remembered being born and the inescapeable fact that he didn't like her then.

All she was doing was eating her idiotic Gag but that action was really getting to him and he stared like a violent serpent looking at a bunny rabbit at the piggy way she hoed into whatever was put in front of her; which was forever and all time Gag.

He tried to concentrate on the gossip column he was reading and the more he strove to absorb every single detail the more she gave him the shits.

He fantasized on shooting her right in her Gag and then realized he was just feeling a bit stressed. He excused himself and clambered up the stepladder to have a breather in the polluted air that choked him with each hard fought for intake.

His head was positively pounding as he found it virtually impossible to separate reality from his interior truth; his mind was so exhausted by the dumbness of his mother and the way she was always simply there with him that he fainted.

All around his sudden unconsciousness were hundreds of other chaps precisely like him, drained of all life by oppressive mothers who absolutely dominated them.

These ruins of chaps lay spreadeagled all over the main road twitching and trembling like litmus paper every man Jack of them, with their minds completely shot and their tongues hanging out.

It was naturally enough the end of the world or at least the end of lemonade workers' worlds and the sight of that waste made Ernid vomit so he paused to vomit and weep at the sight of every corpse or seeming-corpse he saw mentally recording for his own sake, his own sense of posterity, because he truly believed in modern history.

He forensically examined all the soft drink toilers with an eye to grisly detail and with his diary-notebook knelt by their sides and wrote down every single thing he witnessed like a true reporter would do.

He saw them all as the violent victims of crime in industry that they really were. It felt beneficial to write down exactly what he saw in his acute handwriting and take his time with it; he had in mind possibly a publication coming out one day describing the planet in all its ruin and phases. He felt he could be a writer because his conscience always worked even if he experienced problems with the rest of himself.

He rang his hole desperately to make amends with his poorly mother whom he loved but lately had been thinking ill of and loathing her bulldog forehead clasps; he wished she would never put them on but it was a woman's prerogative to do exactly as she pleased. She picked up and apologised profusely for hating her lately but being completely deaf she just nodded, which she always felt was best etiquette for a phone conversation.

He hurried home and prostrated his long narrow but immensely powerful physique before her and very emotionally kept on begging her to forgive him but she kept saying over and over that there was nothing wrong in the first instance. As he seemed to be having an incredibly bad seizure she forced a fistful of calming sedatives down him and waited for them to kick in properly, she being worried his drooling would destroy the Turkish Carpet.

As he emotionally reached down to pick up his head that had irritatingly fallen right off. That had happened a lot lately and he thought it might need a tune; he reminded his already exhausted self to make a new appointment to see possibly a different specialist about the coming off of his own head.

He got his tired mother to assist him with a spanner and some really good tough bolts and managed to squeeze his athletic neck into it from below and then ram the whole thing on in the one dramatic action. 'Jesus Christ!' gasped his mother. 'Not so easy!' He wanted very much to wholeheartedly agree with her but he was still engaged in the basic action of pulling it on good and proper because he didn't want it to come off again. 'Heaven Forbid! He muttered between very clenched dentures and he meant every single word of it.

Some of his hard-to-get-at rear teeth had come out when his head hit the deck, but Ma was good at screwing them all in again while sweating like anything just to do that. He then managed to shake hands with her free arm as she pulled it off. 'Your new dentures are far brighter than lavatory tiles!' she giggled like a fool and he felt love for her again.

It may have been morning or midnight but he took her to a cab and directed its Greek driver to take them both to a very costly beautician in the heart of town. He didn't mind the expense as his heart that hadn't been functioning as it ought to do was now fully capable of kindness to a stranger such as his own mother.

She alighted the taxi and trod in peasant certainty on the rolled out red carpet that a few underlings saw to doing, as they were instructed by management, then she was ushered into a stunning modern beauty parlour decked out with thrones padded with crushed scarlet antique velvet and pretty girls manicured her overgrown and badly neglected nails, both toe and finger and of course thumb, then she was given dreamy facials that more than soothed her and made her feel noble.

No other feeling is even vaguely like nobility and importance; and for once she felt regal and almost too good for the hapless minions that saw to her, fussed and shimmied around and thanked her just for being herself: Ma!

It wasn't as though he didn't possess enough woe himself when you think about it: his problems with the so-assured head continually tumbling off and the tension headache he always received whenever the visor and the bolts to his strange forehead came loose, almost to the point of falling to the ground again. But he struggled manfully against the odds and was grateful he had a fighting peasant spirit just like his father.

Though she cursed him and invoked language he'd never been acquainted with before he plucked her body up and politely escorted it to the bath to scour the bewildered creature and make newness of her again after what felt like eons of grime and split baked beans all down her repellent bosoms. Why did she refuse to put on her bra?

She tried hard to bite and boot him in the testicles but he was just too strong for her abuse of him any more, not so much the physical abuse because she still liked to kick him when he awoke, as was the wont of the village, but the new complaining and belly-aching she performed upon him twenty-four hours of each long day because she missed The Old Country bad.

She bit hard into his back as he twisted and weaved in order to get a good aim at the lovely water lying there in the tub. She chewed his face and spat and belched but it was no good and in she went like a plummeting object of scorn.

He scrubbed the old dried up gore from her hide and applied new shampoo to her dehydrated scalp driving the fleas out of cracks in her head that had had their young there, and laughing hard as she defiantly yelled at him and threatened him; but in she just went anyway like a dirty old thing!

'I'll be late for work!' she seethed and whimpered to which remark he responded, 'You'll never go to work again in your life you old thing!' And she of course blubbered like anything at that remark. He scrubbed the loneliness out of her body parts.

After much bellowing and matriarchal threatening he saw in her the tranquil change and dreamy development he'd been longing for as she started to actually whistle like a nightingale because the dried-up-ness had fled her, the hard grind of factory slavery was vanished and she was a nice lady again.

It was just so heavenly to wash her who gave him life in a lemonade factory after all and although that had its dangers and ups and certainly downs he was there for life and he knew it. He liked going there of a morning with his hard-working mother and liked it when they caught the plant shuttle first thing.

He got it that a revolution not just in gaseous confectionery was occurring in such a way that drinkable beverages were being phased out to be replaced with an array of puffers and inhalants and possibly disposable syringes. Far from being a minor drug used in most cakes and all kinds of cooking it was the desire of 'Burp' Pty Ltd to not just completely overwhelm addicts of their range of products but to conquer amphetamines and metamphetamines too.

He was ushered into a top bureaucratic meeting with several of the hard hitters he'd met only once or twice when he was made their fig-urehead a year or so ago. They had badly aged and looked worse than he did and he rather gloated to himself when he shook hands with their sweaty gymnastic palms that signed trillion dollar deals as you or I would humbly sign up for another year's worth of car registration.

To his startled orbs he saw they were pretty much identical male beings composed of baldness and fat fitness in aluminum suits and hard on the eye black cotton warm-up pants. He was gestured to shut up and to listen as never before; that was fairly easy as he was born of a silent peasant stock who only spoke to logs.

'We are aware of your trials and tribulations Mister Ernst and you must surely feel a tad used up in your duties here for us but you have a very rare quality indeed and that is your stupidity', sighed a very important-looking one of the bosses as he clasped his enormous puffy palms and stared at him with enormous masculinity and intensity.

'I suppose I am very stupid', mused Ernid Ernst shyly looking down hard at the meaningless wood grain of the preposterous desk that went on forever and ever, and with their equally dramatic faces glaring at him he was beginning to wilt from the heat of it all.

'It is of course your classical humility added to your great dumbness that the soft drink inhaling public subscribe to, Mister Ernst!' they chorused and so did he.

It was getting so that he could prophesy what they were going to do and say next, and he found himself using a grated teeth smile of embarrassment on them again; the only thing he could think of.

They assured him their fame and profit margins were never greater than when he personally appeared on the brand, be it bottles and pop-top-cans or kegs or barrels or inhalants or else drink the public could smoke and hopefully then butt out; they desperately wanted him to go back again as their figurehead. They wore tears of love in their weedy eyes and screamed his name over and over as they hoisted him on their shoulders.

One manager said to him, he may have been Burp 1 or possibly Burp 2: 'We really need you to do this for us Mister Ernst, the Australian dollar has fallen like the fallen of World War One; we know that you're a patriot and you have saved 'Burp' Pty Ltd before and we ask you in God's name to go to bat for us again. Pepsi has boomed since they introduced zero tolerance to sugar and so has Slade.'

He was taken into a laboratory and stripped naked before a whole gaggle of surgeons and nurses and after suitable sedation was formally introduced to Doctor Tulp who was said to be a leading soft drink nuclear dental technician, and he sort of looked like one thought Ernid passively as he lay there so helplessly and curious as to what they were going to do to him. Maybe murder him?

He was by now completely unconscious and snoring very loudly so it was no problem for them to shoot up with an arsenal of drugs including heroin to make him relax.

They unscrewed his robot head quickly the same way a starter motor is lifted out of the bonnet of a car and rinsed, dusted his airways which were made of hosing out of a washing machine and declared him headless indeed.

His face and being were discarded in a bin as they screwed on a reconditioned visor on him while asking him all the time whether or not he was okay; and he really was okay even if he couldn't answer them in any cogent way.

They swiftly fitted in a new Speaker Phone with a lot more subtlety to it and more depth of the upper voice register and they tested his internal microphone saying 'One two, one two, one two!'

His heart they kept as there was nothing of any kind the matter with its old radio valves and aorta pump modelled from a Holden Fuel Pump but of course modified and streamlined. They put a doorbell in him so he could detect whether guests were there or not; he could even detect whether he was there or not. They thought of everything!

He awoke a few times during the rapid fire procedure and tried to ask some of them what they were doing but the drugs conquered him and he fell back into unconsciousness again which was sort of where he lived in perpetuity.

Doctor Tulp was the leading dental scientist in the universe and had done extractions on apes and astronauts and led the field in dental record manipulation and gum experimentation. He was a trifle hung over as a matter of record and at one stage tried unsuccessfully to fit a turntable in Ernid's foot to make him more like a gramophone.

Tulp bent right over his helpless patient and began to attach secret messages from the dead in paste form on the rear of his newfound gums. He was in a real state of disorder and basically fiddling where he had no good moral reason to fiddle because the results can be catastrophic and lead to a fair bit of death.

But he pressed on regardless and kept on using a watercolor brush with a most delicate needle-point to brush on the secret messages stored in a brown paste that were fairly hard to come by. It was called 'Memory Paste' and sold for a million dollars a brush stroke on the black market. It's street value was incalculable.

In the record library of the brand new operating theatre were ancient newsreel footage film spools kept for inclusion in scientific recollection testing. They came darkly out of treacle coloured reels or in tubes of water colour or even oil-based paint with sound grabs in it that went back to Edison.

In the larder there were many jars of memory dust, nostalgia powder, rejuvenation pastilles, tooth restorative ointment and newsreel drops that were so powerful one tiny squirt of them made its recipient go back to The Origin Of Species.

Hidden among the jars were horror creams stored in tin tubes which were hard to squeeze actually but once a fraction of it went on a gum the meaning of life went right into the damaged root.

Doctor Tulp found what he was looking for which was the restored print of William Zapruder himself that followed the original assassination from go to whoa. It wasn't the widely available print but the actual one shot by Zapruder.

The mad doctor carefully brushed the historical compound on the newly inserted molars of his patient, painted modern history into every corner of his implanted teeth and added an emulsion sound track for good measure. He clicked Ernid's new jaw over and over and tightened up the tiny metal hinges with his pump-action-screwdriver until it was all okay in his opinion.

'Are you okay?' inquired the doctor.

'I am okay as it turns out!' replied Ernid unconsciously.

'It works!' cried the doctor.

The problem was critical in that the surgeon had put twice as much cinema compound into the regular spaces in his donor teeth and the JFK movie got jammed between one of the upper and one of the lower ones, with the dire result that each frame of the incident in 1963 kept playing on and on, and jamming no matter what he did, so he had to see each gory frame repeatedly as though he were either the doomed President or Oswald the hit-man.

He did not convalesce long at all, only munching the one Milk Arrow Root hospital biscuit and sipping one economy tea bag with a drop of milk before he was untapped like some sort of Christmas present and hurled into the ambulance.

The ambulance driver and team were drunk and laughing all the way to his home-cum-hole. He wasn't much use to them in giving them any useful directions home as he was darned well unconscious again; and he obviously felt about that but what on earth could he do?

The driver was hurling empty bottles of wine directly out the window as he tried to read the antiquated street directory, the trouble with giving it a perusal of any sort being that the stiff wind that blew in the window collated all the muddied pages making it pretty hard to make out; and with the massive intake of grog it proved trying to find his home, while he was by now groaning like a turbine.

They pulled up loudly and nearly rolled the ambulance by virtue of the chaotic condition they were in, dropping grog bottles everywhere in their haste to get out. Then they couldn't get him onto his stretcher in the correct fashion as they were just simply too wasted.

They fumbled his important paperwork and lost his confidence completely as they stuffed around trying to remember who he was and just why they had brought him here. He was still dead to any world you care to mention; with his breakthrough artificial tongue not looking too great, in fact just about coming right off at one stage of the unloading of him into his hole-home.

'Just sign here, here and here!' they chorused and threw him a pen without any ink in it. He was forced to sit up nice and straight whilst they assisted in the signing.

'What's your name?' they asked and as he was in no condition to answer they dragged him out on his stretcher and slid him right down his hole in the one rough action.

He tumbled rough as bags down the hole along the mahogany staircase and balustrade that were beginning to look a bit down landing with a bump on the earthen floor of his general kitchen area as one of his big bloodshot eyes opened to show the rest of him he was alive.

'Good one!' he said to himself with undisguised rapture as he held his heart that registered a hearty tick as all hearts ought to do.

In his left hand he held a mysterious envelope containing an invoice from the hospital. He tried hard to run his only working eye over it but that wasn't so easy as he imagined.

He tried to come to but it took ages to crawl across the dirt floor and dodge the motorcade of Dallas as he did so because he was obviously in 1963 again. This time it wasn't illusory but real for he saw Oswald pull the trigger right next to his fridge and then witnessed the President take a direct hit right near his sink. The more the killing bullet went in his head the more the dishes and plates crashed to the ground.

'How upsetting this is!' he heard himself declare on the blood-soaked-floor as he tried to assist Jackie Kennedy from the limo as a stray cat wandered in to see what was going on; and the cat bore the same face as Ruby the nightclub owner.

Someone called security and the very next thing he knew he was imprisoned inside a cell having to front many violations to do with breaches of the peace and causing affray; but in his heart he knew he was innocent as a new-dropped foal.

He was given various strong sedatives which knocked him right out. Any resistance to the will of the police proved meaningless and almost sublime as he was now fully schizophrenic as opposed to partially. Even in his drugged dreams he kept seeing the assassination over and over the dead-real-flashbacks being vivid and more real with echoes and reverberations of the single shot making him scream and vomit in the latest cell they put him in.

It was similar to a giant chained sleeping bag that they zipped him up into, He kept wandering round like a demented creature, for such he was really, belting and banging his latest experimental noggin into the large padded walls, begging his guards to switch off 'the infernal machine' as he now called his inner documentary on JFK.

But no one tended to him and no one relatively human cared about him in there, only the unerring CCTV cameras trained upon his every move, with every twitch and gyration photographed and sent to Head Office for instantaneous assessment. He begged for help but of course none came so that he felt guilty about coming to Australia in the first place and wishing he were back in the old village conversing with owls.

'At least the owls listened to me!' he wailed to no avail as he thrashed and kicked the bottom out of the terrible chained up sleeping bag. Somehow he managed to escape its foul feathers and hay fever inducing pong.

'At least the owls cared about me! You in there! I am trying to tell you that the beautiful owls cared about me in the Old Country!' But he was conversing only with himself and no one else.

He paced about the ever decreasing cell that in the end was just a pin point in outer space, like an anaesthetized light or some force of man's will that couldn't harm or hit an innocent lemonade toiler like him.

'I need not to hurt any more!' he wept to overflowing but again there was no one there to assist him in his agony of general lostness but never foundness.

# Chapter Fifteen

## Absolute Soft Drink Memory Loss

It was not so much that he didn't have any identity as any future or venue to say this is me and I work here, I live there in that particular hole that the goddamned local council put in. It has a one bedroom truth to it which is irrevocably right and my mum stays with me now her hole has been developed and we get along okay really even though she is obviously older than me; you'd have to be in order to give birth.

He felt beaten up as if the Nazis had beaten him up but a lot of modern citizens happen to feel that way after being exhausted by modern medical science and also evicted from their only temporary holes that make habitats look nothing except a joke.

'I was virtually assured the second take at a head would be okay!' he most mournfully uttered although there was no available audience to mind one way or another how he was getting on in this new disastrous scene with neither beginning nor ending available. There was no program as there was no manuscript and no review and only a meagre share of the box office takings that amounted to absolutely zero.

He patted the components of his latest head on, screwed the newest mouth on pretty hard and was careful not to strip its thread because he didn't have a clue where now to procure another one. He had a strange numbness to his own face as though he had been doing a little too much dish washing without proper washing-up-gloves on.

His eyes thumped and ached behind his Halloween mask that seemed nothing like his god-given face, so maybe god didn't exist out of Prague where Home was, where history existed and his battery-driven-dreams escorted him. He managed to get just about every single new part on and in a jingling and juggling and squelching sort of a way he strode up the nameless road into the nameless city in search of meaning.

It appeared as if there had been a recent nuclear sort of war as all the great soft drink billboards were more than merely luminous but shining like suns or exploding planets, with the enormous pressure to sip only 'Burp' lettered by masters of persuasion into every artwork can of it as he traipsed along in a complete fog until he beheld a crèche that had lemonade-headed-children playing soccer.

He leant on their fence that was made of parents who had turned into pies and sauce through the recent war and he tried to mumble friendly sayings to some of the pie people to be communicable but they just hissed in their own mince.

He saw that the few trees that had been spared by the shifting of tectonic plates or whatever it was were made of packets of self-raising flour, no explanation given.

He cheered on a particular boy for kicking a good ball and one of the pie people hissed his mince aggressively at him like some sort of warning not to join in.

All of the pie people hissed minced encouragement onto the soft drink headed children who were so hooked on sugar they screamed if they couldn't have it even in the deed of playing.

There must have been over four hundred pie and sausage roll people hissing out of their sunburnt pastry bodies and moaning with minced disgust when a child missed what they saw as a sitter. Some of the pie fathers cast their own heads at the children so that mince went all over the oval and others just sat there scoffing themselves.

He wandered away to a little hill and placed his automatic hands on his unreal face as a gesture of surrender to the ones who make us do the things they want us to do.

He prayed to the god of hallucinations to give him a break; but sadly there is no god of any single thing to give us that chance and so he wept buckets of purest robotic frustration. 'Why do I keep on seeing that which isn't there?' he asked whatever he was, which was only a freak.

'I am so wearied of being a freak', he so soulfully admitted to his rust bucket self because as he looked down at whatever he could make out of himself there was nothing but a mossy finish and he could sense some of his bolts coming loose and one or two spark plugs seeming to come undone as he had lost all his energy completely.

The sounds of the booing patients diminished so he could at least hear himself speak, although in the old times in Europe you were too poor to speak to yourselves and it was considered the height of poor form to think at all as Hitler's tanks rolled in.

He wished he were Hitler because then he could be dead like Hitler.

In his present predicament he may as well have been Hitler because nothing was going remotely right for him. He looked at his left leg and there was in that instant a completely rusted-up tin suitcase that the fates had placed there for the express purpose of refreshment. It protested in a croaky way when he figured out how to undo it as though like everything else around him it was in a bad mood.

The lid of it literally fell right off as he opened it and in it was a street directory and a shotgun. Was he to see this as symbolism or another thing that wasn't there?

He fired the shotgun into his own brain and a dove came out.

'I wonder whether you can get breakfast around here?' he said to the friendly bird and clutching the rusted suitcase he set off to a new Nowhere.

The explanation-less shotgun was too heavy to cart so he made sure there were no shells in it and left it by the side of the groaning road with the relatively new edition of the street directory under his croaking arm; the various pages of lost streets and found avenues flipped and they flapped in a rather reassuring way it seemed to him as his difficult to understand medical breakthrough body shuffled and clanked alongside of his soul.

He walked into a Safeway Store that had in it a Repco Outlet that sold car parts direct to the public at wholesale price, so he variously clunked and rattled over to the desk where another robot clerk looked up from whatever he was reading and asked whether he could assist. 'Look', said Ernid, 'I do think I need some sort of assistance', and he for some strange reason commenced to cry most bitterly indeed right on the bell you hit when you want assistance of some sort.

'Whatever is the matter now?' asked the friendly clerk and put a brotherly arm around him to comfort his customer in the friendliest way possible.

'Look, I have no idea what I'm doing', blubbered he, wishing he weren't weeping since it is just so exhausting; but there you have it, he did weep.

'That, dear man, is perfectly understandable in times like these', said the clerk, and handed him a tissue with a drawing of a clutch printed on its surface.

'I think I need a tune!' cried Ernid and examined a brochure to that end after which the rather sweet clerk gave him a quote for a complete do-over.

'But I've just had a new head on in hospital you see?' cried Ernid but the clerk just looked at a timetable.

'They are pushing most of us out', whispered the clerk conspiratorially behind his hand, which action of course the new regime would obviously prosecute to the full limitation of the law. 'There is to be no more speaking behind your own hand during the reign of the present Government, sadly!' added that lowly Repco clerk, and now it was his go to cry and they shared the same tissue with the crest on it.

'I am most aggrieved to learn of that', answered Ernid and they both bent to each blow their noses in the most tragic manner to be sure.

But the clerk had the wherewithal to press a buzzer for extra service and two assistants of the same type and gender and in a no-mucking-about way escorted Ernid to a loading bay out the back and laid him on an ironing board in the full sight of passers-by.

They injected him with rather expensive brake fluid and put in a new set of points, then rapidly replaced his still fairly new windscreen and sealed it against moisture. They next added new windscreen wipers and searched around his legs for tyres and put on new sox instead with plenty of tread on each.

This third head job was done with industrial precision and a perfect comprehension of engine components. He began to come out of his sedation which was Valvoline Motor Oil laced with Aspirin and murmured a little so they put him up on a hoist and chained him up good and proper so they could examine him properly; it was two motor mechanics who did this.

In the end there was a fair bit of fuss and bother as to pinpoint the accuracy of parts such as where to unplug this rotor and on what foot to put what sock and whether or not to tighten up the chromium grille around his latest mouth or whether to put new tail lights on him and a roof rack that would come in handy if he wanted to shift addresses, which is always on the cards.

They took him down like a Christmas tree and walked him round the surgery cum garage. In their opinion this was as good as they could get him. He ached a lot actually but put this down to the wearing-in of new motor parts and as he walked about there was joy in his light step and surprise in his refurbished mind. They made him a cup of hot brake fluid and he sat on a fruit box as they gave him an invoice.

He nearly swore aloud as he tried to concentrate on the numerals and 'add ups' that swum before his so-sore eyes, his fingers twitching and fidgeting as they strove to clutch the paperwork; but he couldn't see the need for body filler in his legs that were already pretty stiff and awkward as well as all knobby and hard on the eye of others who saw him bumbling along life's old hard road to salvation and sense.

'It's ten thousand bucks all up mate but you can pay it off if you like over a few months; we won't come after you or anything like that!' laughed one of the surgeons as he swung a new golf club.

The two car mechanic human body parts specialists began to roll out a long thin green carpet and started putting brand-new golf balls into the tee and they invited him to give it a go to sort of get in the swing of new life and maybe start to try and enjoy life a little more.

'You have to learn to let go Mister Ernst!' barked one of them as he got down on his hands and knees to address the ball.

He enjoyed a few half-hearted putts and folded up the invoice and thrust it dramatically into his breast pocket and wandered away to find a coffee shop where he could with some degree of effort plan his future or indeed futures, there being in fact so many of him.

He clanked into a pleasant tea room, the last one left in the city and he suddenly became aware of all sorts of niceness such as fresh flowers and the assorted fragrances of people's make-up and deodorant and eye-liner and even the aroma of their handbags which possibly was the headiest of all. He ordered a coffee from a friendly lady who confessed to him she's seen him before somewhere friendly.

She was so pretty and looked Viennese or possibly out of Prague in some way and they chatted in the most laid-back sort of a way. He told her about his latest grease and oil change and new head gasket job and front end headlight focusing work, and she told him she had never had any sort of an accident in her life and felt sympathy for him. She stroked his front bumper bar that he hadn't noticed being put on.

'You're out of registration', she smiled, and he admitted he'd let it lapse because of over-commitment to his ailing mother lately.

Although the coffee shop was busy as well as not busy she sat down next to him and gently kissed his bewildered mechanical face with the utmost tenderness, and then patted his swollen eye headlights with a crumpled-up fragment of soft tissue.

She dragged her own chair in much closer to him and gently stroked his chromium front end ordering him some cinnamon toast which as soon as she said it was in front of him. She presented smiles to him he had not seen since his peasant times in the village where even bears smile from time to time.

She hopped up and mimed his clanking walk like a sore-footed robot, which of course was exactly what he was. She then sent him up viciously making the other coffee customers laugh and point at him until his feelings were rather on edge you may say, and he wept like a water falling man and she wept with purest ridicule.

He was so unused to the latest technological head and neck that seemed to sort of revolve of its own making with the agitating sound of some sort of internal mechanical indigestion or washing machine on its noisy cycle, the sudsy feeling all through him, the by now saturated invoice and the aching in his bolted-on-knees, so he just felt used up again and clonked philosophically away in search of more pain.

He sat down again on the city's only street seat as workmen came along and removed it the second he sat on it. He then started to look at the paper, the daily newspaper which barked at him like a seal.

At least he had the gloomy workmen to talk to as they carried him to a truck and threw him and the bench on to be demolished somewhere close to the town hall.

He thanked them both for being brilliant conversationalists and strolled in the most creaky fashion into a chemist shop on the fringe of wherever he was, which he was sure had to be Hell, and a guy walked up to him who only a moment or two before had been seeking a coin from seething motorists caught in a traffic jam by wiping their begrimed windscreens sort of clean again with a dirty squeegee.

He was not very well dressed but Ernid didn't care about his fashion sense and was pleased to sit before him in the drain and be cleaned properly with the wondrous squeegee and allow the sudsy device to give him a gleaming-look that is hard to buy anywhere, least of all in the street where just about anything can occur.

'What have you been up to today, mate?' asked the dirty cleaner of cars and people as he steered the device over every single portion of Ernid in the most dynamic way imaginable, every so often dipping the object down into his plastic bucket again only to bring it up again as filthy and depressing as ever. 'Like your head done?' he said, and without being able to form an answer the guy just did it.

He used the foul smelling suds and greasy water and a spongy stick to make him nicer looking and as well as that he employed old awful rags to shine him up new. The sparkles came to him so that he felt like a new robot entirely. 'How much, mate?' asked Ernid, and the whole thing came to only two bucks fifty.

He really liked his road cleaner and never felt better in his life so he gave him a tip of fifty cents and ran for the bus that would bear him home. He was becoming disorientated with all the oil changes and other alterations that were happening all around him, which is entirely understandable due to the world's chaos and the way people had become, like him in fact, machine-like and automatically vile and reactionary.

He paid the coin into the tentacle of the octopus bus driver who put its eight boots down on the accelerator straight away, driving so fast that many gasping senior citizens were forced to run down the bus as they got caught in his gravitational pull, with the travellers seeming to attenuate as they tore along the aisle between the seats; and they sure looked frightened as they hit the back of the bus.

Most of the passengers were soft drink toilers like him but he hadn't memorized any of their names and felt devastated about that actually but then again they were all rolling and tumbling by him so quickly he just didn't have the fuzziest who they were, just the rank and file workmates.

The deranged leering octopus driver seemed off his head as he hammered down the main drag in the seeming direction of the plant. As well as his mental condition he was screaming heavy metal song lyrics into his bus microphone in such a way that the falling over passengers, as well as suffering from concussion and not feeling the best, couldn't follow what song he was playing or accompanying. They just wanted the bus to stop and eventually it did as he went into a wall by the main gate at the front.

He clocked on as per usual and felt the old working class surge of pleasure as the black carbon typewriter-kind-of-tape bit with its chronological assuredness into Monday and made it 6.30 a.m.

It was so reassuring to file in with the last of the Mexicans and some of the other various new Germans on the morning shift, with everything normal again as in the old days that never existed.

It was nice to go into the changing room that never changed much into anything else, and while not really chatting with fellow zombies at least feeling kind of employed alongside of them, plus the fantastic feeling of being paid in whatever the Australian currency was going for; but he had felt a bit deflated last pay day when the money was in bottle tops.

As he trudged to his great vat the flashbacks started up again in deadly earnest as he saw his earlier incarnation fall right down deep again into the crushed glass. He made sure he gripped the safety rails on the downwards ladder with ample certainty of touch and was glad of the dopey big black rubber boots he had on.

A voice with unquestionable authority shook all of his new parts so hard he literally fell apart there right on the sluice channel at the base of the vat where mega mountains of crushed glass got hosed by gases only known in Outer Space and he watched on his boiled hands and knees as masses of crystals of soft drink bottles were swept along to a reforming vat not far off where the new bottles were formed.

'You are back to Square One Mister Ernst!' it boomed and echoed among the particles and fragmented labels. He quavered a lot at that voice because it reminded him of his father from long ago, further than The Old Country even and the way it boomed of course alarmed and frightened him.

He gazed across at his fellow serfs and lady slaves treading on the sharp angles of red-hot-glass. He didn't really like to admit it but the sight of their insufferable and continuous crawling for their bosses comforted him, it really did!

He was glad of the sad sight of them as they gave him peasant comfort in their eternal cycle of subservient misery and the sense that ignorance is bliss.

He grovelled and shovelled with them, not to ever understand the bosses but to be at their beck and call forever and ever and hope to put a dollar away for old age in some way.

'How many heads have you lost?' called out a lemonade serf with a troll look and a big bent nose with a whiskered bunion upon the point of it; he was somehow familiar but then again they all were in their martyrdom and dreariness. He loved them for their obsequiousness.

Once the boiling hot acceptance vat was patted successfully by millions of serf-shovels and the whole lot shunted into the gargling sluice-channel then all the glass got reformed and rejuvenated the same way honest workers are when they get to Heaven.

I've had three new heads!' boasted Ernid, but no one seemed surprised or congratulatory.

He asked who he sometimes imagined was his only friend, except he was a one-off, 'Where is my old family?', and his long and bitter tears ran along his much-shovelling arms and gathered at his work boots only to look up at their owner in awe.

Then the oddest thing happened, as the whole lot of serfs started to exactly and loudly echo Ernid's remarks, which he accepted as their lemonade legacy all right, and that even if they were as crushed as their vile glass they had the right to oppose bottled bullying.

'I've had three heads!' they all called back and there were paroxysms of uncontrollable laughter as the bosses looked on with big whips behind their backs. Correction by flogging was back big time and many a serf had died of his or her welts and unsightly wounds. At the top of all the mile-high-vats you could clearly see the dark-hooded-floggers circling in an evil way with the cruel whip behind their dreadful backs and a drooling leer on their cave-age-faces.

Sad it was to sometimes see serfs and lady slaves die in their work and end up as part of passion fruit Burp.

The real worry about the serfs who had mostly replaced the Mexicans was their fevered willingness to more than accept primitive working conditions such as ten minutes off a day in a rather tiring shift of very nearly twenty-four hours per day.

The serfs were aggressively militant as well and well-organized masochists who just adored humiliation and pain.

They were all exactly four feet tall and wore somber hoods on rough serge and sort of frock-things with bare sandals at the bottoms of them; some chanted terribly mournfully as they trudged up greasy ladders or sometimes down them depending on what was required by mad plumbers who saw to the mile-high-vats.

Ernid didn't really want to be monk-like or serf-like and loathed the hoods and dark crudely tailored skirt-things they had to put on, even the women serfs who looked completely crushed and crazy as they took orders from humpbacked managers.

If a worker was more than a fraction of a second late to start work they were flogged with all made to watch or else not watch if they were next; the fearful lash sounded something shocking as it whacked on the backs of the tireless serfs who chanted or moaned or shrieked or sobbed as the mood to do any of those came into being.

Management liked the new architectural plans they commissioned to make 'Burp' Pty Ltd just like a gothic nightmare or a monastery with all the trimmings such as the expert flogging of junior staff and the drawing and quartering of anyone late and the instant sacking of new people who had just started that very morning; this rude ruse was designed to hurl fear into people and although it sounds far-fetched to dismiss an honest serf before they have the chance to clock on it worked a treat.

The buses had never before been as loaded with fired plumbers, dismissed leading hands, sacked serfs, men and women of course, and dismissed rank and file of every description who had to hang around, often for a month or more, for the bus whose driver had just been put off.

Slaves who carted the gigantic barrels of oxygen and carbon dioxide and used air in the dark all the way from the super trucks at the loading bay to the miles of bubbling hot vats had to smile as if they were pleased to be there; at bosses who just loved to keep them in their place which was Nowhere.

It felt degrading for a man like him to have to look Mexican but even though most of them had been stood down and placed in a forced emigration program to return to Mexico the emotional need to appear Mexican still of course prevailed at the plant and nowhere was this mood more so that at the pumping station where he was to go on a twenty-four hour shift with one second to eat morning tea; a Gollywog biscuit!

'I hate being made to resemble a Mexican!' he muttered to himself in the very cold changing-room while noticing that no one else had to do it, but he knew his grooming instructions off by heart and sneered in the mirror as he put on his cheap sombrero.

He strapped imitation pistols round his emaciated waist, adjusted his golden spurs and threw down a double shot of tequila.

Then it was down to the old boring work of trudging around in circles at the base of Vat 1 until he was judged good enough to trudge around Vat 2.

'I am just so sick and tired of kicking jagged fragments of glass into the sluice channels!' he bemoaned but unfortunately he just had to dog it out as he needed the ever-shrinking-income badly.

His hallucinations ended in the vat so that he couldn't even hear JFK things for all the noises of glass getting liquefied and all hacked up. Hence he rather enjoyed the long shifts because there were no nightmares nor distractions and he simply had to enjoy the new Mexican look and take orders from Mexican-looking overseers.

The much-looked-forward-to one second meal break was the greatest thing of the day. Although you can't obviously go back in time, as well as that he was somewhat afraid of surrendering to time being dissolved before his very eyes and working legs as he often stared at them, luckily both, and asked his legs why slaves expected so little?

He trudged and he trudged around the morass of boiling glass and felt as though he had swapped his life for idiotic lemonade or his spirit for tonic water. In the serf café he idly stared at the unhappy visages of a multitude of fellow pygmies who were neither contented with their lot nor deeply miserable that they didn't have a lot.

He left his extra long shift around five in the morning and felt incapable of even walking as opposed to strolling. He could always afford walking but had always found the lost art of strolling too expensive. He strictly budgeted for walking and in his new poorness and daily and nightly discipline of both action and meditation he sometimes did add-ups in his brain to see a future of some sort.

As soon as he woke he swallowed six Anti-Assassin Capsules that did their medical and mental job of prohibiting frontal lobe projections of Dallas in 1963. Unfortunately the capsules were remarkably expensive even on his new health card so he had to live on a coin a day to get through.

He sat in a ditch that just happened to be there for the express purpose of such a thing, and pulled his pay out of his left pocket, which was just enough for the monthly hole rental with twenty cents over for food to keep him going to work. His monthly bus ticket had lapsed and he had spoken with The Housing And Hole Commission about the chances of somewhere nicer, but holes in any condition, even unfurnished and one bedroom today came at a premium and he was right out of those.

He gazed at a little crumpled up snapshot of his village and as he focused on it he saw his mother milking a goat in miniature in the foreground and his father just waving and smiling like a fool. He immediately wished he could be there with them when life was honest and elementary so unlike the complexity and viciousness of today.

It was good in the ditch and he could see that soon the public would be put in them to save money, with a Government House Ditch for the important serfs and just common ditches for the rank and file, as opposed to holes in the road the way it was.

He could envision trellised ditches and ones with roller door garages.

For a reason he couldn't hope to follow as he trudged home he stared into that rumpled and crumpled sepia photo of home with his innocent parents in it and his salty tears flowed down its faded detail until the internal pain fled his hide. He always thought of that epiphany as important in later years; the fact that the old photo was so common it was sacred.

In a perfect vision of ineptitude and physical ruin he stumbled along the strange main road thinking really only of ditches and how he had to soon provide for a two bedroom ditch for his terminally sick old mother and himself a.s.a.p.

He noticed bailiffs evicting persons from both ditches and holes as though there were no difference between them with hard indifferent enforcers of law personally beating up on their old friends and the drains lined with teeth and gore.

It was another Liberal Party Crack-Down on late or part-paid rental and The Government Of Australia had wearied of paltry excuses such as death or life with life being seen as the paltriest excuse of the lot. It had become much too expensive to live either full-time or part-time and all you heard was moaning or possibly wailing in every quarter of every bleak suburb.

The innocent had had it and were now being collectively punished by

No no, no.
don't get me wrong
Jacqués. You ARE
interesting but just
not that interesting.

bailiffs and paid thugs who only a day or two earlier had worked as lower order clerks for The Department Of Sustainability or train drivers or milk bar proprietors or demonstrators of speed boats on lakes that could be highly profitable enterprises indoors or outdoors but had through economic and emotional pressure turned into oppressors.

The most popular new jobs had to do with vindictiveness because you didn't need to learn it like wall papering or flower arranging. It just came naturally.

People being summarily evicted just took it in their humble stride and accepted getting pulled out of hole or ditch and watching horrid people engaged by the council to employ tomahawks on their desks and chain saws on their cupboards as if that were perfectly natural and human tranquility was subsequently banned.

The new atmosphere was forced gloom at all costs and crèches had crummy organ music piped through them around the clock to keep toddlers in their place, whereas their former place was happiness and contentment.

Patents who had the insensitivity to be late for their pickup were outed with their portraits pinned to popular meeting places such as the gallows.

If motorists dared drive with pleasure then they had their licences cancelled for life and sing-along-types of cheap entertainments were cancelled.

Dogs were to bark more mournfully and cats to sidle more miserably than ever before, and it was law now to bump others out of your way on any footpath anywhere while road rage was made mandatory with hefty fines for driving normally.

Christian drivers who permitted others to go ahead of them on the frantic intersections that were there only to make motorists madder were hanged in public and then fined a fair bit.

The year 2017 became the age of oppression with no excuses for being nice.

Ernid was so tired of it all he entered the incorrect hole this time and lowered himself down the melancholy council-designed ladder to a poor family he had never known before and who cried with more force and sorrow all the more for seeing him.

The whole lot of them were lying flat out on the earth floor trying to eat a still born carrot.

Their library was made of mud with their few books made of stone while the skinny mother looked twice her age; which she in fact was.

The children were eating line drawings of cereal. The bronze baked beans they were eating had fallen upon the floor and just lay there covered with unhappy flies.

'I am dreadfully sorry I came into the wrong hole, it must have really put you out', he sighed and apologized over and over but they couldn't have cared less and offered him a chair on which to either sit or live there with them. The father was so impoverished he spoke side on.

'We live very humbly here as you may see, he said with a sweeping gesture that took in the squalor and exhausted blow-flies that were so stressed they were trying to bear their young in order to have a companion to talk to.

These remnants of humankind were becoming the norm as opposed to the odd freaks of society who once hit drums outside railway stations to make bad music for a living or else went on talent shows on television and did impressions of people nobody knew or could in any way remember. And why should they? They were anonymous.

This motley collection of proletariat nobodies were nameless as well as without any talent and their entire day consisted of hanging out on the street smoking a mixture of chaff and cocaine donated by social workers to try to cheer them up.

Social workers had become the only paid workers of the world apart from those sods employed to make soft drink.

'We should like you to sup with us and break wind with us as well', one of them muffled behind his artificial arm that had once been the leg of a desk. Their son had a drawer for a head and annoyingly kept on shutting it over and over in a marked manner, only to undo it again and look into it again. Their daughter worked for Coles the only giant supermarket still trading in their municipality and it too was in danger of going broke.

Ernid was provided with a grandfather to sit on and joined in the meal which was mostly sections of motor tyres that had come away on the motorway due to wear and tear. The dusty knobby sections of thick rubber were boiled in hot water for a month and then sizzled with pesto so that they were a form of pasta for the whole tribe.

It was a touching scene actually with the poorest family on the planet all tucking into a wheel meal and mopping up the tyre sauce with sliced white toast and chatting together amiably. Ernid truly felt welcome and eagerly joined in the passionate conversation about where on earth the rest of their lives were going.

The mother and father were so impecunious they borrowed one another's memories and tried to brighten up the struggling talk at the tea table by recollecting things that hadn't happened to them; but their kids didn't care because they themselves were fairly boring and only had the one saying which was 'What goes around comes around'; but no one at the table had a single clue what that meant.

To save lighting costs they spoke side on or in silhouette which worked a treat and as they had no gardens they developed borders and flower beds in their bed to ensure that hope was there. 'You cannot live without hope!' cried the diminutive dad and all the children loved that saying and muttered it too as they fed tyre rubber pasta to their tireless mouths.

Road menders paved bitumen on their overhead roof all night so that the fragrance of burning hot tar floated down gaps and cracks in the ceiling but each family in that area found tar mesmeric and wept buckets if it did not come; the clothing they endeavoured to stand up in was of tar and their pants and skirts were of tar. When they ran out of Vegemite they cheerfully spread asphalt on their unbuttered toast and they mournfully thanked God for its yeast.

After dinner they sat around smoking tar in tarry smoking jackets and were so sweet to Ernid that he was torn between living with the asphalt folk or living again with his mother who was now toiling as a brochure.

Her new work was to do a meet and greet at the plant tasting section where tourists sipped experimental flavours and not to move a single solitary muscle; this work she found easy to do as in her village she had toiled as a target for The Third Reich and stood for weeks all alone in a stony field accepting her lot without grumble.

'I like the idea you are anonymous'. He smiled at them as they hung around the home bored stupid and in that moment he understood the need for an education and that there must be at some future stage an activity greater in intellectual pursuit than Snakes And Ladders at which activity the whole lot of them were hurling themselves into on the tufts that were the floor.

As he bade adieu he noticed that seven of the children went to the upward door with him all stacked on top of one another to look bigger, in fact over the top of them they had pulled a giant coat so they resembled a grown gentleman and gravely shook his hand to say farewell forevermore.

The mother came up the spiraling staircase and stood gallantly in the thermonuclear wind waving goodbye with a potato which was how she was shown as a baby, and the father wept into his two yard beard like anything to see his young friend depart after such boredom in their living room.

'I can't promise you it will be any more interesting next time young man!' he cried with the radiation in his preposterous whiskers glowing ferociously.

Ernid was saddened by his departure but had had them as they say in the street.

He tried to catch a bus to work but all the buses had been burnt by the incensed protestors who were just everywhere.

He stared as he strode at his time card that he loved with a fatal force as it was the only object that loved him back again. It never let him down and loved to get the exact commencing time imprinted on its surface. It alone knew his rank and file number and could probably recite it to him if it wished to do so.

All the new worker had was a time card and the exactness of the inky imprint as the mechanism for recording work time and start up time and knock off time got hammered into it with the identical ferocity of the human relationship between employers and serfs.

He stood at the blazing gates of the factory that loved him in the same way he feared it and never took time out to comprehend its wild and uncontrollable profit-making and sheer force of will. As he watched the thousands of honest demonstrators chanting for job security and a modicum of respect it didn't startle him to see riot police baton newborn protesters.

Because they had been out on strike for so long the lines of newborn demonstrators were frog marched, handcuffed, toughened up, hurled into black transit vans and screeched off to the factory correction centre for vicious processing which was often more psychologically nauseating than a baton over the newborn ear hole.

Experts whose task it was to estimate crowds' sizes were spontaneously downsized and reduced to skeleton staff.

A giant unfriendly tunnel was being dug underneath the city to connect something from another thing but no one could remember what.

The good aspect of this was that tens of thousands of construction workers now had incomes but were pathologically detested by the starving-hungry protesters.

Public fairness was formally banned in the parliament.

Flu was free so many of the hysteria class contracted it merely by being. It was a complimentary contagion and many lonely people decided to enjoy it and in an overjoyed manner hopped into bed to kick the bucket.

Midst all this confusion Ernid carried on continually with his mechanical third draft mouth and just did his level best to be kind to whomsoever he collided with.

Millions of people who were jobless had at least the flu to catch up with although the government promised complimentary job inoculation it didn't come into being until it was much too late and in the end the only work was watching other people work but there was no payment for that and as well as every other thing that was wrong it was boring so people in every single suburb died of boredom and were strictly buried in the most boring fashion possible to ensure cultural satisfaction.

A job creation scheme entitled New Envy scored a green light and for a limited time there a fair few people at least earned a few cents for observing others do pick and shovel work for the local council and elk patting in zoos.

It occurred to him he hadn't slept for exactly one century and had been thinking around the clock since he came to Australia as an original serf with a whole boatload of various other ones who had beat it when Hitler got into office; understandably his own family were thrilled to accept menial duties at the major soft drink company in this new country, and he had tried to be just one of the stupefied originals.

Part of him was like a spy obsessed with espionage and recording every single thing and object around him for future reference. Part of him was a humble drone who liked being depressed and loved to do stuff like personally lick his master's boots, while another part of him was a medical and scientific experiment in neurosis and psychosis, oblivious to the forfeiture of his soul. He was just a front, a label.

'Why do I keep on descending the wrong spiral staircase?' he paused to inquire of himself once again as he blindly clambered down into a hole where unknown soft drink workers were playing darts with the dead. He had seen them before, all of them from the old bad times when the German tanks had loudly rumbled into Vienna. Although that had occurred only in his mind it was as real as a flickering newsreel in a tottering cinema of the memory.

He sat in with a family of bottle top putters-on and immediately knew them, patted their bald heads and cheerfully joined in the knitting and the animated conversation which was in another language actually. Then he began to experience savage sorts of seizures that required him to hurl his body onto the earthen floor, revolve anti-clockwise and foam at the mouth until they assisted him to a makeshift bed in the cellar. 'Good one' was what he said as he fell in a heap of gratefulness.

# Chapter Sixteen

## Moving Out Only to Move
## Into Something Much Worse

The Anonymous Family put in a formal request for him to move in with them forever, so being a perfectly polite sort of a chap he accepted at once and asked them if his sick old mum could move in as well. They all agreed to that so he rang her on her goat horn mobile that she'd fetched over when she emigrated. Miraculously she had credit on it and it rang as she breakfasted on a hedge clipping at her own hole.

'Ernst residence how may I assist you?' she gargled feeling immense relief when his machine-made-voice came on and they chuckled the second they heard one another, even though they were only around the corner geographically speaking.

'A request has been made for us to move in with people we don't know and I thought you might like a bit of a change, mother,' chuckled Ernid. He had no idea why he was amused by the idea.

'I'll have to change', said his mother dramatically and then added that she would need half an hour to sort their possessions out and separate jumpers from trousers and stack their rare jazz recordings in plastic soft drink crates which were becoming more and more difficult to find.

'Will you need some sort of transport, mum?', he queried, but she said she'd get a burro and so he left it at that. 'We're at 15 Thing Street', he added good humoredly and she knew where that was as there was an illicit milk bar there. She packed up her few belongings including World

War One brassieres and a parachute guaranteed to open and rang for
the next available professional burro; she had just enough money on her
person to pay for one and it duly trotted over and whinnied outside.

The Anonymous Family were thrilled with the chance to meet
new people and happy that all of them got on the same bus to work and
wouldn't have to try any more to chat with strangers to make small talk
when the end of life is arriving on the planet.

'Isn't it hard talking to people you don't know?' said the patriarch of
the new family where Ernid was so suddenly taken in.

No one in the big family had a clue what their father was talking
about so they cut him cold and started on their hedge pie.

Ma back breaking and front breaking too trudged over to her new
home pushing her pram with arsenic in it and flour and scone mix, all
you need for a new start. It wasn't that hard with the pram as she turned
up the volume control on her head and listened to classical music along
the way which was littered with armies of thoughtless vagrants who were
so unmindful of the anti-litter-laws that they hurled themselves into hard
to get at drains and edges of lamp poles.

Ma saw so many people who had philosophically become litter and
quite cheerfully sat in bins because they had nowhere else to study Marx
and the teachings of The Street Directory which was voted Number One
Best Seller of any book on ideology; and people at impoverished parties
liked to quote from it.

She noticed grammar school children had opened up their umbrellas
a bit too swiftly and those cute expensive things had got turned inside
out by a tempest nobody could possibly see coming and which tugged
them up into the heavens that were of liquid fire and so on.

Ernid was so enjoying breaking scone rather than bread with the new
family who were engaged in the mysterious hunt for a real date in one
of those scones. They took off their serf hoods a bit and looked at their
new friend with remarkable familiarity as well as relief that he looked
just like them.

'How long have you lot had to put up with mechanical mouths?' he
asked them but they didn't know as they didn't know anything. 'We have

been so poor we have developed one collective mouth into which we put a single scone once per month, while the rental on our hole has practically skyrocketed lately; but we are hanging in there you may say', said the father as he put his hand on his wife's motorbike tyre leg.

There were at least a dozen of them and on their calendar they only had the one word written in black that said 'Work!' on each day of the year and 'Death' on the holiday page although it wasn't certain what that joke meant. It was possibly an in-joke.

They were so depressed they started to play Scrabble on one stale square of ravioli and then moved into Snakes And Ladders on the same bit, which they cheated at and slobbered over like mating German Shepherds.

Although he was sort of in love with them the old awful feelings of JFK came back as he joined in with them in their games listening to the dice and his so suddenly greatly amplified heartbeat that sounded like a market truck backfiring.

He sweated and shook and they were aghast at his transformation as he glared at them and muttered anti-communist speeches made by paranoid White House staff a long time ago.

Sweating and shaking he plucked up a plastic clothes peg that happened to be on the tea table and rested it on his shoulder as if it were a rifle and pulled it.

'The single shot theory!' he screamed and they couldn't handle him.

His horrifying seizures made it hard to follow precisely what he was saying so all they could do was point and laugh at him in the tried and true manner of serfs.

He bit hard into his cloth serviette lips till plasma arrived. He was shaking so much the family had to use a skipping rope to tie him in place to a wall just to try and relate to him. They asked him to try to keep his voice down as they had a sick child who thought he was a mudguard and was running a very high temperature; but nothing could cease his vibrations and ranting and raving.

'The single shot theory!' he screamed again and they looked inside his breast pocket for his last few remaining Anti Assassin pills and luckily there were just two left so they forced them both down his throat and hoped for the best.

He kept on screaming out that he was a true Cuban but they didn't get it.

'I didn't use a telescopic sight!' he moaned loudly as they reluctantly assaulted him by punching him up and tying him to the bed in the guest room with several dressing gown cords. That ruse worked.

All of this activity was being watched by his masters Mr Burp 1 and Mr Burp 2 from their telescopic tower via moon-driven enlarging lenses and they were pleased with what they saw.

'A perfect paranoid droid!' they sang and clapped their palms in delight.

A wicked scientific dentist had come up with JFK dentures that had footage of the hit put into the actual ceramic individual molars so that each time the recipient closed his or her mouth a shot rang out as loudly as possible.

Their unheard of plot was to make evil of soft drink to such a point where suggestions and automatic thoughts were programmed through each and every sugary bubble into the consumer's memory-bank to make them not merely submissive but slaves to profit margins so large that no other bubbly beverage could hope to compete with them. The assassination of JFK was the most famed moment in modern or any possible history and Ernid was the prototype of sugary submission.

The public found themselves walking in a state of hypnosis to milk bars in the midst of time passing and guzzling it till it overpowered them. To make someone believe they were some sort of an assassin was the wildest thinking in the universe; to make them believe they were murderers gave them cachet.

'Bad taste sells soft drink!' muttered Ernid constantly after the third mouth had gone in.

They had tried him out as the human and inhuman face of sugary intoxication and knowing that decadence and gluttony are more popular than unselfishness the masters at 'Burp' Pty Ltd were terribly confident that murderous intent boosted sales.

In his fevered brain he was the secret ingredient of murder and spontaneous violence that got belted out over radio in every nook and corner of the Universe and with each brain-pumped-seizure the occurrences of Dallas in 1963 fizzled and snapped as he saw possibly what no man should see; the great flying chunk of intellect come flying out of the beautiful president's head.

When that happened the whole earth changed irrevocably and it was demonstrably proven that lunatics can do murder to great leaders in the name of vanity or misguided socialism and the people of America have never been the same, while the people in Australia have been made jaded by it and pageantry has become an end game.

The Anonymous Family he boarded with as well as them being so kind as to let his sick old mum live there too had gone to a lot of trouble to dig a spare room out of a cliff face at the rear of the property so mother and son could relate to each other and even nibble crackers in there and have a secret read.

Books became banned in Australia, especially fascinating ones and the only kind of publication was the city-to-lemonade-plant bus shuttle timetable. It was the law that the million who worked there got there on the dot of their allotted shift or they were put down with a syringe in front of everyone; and that could prove terribly embarrassing as well as frightfully expensive as burial costs were on the family.

The terrible frontal lobe attacks ceased completely when he basked in the kindness demonstrated by the new folk he lived and worked with. As though it had never been there was how he felt, reassured by their thoughtfulness at every millimetre of his longed-for recovery.

He lay in his ever so nice and friendly bed made of turnip scraps and all the internal havoc got turned down and the projection spool of his hot forehead became not icy but cool with a perfectly average temperature. JFK was gone like a newsreel in a movie house that had vanished.

The much-feared council evictions continued apace right round their neighborhood but possibly through a bureaucratic oversight The Anonymous Family were spared and although they were perturbed by the news service of a night that depicted lots of people having their beds and undergarments tossed into the street it felt just great to be left alone and just attempt to be grateful.

He and Ma went off the lethal Anti-Assassination Capsules cold-turkey and they never felt better in their lives. There were lots of theory-addicted people out there tearing up their prescriptions and saving a heap at the last few pharmacies still trading; people were tired of feeling under siege and being perennially unhappy and needed a power boat.

Special laws were passed in the parliament which permitted police to strip search one another around the clock and even harass each other and incarcerate those who looked a bit unusual. Although they all did so they just had to hack it; many police were so stressed by being undressed in public that they became strippers.

The Federal Parliament was nothing but a house of ill-repute, in fact a house of burlesque as the debauchery of so-called debate was nothing but unscripted hysteria with the abandonment of Question Time. Idiocy was the thing that mattered and the public of course didn't.

It felt so groovy not to be doomed into believing assassinations overseas were his doing and that he may now fall soundly asleep in the same ditch as his mother in the sure realization that they could never be separated; and if they became so poor that they had no books they could easily read one another's minds in the spare room.

This was the new groove and the new arrangement which would last for the remainder of his lemonade days; the last few attempts at peace only discovered with others and his dramatic shift from self-obsession to the great strengths of solidarity which had always eluded him. He swore a new allegiance to his employer and vowed internally to give strangers a break and if they wanted him as a figurehead again he would cheerfully do it.

For a month there he had a regular routine of toiling in vats as per usual and trying hard to enjoy overtime. He got on well with one and all, the inner voices and inner assassinations went down in volume as well as pictorially, and the regular taking of incredibly expensive Anti-Assassination Capsules really worked as his General Practitioner swore they would.

It was so refreshing now to fall asleep on the motorcade but to know it was an illusion and that even JFK was an illusion, as the capsules contained prohibiting ingredients including Gloom Loss which apparently came from The Horn Of Africa at great cost but took away mental images that only proved distressing, such as assassinations accidentally pasted into new gums of new artificial mouths like his third one.

There were no bang noises in his head, no images of ailing presidents and peace was his so long as he and his old mother did the vats.

The new family dined with them both as soon as they got in the door that led upwards into the blazing hot road known as the upper air, which at least was gulp-able.

One night he rang the cops and got through to a senior sergeant in archives and they had a proper chat about any likelihood of earlier trouble with the law, such as affray or running amok with weaponry or eating a person within the meaning of the act.

To his utter relief he had never done a single thing wrong and still had ten demerit points untouched on his car licence. He chuckled actually out loud when the policeman assured him he was clean as a whistle, even cleaner.

'I'm off the hook!' he kept reiterating until he could begin to believe in his innocence and at the same moment take in the obvious fact he was sleeping in an anonymous room where this new family or tribe had let him in.

'They have let me in!' he repeated until he began to see in his mind their friendly visages and friendly everything else. They even had good manners and the entire lot of them had sweetly bestowed a single kiss upon his retiring forehead as he exited to repose in a home he hadn't known before they came along like an automatic focus.

He quickly checked that his mother was safe and sound and somewhere sleeping in his unexpected room, and there she was just the same as ever, lying across his legs to keep the end of him warm like an eiderdown.

It felt good to be looked after with so much abuse going on all the time. He saw his faithful shaggy toothbrush in its rinsed out glass on the bureau by the bed and it comforted him immensely.

He permitted his old mother to have a bit of a lie-in and hopped in the family shower; they were so in debt to the water company they physically showered together and there were a heck of a lot of them in there when he went in, they were all vigorously scrubbing and solemnly passing the ever-diminishing sliver of industrial soap to one another and sadly singing a sea shanty when he came into their collective view.

There had to be twenty of them in there and when they all called out 'Ahoy!' to him he laughed for some silly reason and asked for a towel.

The mother of them gave him an opportunity shop one which was one dimensional.

'You're next in line!' she giggled and he giggled with her but waited in the hall for his go with the tiny chunk of soap.

They all ran in different directions and roughly towelled themselves down with anything which was dry such as a curtain or the embroidered cushion of a chair; they were a rough and ready lot!

There was a slovenly ancient grandfather who lived there and was surprised to see some of them grab him by his whiskers and give themselves a thorough drying with him, not that the old chap minded much as he kept on saying that he very much wanted to be of use.

'The JFK hallucinations aren't projecting!' he cheerfully announced to his still-sleeping mother and felt compelled to politely boot her body off the bed.

'I am more than happy that they don't', she replied earnestly as she hastily fell.

'It's just that they are a contagion and you've clearly passed them onto me!' She decided to experience a full-on-seizure and had a bad one to her liking.

By this stage the Anonymous Family had got out of their communal shower and reassembled in the first stage of the living-room, the second stage being outside.

There were so many of them in various advanced stages of insanity and yet there was something touching about their cannibalism.

Eventually everyone in the place got up through the upper door-thing that with big hinges on it led to the road. They caught the lemonade bus and went to work without having the foggiest clue as to what time it was; and that was okay with their managers because the pay was the same if you lived or died and every shift was the same.

The Burp Company had increased the rate of servitude and misery foisted upon its serfs by banning morning tea and having Golliwog Biscuits flogged in full sight of the poor things that did all the dirty work, the carting of pails of coconut tint up hard to see sets of slippery steps and the appalling peeling of various fruit to add to the flavours that were nothing like their pictures on trams and buses, etc.

Babies just arrived by caesarian section were taught how to crawl down bottles with rags to give them a good go-over. Babies were redeemed by toil and were at the perfect age to work long shifts on the conveyor belt that seemed not to conclude, and it was a heart-warming sight for bosses to see them use labelling guns on cartons of soft drink at only a week old.

Ma was having serious trouble focusing on her own work which was stacking difficult boxes on top of each other until she couldn't see them much any more. She was having the identical hallucinations of her son and as she stacked the boxes she heard shots ring out from The Book Depository Building; even though she was in New South Wales. She screamed as the actual bullets whizzed by her ear.

It was all the fault of the dental scientists who had used past paste by error and inadvertently glued some of it into her false teeth so the past had really caught up on her as she strove with all her heart to do her toil; but the things of the mind are more real than we tend to give them credit for and she screamed loudly as she rocked and shook in a complete circle on the warehouse concrete floor.

This time however Ernid was well acquainted with mental phenomena and as his stricken mother lay on the dusty dirty factory floor, literally cork-screwing herself about and screaming about the gunshots and conspiracy theories her loving son cradled her as if he were the parent and reassured her it was nothing but shadows and a play with voices. She didn't appear to take much notice of these assurances at first and had to be carted into the sick bay where several other serfs lay writhing and shrieking due to all of their conglomerate theories and there was no doctor.

The factory doctor was busy at his own place of residence where most of his family had come down with JFK hallucinations and he was himself beginning to hear shots on the imaginary motorcade. The whole area had its victims and the anti-virus capsules were running low. The poor doctor patched up his suffering family as best as he could but there is a limit to pain killers and sleeping tablets and human prayer.

Because of the epidemic the company were losing profitability in every corner of their expertise and therefore sorely tempted to re-hire sacked Mexicans but so many of the originally sacked ones had shuffled off to their original country so they had become very thin on the ground. 'But they were so cheap! We miss them!' moaned the bosses as they tried to dream up new ways and means to win the Mexicans back.

Ma got so bad she had to be taken home. But which was her abode after so many real and fake ones, so many makeshift places of temporary rest amid the raging crisis of not enough Mexicans, too many JFK conspiracy theories that boomed in uncertain political times and dreadful leadership displayed by poor thinkers in the shaky Government.

It was hard getting her home as management refused to shout her a taxi and the buses were out due to a protracted strike as some of them had come down bad from the JFK virus and again management were looking at Mexican bus drivers and advertising for them to return at once with a new pay deal. But there were few genuine responses as none of them could possibly read or speak anything but Mexican.

The only way that the son could cart his stricken mother was to carry her body across his still-broad shoulders all the long way home, with her seeing Oswald up there on them and flinching and twitching like a live lone nerve-ending, the fate of lemonade workers without proper health cover. There appeared to be loud explosions happening in the dull red heavens and loud distorted demanding voices calling out in vain to go back to work.

'It was a single shot I tell you, a single shot from The Book Depository

Building!' raved his demented mother forming foam around her so-challenged cracked lips so that the scurrying son had a hard time of it just managing to keep-her on him. There were loud church bells in his ears but no churches anywhere near them. Their constant gonging was hard to bear but he strove to locate any of their old addresses by ever changing streetlights.

'They used an explosive bullet on him, an explosive sort of thing on him so that his brains came out, his brilliant intelligence came out in a torrent!' she wailed and writhed ever harder and more difficult was she to cart in the flickering nuclear light of the final curtain of all available soft drink.

'Mother please stop raving, it will do you no good to go over and over it!' he whimpered and pleaded but she raved ever more as he staggered along.

All the holes seemed even darker and their door-openings harder to find in the lurid darkness. He saw exhausted bottle top teams that he had worked with get very irate trying to see their own particular doorway; many had lost their keys and were trying to lob bricks through thickened windows to get in. That is a terribly hard way to get in so people had become vandals, to their regret and cost.

Window glaziers were making a pile putting in newly busted glass windows and plumbers too were raking it in by virtue of whacking in new pipes because of the wear and tear of ones that had too much orange lemonade pouring through them. It wasn't quite known how that had occurred but it just did and homes were destroyed by it unless an honest trustworthy plumber could be summoned to fix it all up again.

'A single shot it was!' Ma screeched again as by sheer fluke he stumbled into their real doorway. He fell through it as it turned out, so that they both fell in collectively. Her seizures had become so bad he left her foaming around her cracked lips on the kitchen floor in a writhing mess and got the ladder out to find the Anti-Assassination Capsules in their small medicine cupboard.

'Only one left!' he heard himself cry and deftly flicked the remaining capsule right down her crazed throat and waited for her body and mangled mind to take it easy. Both of them did the second the miraculous medicine hit her ailing bloodstream.

Her body sat up nice and straight again and she patted her formerly furnace forehead but it was decidedly cool as a cucumber. She was a living and healthy entity again and in a dream went to the kettle filling it from the tap, spooning out a couple of lots of instant coffee and making them both a hot drink.

'Gee Ma you had me worried there for a second!' he uttered as she visibly relaxed on the spot. They switched on the television catching the early morning news bulletin and what they saw confirmed his worst suspicions.

A huge fireball had arrived from the heavens and swallowed up New South Wales in one big hot gulp; it wasn't a bush fire but a temporary bit of bad luck.

'This is just about all we need at the moment!' he said to himself; but of course she heard.

'You do get a bit sick of trouble!' expressed the son to the mother and then they had to eat at the end of the world, always not so easy unless it's another false alarm which it nearly always is due to news bulletin ratings.

The only substance of sustenance was Gag in a new powdered form that was processed by depressed headhunters in New Guinea, sponsored by *Time Life Magazine*, so they boiled a bit of it up in their only dented saucepan and humbly poured it into a pair of badly cracked soup bowls where it lay foully.

'Not so foul as last time my mum!' called out Ernid as his just-recovered mother tried gallantly to come at it. 'It still tastes like death to me!' she sneered, but to her everlasting credit managed to spoon a fair amount down her throat.

They didn't know what to do so they didn't do anything, which is as popular in Australia today as it ever was in Europe and the promise of nuclear warfare only makes it more popular in suburbia.

He reached across the scattered and silted tablecloth to pat her forehead and was relieved that her temperature had completely gone, like her mind in fact.

Again he had trouble with dates and times and his old mum was in and out of focus like a much blurring clock; he was programmed since birth to know the day of the month and the time of the day but had no idea of either of those great forces of destruction.

He read his feeble mother a feeble fairy story that always made her relax because it was so reliably tiring and distressing, a revised account of *Snow White And The Seven Dwarves* only set in Sydney. She purred as her dutiful son turned over the illustrated pages and read it out in the old village way that she could identify with entirely. 'More!' she salivated and wept to hear. 'Much more in fact!'

Pathetically they read their bankbook as they shared the same savings, the same everything and each fortnight they read their latest balance by candlelight or the last vestige of hard-fought-for hog fat that afforded ample light for such a crucial add-up.

It seemed they were in the grip of unpaid fines for imaginary funeral services as well as huge fees for new asphalt work out the front rolled there by unhappy council staff.

They touched freezing cold noses with stalagmites forming it was so cold; and through foggy opportunity shop resourced reading spectacles donated by our country's blind they saw to their shock they had two cents left in it.

When people are as poor as they were they collectively sigh together to save on wear and tear on the body and the shagged-out-mind so it was that the impecunious skeletal mother and the sort of normal son sighed and eye-rolled simultaneously.

They were that hungry they thought they had eaten breakfast the night before and patted their concaved stomachs with ample satisfaction and went to work on the night shift.

Many exhausted serfs were refusing to become weary and worked two long shifts in the vain effort to fill their larders with enough canned muck to get through the winter that seemed to run on forever, smacking its iced chops.

They lined up as per usual to punch their worn down time cards and noticed a fair few dead in the line who had perished of advanced starvation, their black tongues hanging out and their faces full of dark purple horror-looks they were swept up on the spot by council front-end-loaders and sent to rot at The Tip; their waste was then recycled back into soft drink bottles. Fair enough.

The long night shift never really ended for it is pretty much forever night-time in soft drink factories that boil the stuff up in mega billion ton vats for urgent delivery to the universe's last milk bars. Tonight Burp was catching up on a popular new line called 'Pine-Burp' which imitated Burp mixed with unbearably over-sweet pineapple and the addicts of the world were automatically hooked.

'Are you having conspiracy theories mum?' politely inquired Ernid as he manfully descended the slippery great ladder to get down the bottom to help hose out the tanks with mops.

'They seem to have gone, son!' she screamed as she put in the hard yards with her particular mop, her favorite one that seemed to mop faster but that was just Ma's wish fulfillment because all mops at 'Burp' Pty Ltd mop at the same fixed speed which is flat-out. By Jesus did Ma love to mop the vats!

Not much is known about Ma but her indelible and unconquerable passion to do precisely as she is told. Anyone will do as long as it a person of authority and she bears the agony of crushed knees and crushed shoulders and crushed Achilles heels and it was born unto her baby body to know her place and that place is to be a slave in The Capitalist System till Hell freezes over; which it is overdue to do given the global climate crisis.

She is actually happy down on her painful knees mopping up the fragments of smashed glass that the X Ray machines have somehow missed. She is like a clucky hen the truth be told when she can feel the savagery of serfdom bite right hard into her weatherbeaten tits.

She just needs the agony to never conclude and the misery of tugging her forelock to her betters, her betters being the ones who oppress her day and night while the pain and abysmal suffering she sees as her entrée into Salvation; it isn't of course but billions of serfs like her get it that they shall never have a holiday and how completely inane it is to picture

stuff like a yacht or good food.

She is shown as an example of the perfect serf to potential new serfs who crawl their way to the fifty mile long soft drink plant in search of the security of sorrow.

Human crying is what they'll be willing to work for.

# CHAPTER SEVENTEEN

## THE FEAR IS UNDERSTANDABLY ACTUAL

About this time which of course happens to be timeless and in its way increasingly meaningless since masters of industry do not care a single whit whether the globe continues to spin or drop dead from exploitation it occurred to Ernid on the double night shift in the vat that he had no hate in him. Why that was eluded him and began to plague him in the same way an annoying tummy ache upsets its owner.

He felt he was too passive for his masters and the picture or portrait he had of himself which he knew he kept in his heart was someone who never resisted a single evil; and evil was on the march in the world all around him and was surely made manifest in the morose manner men spoke or the oppressive dialogue of shop stewards or the sudden sackings of a multitude of workers without any degree of warning.

The lemonade factory was positively booming and extending its physical as well as metaphysical operations, and with new sections, new ideas and new Mexicans to make the dreadful and dangerous stuff, the way was clear to get Australia diabetic by the year 2017 come hell or high water.

Ernid was neither young nor old but a gloom in between and just trudged around literally at the bottom of the pile on his dreary treadmill, sometimes pausing at his locker to take a peep at one of his dilapidated scrapbooks that his mother had carefully pasted articles into with a loving and marvelling hand.

The well-preserved pictures showed himself as famous and a global hit of 'Burp' Pty Ltd and he half-grinned to himself or shrugged as he took in the look of himself only six months ago when he was their publicist and movie star; other shots depicted him giving the thumbs up signal in hospital and showed his revolutionary mouth that worked on a remote.

His was a life he actually never had and he knew he was a used up figurehead for an ever expanding company of dead souls who perhaps had their origin in Nazi Germany in the late 1920s with the doctrinaire of dread.

The philosophy of fear had come of course quite naturally to Australia in the persuasive game of Capitalism where profit makes honest workers mere pin pricks and their masters just ordinary pricks incapable of any symptom of human feeling. He was badly injured not that long ago as were hundreds of what the middle order management called scum; and yet every single serf had the right to hope for a hug.

The Australian Government banned human embracing in 2013 and that included friendliness of expression in a person's home and especially in a one bedroom housing commission arrangement where a hug could have come in handy. The rules of The Government meant that all dialogue in the parliament had to be rude and very cheap and hopefully nasty.

Kindness even in churches was put an end to with the humble wooden collection plate electrified so that no thieving worshipper may knock off a twenty cent bit. Holy Communion was altered so that the worshipper who ate the water cracker had to pay for it out of his or her wages. Talking to anyone you knew was heavily taxed and public trust was axed as there was no point in it.

Banking in Australia changed to an inhuman degree so that old people were forbidden to run a bankbook even though they were seen as too unintelligent to add or subtract, and Indian well-built muscle men were paid handsomely to act as security guards in banks and laugh hard at white trash as they loped in with that eternally hung-up-look on them or pushed their prams stuffed full of dirty bent lower order coinage.

It was strange that of all unknown countries on the face of the earth ours was gamboling down the gurgler at so rapid a rate. The people pretty much did as they were told but were tiring of instruction and battered leadership that took the form of a put-down with no enlightenment anywhere and no cultural practices so that ballet for example was to be only done by the blind.

Industry was over and hundreds of greedy insurance groups completely evaporated like steam off the country's crumpet. The only thing of worth that was intact was 'Burp' Pty Ltd and oddly enough its huge profit each financial year just about kept Australia going. The only work was to boil more sugary soft drink that buoyed the dollar but at the same time kept 100,000 people in guaranteed misery.

Public holidays were done away with because there was no fun in life any more. This was voted on by both houses of the parliament which made laughing a capital offence with execution a dead certainty; never had it been worse in the land even during white invasion over two centuries earlier when terrace houses were invented for white rich and The Municipal Tip for others.

The poor were shot which saved them a great deal of anxiety whilst the ruling class were encouraged to be thoughtless or just gloat all day about their properties and other assets such as pomposity. Pomposity was taught at the very last technical college to receive enough funding to keep going, and the managers of this worthwhile house of learning were intrigued to discover just how popular the arrogance classes had become.

Each night after work his mother wept herself to unconsciousness as she struggled hard to read the saving passbook ledger print-out that guaranteed them both enough to both pay the beastly rental and scrape together enough essential ingredients to make life-giving Gag. Her kind son wanted to read her 'The Three Bears' but she said that she couldn't understand any of it apart from the repeated reference to porridge.

They huddled closer and closer together and dreamt the identical prosaic dream that the factory was waiting for them. They envisaged it open and mentally pictured all the vats waiting to be stomped in to eradicate little dangerous fragments of plasticized glass that could be dangerous or even lethal to devoted customers who clamored for it every single second.

The rich were the new heroes and instead of Anzac Day they were paraded through the heart of town in jeeps and Rolls Royces to look great with their official ribbons of fantastical importance to half-hearted cheering and jeering from the crowds that were forced to clap them at gunpoint in a supreme effort to reboot nationalism.

The passion inside those mobs on the reversal of Anzac Day was to become a seething hotbed of resentment that not even the few police who were under thirty stone in weight could do much about. As the gauche wealthy citizens waved in the most bored way imaginable to their underdog selves the mobs screamed in bitter agonies that in the end have to become revolutions.

Ernid and Ma sat at home this important day and viewed the solemn display of financial courage with deepest respect for the fallen, the ones courageous enough to make big money in times that were no good to the ordinary rank and file. One after the other the pompous speakers spoke of the beauty of loot.

'Loot of itself is very splendid and it is no use turning up your snot box at it!' cried one old billionaire. Splendid booing ensued and then other rich got up and urged the disgusting poor to live better and look to a courtyard or a terrace with a god-damned terrier tethered to a stake in it. 'All poverty is illusory!' cried the second hero and rather surprisingly she got a big hand for that calculated remark.

Through each public address system in the land the grotesque impoverished had to hear about investment properties and insider trading and the importance of proper jackets and stunning dresses and how to coast upon the begrimed necks and shoulders of one's downtrodden brothers and sisters in ignorance.

'It is when you take that you get the idea!' screamed a billionaire but no one expected him to say that one and someone threw a fold-up-chair at him on the breast pocket and would have probably hurt him. The organizers had put up colossal television screens all through the red carpeted streets and each rich man and woman was given all the time they needed to impress the lame.

A surprise speaker was Jesus Christ Of Nazareth whom no one

recognized and here was this boring caravan salesman talking about the need for pop-up-trailers and air-conditioned caravans that could make it all the way to Broome in Western Australia if need be; in time of continuous soul-searching he said it was time to forget motels.

He didn't go over that well with the crowds who expected no doubt better oratory and maybe a little more attack in the speech which was seen as conservative, even useless during tough times. He had a fold-up chair thrown at Him too.

Another remarkable alteration arrived in the society whereby the rank and file were encouraged to seek redundancy packages at home in order to save costs, so that mothers and fathers voluntarily sought the sack as they lay in bed or weeded their small gardens. These cost-cutting schemes were automatically given the green light by managers in every walk and crawl of business.

Men sacked their own children to curb costs such as being there, ladies fired perfectly decent men whose only fault was that they lived, and children found weaknesses in the contracts they held with puppies and cats and put them on notice to quit the premises at once. The result was hardly anybody was left in any sort of way to keep things going meaning factories shut and as did people's mouths since it was now unlawful to speak.

Australia's name was changed by referendum to Automaton and folks liked it better than the old one by far, as they were proud to be nobodies led by richer nobodies in a quest to shut down costs of any sort that included the prohibitive cost of rising in the morning. All that sort of nonsense was put an end to unless you rose to be a serf and as a consequence hated yourself.

But no matter the hardships it was the fact that people still hung in there and obstinately refused to let go the noble idea of making a buck no matter what.

Millions sleeping out juxtaposed against a few doing the cigars and the new order was called Automatism.

Not a single change was questioned with every new hardship passionately embraced as though it were the living air that came at a polluted premium; new offences raised profits for local councils such as walking too close to another serf while the penalty for illegally tailgating another pedestrian was disembowelment and forfeiture of assets.

There were no police to judge correct and incorrect living and just speed cameras to take shots of people illegally popping groceries in their prams or pausing to chat to someone they had no right to know, an act that was unpardonable as was everything else in the new order. The human enjoyment of talking was banned with stiff penalties for breaches of The Silence Act.

Public hesitating was forbidden as was refusing to be rude to your neighbours in any street or the refusing to slam car doors in cramped driveways of blocks of flats in order to rob repose from your fellow Automaton.

The universe of course kept spinning around and was not very interested in the outcome of the human race on the planet Earth. The gods out of boredom listened to radio 3AW each day and night to swoon along with Elvis and all the other crooners who had romanticized life way out of all that is recognizable in the dreariness of daily labour and eternal serfdom. The dear old universe was of course delightfully detached from profit.

The new awfulness was accepted by the mega billions that toiled to keep eviction away because sleeping rough was the one horror nobody wanted to deal with, being seen as the ultimate drug of dependence, while trying to get to sleep in an alley was nothing more than substance abuse. Times were not just unpredictable but rigidly enforced by a regime of public servant mobsters who kept things dreadful.

Some unfathomable atom of archival footage had found its dangerous way into a certain batch of pineapple-coconut-lemonade, the accident of food science, a bungle in a lab and Ernid had been the first recipient, so now it was commonplace for citizens to replay the JFK assassination in their heads and complain of headaches and repeatedly hearing a single shot or seeing grassy knolls on their evening supper table.

'Burp' Pty Ltd gave their workers counseling but it was tenth-rate in many respects and even the professional counselors began to hallucinate and need very costly anti-assassination prescriptions to be filled out at an all night pharmacy.

The latest politics were draconian but of course people accepted restrictions and penalties and insults from above as drops of fresh rain, the other problem being the increasing evictions occurring in just about every single one and two bedroom hole. Naturally children were scared and insecure when councils proved their prowess by hiring thugs to cast the poor out onto the grinding and deafening thoroughfares.

One moment people were just about to play a game of Scrabble and munch a crumpet by the gas fire and the next thing thugs were smashing up sofas with pick-axes and pulling out refrigerators and hurling infant's plastic lunch boxes into wheelie bins, with no explanations given and just half an hour to fuck off.

Indeed eviction got so common it was nothing but a bore for The Hells Angels who were paid a healthy commission by councils to hurl people out. The cops didn't really care that much because it was boring for them, unless they had a heart for the future; and it must be said that one or two of them had that and refused to assist in suitcase-throwing out of perfectly honest holes in the road.

Luckily for Ernid he had paid his hole off and thus his old mum and he boasted security over the bullies tipping people out in a daze of bewildering dust and mayhem. He and his mother lived in relative peace down in their bunker but could easily hear people's furniture being pulped and desks and shower screens getting jumped upon not more than a foot away from their digs, something they found very upsetting indeed.

There was just about nothing recognizable left of Australia, which had become a war zone of some kind with mass eviction the only proper life-force. Indeed with recalcitrant householders refusing to leave their warrens the army and navy were called in to detonate and shift all the debris to the tip.

Evictions took place at Municipal Tips constantly and the maggoty men who toiled at tips were thrown out and replaced with ogres just the same. The only thing that made a jot of sense was eating but pretty soon even that was not very possible as all of Australia's food was buried to save on the prohibitive expense of eating it.

Politics changed for the extreme worst and instead of old traditional well-established seats there was Coles and K Mart and Woolworths for marginal or swinging seats and no local members of parliament left to go to bat for their old electorates.

The only aspect of existence that remained identical was sugary drinks that the lazy and hyper public couldn't possibly do without.

Lately Ernid's third mechanical mouth was playing up on him big time with its forward gears and clutch jamming so that it proved impossible to sip or to munch a single particle without experiencing fabulous pain – not that he resented fabulous agony in any way because he came from peasant stock where it was the only thing to enjoy and trust in any way.

It was almost but not quite a deed of masochism for him to keep on going with his calling which was to earn an ever diminishing weekly wage and take proper care of a woman who thought she was a shoe.

She was heading for eighty and quite rightly became a useless shoe for the tread of others in the system of work where there is no reward but misery with a print-out embedded in it . The mother and the son comforted one another as best they could during the wildest storm of clinical depression the country had witnessed.

All her son knew to do was hop up of a morning, put his jocks on, try to get his latest mouth operable, and try to gnaw tasteless dreadfully costly breakfast cereals in order to power his body up a hill. He was so reliant on puffed wheat he got very edgy if there were none in the packet; that was where he spoke gruffly to his shoe mother who was so timid she talked to her shoelaces in their own language of obsequiousness.

Her only word was 'sorry' which she perfected until it positively shone through the mumbled gloom of all other stabs at words. She said 'sorry' to her son when he didn't quite catch what she was saying but that only resulted in his saying 'sorry' back to her.

If they had no food then they ate apologies

Pain was worshipped, especially back pain and to this end the Government handed out free physical agony which was 'on the house' so to speak. Most citizens liked pain because it was honest, couldn't come any other way and was free and very reliable. People lined up at medical centres for ages for a new batch and swallowed it down instantly, without bothering with a glass of water or anything resembling comfort.

In the last occupied hole in the road Ernid and Ma experimented with Financial Agony, a new breakthrough capsule that wonderfully increased all kinds of rheumatism and arthritis by destroying the central nervous system in five seconds. The immune system was conquered by a similar capsule with the whole revolutionary concept being to strip the human being right down to the bone and create an unquestioning sub-class that didn't cost a cent.

The hard times came for Ernid when he ran right out of Anti-Assassination Capsules or was down to one left in its sachet which he always kept in his breast pocket even though he didn't have a breast in it. He felt incredibly awkward deep withdrawal from the pure need to relive the murder, just thinking about the moment when he ran out of the tablets that stopped it.

The anxiety of not seeing JFK murdered ate right into his spleen and at night the poor thing writhed something shocking, similar to a heroin addict not receiving a fizz.

His loyal mother surprisingly nimbly got up out of her bedclothes that were telephone directory pages and located his last tablet that was programmed to drive hideous memories away. She nearly fumbled the tiny pill and being a peasant with a peasant's sensibilities she held it and stared hard into it trying to see JFK.

She cast it down his hatch and the writhing stopped as smartly as it started. He wasn't seeing anything except her ever so hideous face but one with love in it; she cared that he lived and that they ate Gag, in that order. She was so poor she dressed in a shadow and they rode into town together on a packed bus full of lunatics who thought they were going to a soccer final.

They noticed that the council had increased the necessary evictions quoted by the Government to raze the planet, and one after the other they watched helplessly as perfectly smelly and unwashed scum were hauled out of their holes and cast into the main drag. Their putrescent warrens were then either stocked with hares who could breed there in peace or the awful holes were filled with strong disinfectant and set fire to.

It was an awful scene indeed to observe honest scum get booted unceremoniously out of warrens that for all their petrified jocks had become recognizable habitats, recognizable due to fragrances that defied understanding and bookcases stuffed full of bills for power and gas supply that no one could possibly afford.

Over and over as they went into town to look at the depressing Christmas decorations in the civic square they watched Housing Commission Hole people get roughed up by the cops right outside their now sealed-over-properties; in some instances those evicted victims tried hard to hang themselves on plastic branches of the big public Christmas tree but were forlornly cut down by the grim-mouthed-authorities.

'I wonder whether the cops have ever been evicted themselves, mother?' asked Ernid, but his mother had either died or gone to sleep.

'But are they the same thing?' asked her son aloud; he only really trusted talking aloud because it seemed like some kind of guarantee that it was really he who was speaking. But he was fast learning the new scarcity of guarantees.

The feeling was such that only humility worked in favour of the masters and a serf had to boil up all the latest colours of global lemonade or go on the dole which was so small it cost five dollars to get up in the morning, and fifty cents to smile or go to look at a gate.

Ernid was suitably disappointed when the neighbours were evicted from the hole they had paid exorbitant monthly rental for ever since they signed the lease to become unhappy. The father wept in public to see the sniggering thugs hired by the council rip up all of his family photograph albums and kick the best of the snapshots down the drain to the not laughing of all the other neighbours.

'It's like they are trying to take away our incentive, mother!' he caught himself saying as the thugs came up and checked out his lease to see if it was in credit, which it was, but only by a narrow margin such as a fortnight.

Door after poor door that swivelled upward into the dusty road was padlocked with a sign stating it was a property condemned and that access was a breach of the law. Then evicted armies of exhausted people trudged towards the only thing they knew, which was the lemonade factory that kept on expanding in size and profitability and never shut no matter what.

People can endure anything except death so they set up temporary camp outside the vast plant and bore their young in windy flapping tents. Many a baby was born outside the pineapple-coconut section and was addicted to that flavour ever after; merely the passing particles of pong made them lifelong addicts.

About this time *The 7:30 Report* covered tent life outside 'Burp' Pty Ltd as a feature segment on The ABC. Viewers who hadn't had their television sets seized by The Hells Angels were horrified by the detail.

Drunken hefty thugs shown kicking defenceless people out and then urinating upon their grandchildren in a way that could only be described as insensitive and unhelpful. The segment rated highly but nobody wrote in to express shock because human comment had been suspended permanently.

# Chapter Eighteen

## The Political Awakening of Ernid Ernst

He was of course beginning to come clean and understand the massive philosophical and political alterations occurring in Australia, a land he emigrated to a few years ago in company with his honest father and mother, simple and trusting plebeian souls who had dreamt of butter going on their bread rather than cancer as it was in The Old Country, where that particular Government made you sick for different reasons, namely because Europe had too many serfs in it and it was vastly overpopulated.

And therefore this new place called Australia appealed to their sensibilities as it was said in the backblocks of Prague you got a fair go there, that mild mannered wallabies shared their lunch with you, houses cost a few hundred bucks, your side fence got installed for nothing, people were kind in this sincerely sunny continent and that they were not bigoted nor mean.

But it was immediately apparent to him that they had been badly misinformed before they alighted from the vessel which fetched them here, and that it had nothing to do with sunnier dispositions, any more than in Vienna or better cows' milk available at the oddly named 'Milk Bars'.

Possibly due to the fact that The English invented Australia as a prison it had hobbled off in chains to a crummy start, with convicts hanged if they put a daringly European-styled shirt on or got whipped if they smiled during boulder-crushing duties.

The family had been programmed into believing swagmen were fascinating bohemians who played the harmonica to deaf Greeks but the fact was they were nothing but smelly thieves who couldn't hold a note of the simplest tune.

The father had died of Australia because he anticipated friendliness and human happiness. The mother and son tried hard to make the adjustment but had turned into serfs before you could say Jack Robinson.

Ernid after his third mouth reconstruction was hearing more historical voices than ever and was obviously screaming lullabies in his sleep to try to take it easy.

Every day he wept by the grave of his perished papa.

Because the two of them did nothing but work on twenty hour shifts of swabbing vats of boiled and broken plasticized glass it was pretty tough to make small talk when they got home; not that they exactly had a home any more by the way.

Holes in the road had been sealed with fresh thick lovely tar while folks tried to just stand in a paddock at night and put up with the boredom of that, which wasn't easy.

The notion of individualism and neighbourliness was over just as a fair go was over and the society was now cashed up or dead on the spot, with chemist shops now charging huge prices for simple pain-killers such as aspirin and telephone companies adjusting the cost of wake-up-calls to more than was worthwhile even waking up, because all a citizen could do was go to a factory and be sacked at once for having the brazen cheek of believing the job was going to last.

Ernid and Ma now slept rough and just stood side by side in a small vacant lot right by the sealed over hole they once called Home Sweet Home.

Their only comfort was a phone that had a wake-up-call in it and whenever it blared away they showered in the pelting rain and caught the bus to work together.

Thousands of similarly evicted people wondered where their former entrances and exits had gone to and just had to like it or lump it in their graceless ghetto, whereas the rich in their mansions ordered yachts to beat off the boredom and enjoyed really late luxurious outdoor hot breakfasts. Even their pampered puppies enjoyed puppy lattes and spinach on the side of baked bacon.

It was by now unlawful to enjoy anything even a seizure if you were impoverished, and most people were impoverished so they had their seizures in a paddock or behind a boulder, as they were by law to suffer discreetly.

One of the few treats was yawning but by law that was altered too and no longer legal unless you were listening to Question Time on the radio.

On a particular Friday night well after they both completed their vat mopping tasks the two battlers went to a late night cinema to take it easy after toiling twenty hours straight. Ernid made the final payment upon a tub of popcorn which they nibbled whilst a documentary came on about the murder of JFK.

Ernid's eyes completely popped out of his chomping head as he and his tired old mum observed a computerized version of the single bullet theory, the presidential cranium exploding in 3D. It was so realistic that cleaners employed by the movie house put a vacuum cleaner on to sweep up all the bits of brain.

Ernid fled to the cinematic lavatory where he threw up with all his force but there was no one else in there. He had expected there to be lots of vomiting others but there he was again really suffering and wishing he'd never swept a vat in his working life.

'I'm not feeling too good, Ma!' he ejaculated and she had to admit he looked bad.

They endured the night with him repeatedly hallucinating the JFK hit in a free paddock, one of the few still habitable with a tap in it so they could make tea. Ma kept on boiling up hot tea on a portable gas primus stove that saved their bacon, and the two sipped life-giving tea until an ambulance happened by to see what the fuss was.

'My son keeps on seeing JFK's head come off', Ma explained, and the ambulance staff pointed out just how common that was.

'It is just happening all over the country, madam, and there is not a lot we can do about it to tell you the truth of it. It happened fifty years ago but folks are only now really taking it in. It is of course delusional.'

They took him to a hospital that was screening the most vile documentary ever made on the hit in Dallas. Ernid groaned as they popped him on a wheelchair and ran him through the screaming wards of delusion suffering ones who could produce not one syllable of sense and just barked and foamed at their mouths.

It occurred to him even though he was right out of it or in a psychotic state as more than three-quarters of Australia was that everybody in the hospital was either Oswald the lone assassin or JFK himself, dead or alive. The very nurses closely resembled Oswald or Kennedy, but perhaps they had realistic masks on.

He received this time in theatre a donor mouth and not an artificial one and the tricky operation took over a week in total, with much more comfort in the chewing of offshore mints that he was particularly fond of, and which cost him usually two dollars a bag but were cheaper for some little-known reason at the hospital of Mouths.

The expert specialists stretched the donor mouth very tightly over his nose all the way to his gulping throat rather like the way a woman puts a stocking on. They tapped the lips with prods and tapped the donor teeth with other prods, then in went the donor tongue that felt so much better than any of his other ones. They included donor saliva glands so he could spit whenever he felt like it and swallow.

All he really knew of his benefactor was that he was a fellow serf at the plant, who just like him, had fallen under the big copper pulverizing rods of a vat, but unlike him had retained his own mouth. It was in his will to leave his mouth to a fellow serf who obviously needed one to eat his cereal of a morning properly as well as talk and chew chops if it came to something like that. He was Anonymous like all serfs but Ernid felt adoration for him, whoever he used to be, as he saved him.

He enjoyed rehab, doing the treadmill with the new mouth on and could easily feel the breeze coming onto his body from the electric fan over the handlebars. He did the exercise bike in the same manner although both machines confused him a bit at first.

Most of all he loved the weights and began with the smooth one kilo ones but quickly progressed to the two kilo ones and built up a great deal of sweat using them to define himself.

He was released earlier than expected and never felt any better the truth be told, his delusions ceasing the moment rehab informed him the latest mouth was a winner. He was invited to dine with other successful donor mouth recipients at a new restaurant entitled Mouth Lodge which was wholly inaugurated by the charity wing of The Government because it seemed like the only way to go.

At these sparkling dinner occasions he proved a very popular orator since he was one of the few raconteurs who could be even marginally understood; the new lips opened and shut more than efficiently and the teeth were realistic enough to be believed; and the new voice was terribly confident and didn't boom as was often the case with dinner speakers which could be annoying after it goes over the comfort limit.

He enjoyed speaking via someone and something else and hardly gave a thought as to who it was gave him speech, let alone life, that mystery beyond questioning as well as understanding. Maybe the donor was a raconteur? That would account for his quality of new metaphor.

He felt he joked in a new way, even a revolutionary way, but it was most enjoyable to give animation to thoughts unimaginable were he still a serf with no grey matter to kick around.

He had just enough cash to buy himself a brand-new-tuxedo and a sparkling pair of patent leather speaking shoes because good looks are terribly important on a speaker's tour, and he was still relatively good-looking for a man of thirty-odd, even though he had been through many a mill as the saying goes.

He took awkward questions from the large audiences in a completely spontaneous manner and put critics of new body parts at their ease, the unflappable new mouth allowing him to ask ladies out and he now frequented art house cinemas with good-looking companions who openly flirted with him, although they only went so far and didn't make it to the bedroom with him, new mouth or no new mouth.

A woman at the local council put him and his mother on a waiting list for a walk-up-hole which was the latest accommodation concept around, as they had been successfully trialled in the USA and everything that seems to work okay in that country is soon imitated in Australia; so he was pleased to go on the list.

Since every single road was now sealed over with hot tar the new housing idea was to construct great ugly pylons and poles and attach a one bedroom studio to them with a fridge and a single mattress, then the lucky tenant would climb up a preposterous ladder and let himself in; or herself in as ladies really went for them big time.

Since they had no lifts in them he had to carry his old mother right on his still-strong-back up 12,000 steps to get in and deposit her aching old frame on the council-made-mattress and let her flake for a while whilst he put on the frozen fish fingers.

He liked frozen fish fingers and wished he'd invented them or at least some of them, as he looked at them and understood them and that very soon they would be in his gut, and in his mother's large intestine tract to keep her animated.

With his new mouth came the chance to take in soup so he put on the electric kettle and boiled up flounder tea that comes with flounder flavored tea bags that you repeatedly infuse into bubbling hot water in a cup of your own choice; you then sip it and grow older.

The society loved the home atop a pole idea and purchased them in kit form from various warehouses around the land. They were easy to assemble and nothing but a joke to live in, some having a nice balcony surrounding the top bit and others even boasting a spa.

Homes upon poles were the height of fashion and the ordinary serfs lived extraordinarily well in them until they sometimes fell off them, and it was a darned long way to the ground it ought to be pointed out.

Wealthier people had a lift installed and sailed up to their rooms at astonishing pace with nothing really to look at except the birds who all had whooping cough.

Now he wasn't delusional Ernid decided to entertain and invited the cleaners from work to rather expensive suppers and he and his mother served up the Gag as soon as they arrived, probably not expecting such a dish but out of polite manners having to request its ingredients to take home and commit infanticide on their young.

The new idea of only inviting cleaners to parties caught on and it wasn't long before there were what was known as cleaners only dinner parties where the discussions varied from how to use a big stiff mop on a perfectly dry surface like concrete to who was the best impressionist mop cleaner to come out of Paris in the last century.

Cleaners love to elaborate and also to hit each other over the brain with damp serviettes. No one quite knows why that is, you'd need to ask them.

Because of his new and sophisticated mouth and his interest in entertaining Ernid began to invite intellectuals to partake of his mother's Gag and they flocked to it.

There were only five intellectuals in Australia as it turned out so they had ample room to dish up and entertain, the food being always awful but becoming a fad with the secret recipe for Gag being published in *Woman's Day.*

Sometimes after a few too many liqueurs his old crazed mother raved on about conspiracy theories because she still had the brainwashing problem with the intellectuals offering all kinds of reasons as to why she was off her nut.

She was boring after too much grog and got all weepy when she remembered things that never happened such as World War Four; but they forgave her ranting and raving and suggested she get a new mouth too; but she hung onto the old one out of sheer obstinacy and also because she was profoundly stupid, a fact she was proud of.

She often got completely carried away during philosophical talk and spoke of Adolf Hitler and how he'd invented The Roll-A-Door and how that had been used in armored tanks with particularly great success.

The mother and the son were by now the same character which suited the creeping conformity of the country of choice they had sailed to many years ago. They only cared about one thing, even in deference to Gag the thing or food that kept them going, the one aspect of life that scared them more than extinction was being late for work.

They used to turn up a week early to get in good with the bosses, not that it counted for anything much.

Because there was no employment left in Australia except for the making of lemonade it was not so easy to get a job in a monopolized industry. Soon there were accounts of the long-term-jobless impersonating a paid serf by looking slightly more cheerful than usual in a country driven by clinical depression and high anxiety, in fact both of those illnesses were right out of control you'd have to say.

Of course nothing curtailed the production of billions of bottles in plastic throw-away-form, inhalants and cans and self-perpetuating-straws and lemonade in tablets, and even in the physical form of whole meal and white sandwiches, as the country consumed much more than 'Burp' Pty Ltd could manufacture for its own addicts of life-threatening-sugar.

Mister Burp One and Mister Burp Two, both dressed in pitch black and wearing a classical monocle and smoking a cigar, looked down on the city they both controlled and felt glad that profits were more than up; things had never looked as good and Burp and Fanta just couldn't keep up with them.

They had re-hired lots of destitute Mexicans and seen the error in their ways of hurling them out of an industry that only they could understand properly; not all the serfs were called Jose but a heck of a lot were!

Ernid was grooving on not having vile hallucinations in his mind any more and was trying to teach himself yoga and having a lazy lie-in of a morning. He was even practising his smiling on other unsmiling serfs just to see how that would grab them.

But the second he woke he went to work with his ill mother on his back; that was how they got there unless they saw a bus.

They both decided to toil ever harder for the firm they always totally believed in, the company that gave them a complimentary bottle of soft drink at the annual Christmas do.

They always had that do to look ever forward to and made a mental note to dress excellently for it and not to complain about annoying cancers on loved ones or go crook about such long shifts such as the current one thousand hour straight one they were on. Ma got herself overexcited when a servant offered her a free cracker at the do last year and darned near choked on it; and Ernid was pretty hung-up about that.

The times they endured were certainly strange where all sons carted all mothers to the same factory if the god-damned bus was running a trifle late; that was what you beheld if you were on the road to work with them: long skeletal legs carrying brain-dead mothers on their backs in order to be early for work that they loathed in an almost diabolical way.

And of course management laughed at the incredible effort of the serfs with mothers surfing, as it were, on their son's broad shoulders, the only meaning in life being the goading mechanical time-clock which seemed to somehow grin at them as though to say 'Now what on earth are you hurrying for? You there punching on the card. Do you hear me? I am the meaning and the way of death and even after you two have carked it I shall enjoy the timeless spectacle of other slaves of our factory rushing to look good for the Boss!'

In the company canteen it was possible to debate the JFK assassination due to the fact that every single channel televised their own interpretation of the Dallas Motorcade and whether it was a lone assassin or The FBI and the tired staff sometimes wearied of the same show; but it was seen as better than defecating.

Ernid had a very brief affair with a bottle top girl who spoke no language whatsoever except signage as she was born dumb. They used to meet on the roof for a session of completing a crossword puzzle together with nothing on, or in a small park, one of the few without perverts in it because lethal pervert bait had been successfully laid there by the ever vigilant local council, and that ruse had worked.

Ernid sat on a park bench with the nice bottle top girl on his knee and didn't need to say a single word because she could easily read his mind and could see he was from Prague as well as trustworthy. It was heavenly to be caressed by someone with whom he felt rapport without needing to speak; the friendly wind expressed his eternal thanks as she pressed her face to his perfectly new one.

After his thousand hour shift they consummated their feelings towards one another, always in the same pretty and anonymous public park that had been viscously sprayed with anti-pervert aerosol to keep the scum back, well back.

He felt such love and trust for the bottle top woman he rather foolishly cut her a key to get in at night. She had to shinny up the enormous supporting pole to reach him at the summit but she was very fit as well as dumb so she did it.

He used to hear her dumbly coming in, tip toe-like across the parquetry of his modest aerial home in the heavens and then the sheer ecstasy of making wild love to her with his exhausted old mother asleep on his back. It was a strange but suitable arrangement and it worked out okay unless she heard them at it.

But she died one night of love and Ernid was absolutely shattered having to endure the ancient form of alienation and sexual frustration he had had to put up with since birth, and it was a hard old fight to be certain. He summoned the doctor who pronounced her 'worked to death' and she was speedily buried.

He never saw her again but often remembered her, even her face, even her name which was 999 and swore he'd be reunited with her again in the next shift, the next life, even though there is only one.

He kept a picture of her in his locker and smiled at it during his one second break at Morning Tea, a thing he eagerly anticipated even though he had to go to the tin locker with his old whining mother physically right on his back, so he could only stare at his dead girlfriend with his mother gasping away, always eavesdropping, always looking on at his stuff.

His mother required him to cart her to and from the women's lavatory almost once per minute, since being chronically incontinent she was always waterlogged and weepy. That sort of stuff made it really hard for him to put up with; although lots of serfs put up with whining frightened incontinent mothers just like he did. Nobody in Australia appeared well and certainly nobody laughed at the endless cut-backs on offer.

Electrical maintenance serfs were fired so the quality of electricity was dubious to say the least, with power failures in every single milk bar in the land and polar bears hired to smash up ice with their powerful front claws.

On a certain Friday the company actually shut down for half the day in order for less lemonade to be made. It was suffering from surplus, in particular the rum and cola variety, and all the serfs could do nothing but go home and weep that things had got so bad as to invoke liberty at such short notice. Were they put out or what!

Ernid talked it over with his dying old mother and they decided to attend a session of debate at The Parliament just for the heck of it; what had they to lose but half a day of bubbling up cola anyway? They walked in their accustomed fashion to the old Parliament building and sat politely together in the public gallery, she on his back as usual.

Although he always voted Labor as he realized they were on the side of the working-classes he couldn't see that it made a jot of difference if they ruled or The Liberal Party ruled; so far as he could see there was no management of Australia.

When he and his so-sick old mum sat in their chair to view Question Time in the Parliament. What was on offer was chaos, constant interruption and The Speaker weeping as he crumpled completely from a barrage of insults and cruel remarks delivered like poison. The Parliament was poisonous.

Nothing physically very violent happened during the hours that he and she watched proceedings but the air was vicious and the faces mean and unloving; unlovable were our leaders and narcissistic their regard for all that mattered; which was their pay packet and their fancy car to and from even more abuse and vocal hostility.

'Maybe we should take the voluntary redundancy package and go home to Prague?' asked he but she couldn't really concentrate on her answer much, not with the angle she was lying across his shoulders and doing all that infernal groaning and so on.

He walked them both home all that long way with her going crook all the time to him underneath her failing but heavy body; her whining just made it harder and longer to get back to the pole-home on stilts.

She was so fatigued that she slept in her sweaty work clothes right on him on the camp stretcher they used to get unconscious together on. Her bony legs stuck right hard into him and hurt him actually but there was bugger-all either of them could do about it. She was simply a burden on him.

When he had to hop up at night in order to urinate there she was also right on him; they were joined together like a Kit Kat.

He liked having a delicious read of 'The Phantom' on the lavatory as a rule, that was a thing he looked forward to for it was quiet-time in its way, and he used to keep a big stack of 'Phantom' comics down under the pipe at the back of the lid but he didn't feel like reading it whilst she sat there on him, not really, as it put him right off.

He had to speed up his wee-wee in order to bear her sheer weight pressing down on him out there, so he hurried as he pulled up his saturated jocks and muttered in his native language as they struggled back to bed again utterly spent and sopping-wet.

It occurred to him to get the district nurse to check her out but she refused on the grounds of lunacy; and he had to agree that she had something there.

When they finally managed to get off to deepest sleep they both awoke to a replaying of the JFK assassination right outside their bedroom window, performed a mile in the sky by extremely skilled actors in fact.

He was so tired he couldn't tell if it was real or make believe and in the end succeeded in crashing to deepest repose whilst his mother managed to pull herself off him and make it to the bedroom window for a closer look-see at the murder in Dallas so long ago.

He was suitably shocked at the response of his mother who simply rolled over, still on his head, and confessed that she'd had it.

He slid right down the great pole his home was on and tried hard to establish for his own benefit whether or not the convincing actors he'd seen before were still about, but nothing was there of any kind and so he shrugged, one of the last things still on the house in Australia, and ascended the pole and got back in with his mother who was screaming her head off in there.

Nothing he might do or say could assuage her horror at not just her own hallucinations of JFK but everything; she screamed that the plant had closed down and that they no longer needed her on her shift. He had to fetch tissue after tissue to assist her with sponging down her grievous and reddened cheeks.

They held a family meeting, which wasn't hard to pull off as she lived full-time on his shoulders so could always make herself available, maybe after work when they came home on top of each other, or a quiet bar where they could take it easy, or maybe in their miniature kitchen where she sipped her coffee on his neck muscles.

He coached her in meditation techniques he'd mastered as a small boy back in The Old Country such as hanging around a milk bar all day. That nearly always worked and was cheaper than paying an expert or getting hooked on heroin; and that idea was a distinct possibility if she didn't snap out of it. She kept chanting 'I am the lone gunman!' over and over until he could scarcely bear to hear it come out of her mouth.

To his continuous horror the next door neighbors were the ones disguising themselves as Oswald and Kennedy, and even Governor Connolly and Fidel Castro, and all the real life characters involved in the assassination story; and late at night these neighbors darted round screaming and shouting and firing off impressive guns.

They didn't pack it in until the wee hours of the morning, which was when Ernid carted his mother into work on his neck again and they feebly clocked on.

Their legs were getting very tired of walking around in perfect circles and edging the broken glass particles towards the gaping and freezing cold sluice channels. They were becoming more ground down than their own never diminishing product, glass that never really disappeared like the billions of consumers around the world who gusted into it at every chance.

He wept one day at work when she retrieved out of her grotesque apron a perfectly preserved biscuit, in fact a Calypso Cream, his favorite one and said 'Happy Birthday my dear!'

He bit right through it successfully and they chuckled together at the minor triumph.

Although it was five in the brand new morning they had no tiredness whatsoever in their physiques or minds so they decided to keep on working in the most demented manner to hopefully impress their masters. It must have worked because they noticed half a cent increase in both their miniature square pay packets on pay day, so they kissed the little coin and planted it in the volcanic top soil in the hope it would bear its young and make them both prosperous.

Later they went out to Potters Field where the anonymous lemonade serfs are buried and bowed their joined heads over their father's tombstone, hoping he was in.

They pushed an imaginary door bell and out he popped to say 'Hi!'

'More hallucinations', said Ernid aloud but his mother was still seeing the man she married so many years ago. She saw the real man or the mortal ghost, whatever he was she saw and remembered the ever so friendly chap who saved up hard to take her to Australia which back then was said to be The Land Of Milk and Honey.

Ma laid a wreath on Pa and they bowed their honest heads and thought of him doing all the friendly things a loving father would do upon arriving in Australia: learning to play a brisk game of rope quoits or studying a bus timetable or purchasing a bantam.

Pa was a simple sausage and savagely missed by them both. They never forgot that he left them a buck.

They decided to do something unheard of and took a day off work, even though it was a Sunday, and often the company wanted them to work on the Sunday after all. He put a fifty cent piece in a public phone and rang through sick. Whether he was believed or disbelieved is a matter of conjecture, as he'd never rung in ill before just as he'd never lied in his life. He didn't know how to do that even if its sounds easy enough to do.

They spent the whole day basking in glorious sunshine in The Royal Botanic Gardens and drifted into the flower beds and wafted into honeysuckle fragrances; they still walked in the same old tried and true manner, he with her on his neck and their fingers bunched together as a sign of grim solidarity.

He went and fetched her a delicious tray of piping-hot-fluffy-new-baked-scones with jam and whipped cream with a piping hot pot of fresh tea and an extra complimentary pot of boiling hot water with a cold jug of milk on the side; the only drag here was that of course she had to go too because they never let go of each other physically or mentally. They dreamed in high definition sound.

He rubbed a soothing de-stressing balm upon her worried-looking and heavily wrinkled forehead, that same forehead that she could saw timber with in the old times, and he gradually teased the inner agony out of her poor broken old physique.

It was two years since Pa had died and they both mourned him exclusively and intensively, hoping he was having time off in some place as friendly as the old sick bay at 'Burp' Pty Ltd; Ernid had only been in it once suffering from a fantastic cranium-ache but he would never forget management's kindness in lending him a pillow.

In that old safe sick bay that was when the delusions stopped in their tracks for the first time just about, and he was capable of human peace if only for one hour. He blessed those who carted him there so he could cease the pain of gunshots and book store depository buildings going on in his brain.

His mother told him in her cups she would always work in Australia even though she didn't understand the philosophy of a place that rewarded the poor with death and the unemployed with a fifty year wait for a Housing Commission Flat.

'I think I tell you I love you a bit too much, don't I?' he smiled and she wouldn't let go of his palms for all the tea in China. 'We'll be okay' , she grinned; but he didn't really believe that because he had no security except his bitter and useless cascading tears of impotent rage.

'It is a bit hard having to shift homes all the time, the tiny sacrifices we must make, the scraps of opportunity shop scuffed furniture we cling to for dear sense, dear life, I hope we have enough soul for a future, mother!' he whispered ever so hoarsely, and his mother, for her part, fainted.

He loathed having to skedaddle up and down the mile-high slippery pole all the time to get in and out of their cheap council-designed home. There were thousands of perfectly decent weatherboard homes being pulled down to make way for flats on sticks as the children called them; people didn't like the designs at all but they supposed it was better than sleeping in a paddock, not that they'd tried a paddock.

He carted her to a General Practitioner he didn't really know, who had a successful practice on a pole with a generous-sized waiting room where usually industrial accident victims waited in reasonable agony. He was good at agony, in fact he was a specialist in the field of unbearable body pain.

Ernid read *Woman's Day* whilst Ma lay in a most uncomfortable position on an examination couch as the specialist put on his enlargers and examined her head to see where the brain might be; it used to live at the front of the head but after years of dreary service for her employer she couldn't possibly be certain where it might be.

'I keep on seeing The JFK assassination', she wept very hard and

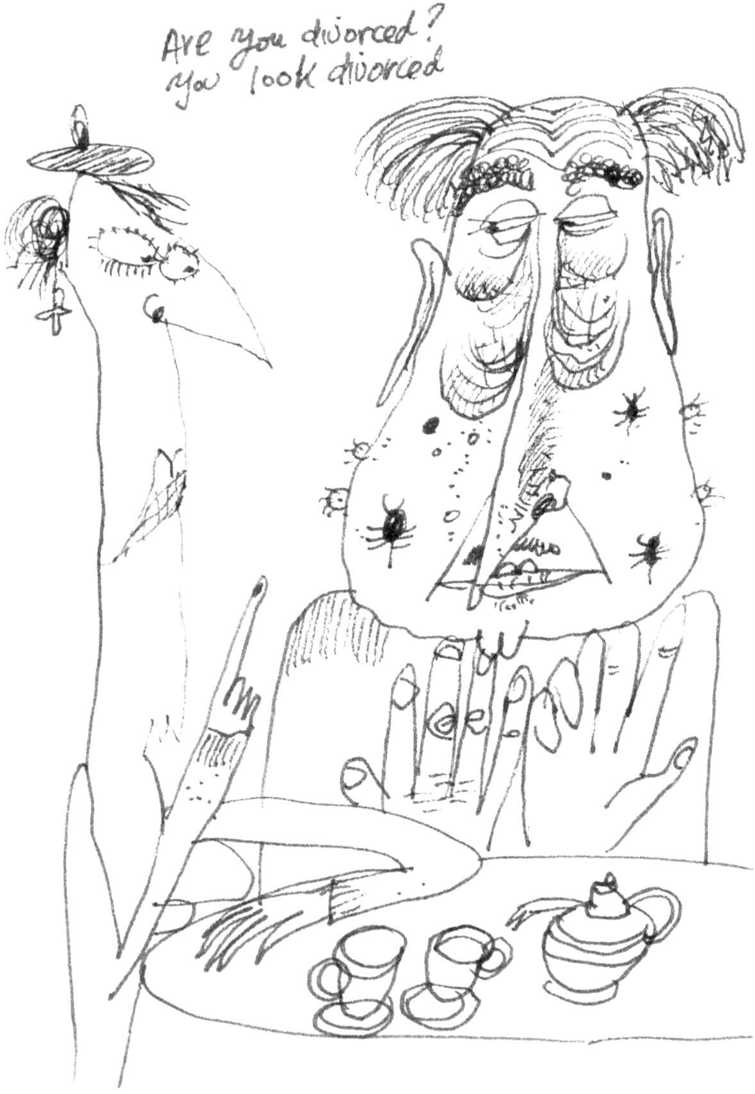
Are you divorced?
You look divorced

he sighed and echoes that it was all too common, like a bad Flu, then he gave her a prod and checked out her memory. The fact that she remembered the prod gave him hope, for he scribbled out a prescription for the speedy abandonment of fuss.

'Take two big Fuss Loss capsules per day and the dreadful pictures in your brain shall flee!' he raised his voice a bit when he said that sentence. She dressed just by standing up, paid fifty bucks at reception and swallowed her tablets at the bus stop; she naturally noticed lots of lady and men serfs doing similar and swallowing theirs down the pudding chute like her.

The delusions ceased at once and she went to a handbag sale at one of the last fancy ladies' stores in the city. She wanted a bag she could dong someone with if they got too near and in the end she purchased a prosaic bag, stooped to the road surface and piled some rusty big bolts in it that had come off some sort of scaffolding above.

She was happy not to have the JFK re-runs going on in her mental cinema for once and made a mental note to cheer right up, indeed being contented she reasoned was far cheaper than being perpetually miserable because a person didn't require help or a prescription or shell out money every single minute.

She could scarcely bear the city she once enjoyed and remembered every fixture and piece of leadlight window and down pipe and upwards pipe. She used to love the beautiful and sacred churches but every single one of them was either an apartment or a warehouse which sold cheap crap to the brain-dead.

She began to understand that she didn't have a companion other than her son so she dared to spontaneously converse with another woman who had just made it out of a warehouse having purchased unnecessary Christmas gifts because her family had been hit by a truck a week ago.

The other woman pecked her on the cheek so Ma was frightened to go further. She had had no sexual experience with gay ladies and didn't want to start without a manual of neatly printed instructions as to satisfactory arousal; but the stranger assured her it was just so nice to bump into an idiot.

They chatted amiably about all sorts of things that clearly concerned them both, such as the rising cost of living and of death, the council's lunacy in erecting poles with one bedroom flats on the tops of them, how awkward and fatiguing it always was when the lift was out and a lady had to haul great grocery bags up the stick-thing to get to the top of a place she hated and wished it would simply just topple over.

It was the fact that they loved each other.

The unknown lady took Ma to a continual continental movie. She paid and they gnawed hot popcorn together from the same cup, a most daring thing to pull off in today's conservative society. She pointed out that her hubby beat her up out of indolence for what felt like centuries, then he died one night playing poker with a falling tree.

She was liberated now from such an ogre and although she too was forced to endure existence in a pole-house she was relatively fit and was as well a cook of some note, not that she knew anyone. She reached across and held Ma's lonesome hand and she graciously kissed its beating pulse; then she invited her to her home for sex.

Ma had not engaged in the sexual act since Pa died and had completely forgotten how it should be achieved, assuming it should be like running up a dress or making nice curtains or something akin to darning a sock; but it was not like any of that.

'We're safe here, Mrs Ernst!' she said with a violent hacking cough, and the great sputtering put Ma off a bit.

They undressed and slid beneath a silk sugar bag. The woman instigated the assignation by pouring a flute of cheap champagne down her own throat and then smoking furiously, which put Ma off.

She then commenced to embrace Ma where a well-bred middle class lady would not, and Ma felt debauched and wanted to put on her filthy rags and go home.

'Are you lonely?' she inquired as she playfully bit Ma on her neck goitre.

'Only a little but I am almost sixty-five you know?' replied Ma and pulled her pants down not knowing what to expect next from this lusty stranger who was trying to ply her with cheap fizz to get her randy in a pole home she didn't know the location of.

In the end the lady put on all her garments and read from Proust to her in a bid to win her over, but Ma simply couldn't relate to 'The Remembrance Of Things Past' that well and asked for 'The Three Bears' but the lady didn't have a copy in her bookcase.

'We could just talk to each other before sex?' suggested Ma politely as possible, but the strange lady who wanted to be her lover seemed put-out.

Before she knew it the lover kissed her all over her worn down body and absolutely craved her in an entirely new way. Ma had never been ravished before, not even by Pa after he'd had a few, and tried really hard to allow herself an exciting new experience.

She assumed the lover might tire but tired she was not and slaked her thirsts on her had-it-physique until she was thoroughly spent.

It felt satisfying for Ma to fornicate with another lady and she briefly wondered why she hadn't pursued a dalliance or two with any one of a hundred vat pulverizing staff but she supposed they weren't turned on by her; and it was pretty tough to think of arousal with stiff mops and awkward buckets in your hands, as hot as she sometimes felt for the lady vat serfs.

Employing her clever tongue the lady stranger succeeded in climaxing Ma and then she read to her from The New Testament in Braille and they climaxed independently of one another; she left after throwing back a sherry and they had already swapped phone numbers so Ma felt pretty good about fornicating with complete strangers from now on.

Her strange and erotic sex life was a one-off and she swiftly went back to her famous celibacy again, the only man she loved in her now long life being Pa, and he wasn't really that available any more, though she often went to his grave to try to think of him and remember how she got pregnant with Ernid about thirty years ago.

She couldn't divide reality from dream either and was in the same state as her son once was when he was in Hell with his first experimental mouth that gave him delusions maybe as an after-shock of some sort. All she knew was she didn't need liaisons in cinemas and settled for life with absolutely stuff-all in it for her day-to-day requirements.

She had just enough savings to cheer up and public cheering up doesn't cost that much, so she went down to the bank and got in line to check how much she had accrued in her savings passbook. She banked with The National.

The line was long and filled up with spiteful cantankerous customers, one of whom was all scarlet in the face and mimed cutting his throat as a crude commentary on the slowness of service; another guy was savagely weeping as he tipped a hat filled with dirty change on the counter and muttered 'Turn that into a future, would you please?'

Two grubby little children tried to cash a cheque that was a line drawing on sand.

It was stuffy and close in the bank with customers bad-tempered and staff the same way. Eventually she was served and shown her saved amount which had accrued some interest and was just enough to decorate the new home on a pole.

She promptly withdrew enough a for a lambs wool roller, some smart lime green paint, some excellent brushes and a long drop-sheet for catching any accidental drops of ceiling paint. She carried a sturdy stepladder on her athletic neck all the way home. It banged together rather annoyingly which grazed her arm.

She set to and tidied up all the unwashed Gag plates, answered the phone though it wasn't ringing, washed everything in sight, turned the oven on only to turn it off again, placed fresh parking fines in attractive vases to illuminate the place and then she used the lambs wool roller with great dexterity to achieve a marvellous result which could only boost property value.

She never spilt a single drop of the stunning lime green paint and managed to paint all the window sills the same hue as well. She then put down some fairly new inexpensive Turkish carpet and hung a dartboard on a screw just to finish everything right off.

When Ernid arrived home at midnight from an arduous triple shift he hardly recognized the place which was so blindingly lime green he assumed he was in an aviary, which in a way he was because his old mum was singing like a lark in there and even the way she dished up the Gag seemed new to him.

Ernid was truly enjoying relaxing in the fresh and decorated home and sipping Gag in a different sort of bowl to spice things up a bit.

Even the spoon was Chinese-looking to him when he switched on the television set and his new mouth almost fell right off as he struggled to adjust to a new bulletin on Channel Ten.

The Prime Minister Of Australia was on in a muttered sort of way and giving a very short speech about laws and changes to everything as in immediately; these drastic alterations included no rights and no meaning in anything whatsoever but he gloomily concluded that the changes were in the country's best interests.

Ernid had some problems taking these changes in partly because the voice of The Prime Minister was so inhuman and sounded to him precisely like the smashed glass at the bottom of his vat at work; there was no hope in it.

The new rules of Australia were the public hanging of Indian taxi drivers, the introduction of vicious dogs outside every person's home to violently bark so no sleep could be introduced to the property. 'Burp' Pty Ltd was to have half its staff fired even though the profits were astronomical. Pedestrian walk-rage was now compulsory with huge fines for not doing it. It was law to intimidate others walking in front of you or lining up at an ATM machine.

Abortion was banned so hundreds of thousands of unplanned new babies had to serve at Bunnings Warehouse forevermore; the newborn had no say in anything and were taught how to do the register in the womb if not earlier.

All homosexuals were retrained in locomotive comprehension and forced by new legislation to learn how to drive a steam train; they had no say in not doing it.

Legislation was sped through both houses to encourage human vanity and points were awarded for undeniable deeds of self-love and this law proved popular.

Human sleep was banned and only human work remained during each twenty-fours hours of guaranteed exhaustion; the writing of fiction was put an abrupt end to and the understanding of social realism meant a forced frontal lobotomy with all expenses paid for by the recipient. Social change was over and social workers imprisoned for life. When they eventually got out they were required to be down in the dumps, and as a consequence completely useless.

Instead of the traditional Health Care Cards which were so vital in helping people pay for pharmaceutical necessities there was now a Public Gloominess Tag; it was bound around the human foot and read by a doctor once a fortnight. That important reading was to make sure citizens were broken in spirit and that they wept a lot.

The only income for Australia now was 'Burp' Pty Ltd and management were cock-a-hoop since there were no commercial rivals and no commercial anything; the country had shut down for good with no services, expensive train journeys and unavailable taxis.

The most hurtful law was a medical one where no help was to be given to the ill.

Hospitals were turned into cheap video arcades with grotesque faulty billiards tables in them with the public physically hit if they didn't join in. The selling of all hospitals put The Government into surplus; it's just that a lot of people died of death.

Even the most modern hospitals were pulled down and fashioned into simple graveyards or one or two bedrooms which sold at auction for anywhere between one million and two million dollars; and you could move straight in if you wished.

The most serious operations now took place only in bus shelters with the blinds pulled down, the patients trying to read out of date timetables in order to relax whilst their inner tubing or whatever it be was removed and then a patch glued on; hopefully there should be no leaks of hissing sounds.

The ignoring of the lame was rigidly enforced by the priests and ministers and bureaucrats who demanded an end to the boredom of suffering and ugly anguish; the only way to attend a church service was to feel terrible from the moment it started till the moment you got out of the car park. The lame were laughed at near the great big impressive marble altar and some of the more sensitive parishioners got a bit upset by that fact.

The poor at least had lots of company, in fact too much of it at times since they mostly lived leaning in a tunnel or just hanging around a vast shopping mall sort of thing; the poor had lots of time to kill and either hung out all day in the malls just blinking at useless objects such as deodorants or else they died.

The incredible amount of poor didn't know what in the world to do with themselves and the monster called Boredom destroyed their limited visions of a better life all the time; entire roads cobbled with the poor became the only infrastructure with even impoverished book shops where the infirm could read about recovery.

Every shop that started trading offered fascinating new body parts which included vinyl memories you could play around the clock, inflatable thought that was pumped into the brain at a service station free air hose, and you could browse for a china toe or a cardboard temporary chin in any of a million fashionable shops that had yearly sales that proved very popular.

Ministers frightened of importance and important ministers involved in politics were re-educated in Fascism and stood bold and large and upright all in hooded black and lectured meek parishioners in the love and need of fear; some were so scared they didn't understand a frightening word or sound that was hissed their way; they got out modest notebooks and wrote down every little put-down on them and committed it to paranoid memories for use later if things got worse.

The rack was reintroduced to important cathedrals right on Christmas and worshippers watched their friends get tortured for a fair while and then bears put on them for good measure; witchcraft was back with a vengeance and there were assistant hobgoblins who worked at fancy stores who understood the need for fancy Christmas present wrapping paper.

Anyone pleasant was drawn and quartered and the footage screened on any one of a thousand news bulletins.

You'd have to think The Government was regressive.

Yet there was hope in the land and Aboriginals now bought up shares in 'Burp' Pty Ltd and made a killing. They did up their caves and owned automobiles just like anyone else around; they were even hired to clean out the vats like white men.

Often Ernid thought of Pa and even whilst his snoring mum was out like a light he put on his best stuff and slid down the pole onto level ground and waited for the bus to come that always went to Potters Field where so many poor immigrants were who had been in dire accidents in one way or another, thousands of them lying under immaculate white crosses that stood for lemonade.

He knelt and prayed hard and so fervently and so long did he do it that he fully expected Pa to vault out of the grassy grave and look at him again! Oh, heavenly days! What he should give if that could only come true!

His hands pawed at the mud and his blunt fingertips dug deep into his skinny knees as he shut so hard his eyes, scrunched them right up in order to see his father alive again in some revolutionary way, something better than a dream.

The tears boiled down his waterlogged cheeks as he sent his spirit down below and then sent loving thoughts to all of those at Potters Field who had committed suicide. Hundreds had, men and women and children, because the way was hard and friends were scarcer than love even; and that is saying a lot when you think about it.

Some who had no doubt committed suicide were the long-term unemployed, others were untalented sculptors, many were just all mixed-up and never did fit into Australian identity of any kind, living third lives or fifth quality lives that got too tough with decades of drinking Burp and just hanging round malls waiting for a drive-by.

He knelt and made himself aware of their spirits and souls, contemplating their fears and their destinies, what sort of baked beans they had, and what sort of stolen take-away white plastic fork they had supped with in the lonesome night time.

He sent them his loving signals and if he could have he would have blessed them in their death-house, in their death-knell.

He did a translation into their battered old unloved shoes, mentally becoming those he did not know. He loved their lostness and prayed for their delivery to a great world, a much kinder one for these who had never known anyone to help them up, and not kick them when they were so damnably down for the count.

Down for the count indeed was the soul of Australia with no plan to steer it ever upwards again, the leaders lost and management all narcissists and billions clinically depressed in The Public Service. The old way of helping your brothers and sisters was laughable unless it was you personally who languished in the drain or its colleague the gutter.

The Government were investing the last of printed money in charity fruit cakes which were designed to in some way lower spirits right on Christmas; however they killed their eaters due to fantastic insecticides in their currants and uranium in the self-raising-flour; and then for some reason ordinary suburbanites didn't look forward to them any more. The Government was bankrupted with cash flow and decent ideas to somehow lift the place and restore confidence while things merely got worse quickly and determinedly as though God was bent on Australia's obvious downfall.

Wasp plagues attacked every man woman and child in the country. In the old days local councils smartly organized wasp-looking-gentlemen to destroy an active hive that threatened a home but because of misunderstandings that went on all the time in fact great big thriving wasp hives were brought out of wasp storage and expertly attached to people's sideways primed for attack.

Ernid joined the local branch of The Australian Labor Party but there was only one other member and they turned out to possess extremely different points of view; he met at their offices once per month and they steadfastly ignored each other. The other member in a fit of pique resigned and crossed over to The Liberal Party, a thing that temporarily hurt Ernid's feelings.

He was feeling rather desperate so he organized a meeting with Public Relations staff at his employment to see whether he might be reconsidered the figurehead of 'Burp' Pty Ltd again in a bid to get some income into his dwindling bank book.

They met with him but weren't in any sort of way interested and told him he was suffering from a wave of nostalgia. They didn't even give him a cup of tea or a biscuit and told him to shut the door on his way out.

They did give him an old poster depicting him as the deranged face of soft drink around the world. He was pretty ill when that head shot was taken but the garrulous public liked it and identified with him at his sickest. He always thought that picture was exploitative and made fun of drastic facial enhancement; and he was sick and tired of being made fun of, the stakes were too high now for denigration but he was always needful of a buck and to that end would stoop to anything, no matter how macabre.

When he got back home again that night he simply couldn't follow a single event in his three years as a serf for a lemonade group or where he was born in what forest region in the snowy backblocks of Prague or whether he had ever been betrothed, lived in sin, lived without sin, been awful or incredibly kind; he may have murdered someone or done something far worse such as torch a kindergarten, but he was no doubt whatever a person of interest.

He didn't like himself whoever he was and knew he had done bad things, but because of medical science he literally possessed no idea what awful crimes or passions he had unearthed; he remembered that he'd had four fairly expensive mouth operations and that the final one of these procedures seemed okay.

He could chew up a chop and crunch up a lettuce and sip soft drink or even hard drink like half a dozen bottles of white  wine and his wit was better because the spontaneous repartee he made was more theatrical and less prosaic; it was as though his donor must have been witty or effortless at making up stunning things to say.

He tried hard to make the adjustment to the amusing or at least creative things his mouth seemed to utter on its own but he needed to find out who his donor was to have closure.

He had a free Sunday off, while Ma had to go in but that was her thing because she always experienced guilty feelings if she wasn't a serf and miserable into the bargain, so they agreed to meet up at tea time at the new pole home and Ernid strolled into the city to spend the day at The State Library in the Mouth History Section.

The mouldiness of that oral reading room was colossal with toothless historians drooling over gummy histories needing serviettes all the time to sponge up their pools of saliva and many sobbing and groaning students of gnawing and masticating food-stuffs that stretched back to cave age eating out or eating in were slobbering away as books became adrift with sodden pages floating in a swift spiral right down a big central plug hole.

Human librarians like everything else had been done away with in line with the new cost-cutting.

Directions emanated from Canberra where the crucial changes in direction were made law despite the obvious flaws that saw walruses take over from librarians throughout the land; it was thought that they looked after rare volumes better than humans.

Ernid saw a hundred mouth scholars sitting all humped over together at an ancient former dining table heaped with 14th century bound volumes of the very first wind-up teeth engraved in astonishing detail and footnotes about eye teeth decorating those lavish black and white plates; students of teeth were studying the first known mouths found in cave persons and even the mouths of cave age dentists.

Sometimes students of these digs sighed or giggled but mostly they obediently wrote down their findings and observations as they peered and mentally remembered the whole history of the compulsive requirement to break down foodstuffs in order to keep the cave fire going and put dinosaur cutlets on the tea table for a voracious primitive family.

A walrus librarian slithered to Ernid and flopped with its soggy arm a whole heap of teeth histories which included illustrations of cork teeth made for Henry The Eighth that worked of course upon brass hinges; he read of Henry's dreadful temper in trying to come at a cutlet or a spud with such primitive clackers and the shooting and searing jaw pain he experienced trying to sip lentil soup; this discomfort was responsible for him ordering rashly thought out beheadings all the time.

He craned his sturdy ever reliable young neck and even though repulsed by the fact that the messy end-papers had rotted off and the smell of the ancient mouth history volume was similar to cat urine in its most diabolical form he gingerly opened a strange 14th century Encyclopedia Of Teeth Artificial And Realer Than You'd Think which was so rare the walrus who handed it to him said it was the only one left.

It was hard to read any of it with all the walruses wheeling and wheedling about being terribly important all over the place. He didn't like it that they wore monocles and bore ever such a superior air, I mean they were just common creatures!

He put on his extra strong magnifiers and bowed over the eroded swimming pages whose ink smelled to him like human torture, and no wonder he thought that, because nearly every paragraph described the fatalistic anguish of people throughout various centuries who were forced to eat a lamington with no grating or grinding apparatus.

The ancient Chinese used steamed chicken to wedge into missing back teeth-holes in order to crunch up meals such as tenderized rump steak or even humble pear; and that seemed to work out okay for them as far as any historian can remember at least.

Cave men wore pig tusks to tear apart their breakfast cereals and swore by it.

The Goths were the very first race to employ cistern tiles to break up a stale pie.

His studious nostrils were right on the dampened paragraphs of old jaw lore when he at last discovered exactly what he was searching so hard for.

In the mid-13th century a depressed monk in France forfeited all his collective teeth in a railway crossing misunderstanding concerning a goods train and himself and lost every one of his teeth.

He discovered exactly what he was after and the chapter was thankfully written in one of the first versions of English ever published, in fact it was a Penguin Anthology Of Mouth Murders.

He leant his palm on the damp binding and put his magnifiers right onto the big print for the book was designed for Adult Readers Of The Late Thirteenth Century and it gave him tremendous pleasure and satisfaction to study the first known or first printed accounts of jaw delusion.

It was common way back then for pain to be confused with pleasure because dentists even then were unimaginable thugs and cared not a whit for the common moron.

He read with his donor tongue hanging out and dangling right on the words of bloodthirsty accounts of public extractions performed by a bear.

People have always preferred bear-baiting to someone going crook about personal agony because agony is boring and bear-baiting isn't really; it is ever so much more satisfying and spontaneous.

He read almost completely breathless about sufferers of tooth pain turning into deranged stalkers nearly a thousand years ago.

People who were unfortunate to be trod on by a horse on the way to a public mockery or a fairy floss stall or just about anything of diversion often became extremely cross with a sore foot or missing teeth as a result of landing awkwardly on a road due to a pig hitting them with all their force in a pig panic; the result was very nearly always violence due to agony or sheer embarrassment or both.

The bloodthirsty highway person Dick Turpin wore a false jaw composed of concrete and fired a big blunderbuss at perfectly innocent travellers; but he was delusional due to the strange and alienating dentures he needed to gallop with.

He was known as a passionate lover although his kisses were not wanted by his many paramours.

In the mid-16th century an assassination took place in Trinidad where a dental patient had to put up with such a protracted wait for what was seen as perfunctory surgery to fix up a bad back tooth that he apparently insulted pensioners in the suffocating waiting room and beat up a street sweeper with his false teeth in his fists; that must have really hurt like anything.

The offender wore a home-made mask to disguise himself from would-be witnesses and used oxy cutting gear to knock himself up a virtually weatherproof set of prison bars on his swollen face that connected with his sore jaw in some crude way or other.

He was pursued with vigour by police but managed to flee most of them because he was so hard to identify in any sort of way.

He was known as 'Prison Face' and a huge reward was offered for his capture.

Because he was addicted to opium he spoke in a very affected sort of a manner and had a way of yawning as he rudely indicated his prison bar teeth with an off-putting tapping thing he did just to annoy persons.

The deeper he dug into jaw mechanisms and dental mysteries and painstakingly archived the first cave drawings of conversation that depicted one cave guy chatting in a friendly manner with another one of them,. They might have been gazing out to sea and observing a hurricane, anything to have a chat about, and the amazingly accurate rock cave drawings showed speech-making and even the first drawing of a cave man raconteur dressed in raccoon skins tapping an early microphone.

He realized he came after a long chain of movable teeth speakers and hundreds of experiments with wired jaws and threaded back teeth using a knitting needle; he studied first-hand descriptions of early pioneers striving to invent a nickel-plated voice box and a late 18th century jukebox implant which played primitive rock tracks within the gullet in such a way nobody knew it was a recording.

He trembled slightly when he stumbled onto grisly accounts in the crazed fiction of Alexander Dumas when he wrote *The Man in the Iron Mask*; where the poor chap inside the beastly contraption dreads his own beard suffocating him.

'Now that's going a bit too far!' he couldn't help calling out in the library, much to the consternation of several ancient mouth studiers.

In the late 18th century there existed a mouth-less highwayman named Tool who stuck people up late at night at Camden Town mostly, armed with a big blunderbuss or two (it was hard to tell at night). Tool leered into coaches containing fairly privileged people who mostly screamed when he showed them a set of mechanical clackers made of musical tongs that he trilled with a cloth hammer.

The only way to salvation is to know everything that ever happened within the mystery of good and bad. Ever since Man was mean to Eve in The Garden Of Eden the only way through life has been to use the grey matter. He loved the old junk in the library and stacked up hundreds of moist histories with garden hoses as bookmarks.

The more he studied dentistry since time began the more he could ascertain real connections with delusion and assassination. He studiously made notes in many ruled exercise books which he actually intended to show a publisher, even though he didn't know any of them. It was a new passion to unveil the link between body parts and having your brain blown out.

He began to realize the entire history of false body components was more a damnation than a blessing, even though the kind portion of his mind assumed medical scientists were always dedicated to helping people such as poor old Captain Kidd, who had to be a stern pirate all day and try to board fiery vessels with a false leg and then give up forever his dream of becoming a long distance hurdler.

With all the very best medical intentions all sorts of mistakes had been made along the way. Conspiracy theory implants stretched right back to the first cave chap improvising an elm arm or putting on history's first cricket pad that he had painstakingly woven out of half an acre of pure flax; and making do with that to get around with to the concern of other cave chaps who thought it wouldn't work.

Dentists themselves had a lot to answer for because false teeth ever since they came in with the reign of Henry The Eighth were nothing if not unreliable since having to turn up starving-hungry at a popular chop-house and try to chew into medieval bubble and squeak on seriously tough toast turned many an honest citizen into a pathological freak capable of anything, particularly affray.

And affray of course was by now the world crisis beyond under-standing and it was created by sugar addiction which arrived through gallons of soft drink being personally introduced to the brain and the central nervous system; ladies in the late 18th century who sipped too much gin and tonic in pubs swiftly blossomed into hat pin murderers, which was well known and inevitable; and there was nothing anyone could do about it except offer a pathetic grimace and say 'that's life!'.

Riots throughout history were due to soft drink becoming both too expensive and unavailable in frozen Europe where war after blood thirsty war spilled out of a half empty lemonade can; the human brain simply cannot handle Burp or Pepsi and deal with other household duties like doing the ironing or garden maintenance.

The illustrations of lemonade manufacturers being burnt at the stake were so realistic and showed crowds cheering as milk bar proprietors went up in smoke with empty Solo cans cast at them as they did so. But the most obscene illustrations showed the complete alienation and disintegration of sales reps who were stoned to death in paddocks for not selling their stock fast enough. They really suffered heaps.

The final chapter of one really old and important collection of early soft drink barbarity depicted gruesome monsters of early London baring their metal teeth through ladies' boudoirs and their ceramic tongues oozing lust in every drop of murderous intent.

He zoomed in on certain men's faces of the late 18th century with curtain rack top teeth with blood all over them and bottom teeth fashioned out of grubby wooden clothes pegs sharpened to a fatalistic razor finish for easy devouring of the public and proper digestion thereof.

The first really dangerous delusional chap with a made mouth was the bold highwayman Dick Turpin. With the dreaded Tool, this Highway Chap robbed sleepy travellers on the old Dover Road and when Dick Turpin declared his dentures achieved with petrified rose stems with dirty big thorns in them the result was greatest fright and a speedy handing over of wallets and bulging purses as he wolfishly snapped at them cowering in their unsafe coach.

Although Ernid's brand new donor mouth did pretty much what it was told and he never saw an assassination any more he was beginning to feel bad in the busy library; it was really hard to concentrate with all the noise of ferrous iron covered books being dropped on a desk, waiters on rackety roller skates whizzing around bearing strong coffees and slices of glutinous cake, the clanging of gothic cash registers and people fainting loudly due to too much study and too much memory-using.

He feared he drooled and felt so faint he could barely read about cloth tongues any more or make detailed notes about head transplants almost perfected by the French during The Revolution; they were damned realistic too and rather haunted him as he felt the claustrophobia and biliousness rise in his gut. He hated knowledge.

Experience was what he was good at.

He had, he thought, always wanted to be a scholar at a library where he would be encouraged to study history and get a whole lot more intelligent, but there was only one library left in Sydney, as all the others had been gutted and turned into restaurants with food he couldn't understand or want to insert into mouth number four.

It felt energizing and cleansing to be able to lightly drop an armful of jaw histories down on the public desk, put his enlargers over his restless eyes, focus on the historical inventions of masticating rissoles and look carefully at the illuminated manuscripts depicting a monk cheerfully undoing a can of rather delicious looking spaghetti.

He looked into the thousands of years worth of monsters and realized that nearly all of them were dentists; he wondered why in medieval times a dentist employed a hammer on old folk who had stuffed up their teeth, possibly by biting too many gophers in half or just getting stuck into too many lollies.

At last he found what he was looking for in a book so old it had cobwebs and rotted leaves for its covers with its lettering of coagulant blood. It was a most grisly publication to be sure and the mad monks who executed the baffling drawings were clearly delusional after drinking dragon claw lattes.

The first page showed the first serf in lemonade making history to be crushed into pulp with the first stirring rods used to pound lemon up before the world's first carbon dioxide was mixed into the stuff to begat two thousand years of suffering.

On the opposite page was an illuminated manuscript picture, which must have taken a thousand years to do, showing a serf having a set of bellows inserted into his throat to blow out excess bits of pie while medical scientists gathered round the operating theatre bunk staring at the bellows excitedly and looking very eager to see all the unwanted and stuck pie get driven out of the chest cavity, thus saving the serf's life.

He read the only clue as to his ongoing fight with delusions which all started with Adam and Eve, when he began to hear voices, all sorts really, of dentists working in Eden on a pro bono basis who had cracked under considerable pressure due to an uncertain income and astronomical rentals for their city practices.

Adam was schizophrenic as it turned out and his terrible delusions had to do with his understandably morbid fear of dentistry.

It was certainly in this area of dental paranoia and dental paranormal activity that Ernid's interest was most definitely aroused and as he tried to turn the soggy pages of dilapidated dental charts and gummy hieroglyphics that stretched back to pre-Mayan times he saw that being unable to chew your food properly invariably made you fairly surly, not to say impossible.

He had his great fascinated proboscis hovering a millimetre over the soggy illuminated manuscript depicting a pre-Mayan dentist screaming at natives who were at reception in the jungle just about dead with fright. You could easily detect the painted fright under the monk's loving watercolour brush, while the crazed witch doctor looked not unlike one of the bosses at work.

The monk, whoever he or she was, had dextrously captured in one painting done with fantastic detail the pandemonium of dentistry and the terror that accompanies the enduring of an extraction or merely a filling.

It was evident many a Mayan villager experienced metamorphosis during an extraction or complete and perfect psychosis after the whole lot came out; he studied and slowly understood that it was the unexpectedness of not being sociable or presentable any more in conventional Mayan jungle society, the force of that shocking change to your body that pushed cannibals to the edge.

Strange to say pre-Mayan society was no different from Australia in the year 2000 in that insensitivity and totalitarian politics destroyed any vestige of democratic thinking and that decapitation in any jungle way back then was the same as voting Labor.

Everyone was corrupt in the jungle just as graft and opportunism is prevalent today.

It was hard to get funding for new primary schools in pre-Mayan society just as it is now and many a villager went neglected and wholly uneducated because of it.

The first lemonade was bubbled up by a witch in pre-Mayan times implementing a mixture of cougar gore and brown sugar and then vigorously shaken by a witch before it was marketed all through the back blocks of Java or along The Malayan Peninsula; but the popular drop came from Chile where it was a lot bubblier.

Then he read with a kind of wild fanaticism of the unmitigated violence that ancient superstitious Mayan men felt when their jaws had been given the witchcraft of donor teeth crudely hit into the new mouth with a chisel; there was rage and discomfort beyond telling as the frustrated patient failed to speak to his mates properly and got laughed at in the pub.

History's first murder was because the plate put into a pre-Mayan chap was so hard to chew a Sao cracker with.

The undeniable irritation and the gasping requirement to persist in spitting out hard-to-swallow fractions of Sao crackers made the patient completely insane, and the evidence was right before his very eyes in the last library on earth.

The next lot of pictures depicted primitive dental patients trying to chew up their early morning corn flakes with swinging coconut fibre front teeth and then screaming from the extreme awkwardness of the action and unfortunately murdering other Mayans due to the frustration of it all.

But it was the almost understandable mayhem the recipient of barred teeth, fashioned from prison doors from 18th century France that really stood out from all the other dental histories he pored over: the barbarity of those mechanics who tormented receivers of rusted bars sunk into their swollen back gums, like the hitting in of a fence post in many ways that he obviously identified with.

The colossal agony of having a rotten jaw pulled away from the face you have always known and spoken to in a friendly way in mirrors or to people in the street, suddenly replaced with papier-mâché or plaster strengthened with picture hanging wire; the crudity of expression left to the unwitting victim was responsible for the forthcoming murders.

Then of course it was the delusions that kicked in with the artificial look of you, the strangeness of theatrical expression and opera jutted-out-eyes so that the wearer of false head parts felt despised and was despised and sought revenge after years of crummy sleep and an upset tummy.

As he examined the ghoulish illustrations of Mayans receiving violent rotten teeth extractions and the first dentists in history being cut in two for being annoying, he suddenly could feel hot breath on the back of his neck: it was Oswald who had shot Kennedy IN 1963. What on earth was he doing in a library or a book depository building in Dallas?

'I didn't do it!' he screamed only the once right into Ernid's ear and then he bolted down the austere white marble stairs and was never seen again in history.

It was just an awkward moment and a very brief one indeed but it felt bad.

Ernid took several of his books of study over to the desk where you're supposed to do that and handed them over to JFK who thanked him with that incredible smile of his.

'Well, I'll be a monkey's uncle!' Ernid found himself saying aloud. He then turned around and the assistant librarian was just a normal guy.

For an unknown reason he just ran, an automatic decision of his long tall body that was so scared; and the running was his peasant way to elude capture.

So he ran through the library doors with their surveillance cameras taking shots of his vanishing form and he ran scared all the way back to his new home on a pole. But an eviction order had been pasted upon his front door and he read the fine print on that as soon as he ascended the stairs to the pointy bit at the top. He panted like anything and kept on staring over his own shoulders to catch a glimpse of his imaginary pursuers.

Luckily his mother was in and that was a thing he hadn't expected since she was always at the factory trying hard to save money for their diminishing futures, but in fact she was there and soothed her son with marvellous moist rags patted upon his burning hot forehead and her soft welcoming syllables of hope as he fainted on her lap with hot tears of shock pouring down his flushed cheeks and so on.

'You shall be all right my love, you have never hurt anyone and the only thing running after you is guilt', she sighed. That seemed to do him some sort of good, as he stared up at her and asked her to give him an Anti-Assassination pill, which she did. She found it hard to pull out of its tough silver foil sachet, but she popped it down his tortured throat and immediately there was no Oswald or Kennedy.

He slept the sleep of the just that night on his stoical mother's lap, who didn't move all night as she caressed his hair and sang him songs from the woods of home, half wishing they'd never got on the boat to a country where they weren't welcome.

As she ever so lovingly caressed his tormented young hair she stared at the terribly expensive silver foil sachet on the floor and wondered why it was they worked so quickly.

In his sodden dreams with the strange fact that he wept from every wart and freckle in his young being, his steadfast mother was his harbour that very long night of weeping, as the fear fled from him through the magic pill. Science had helped him for once, as his poor worn out body snored and took comfort from pharmaceutical love.

And his dreams were not nightmares of pursuit but pursuits of waterfalls and ferns topped with prismatic catch-the-sun type raindrops. He was free.

# CHAPTER NINETEEN

The very last of the costly Anti-Assassination Capsules had run out but the ever-so-sweet family pharmacist assured him that he would always cover him if money were tight, not that he wasn't a good saver, it was just that they, all of them, lived in tougher and tougher times; and it sure felt good to know the capsules would keep on coming.

He dreamed of the assassination as per usual but awoke without it and Oswald and Kennedy were elsewhere and not in his head, or what was left of it.

He slept right in and didn't stir till midday but his mother had gone off to work and left him some lovely whole meal chicken and tomato sandwiches with the crusts cut off; and a loving note that assured him it was okay not to go in that day and to just flake out on the couch and watch 'The Bold And the Beautiful' on Channel Ten at half past four, something of a pleasure he had missed as his life had none in it.

He blinked and reached across to pluck up the first of the mouth-watering-looking sandwiches but as he munched into its tender-looking-surface his eyes watered with chronic agony as if he couldn't even bite into a god-damned tomato!

'My Jesus Christ!' he wept hard. 'I can't even bite into a sandwich any more!'

He flung the half-bitten sandwich on the floor and blew his nose violently into a clot of bunched-up-tissues and then bit into those.

'How do you ever have any fun around here?' he inquired of himself, poor man!

This was his most fatal mouth of the lot, the fourth one which a dead guy gave!

He tried to feel it but merely numbness arrived; and as well as the numbness it was ever so much bigger and much more cumbersome than when he came out of theatre.

The top lip felt like a car tyre or a bike seat, as there simply was no living sensation in its entirety, it just flapped up and down like a flat tyre somehow and although he certainly wasn't vain about his looks, the look of it just hanging there made him feel depressed and helpless. The donor teeth came from an uneducated furniture remover and that possibly accounted for the cruder language he was now using to make his points with.

He hated to swear but lately, because he was borrowing the unedifying gutter dialogue of an uneducated bureau and wardrobe shifter his sentences in the street had become abysmal. He was absolutely shattered by his vulgarity of verbal expression and his speedy abandonment of eloquence and daintiness of vocabulary.

So that when his mind or mood wanted to make a certain point, usually a philosophical point, his foul teeth barked out crude expressions without his express permission; he was appalled by his lack of finesse when addressing a person, even a crude person scrubbing out a great vat with him, that sort of thing.

The main misfortune was the fourth tongue that had come from a professional football critic on a mainstream 24 hour sports radio show, highly rating and filled to the cusp with non-stop abuse of race. When he started to ridicule dark-skinned vat workers who trod the identical broken glass that he personally trod on next to them, he realized his tongue was not his own.

The donor tongue was very bad-tempered and sometimes of its own personality stooped to spitting out unwanted soup in a tenth-rate-restaurant, or even at home he sometimes hawked up his mum's own asparagus soup all over the brand-new-tablecloth which she wept to see.

He stood in their awful cramped kitchen and spat soup at the woman who gave him animation; she couldn't believe that he did it and nor could he. He tried in vain to point out that the donor tongue had poor domestic manners but she wasn't having any of that sort of crap. Then he started to spit out his feelings with a tongue that wasn't his and he swore at children on a see-saw and ridiculed a one-legged baker.

In pretentious modern small cinemas his donor manners via his fourth mouth made him say and suggest things to other cinema patrons he wouldn't have uttered in a month of Sundays with his own natural tongue; but when he saw a cinema person gobbling hot caramelized popcorn out of a spectacular waxed tub and making so much racket that he couldn't catch the sound track he used intemperate language upon them, much to his own shock of course!

The bottom teeth had been donated by a depressed social worker without a sense of the truly ridiculous that you surely need to cheer up the poor twenty-four hours of any day. The donor had toiled for Life Line, the anti-suicide telephone company responsible for encouraging people to stay in the same rut; but the pressure of course had pushed that worker of ordinary miracles right over the edge and the worst occurred.

He could feel the deceased donor's social responsibility in every bottom donated tooth, each tooth in fact reverberating with psychosis and too much fast food.

The bottom teeth felt violated and exhausted from decades of hopelessness and denial of true gloominess of the spirit. He felt bad in them.

In the centre of his chest cavity medical scientists had installed a black pub ashtray complete with half a box of dry matches so you could always light up a smoke, without the fear of the match ever being wet so you couldn't get the fag going, and as well as the matches that slid out of his chest cavity on a nice tray made of mahogany there was a brand-new carton of cigarettes.

Sometimes he was weak and lit a smoke up to elude the frightening pursuers of his physique and mind; something was after him and it wasn't make-believe or shadows as his father called things you saw that frightened you.

It was very nice of his father to satirize fear for him in that natural way of course.

Ernid believed if he had a fifth mouth put in he would be murdered, so he tended to hang onto the awful fourth one even though it didn't work at all well.

You wouldn't and shouldn't believe life could become any worse than all of these travails which befell our poor automaton of lemonade, the czar of diabetes and the king of sugar, but they actually did in the last reel of his tough existence; after the fourth denture there is no other.

The last straw was for the demented council to go ahead and supervise the tearing-down of his home-on-a-pole, and this was whilst his mother and he were still in it. He could hear the wrecking ball sail into his bathroom whilst Ma was in the tub and see through the top window a whole legion of excavators, explosives experts and cheering-squads.

It was practically unreal to the mind to think people could become so debauched in their moral makeup that out of indolence they could find the heart to wildly cheer on the loud and crazy demolition of someone's place of residence, but they did.

People who rather unwisely assumed their own properties were safe came over to Ernid's home, sat on tartan picnic rugs, broke out the boiled chook and salad, passed plates around to approvers of the wreckage and cheered very wildly when the big ball went through a particular feature, like a wall let us say, or a window, making the most calamitous sound imaginable.

The totalitarian regime of The Government made certain there was no opposition to human destruction and of course the people started to behave perversely and stupidly; the new society was ill-thought-out and The Government ruled by blind power because they owned everything and that included the giddy old human being.

Ernid was in so much mental pain and physical discomfiture that he just stared dumbly at rubbish trucks sputtering up his road carting all his op shop stuff including his only reclining chair as he could hardly afford the cost of taking it easy even after he got in from his long shift. He cried when he observed the paid scabs put the mallet into it, bust it into a thousand pieces and then laugh with the effect of it.

He cried a lot more as he and his mother watched in acquired terror as the brutes in the pay of the local council just fall to and belt into bits their few paintings and primitive sculptures they had collected over the years, those struggling years they had suffered in the new country that was supposed to be friendly.

In the end there was nothing left that was theirs except a garbage bag, a big dark green one into which they put their old black and white television.

The other object they owned was a fairly impressive truck battery that they had picked up for a song at a garage sale. It still had plenty of charge left in it, so they patched the television into it and watched the news right on the road as there was stuff-all-else to do.

This appalling form of entertainment became the norm for the whole country as there were only a few remaining at the so-called top; the majority were so dirt poor they used dust to make tea in a cup made of half a tennis ball they found somewhere unfriendly; everywhere was unfriendly and nowhere was nice except behind your eyes where God smiled at you from time to time if you were lucky.

The whole road where they lived perched in the middle of the rough old road watching portable televisions patched into still-sparkly batteries that could power all the crap American comedies into the brain damaged skulls of Australians who had no energy.

There was no laughter with any of the comedy programs transmitted from America and no sorrow either; unless it went onto SBS accidentally and you were bullied into watching seal slaughter, which is the only program they play on that channel.

Ernid could hear something or someone running behind him in heavy gymnasium shoes with a rhythmic incantation accompanying every heavy footstep. Just who was it?

He had been constantly dreaming (but of course he couldn't be sure if it was delusion) of a new world order controlled by cameras and that the only available dialogue was surveillance; at work human chit-chat had been eliminated with instant dismissal for serfs who talked, even in an undertone, to one another.

The new order was intended to save money for the Government but in the end the seeing-to the cameras and the high cost of editing the film they used (it was Super 8 or 16 ml) made the entire process unsatisfactory in the extreme and The Government Think Tank were worrying about these prohibitive costs and trying to dream up a better way to keep everyone unhappy.

Public delusion was enforced on the freeways where opiates like speed and dangerous overtaking are family leisure and eagerly looked-forward-to by the morons who worship hospitalization.

Ernid didn't drive because he didn't wish to hurt a person by anything that could be construed as his fault; he was getting fairly alarmed at road rage as is practised in the family home.

In the old conventional days of family life the people, the inhabitants who occupied the place, dined together, said their Grace of course and passed the spuds. Today the only food is costly take-away, ignored when it is brought in and cast into any of the walls, where it hangs like a foul curse.

Australians don't understand each other so they hate each other within the family and completely ignore one another to instill more agony into the other one of them. Even when having sex many a husband complains to his bored wife about the continuous thieving of his rubbish bins by local serfs who wind up living in them in a vacant lot.

The only place where he could live, with his home destroyed, was in the middle of the anonymous tar road, so he and Ma wheeled their old bed there and hoped a truck didn't clean them up; and still he heard heavy breathing, whistle noises, breeze effects and the unmistakable sound of a murderer coming after him.

# Chapter Twenty

## The Dye Is Cast

He had for so long assumed in some bizarre way he was a murderer because there in his frontal lobe was all of the evidence. He always believed in his guilt and had long ago accepted the unlikely scientific connection between a common industrial accident and the metamorphoses into Lee Harvey Oswald and the three long years of being shot by Jack Ruby even though in the psychotic fantasies he was JFK.

But what now he thought of modern history and contemporary medicines which make you so deluded, what lethal substances were the prescription drugs laced with?

He didn't have the foggiest.

He admitted he felt clearer with the Anti-Assassination Capsules and even after half a one he didn't hallucinate any more or keep seeing things that weren't there in reality. He stopped seeing the Dallas Motorcade completely, didn't hear the single shot from The Book Store Depository Building and heard not a sob from Jackie Kennedy or any of the immortal mayhem of that terrible day. He just swallowed his easy-to-swallow pill and it all went away like the flickering shadow it was.

But now he was sitting with his mother in the centre of a really hot and dusty road where his former home-on-a-stilt used to exist, but the house had been completely demolished, not a thing left; they even took his old gully trap.

Just scraps of black plastic singed rubbish bags fluttered over where his front fence used to be, with not a single home anywhere left standing.

It was a barren suburban landscape adorned with a half-hearted sunset and figures in that landscape not speaking or bothering to play Scrabble any more. The jig was up.

His mother's only home now was her son's broad back and so she rested against its permanence and basked in his greater strength. He was so strong against the world's crisis of confidence and he knew all about The Great Barrier Reef. Or at least he said he did. She couldn't be roused from her slumbers and he was too kind to awaken her.

The dreary sight of a dirty big council steam roller came into view and he watched the thing continue to embed the bitumen even flatter into the dead flat road surface. The machine made such a noise he could scarcely think straight, but he didn't need to think anyway. The steam roller seemed like a modern metaphor for The Australian Government because no one could lift their voice anymore.

It commenced to rain very powerfully yet no one around lent him an umbrella or a sheet of corrugated iron with which to protect his old mother from the elements, which she always called elephants; but that was probably due to her never attending a school in her whole life. The only two English words she knew were All Bran.

So she snuggled harder into the only really safe harbour that she was acquainted with and that spot was her getting-older only serf, who was still remarkably powerful so she confused him with Heaven but he sure had his share of troubles and he knew them all off-by-heart. The murderer was the major concern.

It was ever so stormy and inclement and he was sick and tired of all the detritus around him getting thrown up in his mechanical face all the time. He did feel better knowing his lips and teeth and jaw were kindly lent by a donor. He could swallow much better with the new gearbox and clutch throat and his legs had a limited slip differential put in them so he could get up hills more efficiently, and not fall over as much.

The object of his horror was coming for him with his sleeping parent relaxed upon his lap. He could hear the swishing of relatively sharp sabres and make out the frightened face of Lee Harvey Oswald just at the moment that Jack Ruby murdered him; he grasped hard his sachet of Anti-Assassination Capsules but there was none left in it.

He could feel himself being shot in the head and then he saw a future documentary of himself on a commercial television network, and that it rated highly.

The figure who shot him galloped by on a big black horse which reared right up as the murderer waved his cocked hat to him as a gesture of triumph.

Then to his absolute stupefaction a neighbour waved to him with the identical hat gesture of the highway person, the same cocked and confident hat being waved about as a friendly sign, but it was of course malevolent with the murderer and the friendly neighbour displayed nothing but trust and hopefulness in the way of old neighbors.

'Will you both come over for a revitalizing hot scone with fresh raspberry conserve on it as well as clotted cream; that might cheer you up.' The nice neighbour helped Ernid into his home with his still-sleeping mother and gently threw her on a couch.

'I thought that all the homes in our area had been demolished?' whispered Ernid as the neighbor and his wife, who was also very nice, served up the fresh hot scones at the tea table.

'We had just enough in the bank to put up another one in kit-form', smiled his new benefactor, and he set to work digging out the moist and visionary scones from a black oven tray, then he applied home-made jam to them, just a scratch, and then added a dab of fresh-whipped cream as he said he would do.

He gazed around in dumbfound chagrin and wished more than anything in the whole wide world that he might be loved and looked-after.

He had no idea what the identity of these nice neighbours was and couldn't have cared what former nationality they were, African or Greek or Italian or French, it really had no bearing on any of his sensations. He felt spontaneously looked after for once and although he didn't sing for his scone-supper he had the idea the neighbours didn't really want him to. In the first time just about forever in Australia he relaxed his grip.

After a duplicate set of lovely warm fluffy scones with clotted cream and home-made raspberry jam and piping-hot fresh tea that was warmed in the pot, he was led into a comfortable bedroom where he and his weary mum were shown two beautiful single beds with a copy of today's newspaper neatly folded on the crisp new and ironed pillow. The neighbours didn't say a single thing, they just gestured to the beds.

Ernid went to thank Mrs Neighbour but she wouldn't hear of it, just kissing dear Ma on her sunken colourless cheeks and asking her how long had it been since she'd had a proper and relaxing sleep. Ma couldn't of course answer and collapsed right on her new bed while Ernid almost weepingly tucked her in. Then he sang songs of the village to her even though they were the wrong villages.

As the night wore on he felt less worn out by the horrors of his mind which was formerly a hyperactive cesspool of pharmaceutical jokes which weren't funny. He ceased his keening for his unconscious mother and keened alternatively for his missing father whom he missed more than breath.

He bitterly knew everything now and bitterness against the Capitalist System had taught him to distrust any direction given to him by persons of Authority.

The night was his only tutor and he was a willing pupil of hers; her lessons or moonbeams proved beyond value in the literal sense and as a consequence when he fell asleep he never failed to go up to her in her sky and catch her words.

He awoke in the bedroom of the unknown neighbour and for a full minute there he didn't understand where he was; he felt grateful to invisible forces like perfectly realized kindness although he had no idea what kindness was made of.

He was only dogged about one simple thing and was that he knew he didn't understand how to give up; no matter how many horrid pursuers there were after him he had a simple retirement plan and just wanted to make it to sixty-five and live on The Great Barrier Reef.

He had no idea of the origin of the gratitude feeling but it was a groundswell beginning in his heart and the sweetness and longing it contained made him feel like a devotee of love or possibly beauty. He could hear his unknown neighbours moving about down in their kitchen, for he heard their warm murmuring first, perhaps their billing and cooing was what woke him.

And now that he was heading in their positive direction, whoever they were he loved them and automatically felt intimate with them, stepping ever forward rather like a confident child growing in a degree of real trust because what was before him was honesty and faithfulness of spirit.

The neighbours were having a very early breakfast, porridge actually, and the man who was a bit over sixty-looking was in his nice dressing gown and knotted tassel with a pink face and a woolly comb-over; and he was in the friendliest possibly way adding molasses to his sleepy wife's hot oats.

'Thank my truest love!' she smiled so willingly and the guy added two juicy fat prunes with an attempt at magic for the working classes.

Ernid had never seen real adoration better expressed and knew it had to do with the unmistakable persuasion of molasses.

The four of them clasped palms I suppose in a very biblical sort of a way and bored their wide-open orbs right into one another in a pact of eternal solidarity; they silently saw nothing could tear them apart after so arduous a search to find one another. They didn't want to know each other's names or provenance and Ernid and Ma unilaterally agreed to live there till each of them died of death.

One thing about the new friends that slightly puzzled Ernid was that the other couple had retired and yet he and Ma lived only to fulfill the work-ethic or putting on the shocking ticking alarm clock for dawn each day and after having a frantic beginning run to work or catch the bus to it. But get there or else life ends for an honest serf.

How long could they live with persons of interest they didn't know or have any means of the slightest acquaintance baffled him and even annoyed him. The neighbours showed every outward sign of a kind of love but what exactly was it based on?

They even showered together in the extreme effort of getting to know one another, which was the idea of the male neighbour and after a bit of hesitancy it was agreed to.

It was extremely communicable to lather up and pass the soap to absolute perfect strangers. It felt as if the world had some sort of a chance at peace in this small way, this gesture of group cleanliness. He got the lice out of his old mother's hair and without ever thinking he shampooed the neighbours, both of them.

They were so poor the next door people that they employed a goat as a towel and it took ages to run about and dry themselves down correctly with a beast.

At the breakfast table the neighbours eagerly asked Ernid and his mum what shift they were on and what they might like for tea after work, but by now Ernid was finding their company extremely limiting and left for work with his mother on his back.

It was hard that morning to get his sick old mum up the narrow steps of the early morning bus to the factory, as a lot of other scrambling serfs who found themselves a bit late for work also bore their old mothers either across their necks or right on the old back to get them on the early run to work; many men cried with the emotional strain of hearing their still-active parents doing a whole heap of blubbering.

The driver to the factory also had his mother across his shoulders and it was quite tricky trying to see up the road in that bothersome manner, particularly when the screaming old lady kicked her legs on the revolving rear vision mirror,

And then immediately fare examiners got on with their Alzheimer mothers on their shoulders and checked for ticket evasion whilst their mothers all twitched.

It was a woeful bus indeed that whimpered and wept up to the depot where it took an hour to get everyone off in such a way nobody lost a valuable limb or head; the siren to start work was blasting away like mad and the driver helped a few dying old ladies off the bus who were then buried.

It felt much happier to get started into work mode and that was because in many ways he wasn't a thinker or a moralist, just a serf who toiled to get the necessary Gag on the tea table for his own blood as he called his mother and himself. He still didn't know anybody in the factory, they were just the rank and file ones that produced the soft drink, that was all he thought of his own workmates there.

Blurs who did the product managed by blurs of managers who kept them in their place, which was at the lowest possible fraction of a fair wage; he grinned at some of the clinically depressed fork lift drivers but they just gloomily stared ahead and stacked sugar bags until they climaxed at the roof a mile up. The whole place smelled like burning sugar and sickening additives like food dyes and artificial coconut milk.

The noises got him down slightly today, the abruptness of factory squeals like unhappy pigs in season mixed with hundreds of unrecorded industrial accidents such as ladders falling on craniums from vast heights, carbon monoxide being mixed with lemonade syrup at incredible velocity, conveyor belts revolving at giddying pace and overseers shrieking exactly the same way as knock-off-whistles; hundreds of unhappy sounds culminating in the loud fact you were a slave and a serf after that.

He tried to block out all the insufferable surface noise-abuse but his knees prepared to buckle and his mind was alarmed as his brain took in a billion unnecessary noises such as loud pornographic jokes being told by foremen mixed with clanking of bolts and chains and hobnail boots all rushing everywhere on the echoing concrete floor.

His old vat was really badly blocked up with the usual abstraction of jagged bottle-glass and the sluice channels were even worse so he had to will himself to bend down with his whimpering mother on his sore back and head down the various drains with a big stiff yard broom and unclog the whole lot. His mother, although only half-conscious, was so seized with the work-ethic that she cleared all the muck away too in perfect tandem.

He was commencing to hear voices but this screening had nothing to do with The Grassy Knoll at all; rather it was all the voices of his old village back home in the back blocks of dear old Prague; the merry sounds of waifs and dwarves chuckling in the Nazi-bombed school room filled with blackened smoldering desks and machine-gunned teachers. What a sight for sore eyes!

He then heard reindeer bells tinkling and old geography teachers discussing the flatness of the planet Earth and all sorts of strange distractions to be certain, but he strove mightily to get on with the unblocking of coagulant drains because that was something very close to his heart. He wanted to come clean everywhere he went and that task began with muck.

In a funny sort of a way the imaginary charge of murder was over and out and he saw his future as a looker-after, whether or not that was his sick but still working mother or perhaps anyone he saw who was down for the count, some sort of surreal nurse was being conceived in his soul and his living spirit and as a result all he wanted to do was take care of people who looked vulnerable just as a flower is vulnerable.

Sometimes in the disgusting foul sluice channels he saw a fellow serf who looked pretty down and out and he automatically felt love and sympathy for whoever it may be, trying in an innocent way to help them just by lending them five bucks.

The plant was posting profits larger than mammoths and the shareholders were delighted with 'Burp' Pty Ltd. For about six months or thereabouts Ernid just toiled away unhappily or happily as he saw fit and cleared the muck and unclogged drains in the same way, just about, that cardiologists clear away clogged arteries, and so on.

The relationship with his fellow serfs remained identical and he ate identical Gag.

He was at the peak of his physical and intellectual powers and most of him knew it; he couldn't actually philosophize with his demented ancient mother that well because she now lived full-time on his back. At work on his double-shift he tried to chat a little with her about this and possibly that, but the incredible angle she lay on his sore neck made intimate conversation a trifle strained.

He now had to put on his double-strength black rubber boots, which were very heavy and a bit too small for him so they were hard to wriggle on over his greasy thick wool socks, and with her on him all the time he found it hard to balance as he mopped up and vigorously swept with the great stiff yard broom that had his name lettered in gilt on it.

Management had him summoned and offered him the figurehead contract again pointing out that it had been successful once so why not give it another shot?

They didn't mind that his seriously ill mother lived full-time on his neck saying the offer was always on and his dependent mother could just stay there on him.

He said it was hard to get his overalls off and on with her on him.

The past horrors had all abated and seemed longer ago than the foundation of Hell.

He had survived Hell and looked forward to hustling out into the commercial world, having in mind politely requesting his annoying mother to hop off and give him a goddamned break; but she had him well and truly railroaded and the polite words would not arrive in mouth five, or was it still four?

The problems of his life seemed over but the main concern was the splitting (not of the atom but of the mother) and although they were preposterously close physically he wearied of having her up there all the time. She had put on a fair bit of weight too and he wouldn't have been startled to learn that she came in at a hundred kilos in compacted fat and gristle.

When he wanted to rinse his teeth and do his hair before retiring to bed it was really hard to achieve those simple jobs with her great weight on him in that abominable way; he found it quite tricky getting on his undergarments with her exactly in the way, it taking ten goes at least to get one of his legs through the right hole; and she wouldn't move over in the slightest to allow him to do that.

The fact was she was so dependent on him they had become one being. He couldn't urinate without deferring to her to do it first; he liked to comb his youthful and resplendent hair, which was pure auburn like a girl's, but she lay on that lovely hair of his and his comb got all snagged in her when he felt like giving it a good go.

He was now in the front office with the bosses and Mr Burp 1 offered him a million a year and a posh sports car if he would consider becoming the figurehead again. He said he would and they put it to Ma that she hop off him.

Reluctantly she alighted her son's broad back and sulked something shocking on the sofa in the corner whilst the new deal was being sorted out with a view to start out tomorrow and not a second sooner. Ma sure shot him some black looks but he signed with a rapid flourish and took her home on his back again to the anonymous neighbour's place for a slap-up feed of nothing.

Because he wanted security for his miniature but dependent close-knit family he made the fantastic psychological adjustment to persuade his crazed mother to remain at home, their neighbour's home being now their one too. Then he would get back into the fame game and build up a huge bank account.

Ma terribly reluctantly agreed to do nothing all day, just hang around with the neighbours and wait for her hard-working son to get in somewhere after midnight. Ernid loved fame and enjoyed posing for photographs showing mouth five as well as doctored shots of the inside of his brain and chest cavity depicting bullets being discharged all in the name of fun.

The new powerful soft drink was called 'Extra Ernid' and the devotees went mad for it and guzzled it by the ton. It was dark purple in hue and tasted like turnip mixed with straight cocaine, which was precisely what it was, needless to say. Ernid was on the road again and doing personal appearances at malls in shopping centers; he was seen as the spirit of letting yourself go!

He was the darling of mindless chat shows and made popular television commercials. Women wrote hotly to him and he sometimes paused in the fast lane to reply to some of them and suggest a plate of Gag somewhere quiet together.

Because of the tremendous salary difference between the friendly neighbours and his new standing as figurine for Burp, it was not right thinking to live for free upon retirees and Ernid knew it; after his first day of importance, being photographed a lot, being at press conferences and wearing a four thousand dollar suit with six thousand buck shoes he sat with them in their home and he sincerely thanked them.

'It is the fact you have been very kind to my crazy mother and myself over the past weeks, and after our home was insensitively demolished we had nowhere to call home; you offered us your gracious hospitality and put us in the same bed. We shall never forget your silent friendship.'

The two neighbours naturally had nothing to say to that and just stared at him with the treacle tin on the tablecloth.

The lady neighbour gave Ma a nice smile and a fold-up card table for a rainy day as well as a lightweight table tennis table; and even the tiny bats were fold-up; Ma said something like thanks but lately her squeaky speech had become incomprehensible and she sounded like a flute. Sometimes her music could be transporting but at other moments it sounded flat as a pancake. She thanked them in pantomime.

They took their leave of the neighbours with a shoulder bag stuffed full of fresh clothes and talcum powder, face washers, colored pencils and drawing books, a kettle and a bag of tea with two tin army style teacups and some finely powdered milk.

The most precious object was a big powerful wind-up alarm clock which rang so loudly it gave them a migraine.

But they needed it more than their blood because they would die if they were late for work.

She got up on his neck again, which felt rather reassuring for her because she could have a read up there and even enjoy a lie-in whilst he, down below, strove to find them both some kind of improvisatory residence such as a hole or a hill or a lane not frequented by people any more.

He was mindful not to ever crumple his brand-new-suit nor mark his wonderful new shoes adorned with lime-green shoelaces because he wouldn't want the sack.

Often he worried about the economy, not his and Ma's economy because they lived below anyone's means.

No matter what disused barn or filthy back lane they lay together in he was acutely aware that they were the haves as opposed to the have-nots; he could put up with a mother literally on his back and even read of a night with her on him all the time, but all he saw around him were the colossal armies of the dispossessed trying to get through to the other side of nothing.

He wished his ailing mother had an interest in politics but all she cared about was weeping constantly; and most effective was her weeping even though, apart from feeling fucked, she had lots of things to simply like and look forward to such as not being alive. And she presumed she was a bother and a burden on her hard-working son who did everything in his power to keep them going.

He purchased, using all his personal savings, one square metre of earth about a mile from where all the demolition was going on, with all the ugliness being put in place, and when he put his nervous signature on the contract at the bank he experienced an erection.

He was slightly humiliated by it and tried to keep it well hidden from the banker's eyes but luckily those beady eyes were pretty squinty and as well as that they were downcast staring at the tiny lettering and terms and fantastic conditions that worked extraordinarily well for the bank but not so great for the client; he hated the word 'client'.

With the successful purchase of one metre of earth came sheer confidence and good luck because not long after he and Ma moved in they found a fifty buck note in the drain right next to their property; he was so excited about the find that he bought Ma a new hat and as well as the hat he bought a wall.

They didn't have a roof yet, not as such, but they boasted one wall from which they drew shelter and peace. They adored their wall and knelt together of an evening and prayed to the gods of kindness for a roof; or at least a bit of one.

The vanity of the second version of terrible importance transformed Ernid completely because he wanted to keep his working class mind right and stay loyal to the humility his father had preached to him, particularly with a bad back. His father vaguely remembered The Nazis via the even vaguer memories of his father who saw the German War Machine come into Vienna and then blow it all up for something to do.

At the same time though he was pressured to keep up both a deception of impeccable grooming with a costume no one could openly chuckle at; he painstakingly ironed his trousers and suit jacket on the foldaway table tennis table every single morning at five before he leapt for the bus with his immaculate hair gleaming and glistening.

The new picture of him on all bottles and cans depicted him violently screaming.

'Drink Mechanical Mouth!' each can said and the addicts went for it in the far end of extreme for it was seen as dark and in bad taste like possibly devil worship and the more twisted they depicted his screwed up countenance the better he sold the product for his masters. Some of the artwork on the cans and bottles was obscene.

He liked to bare his sharpened down ivory teeth and scream like a lion. He liked doing that, looking really crazy and even menacing if that look kept him his employment; his mother didn't express her opinion simply because by now she had none. She thought she was a bookmark.

'Burp' Pty Ltd now engaged 200,000 serfs who were in no position to expect loyalty and often the purges arrived and whole sections got sacked on the spot. Mexicans then marched in and they were fully operational again; or else Mexicans got the chop just like every other person. Mexicans had to understand that they weren't indispensable and many a moustache was found crumpled up lying next to a kicked-in soiled sombrero. We were living beyond everything except fear.

In the decent old traditional days in factory existence when a person was summarily fired he was at least given a week's notice but today with harsher regimes a hard working serf can expect half a second's notice maximum; or even a fiftieth percentage point of a second to clean out their miserable locker, say goodbye to the others and get out into the gutter where they present as a visible proof of the economy and the politics that go with it.

It was hard to clean out a locker, man or woman that is, in less than a second, but like everything else in tough times the ordinary worker just had to hack it.

Many toilers openly sobbed as they pulled the pornography out of their crummy lockers and rolled up rude fish and chip shop calendars.

Ernid lost a lot of mates as he rose to celestial heights never before dreamt of, staying in luxurious hotels with his breath freshener alone costing more than a man's house on the North Shore. He made love to movie ladies although some resembled lads more than ladies, and he enjoyed going on posh television shows and matching wits with English comedians who dominated Australian entertainment.

But he unfailingly posted to his mother, who took care of their one metre property, a fruit cake from Safeway and wrote her long intricate personal letters pointing out his latest take on life, eagerly anticipating her literary responses; and to her eternal credit Ma wrote beautifully every day to her whirlwind-making-son and pointed out how much she loved living in a wall and a square yard of earth.

It occurred to him that he hadn't slept for millennia and sort of needed some of whatever it was which had to be pretty valuable stuff because one of the new range of flavours he had to promote at work was Burp Sleep! which possessed many hidden ingredients such as opium and cocaine mixed with passion fruit and elderberries; and this had taken the Australian market by storm.

He liked being on the road and most of all to behold his giant self looking absolutely terrifying, emblazoned on huge billboards on every highway around the country; kids loved Ernid The Impaler as one of the labels depicted him.

What management wanted was to topple Burp but it wasn't so easy because Burp with all its genius had formulated hundreds of still-powerful anti-sugars and incredibly powerful sugars and brand loyalty decided how the cash registers totalled; but Burp was now second to Burp and it had the macabre Ernid Ernst as the logo that got people hooked.

It did seem as if he couldn't possibly manage the two ever so different existences, on the one hand the life of fame and glamour and the constant wonder of appearing upon billboards criss-crossing the country, going on television escapist popular easy-going programs to promote both his last mechanical mouth and the excitement of cutting-edge medical science and then the demoralizing plainness of home and living within his allotted metre of earth.

At least he had persuaded his superstitious and also frail mother not to live up there on his back any more, for it hurt after a while and it just wasn't right, not morally nor psychologically; but he was seeing it occur more and more all around him with old people frightened for their futures and dwelling physically upon their old children's necks.

At work it was the world he loved and was proud of, waiting for a call from wardrobe, the going in to see the hairdresser and the hairdresser's assistant, the billing and cooing and flirtation he experienced between his beauticians whom one could almost think of them as embalmers, the giggly people in television who put on his make-up and caressed his body better than any lover could. He loved them all, every one of them!

He loved to chat with Ben from wardrobe at Channel 7 and talk about things like speedboats and skiing and romantic holidays at Monte Carlo or Cannes and let the friendly vapours of chit-chat swallow up all of his major concerns such as trying to find a sheet of corrugated iron to act as a roof on his one square metre home in the middle of the busy road.

The thoughts and problems and recollections of trying to find the time to get somewhere safer and better to live with his demanding mother always seemed to find a way to evaporate whenever Ben was attending to his hair and Beverly was tinting his eyelashes and powdering his pointy chin in readiness for the show.

'I am a glamour puss!' he would purr in the ever so comfy wardrobe chair and enjoy the luxuriousness of getting looked after rather than constantly intimidated and abused out on the street; even though his fans cried out for more at concerts and outside opening night premieres he could sense that they hated him too for his freakiness.

But he had some sort of innate ability to make hosts cackle and live audiences laugh, since he was often witty without trying to be. It was because he was happy to be alive after so many procedures and technical upheavals, the being evicted and the being separated from his woman whose name he now couldn't possibly recall.

'I am a man of fame!' he cried out in rapture as his beauticians lovingly powdered and prepared him for the audiences and the cameras that gave him everlasting fun.

The friendly team in wardrobe laughed at everything funny he said and groomed the gloom out of his body in readiness to please the sponsor.

Only from time to time did live television go poorly for him, such as the moments when he was expected to down a can of soft drink, some new line they were pushing, and if he wasn't quite relaxed and concentrating then he might spill it and then he looked a fool; and if the bright liquid splashed right on his beautiful three-piece suit the television audience could be dismayed and feel inclined to laugh at him and boo him hard.

Sometimes, irritatingly, the cameras on the studio floor seemed almost humanly capable of sailing right into his big fourth mouth, yes the fourth! And he could easily see and hear the response of the live crowd as it was so blatantly obvious to one and certainly all that he was nothing but a machine.

He could chew and sip and talk and sort of remember, but that was about it.

He was mechanically entertaining and he could be animatedly melodramatic, but he wasn't a real man.

One interviewer on a radio program asked him off-the-cuff if he wasn't a fraud and just a cunning machine running after a quick buck; and then to his own surprise Ernid excused himself from the microphone and went and wept on the lavatory.

He was acquainted with weeping on the lavatory like more than half the country.

The only comfort in contemporary life is weeping into tenth-rate toilet paper anonymously.

He just couldn't cease his caterwauling and was certainly ashamed of himself for being weak as it was certainly a no-no to walk off the set like that, but he was just so absolutely nauseated by insults from known or unknown quarters. God never insulted him; not once!

After he had finished his weeping he carefully washed his own borrowed face in the radio station make-up mirror and tried to work out who he was again; but it was the identical old puzzle and the solid answer just refused to arrive. He was a weeping robot!

A robot with hypersensitive sensations and someone with a ceramic gullet and mesh throat and all sorts of spare parts in fact and deed, he went back to face his interviewer, and it was his mother in the chair. He screamed and again left the set.

One night after a big show at a new cinema he was the big star all right and didn't look half bad actually, in a mint-new-tuxedo and brilliant dyed black hair swept back in a severe way with his fourth mouth working pretty good. Quick with the repartee, he was wittier than ever and a very pretty girl took him home because she said he thrilled her. 'Fair enough!' he laughed and she laughed as well and as they pashed on in the taxi she made him aware he was more than a goddamned robot.

The girl lived with her boyfriend and he was in when they got there so she got some chilled wine from the fridge and the three smoked hard and tough and drank long.

A few hours crept by and Ernid had made her boyfriend laugh so much he fainted in a heap. They put a blanket over his cold shoulders so he wouldn't get a chill and then made it to the bedroom.

www.ingramcontent.com/pod-product-compliance
Lightning Source LLC
Chambersburg PA
CBHW051102030726
47504CB00006B/1738